BETTY
BOO

Claudia Piñeiro

Translated by Miranda France

BITTER LEMON PRESS
LONDON

BITTER LEMON PRESS
First published in the United Kingdom in 2016 by
Bitter Lemon Press, 47 Wilmington Square, London WC1X 2ET

www.bitterlemonpress.com

First published in Spanish as *Betibú*
by Alfaguara, Buenos Aires, 2011

Bitter Lemon Press gratefully acknowledges the financial
assistance of the Arts Council of England

Work published within the framework of "Sur" Translation Support Program
of the Ministry of Foreign Affairs and Worship of the Argentine Republic

Obra editada en el marco del Programa "Sur" de Apoyo a las Traducciones
del Ministerio de Relaciones Exteriores y Culto de la República Argentina

A CIP record for this book is available from the British Library

ISBN 978–1–908524–553
eBook ISBN 978-1-908524-560

Typeset by Tetragon, London
Printed and bound by CPI Group (UK) Ltd, Croydon, CR0 4YY

Supported using public funding by
ARTS COUNCIL
ENGLAND
LOTTERY FUNDED

Claudia Piñeiro lives in Buenos Aires. For many years she was a journalist, playwright and television scriptwriter and in 1992 won the prestigious Pléyade journalism award. She has more recently turned to fiction and is the author of the novel *Thursday Night Widows* – awarded the Clarín Prize for Fiction, *All Yours* – winner of the German Literaturpreis, and *A Crack in the Wall*, all previously published by Bitter Lemon Press.

Also available from Bitter Lemon Press
by Claudia Piñeiro

Thursday Night Widows

All Yours

A Crack in the Wall

To mis amigas, all of them, just because.

To Silvina Frydman and Laura Novoa
They and I know why.

"(…) in his crime stories for the newspaper, he tells the readers what happened and how, but he always arrives after the crash or the crime, he has to relive it imaginatively with witness statements and evidence. Never, until now, has the event unfolded before his eyes, nor the scream of the victim entered his own reporter's ears."

ANTONIO DI BENEDETTO
"Falta de vocación", *Cuentos Claros*

"The microscopic debris that covers our clothing and bodies is the silent witness, sure and faithful, of all our movements and all our encounters."

EDMOND LOCARD
Criminalistic Treatise

"The story goes on; it can go on; there are various possible conjectures; it's still open; it merely gets interrupted. The investigation has no end; it cannot end. Someone should invent a new literary genre, paranoid fiction. Everyone is a suspect; everyone feels pursued."

RICARDO PIGLIA
Blanco Nocturno

1

Mondays are the days it takes longest to get into the Maravillosa Country Club. The line of domestic staff, gardeners, builders, plumbers, carpenters, electricians, gasmen and other assorted labourers seems to go on forever. Gladys Varela knows this all too well, and that's why she's swearing to herself as she stands facing the barrier, from which a sign reading *Personnel and Suppliers* hangs, behind another fifteen or twenty people who are waiting, like her, to go in. She curses herself for not having charged up the electronic card that would grant her automatic entry. The problem is that the card expires every two months, and the times at which you can make an appointment to reactivate it clash with the hours she works for Señor Chazarreta. And Señor Chazarreta isn't a very nice man. At least he doesn't seem so to Gladys, who finds his face intimidating. She can't decide whether the way he looks at her is surly, dry or tight-lipped. But whichever it is, he's the reason she hasn't yet dared to ask if she can leave early or have a break to go to the gatehouse and renew her entry card. Because of that way he looks at her. Or doesn't look at her, because in actual fact Señor Chazarreta rarely looks right at her, rarely looks her in the eye. He just generally looks, looks around, looks into the garden or looks at a bare wall. Always with a long, unsmiling face, as though he were cross about something. Mind you, it's not surprising, given everything that's happened. At least her entry card is signed, that's one thing; it means she has to queue, as she is in fact doing, but that nobody will have to call Señor Chazarreta to authorize her entry into the private neighbourhood. Señor Chazarreta hates being woken, and often sleeps until late. Sometimes he stays up into the early hours. And he drinks. A lot. Gladys suspects this, anyway, because she often finds a glass and a bottle of whisky in whichever part of the house Señor Chazarreta crashed out the previous night. Sometimes it's the bedroom. Other times it's the living room, or the veranda, or that cinema they have on the top floor. Not they, he, because Señor Chazarreta has lived alone since his wife died. But Gladys never asks about that, about his wife's death; she neither knows nor wants to know. What she saw on the news is enough. And never mind what some people say. She's been working at the house for two years and the Señora died two-and-a-half or three years ago. Three. She thinks. That's what they told her, anyway; she can't remember the exact date. Her duty is to Señor Chazarreta. And he pays her well, promptly, and doesn't make a scene if she breaks a glass or gets a bit of bleach on an item of clothing or slightly burns a cake. Only once did he get cross, very cross, when something was missing – a photo – but afterwards he realized that she wasn't to blame, and had to admit as much to her. He didn't apologize, but he acknowledged that it hadn't been her fault. And Gladys Varela forgave him then, even though he hadn't asked to be forgiven. And she tries not to think about it now. Because she believes that forgiveness means nothing if you continue to dwell on your grievance. Chazarreta may have a face like a wet weekend, but what boss doesn't? There's too much misfortune in the world to go around smiling.

The queue moves forward. One woman's angry because her employer has barred her from entering the compound.

Why? she's shouting. Who the hell does she think she is? All this for some shitty piece of cheese? But Gladys can't hear how the guard on duty responds, from his side of the window, to the woman's furious questions. As she storms past, Gladys realizes that she knows this woman, from the internal bus or from walking alongside her the first few blocks inside the club; she's not sure, but she recognizes her. There are still three men ahead of her in the line, who seem to be friends or somehow to know each other, perhaps from working together. It takes longer than usual to process one of the trio because he isn't registered, so they ask for his identity card and take a photograph and they tape a serial number to his bicycle to make sure he leaves with the bike he brought in. Then they telephone the property's owner to get authorization for him to enter. Before letting him go they note down the bicycle's make, colour and wheel size, and Gladys wonders why it was also necessary to issue a serial number. Is it in case the man finds another bicycle, exactly the same but newer and in better condition, and tries to take that one out? That would be some luck. You'd have a better chance of finding a lottery ticket with a palindromic number on it or of getting a full house at bingo. But the men don't question the need for this number, much less complain about it. It's the way things are, the rules of the game. They accept it. And in a way that's right, Gladys thinks, because it means when you leave you can prove that you haven't taken anything, that you're decent. Better for them to make their notes now than go around making idle accusations later. That's what Gladys is thinking – that they shouldn't make idle accusations – when the woman who was shouting in the queue a few minutes ago comes up to her. If you hear of any work, will you let me know? she says. And Gladys answers yes, that she'll let her know. The woman holds out her mobile and says: Take my number. Gladys takes her own phone out of her jacket pocket and taps in the numbers that the other woman reels off. The woman asks her to ring the number then hang up, so that she'll also have her number. And she asks her name. Gladys, she says. Anabella, says the other woman, put it in: Anabella. And Gladys saves that name and that number. The woman isn't shouting any more; her anger has given way to something else. A mix of rancour and resignation. After swapping numbers with some other women in the line, she leaves quietly.

When her turn comes, Gladys hands over the document. The guard enters her details into a computer and straight away her face appears on the screen. The image surprises her: she looks younger in that photo, slimmer and with blonder hair; now she remembers that she'd bleached it the day before they registered her. But that wasn't so long ago. The guard looks at the screen and then at her, twice, before waving her through. A few yards further on another guard waits while she opens her bag. He doesn't need to ask: Gladys, like everyone in the queue, knows the form. As she struggles with the zipper it sticks and she has to tug harder at it before the teeth come free. The guard moves her belongings around in the bag to see what's there. She asks him to make a note on the entry form of the phone in her jacket pocket, her charger and a pair of sandals she's carrying in her bag. And she shows him these things. The guard writes them down. The other stuff doesn't matter: paper handkerchiefs, some sweets half stuck together; her wallet containing her identity card, a five-peso note and coins for the bus fare home; her house keys; two sanitary pads. Those don't need to be logged, but the phone, charger and sandals do. She doesn't want any trouble on the way out, she tells him. The guard hands her the completed form and she puts it into her wallet along with her ID, forces the zip closed again, and sets off.

The three men who were in the queue with her are walking just ahead, jostling each other and clowning around, laughing. The one with the bicycle pushes it, so that he can walk with the others and chat. Gladys speeds up; this Monday queue has made her later than usual. She passes them and one says: Hello, how are you? They don't know each other, but Gladys returns the greeting. He's not bad-looking, she thinks, and if he's in here it must be because he's got a job. She's not thinking of him for herself; she's already married – just thinking. See you later, says the man, who's behind her now. See you, she replies, quickening her step again to put more distance between them.

When she gets to the golf course she turns right, then right again a few yards later. Chazarreta's house is the fifth one down, on the left after the willow tree. She knows the way by heart. And she knows which door Chazarreta will have left open so that she can enter the house without ringing the bell: the one that leads into the kitchen from the veranda. Before doing that she picks up the papers – *La Nación* and *Ámbito Financiero* – in the entrance hall. Chazarreta must still be asleep, otherwise he'd have taken the papers himself to read over breakfast. Gladys looks at the front page of *La Nación*, skips the main headline, which alludes to the president's most recent sworn declaration of assets, and goes to a large colour photo under which she reads: Two buses crash on Calle Boedo; three dead and four seriously injured. She crosses herself without really knowing why; on account of the dead, she supposes. Or for the seriously injured, that they may not also die. Then she lays the two newspapers down on the kitchen table. She goes into the utility room, hangs her things in the closet and puts on her uniform. She's going to have to ask Señor Chazarreta to buy her another one; now that she's put on weight the buttons are straining over her bust and the armholes cut off circulation to her arms when she lifts them to hang up washing on the line. If he wants her always to wear a uniform, as he said on the day he hired her, he'll have to pay for it. Gladys looks into the laundry basket and sees that there isn't much ironing to do. Chazarreta is very tidy and usually brings in all the washing that's hanging up at the weekend, but she'll go out to the back patio anyway to check if there's anything to take down, just in case. After that she'll wash the dirty plates she saw out of the corner of her eye in the kitchen sink. And next she'll do the bathrooms – her least favourite job – to get them out of the way.

As she suspected, Chazarreta has indeed brought the washing in. There aren't many dirty plates in the kitchen sink: either he did some washing-up at the weekend, or he ate out. She leaves the plates, a glass and some cutlery to dry on a dishcloth so that they won't slide on the black marble work surface, then goes to the utility room and comes back with the floor squeegee and the bucket, with cleaning products, cloth and gloves inside it.

As she's walking down the corridor, she passes the living room and notices Chazarreta sitting in the green velvet armchair, the high-backed one she thinks must be his favourite. The armchair faces a picture window that looks onto the park. But this morning the curtains are still drawn, so Chazarreta hasn't sat down there to admire the view; more likely he's been sprawled in that chair since last night. Although the chair's high back and the dim light obscure her view, Gladys knows that Señor Chazarreta is there because his left hand is dangling over one side of the chair and, beneath it, on the woodblock floor, there's a glass on its side and some spilt whisky.

Good morning, Gladys says as she passes behind him on her way upstairs. She says this quietly enough for him to hear if he's awake but to avoid waking him if he's still asleep. Chazarreta doesn't answer. He's sleeping it off, Gladys thinks, and carries on. But before going upstairs she checks herself. It would be better to wipe up the whisky now, because if the liquid lies on the wax floor for too long it will leave one of those white stains that are so difficult to remove without applying another layer of wax. And Gladys doesn't want to start the week waxing floors. Retracing her steps, she takes the cloth from the bucket, bends down, picks up the glass and wipes up the whisky beside the velvet armchair, pushing the cloth blindly ahead of her. But straight away the cloth meets another spill, a dark puddle she can't identify, and quickly she drops the cloth so that the liquid soaking into it won't reach her hand; instead she touches this liquid, fleetingly, with the tip of her index finger: it's sticky. Blood? she wonders, not believing that it can be. Then she raises her gaze to look at Chazarreta. There he is, in front of her, with his throat slit. His neck, slashed from one side to the other, opens like two near-perfect lips. Gladys doesn't know what it is she can see inside the wound, because the sight of that red flesh, the blood and the mash of tissues and tubes is so shocking and repellent she instinctively closes her eyes, simultaneously raising her hands to her face as though closing them were not enough to stop her seeing, and her mouth opens only to let out a muted groan.

The repulsion doesn't last long, however, because fear overtakes it. A fear that isn't paralysing, but galvanizing. And so Gladys Varela uncovers her face and forces herself to open her eyes, lifts her head again and looks straight at the ravaged throat, at Chazarreta's blood-stained clothes, at the knife his right hand holds in his lap and at the empty

15

whisky bottle tucked in beside his body, next to the armrest. Then she gets straight up, runs into the street and screams. She screams and screams, determined to keep on screaming until someone hears her.

2

At the very moment Gladys Varela is screaming in a cul-de-sac at the Maravillosa Country Club, Nurit Iscar is trying to restore order to her house. That is, her three-room apartment in the poorest – or rather, most run-down – part of the Barrio Norte, French and Larrea. She doesn't know yet that Pedro Chazarreta is dead. The news is going to spread fast, but not that fast. If she did know, she'd have the television and radio on, following every update. Or she'd go on the Internet, to an online newspaper, and find out more details of what happened. But Nurit Iscar doesn't know. Not yet. She won't find out for a few more hours.

The house is a mess. Half-empty wine glasses, yesterday's disembowelled newspapers, crumbs on the floor, butt ends everywhere. Nurit Iscar doesn't smoke, never has smoked, and detests the smell of cigarettes. She hopes that allowing others to smoke in her house is therefore a sign of love, and not submission. Love or submission: it's a question she often poses herself – and not only in the matter of cigarettes – without yet having arrived at a satisfactory answer. The day before, her friends Paula Sibona and Carmen Terrada – both of whom smoke – had come over for their monthly get-together, which takes place on the third Sunday of every month and has been a fixture for two years. Not that they don't get together at other times, for a coffee or to go to the cinema, for a meal or on any number of occasions which conceal a secret purpose: to let time pass, as it inevitably must, but in good company. The third Sunday of the month is different, though. Sometimes Viviana Mansini joins them, but not always, and they are grateful for that because, while Viviana believes them all to be intimate friends, the other three don't feel the same about her. When Viviana's with them the talk tends to revolve around her, and she's always making some observation which, however innocent it may sound, feels like a kick in the ovaries for one of the others. Like when Carmen was complaining that she'd been anxious about a small lump in one breast until a medical test revealed it to be merely dysplasia, and Viviana Mansini replied angelically: I know what you mean. I felt the same a couple of months ago when I had that biopsy, I don't know if you remember, no, you obviously don't because you were the only one who didn't call to find out what the result was. And in the silence that followed, Carmen looked at her as if to say "thanks, bitch", but she didn't say anything. In fact it was Paula Sibona who came to her defence and, imitating with difficulty the same angelic tone said: Obviously it went well, Vivi, because your tit's all there. And she emphasized the point by grabbing her own breasts and moving them gently up and down over an exaggerated compass to illustrate the generous heft of Viviana Mansini's bosoms. But, besides sparing them her sarcasm, Viviana's absence means they can criticize her, too. Because, as Paula Sibona says, It must be my age, but bitching about Mansini gives me almost the same adrenaline rush as fucking. And that Sunday before the Monday that Pedro Chazarreta turned up with his throat slit, their monthly gathering was confined to the inner circle – no Viviana Mansini – and took place at Nurit Iscar's house. They rotate houses every month, but the procedure is always the same. They meet before lunch; the lady of the house buys all the papers – and all the papers means *all* the papers; then, while she cooks her speciality, which in Nurit Iscar's case doesn't extend much beyond steak with salad or spaghetti carbonara, the others pull apart the newspapers and read articles with the aim of selecting a few to read aloud. This exchange takes place after lunch, over coffee. But they don't bother with any old news. Each of them, as with the cooking, has her speciality. For Nurit Iscar it's the crime stories – not for nothing was she considered, until a few years ago, "the Dark Lady of Argentine literature". Although that's past history for her and something she'd rather forget, she can't resist serving up "blood and death" when her friends demand it – so long as it doesn't involve writing fiction. And better still if there's sex, Paula Sibona usually says. Carmen's speciality is national news, and her greatest pleasure is finding inconsistencies in the declarations of politicians: syntactical errors and – why not? – howlers. The one she has the most fun with is the mayor. Someone who can't speak shouldn't be in charge of a city, she's always saying. And, far from being elitist, her observation alludes to the obvious contempt a certain affluent social class – from which the mayor hails – feels for language (words, meaning, syntax, conjugation, use of prepositions, solipsisms) and which she, a secondary-school teacher of language and literature for more than thirty years, refuses to countenance. Paula Sibona's choice of news, in contrast to her unsuspecting friends, has less to do with her personal interests than with her love for Nurit Iscar: she goes for theatre and cinema reviews, and entertainment in general. It's true that Paula is an actress (although, can she still be an actress if it's nearly two years since anyone called to offer her a part?), an established actress who, as the years have passed, has slipped from playing the lead parts in soap operas to being "the mother of" and thence into unjust oblivion. If there's anything that holds no interest at all for Paula Sibona it's reading the papers. They make me feel ill, she says. But she's still an enthusiastic member of the group, secretly hoping that the items she chooses to read aloud may help her friend Nurit to exorcize a hurt caused her – Paula believes – by the press. A pain. She doesn't know if that's achievable, but she won't give up nevertheless. Because Nurit Iscar, the Dark Lady of Argentine literature, married until five years ago and with two sons finishing school and about to go to university, fell in love with another man and then, as well as getting divorced, wrote her first romantic novel. Which, on top of everything else, didn't go well. It didn't go well in terms of plot, or critical reception, or with the legion of fans anxiously awaiting a new Nurit Iscar novel. Unfortunately her own love story didn't have a happy ending either – and that's something else she'd rather forget. Some of her readers stuck by her, but many others were put off by a novel that was so different to the others, and lacked the one element they had hoped to find: a corpse. And then the critics, who had largely ignored her up until that point, went in for the kill. "This attempt to be literary falls flat." "Iscar should have stuck to plotting, which is supposedly her strength, and left the metaphors, the poetic pretensions and the linguistic experimentation to writers who understand these things, either through study, instinct or talent – something which, if she has any, is not discernible here." "A novel that deserves to go unnoticed, a forgettable novel." "It defies logic that Iscar, having struck on the magic formula for a bestseller, should now attempt something about which she knows nothing: writing serious literature." And there were plenty more like that. Nurit has a box full of cuttings relating to her last novel: *Only If You Love Me*. A white box, really big, not like those ones people keep – or used to keep – their love letters in. It's tied up with a blue silk ribbon that she plans never to untie again. But she keeps the box, almost as though it were evidence of a crime, although she doesn't know which was the worst crime: writing the novel, reading the reviews, or letting herself be so affected by them. It was those reviews, together with the failure of the love affair that led her to write that ill-fated novel, and the murder of Gloria Echagüe, Chazarreta's wife – a case Nurit had declined to cover for the newspaper *El Tribuno* because she was so absorbed by *Only If You Love Me* – that prompted her to "do a Salinger" (albeit in a Third World/female/crime-writer-ish way), locking herself away for ever, far from the world to which she had belonged up until that point. The difference, though, was that she had neither Salinger's fame nor sufficient savings or royalties to finance her exile, so she had to look for a job that would allow her to pay the electricity and gas bills, to do her supermarket shop and all those other things for which one needs a salary or money in the bank. Or in the wallet. And since the only thing she knows how to do is write (although, after those reviews, even her aptitude for writing has been thrown into question), that is what she does. But under other people's names, as a ghostwriter. She prefers the Spanish term for this: *escritora fantasma*, something applauded by her friend Carmen Terrada, who to this day defends the use of their native tongue against the anglophone invasion, a battle she knows to be lost but which she finds romantic. Paula Sibona won't accept her friend's reluctance to go back to doing what she enjoys – writing her own novels – so she keeps trying to show her the small-mindedness of some reviews which seem to have been written more than anything to flatter their authors and make them famous. Or notorious, like Lee Harvey Oswald or Mark David Chapman.

21

And Carmen Terrada offers up a more erudite comparison: how Jean Genet stopped writing for five years after being "stripped naked", to use his own words, in an essay his friend Sartre wrote about him. But just remember that they are not Jean-Paul, Nurit, dear, and you are not Genet.

After emptying the ashtrays and airing out the room to banish the smell of cigarette smoke, Nurit Iscar sweeps the floor. Then she washes some plates left over from the night before, puts the tablecloth in the washing machine – she'll set it off later when she's gathered more dirty laundry – and dumps the scattered Sunday papers into the regulation black bag which, in a few minutes, she'll take out to the landing with the other rubbish. Only moments before, Gladys Varela was doing precisely the same chores for her boss, Pedro Chazarreta. But at this moment, as Nurit Iscar ties up the black bag full of newspapers, Gladys Varela isn't doing anything, apart from crying, as she sits in the electric buggy one of the Maravillosa guards drove over in, minutes after another resident called to advise security that a woman – a domestic, he said – was screaming like a lunatic in the middle of the street. Soon afterwards a van arrived, bringing the head of security and three more guards, and they offered to drive Gladys to the infirmary. But there's no way she's leaving until the real police come. The Buenos Aires police. She tells them she's not moving an inch. And this time the guards also seem to be more cautious. Once bitten, twice shy, the security chief tells a neighbour who's come to ask why nobody is inside the house with the body. Nobody with a good memory is going to repeat the mistakes made by the guards who came to that house on the day Gloria Echagüe died, three years ago. They aren't going to approach the scene of the crime or let anyone else near it. They aren't going to move so much as a stray hair that may be lying anywhere in the vicinity of the victim, much less allow anyone to clean up the blood, or place the body on a bed; any request not to inform the police, with the argument that everything was "just an accident", will fall on deaf ears. If necessary, no one will breathe until the patrol car arrives. They made that mistake once before. And although nobody mentions it, although guards, neighbours, the odd gardener, the maid who works in the house across the road and Gladys Varela do no more than exchange silent glances while waiting for the Buenos Aires police to arrive with the district attorney, everyone has the strange sensation that, this time, someone is giving them the chance to get things right.

3

It's a few hours later, in the afternoon, when Nurit Iscar takes the bag of Sunday papers out to the landing for the concierge to pick up with the other rubbish, and she still doesn't know that Pedro Chazarreta is dead, his throat slit from side to side. She's going to find out soon, though, in about a couple of hours, when she takes a break for tea. Because the news has started to spread. And soon after Nurit concludes her cleaning effort and remembers to pour a bit of water into the plant pots that adorn her balcony – she's never been what you'd call green-fingered, but she's aware of those plants as the only other living beings in her home and she's determined not to let them dry up – in the newsroom of *El Tribuno* newspaper the internal line 3232 lights up on the telephone that sits on Jaime Brena's desk. In the world of crime journalism, he's better known as plain Brena – but he's not actually on Crime any more. They moved him to Society. It wasn't a move, it was a demotion, Brena likes to point out. But on one of those occasions his (and everyone's) boss, Lorenzo Rinaldi, snapped back: What are you complaining about? On any other newspaper you'd be on the Society desk too, or haven't you noticed that almost no leading newspaper has a Crime section these days? They put the crime stories in Society or News. It's thanks to this change of section that, when his internal line starts ringing that afternoon, Brena isn't writing a crime report but studying a survey that claims 65 per cent of white women sleep on their backs while 60 per cent of white men sleep facing down. And his first reaction to this revelation is a mathematical niggle: why not say that 65 per cent of women sleep facing up and that only 40 per cent of men sleep in the same position? Or that 60 per cent of men sleep facing down, while only 35 per cent of women sleep in that position? It's like when the weather forecaster predicts a 30 per cent chance of rain. If it's only 30 per cent, wouldn't it be more useful to state "70 per cent chance it won't rain"? What's being highlighted in each of these cases? The difference? The coincidence? The majority? The minority? A desirable or undesirable outcome? What really rankles with Jaime Brena is that, at least in the survey about white men and women's sleeping habits, nobody thought to ask themselves those questions before writing up this wire story. Whoever wrote the headline will have phrased it that way because that's how the information came to them. There's hardly any time these days in an agency or newsroom to think about syntax and vocabulary, only spelling. Barely even that. The agency story with the survey findings comes furnished with quotes from researchers at the University of Massachusetts who suggest possible sociological, cultural and even psychological reasons to explain their findings. Is this news? Jaime Brena wonders. Who really cares what percentage of people sleep in which position? Were other races not included in the survey because the researcher couldn't – or didn't want to – include them, or didn't care? Now that could be a news story, the reason why some races – or one, whites – get studied and not others. Or perhaps no other race was surveyed because the only people willing to contribute to such a stupid enterprise were white, he decides, picking up the phone which was ringing until a second ago and saying Hello? But by now there's nobody at the other end, just a dialling tone. Brena uses the interruption to stretch his arms above his head, interlacing the fingers, turning the palms upwards as though aiming for the ceiling, cracking the knuckles and so easing his lower back which, at sixty-something, doesn't respond well to so many hours sitting down. Tell me, why do 65 per cent of women sleep on their backs and 60 per cent of men on their fronts, he asks Karina Vives, a journalist on the Culture section who sits at the desk on his left, next to one of the few windows in the newsroom, the one that looks on to the boulevard. And Karina, who has known him since she came to work at the newspaper eight years ago, and who knows what it means to Jaime Brena to have been forced out of Crime in order to write up stories like this one, puts on a gormless expression and guesses: Because squashing your tits hurts more than squashing your dick? then waits, po-faced, for his answer. It's prick, girl, prick, Brena says, and with a look of distaste starts bashing out on his keyboard the title of the piece and an intro: Women Upwards, Men Downwards. The headline will only confuse readers, but it amuses Brena to imagine the wild scenarios their misunderstanding may conjure up. How long is it since they moved him to Society? Three weeks? Two? he wonders, scratching his head with a black pencil, though not in response to any itch. He can't remember. A long time. And all because he went on that cable show, the one with two armchairs and a lamp for a set, and said: I work at *El Tribuno*, but I read the competition because I trust it more. He's still angry with himself. It was a stupid thing to say, Jaime Brena knows that. But he'd been out to lunch with a colleague and there'd been wine, a lot of wine. Too much wine. And anyway, what he had said was true. That's not in dispute. Several of his friends had switched papers in recent months. Some colleagues from work, too. But nobody apart from him was stupid enough to own up to the fact. Much less in front of a television camera, whether cable or terrestrial. So much news about the president's assets, the president's broadsides, the president's teeth, the president's business dealings, the president's shoes: it got boring. The president's teeth and shoes are of absolutely no importance to him; as for the rest, the first time it's news, the second time it's repetition and the third, if it takes up half the front page and that same day the death of the president of a European Union country and his official retinue in an air accident doesn't make the front page (or does, but in a tiny space) it's something else he doesn't dare find a name for. But not news. That's his hunch, anyway. His take. He liked it when *El Tribuno* used to lead with an international news story. Or a sporting one. Or crime, of course, because then he, Jaime Brena, would be writing that lead piece. That time is long gone, though, as Brena knows only too well and, worse, he suspects that it may not be possible to revive it. At least not for now. If it does return, he doesn't expect to be around to see it.

He opens his drawer and takes out the voluntary redundancy papers. Perhaps the time has come. Perhaps he should do this once and for all: take the money and run. If I had any sense I would, he tells himself, but I've always been a bit of a tit. Or a complete tit. Brena's been working at *El Tribuno* for eighteen years. He learnt his craft there. And while he can imagine reading a different newspaper every morning – in fact he does – he can't imagine working in another newsroom. Even though having to see Lorenzo Rinaldi's face every day makes him feel ill. Very ill. One of these days he'll tell him to go to hell. He doesn't know when, but it's going to happen. It's just a matter of time. And space. Because you can't tell a man to go to hell anywhere. Not in a lift full of people, for example. Brena, I'd like you to cover the National Festival of Patagonian Lamb in Puerto Madryn. Go for two or three days. Get out of town – have you ever been whale-watching? You're going to love it. And Jaime Brena who, as Rinaldi knows, hates leaving town and cares very little about whales and even less about Patagonian lamb, would have loved to reply: "It'll be a pleasure, Rinaldi, and why don't you suck my dick" – but there wasn't enough room. Because after a retort like that, you have to be prepared to get thumped. Anyway, that would have been the end; that would have been tantamount to emptying his drawers and walking out. And if he's going to leave, it won't be with only the scant contents of his desk. Gustavo Quiroz from International News got a cake, as did Ana Horozki from Travel. Apparently even Chela Guerti walked off with a tidy sum, three years after her exile to the back page. They get rid of salaried staff whose pay has gone up over the years and replace them with recent graduates who can be paid half as much. That's what they're paying for – to get rid of people. Never mind that the new recruits can't conjugate a verb or differentiate between advise and advice, or that they get Tracy Austin mixed up with Jane Austen. Somebody will pick that up later down the line. And if not, too bad. What counts is – slowly but surely – to get rid of everyone old and expensive. Mind you, Brena would be willing to bet that Rinaldi isn't going to wave him off with a fat redundancy packet, that he won't get even a fraction of what's been approved for the others. He'll get his retirement money, but it'll be the minimum amount required by law, maybe less. Jaime Brena picks up the receiver and calls Personnel. When does this voluntary redundancy thingy have to be signed by, sweetheart? You can take until the end of the year, if you like. It depends on how you feel yourself. I don't feel myself, my religion doesn't allow it but I might be interested in voluntary redundancy, he tells her, and he hears her laugh at the other end of the line. You never change, Brena. If only, he says. And he means it. He wishes he weren't changing, but for a while he's been feeling older. That he can't get away with playing the fool like he used to until a few years ago, and with pretending that he's ten years younger than he really is. Better still, pretending to be ageless. Age used to be an irrelevance to him. Strange, then, that he's started to feel so old. Too old for everything: for work, travel, even for girls. It's not only a feeling: in the last year his body has visibly aged. He sees it in his abdomen, which protrudes just below his chest and sinks undifferentiated into his belly. Why, if he's never been fat? And in his hair, which isn't yet falling out copiously but which is beginning to look thin in the area that will one day inevitably be bald. And in his bum cheeks, which – although he tries not to catch sight of them in the mirror – he knows to have fallen like two ripe pears. Or two tears. What do you expect, you're over sixty, he tells himself by way of consolation, only to realize immediately that this is the very opposite of a consolation: he doesn't want to be over sixty. Brena puts the forms back in the drawer and gazes over the desk partition at the boy they brought in to replace him on the news stories that used to be his: violent crime and assault. A nice boy, but wet behind the ears. Very soft. Generation Google: no legwork, just keyboard and screen, everything off the Internet. They don't even use a biro. The boy makes an effort, it has to be said: he's always the first to arrive, the last to go, and Rinaldi is squarely behind him, making it look as though the Crime section can run perfectly well without him – without Jaime Brena, that is. Well, these things happen sometimes; you can land up somewhere fulfilling a function quite separate to the job for which you were taken on and with an ultimate objective you know nothing about. You can end up being someone else's puppet and that, he believes, is what's happening to the boy in Crime: Lorenzo Rinaldi is using him to stamp on Brena. But even though he has the boss's backing and doesn't suspect the machinations behind his appointment and new position, the boy seems very lost, almost dazed; he misses important things and, even though he doesn't make the clumsy mistakes typical of a beginner, there's a whiff of insecurity in the way he writes, a hesitancy that doesn't escape Brena. For the first time, the competition is breaking important crime and assault stories before *El Tribuno*. Apparently the boy will say: I wasn't happy about running it, it was an unreliable source. Or: It didn't strike me as relevant. Or: I had a lot of copy and not much space, so something had to go. But Jaime Brena doesn't believe him; he suspects the real problem is that the boy doesn't have good contacts. And a good crime reporter depends on contacts passing on leads that, sooner or later, will blossom into stories. Better still if the info is exclusive. Because if you have to wait until they lift the gagging order, you're toast. It doesn't matter if the contacts are police, lawyers, informants, judges or prisoners, so long as they have the right informa- tion. Sometimes he thinks he ought to help him. The boy. Then he thinks, why should he? They didn't assign the boy to him. Let Rinaldi train him up; after all, and though Rinaldi hasn't said he's the Crime Editor and doesn't appear as such in the paper, he seems to be acting as the head of that leader- less section. But Brena reckons that Rinaldi's less likely to give the boy a training than a kick in the teeth, sooner or later, once he's outlived his purpose. A painful kick. The worst of it is that – although Jaime Brena doesn't want to admit this – the boy inspires mixed emotions in him. He doesn't entirely dislike him. He reminds Brena of his own first steps in journalism more than forty years ago. Forty-four years: an eternity (why shouldn't he be expensive, why shouldn't they offer him voluntary redundancy?). The difference between him and the boy is that he had mentors, both in the newsroom and out in the world, and since he'd come straight from school, he had none of that virgin petulance that some of the university graduates arrive with. The boy's all Google and university and no street, Brena thinks. He's worked in the crime section on a rival newspaper, alongside Zippo, a long-time colleague with whom Jaime Brena has a love–hate relationship. Brena knows that working with Zippo amounts to little more than a secretarial role, because the man doesn't even trust his mother. Just at that moment, as he's thinking about Zippo's caginess, the boy looks up, sees Brena watching him and acknowledges him with a quick jerk of the head, and Brena returns the greeting, making a hat-tipping gesture even though he's not wearing anything on his head. From his desk, Brena calls over: Got anything for tomorrow? Nothing weighty, the boy answers. Nothing weighty, Brena repeats. Why not see what's happening in the rest of the newsroom, he suggests; do you know what the most important element is in deciding whether a crime story deserves to be news? The question catches the boy off guard, and even though it's the equivalent of that old favourite – what colour was San Martín's white horse? – he seems flustered and unsure what to answer. Then reluctantly, as though Brena had sprung a surprise exam on him and he were scared of flunking, the Crime boy opens his mouth to answer and Brena immediately warns him: And don't say "the place where the crime took place, the people involved, the gravity of the deed", because you're not at university any more. Jaime Brena waits. The boy thinks. Or tries to think. Brena says nothing, but knows that if the boy

31

panics and, just to prove he knows something, spouts that five "w's" rule "who, what, when, where and how" (though strictly speaking the last one's "w" goes at the end), he'll have to make an effort not to slap him, both for the wrong answer and for giving it in English. Brena wonders why some people, though not everyone, add a sixth "w" – why – and others don't. Perhaps because it is the hardest question to answer, the most subjective, the one that requires you to get inside the head of the criminal. Come on then, Brena chivvies. No, I don't know, I can't think of anything else, says the boy, giving up. Brena smiles and then declares: The other stories circulating in the newsroom that day. Never forget that on a quiet day some bastard's going to spring out of nowhere at the eleventh hour demanding you give him something – anything – to put on the front page, and you're going to have to think of something on the spot. I think they've got tomorrow's cover sorted, says the boy, the sworn statements and the personal fortune amassed by a prominent civil servant in the Ministry of Finance. Wow, that's massive, Brena interjects, not trying to hide his sarcasm. Didn't that story run last week? Yes, but some of the details have been confirmed now. I see, so this is how they hope to stop losing readers, and then they go blaming the Internet and online new sites for their falling sales. In this country, everyone's busy lining their pockets. Since when is the increasing wealth of one senior civil servant big news? And two weeks running? Jaime Brena shakes his head and shuts up, he's tired of the subject, bored by it. God knows why he always ends up ranting about the state of modern journalism. Doesn't he perhaps share some of the responsibility for it, through either his actions or his omissions? He tries to change the subject, but nothing comes to mind. He gazes at the Crime boy for a few seconds, as though wanting to give him some advice, to orient him a bit. But his fit of bonhomie goes unheeded and so Jaime Brena returns to his survey on the sleeping habits of white men and women.

The telephone rings again, and this time Brena gets to it in time. Jaime Brena speaking, he says. Comisario Venturini, says the voice at the other end. Comisario, repeats Brena. How are you, my dear? I'm well, but poor, Sir, and you? Same story here. It pleases Jaime Brena to hear this voice. It's something like a Pavlovian reflex, making him alert, tense, but excited, almost happy; some substance – adrenaline? – is released inside him. I've got something for you, Brena, says the police chief. Something that's going to cost me a traditional *asado* and a fine bottle of red? An *asado* with champagne, I'd say. I'm all ears, says Brena, just for the pleasure of it, because he knows that nothing he may hear from the police chief – or any of his other contacts – is going to find a place in the Society pages. He still hasn't told his contacts about the move; he can't bring himself to deactivate them: he's known some of them all his working life. His pieces for Society don't have a byline, so to all intents and purposes he's still the newspaper's chief crime correspondent as far as anyone outside *El Tribuno* is concerned. I'm listening, Comisario, he says, tearing a pink piece of paper off his jotter and ready to note down whatever Venturini is about to tell him. Somebody you know very well has just turned up dead, Brena, but don't worry, it's not someone dear to your heart. Who? Chazarreta. Chazarreta? Found with his throat slashed. Talk about a coincidence! You said it. And this is from a good source? I'm standing in front of the body right now, staring into the wound, waiting for the forensics to arrive. Where exactly? In his house, in La Maravillosa. And why are you so far out of your jurisdiction? One of those strange coincidences of life I'll tell you about some time.

You know the house, right? You came here to interview him the last time. Yes, I know the house. The maid found him. The woman gabbled on for twenty minutes without drawing breath or saying anything useful, and now she's gone into shock. Any hypothesis? Lots, but nothing substantial. I was hoping you'd give me your thoughts, Brena. You've caught me on the hop, Comisario; give me a bit of time to digest the news, then I'll call you back. OK, my dear, I'll be at the crime scene a bit longer. If you think of anything, call me. I won't tell you to come over, because the attorney's due any minute and they're not letting so much as a fly in the front door, not after what happened last time … I understand. Looks like I got you an exclusive, eh? And I'm humbly obliged. Call me. I'll call you, Comisario. Anything else? Yes, Dom Pérignon, Brena. Short ribs, pork belly, sweetbreads and Dom Pérignon. Consider it done.

Jaime Brena puts down the phone and sits staring at the paper, wondering what to do. He knows that what's landed in his lap is a bombshell. In a couple of hours every newspaper in town will be on to it, but as in all things, he who strikes first strikes hardest. Although some may say – Rinaldi said it himself, at one of the last front-page meetings Brena ever attended – that since the explosion in online news on the Internet, the concept of an "exclusive" lasts no longer than the time it takes to copy, paste and press Forward. Any old-school journalist, and Brena counts himself as such, still cares about exclusives. The death of Chazarreta's wife, three years ago, had the whole country on tenterhooks. And although not enough evidence was ever found to charge the widower, 99.99 per cent of people have always believed Pedro Chazarreta to be the murderer. That percentage includes Jaime Brena, who not only covered the investigation for *El Tribuno* but also led the way for other newspapers, from the day of the murder to the closure of the case. When this story appears in the papers tomorrow, Brena knows that people will say justice has been done. Even though one can never be sure of what is just, or of anything. True justice for someone who ought not to have died would be resurrection, not that someone should kill her assassin. But Brena doubts that kind of justice has ever been conferred on anyone, Jesus Christ included. He walks over to the boy's desk with the pink slip of paper in his hand. Hey, have you got a minute? he asks. Then he catches the boy minimizing the window in which he's been writing so that Brena can't read it and, even though he says, Yes, of course, Brena thinks: Bad attitude, kid, crumples up the note, throws it into the wastepaper basket beside the feet of this apprentice of criminal journalism and says: Nothing, it doesn't matter. And he goes straight from there to Karina's desk, flashes the box of Marlboros he's just taken out of his shirt pocket and asks: Want to come? And the woman gets up and goes with him.

Outside there are at least three other colleagues smoking. The ban on smoking in confined spaces in Buenos Aires has sparked a pavement culture that Jaime Brena quite enjoys. They sit on the kerb. How's things? asks Karina, hesitating briefly before taking the cigarette he offers her. Fine, he says, lighting his own. What did you decide about taking redundancy in the end? I still don't know. Sometimes I'm sure I want it, and other times I can't picture myself not coming here every day. Brena takes a long draw on the cigarette, then slowly lets the smoke out. Besides, I'm sure Rinaldi won't want to give me the same payout the others got. But you deserve it, more than anyone. What's that got to do with anything? Is being deserving any kind of guarantee? You're right, the girl says, and she puts the cigarette in her mouth for Brena to light it. What about your love life? Ah, that's one area in which I have taken voluntary redundancy, he says, and the girl laughs. He flicks the lighter until a flame leaps up, and she moves closer. You don't fool anyone, Brena. No, seriously, I just want a quiet life. So no more Irina? No, God help me. They smoke together in silence, looking out into the boulevard. Know what? says Brena. The other night I went down to buy something to eat and I passed this guy who was walking a dog, a beautiful big one, must have been a Labrador. And who was this guy? Never mind the guy – it's the dog that was important; I thought that I'd like a dog like that too. Perhaps I'll buy myself one. Oh Brena, you're crazy, you'd never have enough patience for a dog. What do you mean? I know you; after two months you'd be taking it back. Well, a dog isn't for life, not like marriage; if it doesn't work, it doesn't work. I'd find it easier to dismantle a marriage than to take a dog back, she says. Who do you take it to, anyway? But you don't know what it's like dismantling a marriage, he says. I don't want to, either. Brena takes a last drag and stubs out the cigarette in a trickle of water running under their legs beside the kerb. She's hardly smoked her own cigarette and is now playing with the ash. He looks at her, then says: Chazarreta's been found murdered, with his throat slit. Pedro Chazarreta? Yup. I don't believe you. They've just called to let me know. Front cover tomorrow, says Karina. Of *El Tribuno*? Only if the boy wakes up in time, says Brena doubtfully, and I wouldn't bet on that. Yes, he needs to wake up. Now the girl extinguishes her half-smoked cigarette in the running water. You hardly smoked it, he says. I had a few puffs, but my throat hurts a bit. Shall we go in? Do you know why I think women sleep facing up? Brena asks. Why? He looks at her, takes a deep breath, then, smiling, says: No, nothing, forget it. He gets to his feet and gives her his hand, helping her up. Are you going back in? Yes. You're not? I'm going to take a stroll around the block first. Will you do me a favour? Brena asks. Yes, of course. When you pass the boy's desk, will you tell him from me that there's a crumpled bit of pink paper in his bin and that he should read it? Yes, I'll tell him. Karina grasps his hand and holds it for a moment as though poised to tell him something else. But in the end she only repeats: Sure, I'll tell him. And walks away.

Brena could walk in any direction because – as he's all too aware – he's got nowhere in particular to go. Finally he decides to walk east, so that the sun will strike his back and not his eyes. It's not too hot, but the sunlight's reflection on those light paving stones has been making him frown for forty-four years. And today he doesn't feel like frowning. He turns his head one way and the other to stretch out his neck, fills his lungs with air, pulls his trousers up around the waist. He looks back over his shoulder to check that he's alone, that nobody is walking nearby. Then he holds his right hand a little in front of him, with his arm extended and his hand in a fist, and keeps walking in this position as though something were pulling at the end of a lead. His imaginary dog.

4

Nurit Iscar is working that afternoon on the book she's been commissioned to write: *Untying the Knots*. She hates it. The commission came from the ex-wife of a transport tycoon who, during and after her divorce, experimented with alternative lifestyles she believes to be "unique" and found "soul solutions" she wants to share with others. You won't believe the book you're going to write when I tell you my life story, she said on the day she interviewed Nurit for the job, never guessing how many times this particular ghostwriter – and other writers besides – had heard that same phrase or similar ones from other mouths. "If I tell you the story of my life and you write it up you'll win the Clarín prize", "My friends all say I've got enough material for a novel", "I'm going to tell you something – write this down and there's your next book – not just your next one, there's enough for at least three volumes!" Why do so many people think their lives are unique when I think mine's just the same as anyone else's? she asked herself then, and still does every so often. At least she's finished the stage of interviewing the "author" and now needs only to transcribe the tapes and start writing. The best bit. Playing with words, putting sentences together, conjugating verbs. Writing. And the transport tycoon's ex-wife is paying well. Very well. So Nurit tries not to think too much about "the message" that this woman hopes to get across, or about the knots, or what she means by the words she chooses, but rather of how they sound, how they sing, how one bounces off another, finally creating a melody that *Untying the Knots* doesn't deserve. It's for the words that she keeps writing. Not for whatever the transport man's ex-wife "wants to transmit". The sooner she hands in a finished draft, the sooner she gets paid. The problem looming is that after *Untying the Knots* there's no other work in view. But she doesn't want to worry about that yet.

By mid-afternoon, Nurit feels sufficiently lazy or bored to need an excuse for a break. Time for tea, she tells herself. A glance at her watch confirms that it's the right time, ten past five. At that very moment the boy in the Crime section of *El Tribuno*, having minutes ago uncrumpled the pink paper Jaime Brena threw in his wastepaper basket, is googling different combinations of keywords all plucked from that same note. But nothing useful comes up – it's all old, relating to the death not of Chazarreta, but of his wife. He checks Twitter, but nobody he follows has written anything on the subject. For a moment he wonders about tweeting something himself: "Anyone heard anything about Pedro Chazarreta being murdered?", but he dismisses the idea, realizing that it would mean alerting everyone else to a piece of news that appears at the moment to be his alone. And Jaime Brena's. The boy asks Karina for Brena's mobile number and she's annoyed by the way he asks for it, so assertively and cocksure, as if she had no choice but to give it to him. But she gives it to him all the same. It's always switched off, she says, but try anyway, if you want. Yeah, it's off, says the boy, swearing. He leaves a message on Jaime Brena's voicemail and tries his luck with Google again. And with Twitter. By the time Nurit Iscar has her toast ready on the table with her customary low-calorie jam and cream cheese, it's dawning on the boy that Jaime Brena has no intention of returning his call, nor perhaps of returning to the newsroom for the rest of the day. And without his help he can't get much further than what's on the crumpled piece of paper. Worse, he's wasted valuable time trying to track him down. That's why, while Nurit is adding a little more milk to her tea – she's given up coffee not because of insomnia or acidity but because someone told her (and she has no idea if it's true) that it causes cellulite – the Crime boy is striding down the corridor towards Rinaldi's office: best to bring him up to speed, he thinks, and get his opinion on which contact to call. Before going into the office he checks Twitter once more on his BlackBerry and now it is there: a tweet from a young radio and television journalist, a tweet that's already been retweeted several times, too. Just one line: Chazarreta, widower of Gloria Echagüe, found with his throat slit. Nothing more. The boy knocks on Rinaldi's door, waits for the words "Come in", then launches in, silently grateful that his boss isn't a techno-junkie.

Neither Nurit nor the Crime boy knows this, but just arrived at Chazarreta's house is the attorney, whose first complaint is that the crime scene is too busy. Milling around Chazarreta's body are: a group of police officers from the local station and their chief, Comisario Venturini, who, amid much friendly back-slapping, is explaining to the attorney that he was in a meeting at work when a colleague received the call informing him about the incident and he didn't want to miss the event; two more police chiefs from nearby stations who somehow got to hear about the case (they don't say how); the emergency ambulance crew that was contacted by guards from La Maravillosa, in line with the club's policy that they be summoned immediately following every verified accident – the very same service they called when Gloria Echagüe died; the homicide team, which is already drawing up a summary report; the forensic team, which arrived minutes before the attorney; a photographer; a planimetric surveyor; doctors; a biochemist; tracker dogs; a ballistics expert (who's present even though a throat-slitting may not seem to require it, in case there's also some stray bullet); and a neighbour from the club, acting as a witness and signatory to the summary report. The Criminal Procedure Code for the province of Buenos Aires doesn't require a witness, but it's better to be safe than sorry, said one of the police chiefs, and the others agreed. This case is going to have even more repercussions than the wife's, and we don't all want to end up with egg on our faces again. Hey boys, couldn't you think of anyone else to call? jokes the attorney as he makes his way towards the body. He walks around the armchair, studying Chazarreta's corpse from different angles, then after establishing which police chief is in charge, asks this man a few questions while observing how the neighbour who's been called in as a witness – who's nervous and reluctant to look at the body – drops the wrapper of a sweet he's about to eat onto the floor. The attorney points at the paper and says to one of the dog-handlers: Pick up that piece of evidence, it may lead us to the killer. The neighbour, nearly choking on his sweet, immediately bends down to pick up the paper.

Nurit Iscar spreads another slice of toast with cream cheese and low-calorie jam, puts it on the plate, then picks up the television remote and looks for a news channel. She skips from one to the next, trying to find something worth watching. The National Lottery results don't interest her; a raid on a sports shop less so; the Buenos Aires to Montevideo regatta not at all. But on Crónica TV, a red banner across the screen chills her: *Breaking News, Pedro Chazarreta found dead.* Nurit has to read it twice. Pedro Chazarreta found dead. Dead. And the newsreader's voice says: The widower of

Gloria Echagüe has died in tragically similar circumstances to his wife, from a fatal wound to his neck. Nurit calls Paula Sibona because she needs to tell this news to someone, but there's no one home and she doesn't leave a message. She can't reach Carmen Terrada, either. She scours the channels for more information, going from one to the next, back to the first, up and down the schedule, finding nothing. Minutes later, in his office, his back to the Crime boy (who's glued to his BlackBerry again), Rinaldi is doing the same as Nurit, but with better luck because even in those few minutes the news has spread to every channel. And this despite the fact that no journalist has been able to get into Chazarreta's private neighbourhood. The only mobile unit to get there so far is outside La Maravillosa, transmitting what little information can be gleaned at the barrier. These are the club regulations, the security officer keeps explaining to the reporter who's demanding to be let in. Rinaldi goes to a news channel that belongs to the same media group as *El Tribuno* while saying to the boy: Tell them to get me the TV news editor urgently. On the screen the newsreader is asking: Can we be sure that Pedro Chazarreta died as a result of having his throat slit? Yes, replies the Crime correspondent, as a picture appears of La Maravillosa's entrance sign bearing the words *Members only beyond this point.* There's still no official confirmation, but reliable sources have informed us that Pedro Chazarreta, whose recent trial for his wife's murder was dismissed on the grounds of lack of evidence, has been found dead with his throat slashed this morning, at the home the couple shared until three years ago, and in an armchair that was only yards away from where his wife's body was discovered. Then, lacking images to accompany their report on Chazarreta's death, the news channel run some relating to Gloria Echagüe's death instead. They've still got nothing, Lorenzo Rinaldi murmurs to himself while the Crime boy keeps trying to contact the TV news editor. For those viewers who don't remember the crime that had us all gripped in 2007, says the newsreader, half-smiling while waiting for the archive footage.

A reporter reprises the details of the case, explaining how Gloria Echagüe was found dead three years ago from a wound to the throat, also apparently the cause of her husband's death. Her body was discovered by a cousin, Carla Donatto, also resident in the Maravillosa country club, who had arranged to drop by for coffee early that evening. Gloria, who went to the gym at three o'clock every Sunday and followed her fifty-minute routine with a sauna, had evidently told her cousin to come at six o'clock. So it was Carla Donatto, who is married to Lucio Berraiz, ex-business associate and friend of Pedro Chazareta, who discovered her cousin's lifeless body face down, surrounded by fragments of glass in different shapes and sizes and lying half in, half out of the house across the French windows that separate the Chazarretas' veranda from their living room. She was wearing the same exercise clothes in which she had left the gym: trainers and a black-peaked Nike cap, which was still on her head.

Questions still remain about the case, says the reporter. Why, that Sunday, had Gloria Echagüe decided to enter her house by the French windows, when she always used the side entrance leading into the kitchen? Why was there no pool of blood under the body, as one would expect in the case of a throat-slashing? What was a stone ball, identical to the decorative ones in a bowl in the hallway, doing in the living room? Why would Gloria Echagüe, who according to statements from her friends was so careful with her woodblock floor, have expected to find the French windows open on a day of unremitting drizzle and 90 per cent humidity? Which part of Gloria's body had broken the glass? Her knee? Her forehead? Why, then, were there no other wounds on her body? And what were those small cuts on the palms of her hands? Which of the pieces of glass around her had made such an even, clean gash, parallel to the hypothetical line of the dead woman's shoulders? Why did the wet veranda show no muddy marks or footprints on such a foul day?

Apparently nobody had thought to ask these questions that Sunday. At least it seemed that nobody had asked them. Carla Donatto immediately called Chazarreta's mobile; he was buying wine in the country club's store. "Come quickly, Pedro, come back to your house. It's Gloria", she screamed, according to the statement that would be read out at the trial. And Chazarreta took seven minutes to get there. He was at the checkout when he took the call, whereupon he paid with a card (his till receipt showed it was 18.15), got into his car and drove straight to his home. Exactly seven minutes, according to the transcript. Two minutes at the checkout, one minute walking to the car (which was at the far end of the parking lot), a minute to load the wine bottles into the boot, a minute to pass the clubhouse at a time of day when priority has to be given to the children coming out of their activity session and two minutes to cover the five blocks that separate the store from his home at the maximum permitted speed of twelve miles an hour. Seven minutes.

Carla Donatto's husband took care of the funeral arrangements, including obtaining a fake death certificate stating that Gloria Echagüe had died of natural causes. Everything was done at lightning speed, and Pedro Chazarreta's wife was buried in less than forty-eight hours. But a week later Gloria's mother, who lived abroad and with whom her daughter's relations had cooled since her marriage to Chazarreta, began to have doubts. She booked a flight over, went to visit her daughter's grave, asked some questions. The answers didn't convince her. Her doubts grew. And eventually other people came to share them. The attorney requested the body be exhumed, and after forensic reports and other legal procedures the truth came to light: Gloria Echagüe had been murdered outside her house, then dragged to the position in which she was found after someone had broken the French windows with a stone ball. The murderer – perhaps with accomplices – meticulously cleaned away the blood that had stained the veranda, wiped away footprints, staged the crime scene and left only then, without anyone having seen them. The murder weapon was never found.

The TV shows photos of Gloria Echagüe, photos of Pedro Chazarreta, photos of them both together. Photos from their youth, more recent photos. Photos of Gloria Echagüe with some female friends. Photos of Chazarreta with male friends. Photos of the couple on their wedding day. Holiday photos. Photos of Chazarreta on the day of his wife's funeral. Photos of Chazarreta on the first day of his trial. Photos of Chazarreta being taken into custody. Photos of Chazarreta being freed. A brief commentary from Jaime Brena, the only journalist who managed to interview Chazarreta at that time. But of course nobody yet has that killer shot: the one of Chazarreta dead. Cut.

Then Lorenzo Rinaldi says to the Crime boy: We're not going to be the first on this, but we've got to be the best, and he takes the phone out of the boy's hands.

Nurit Iscar goes to her computer and types in, one by one, the addresses of the online news sites that come to mind first: *La Nación, Clarín, El Tribuno, Página/12, Télam, Tiempo Argentino, Perfil, Crónica, La Gaceta, La Voz del Interior, La Primera de la Mañana.* And all the while she's thinking how many people, when they hear the news, will say justice has been done. This is the same conclusion Jaime Brena reached several hours before, when he was jotting down the information Comisario Venturini gave him on the pink notepaper he later threw into the Crime boy's wastepaper basket and which is now on Rinaldi's desk. Because even if Justice, in the strictest sense, the Justice of judges and courts, freed Chazarreta for lack of evidence, most of the country, rightly or wrongly, still believes that it was he who murdered his wife, or had her murdered. For her part, Nurit Iscar keeps an open mind precisely because of that lack of evidence. She understands the others' argument: why pretend something was an accident when even an idiot can see it wasn't? Why not immediately get the police involved? Why obtain a false death certificate? Can people who were educated at the best schools and universities really be so stupid? But the compelling evidence is still missing: a murder weapon with prints, a witness, a DNA sample from a strand of hair, a drop of sweat or blood, anything to condemn Chazarreta irrefutably; and so she – though she may be wrong – prefers to leave room for doubt. It's right to be doubtful: what she feels, what she intuits, isn't important. Not without proof. It doesn't matter what she thinks of Chazarreta. Everyone is innocent until proven otherwise. And she doesn't know if Pedro Chazarreta is innocent; only that it hasn't been possible to prove he isn't. The same can't be said of Jaime Brena or the other 99.99 per cent of the population: they have absolutely no doubt that the man was his wife's murderer. Or that he ordered her death. Or that he knows who did it and why, and he's keeping quiet about it. It all amounts to the same thing: he's guilty. Justice isn't democratic, though; one can't vote on a person's innocence or guilt the way one votes for a president or a governor. If it were, if justice depended on tallying up the votes of public opinion, there would certainly have been more than a few mistakes. Mistakes get made, even as things are. As Nurit scans the news bulletins for more information on Chazareta's death she considers the different reactions people will have when they hear the news. "Justice has been done"; "What goes around, comes around"; "God is just"; "You reap what you sow". Some of them will have learned the news at the same time she did, or will find out when they watch the evening bulletin, or from the morning newspaper tomorrow; people in the flat opposite hers, or the one downstairs, or the one in the next block, people in the corner café. She double-clicks on the homepage of the *La Primera* newspaper and sees that there's a short report by Zippo. As she's starting to read it, the telephone rings and, although she doesn't answer – she never answers without filtering her calls, so that she can hear the voice and decide whether or not to pick up – she pauses for a moment, not wanting to be distracted from her reading and confident that, once the speaker is identified, she'll reject the call. But the voice, *that* voice, and the way it names her, chills her as surely as it did a moment ago when she first read the headline announcing Pedro Chazareta's murder. More so, even. Hello Betty Boo, says the voice; and then: Call me. Chazareta's been murdered, and I'm hoping this time you won't let me down. Then he hangs up. There's a dialling tone. The answering machine cuts off. The person ringing forgot to say who it was, or rather was certain that Nurit Iscar would know who was making the call. And he was right: she knows. He doesn't need to tell her. There's only one man in the world who, even today, can call Nurit by that name, Betty Boo; a man whose voice alone can send shivers into places inside her that Nurit Iscar had almost forgotten existed: Lorenzo Rinaldi. It's because of him – and to a lesser

47

degree Chazarreta himself, or at least the crime that most people believe him to have committed – that Nurit Iscar, after a successful literary career (measured by parameters which in literature confer success on some and failure on others) has never written another novel of her own, opting to make her living as the ghostwriter for people who want to communicate things of such nugatory interest to Nurit as *Untying the Knots*. Hello Betty Boo. Nurit rewinds and listens to the tape again at least five times – Hello Betty Boo – as though needing to confirm to herself who the caller really is, even though she has absolutely no doubts on that score.

She doesn't return the call. She knows Lorenzo Rinaldi will call again in a while, in a couple of hours. She knows that Rinaldi doesn't give up easily if he doesn't get what he wants. And she also knows that she, Nurit Iscar or Betty Boo, will have no option but to answer when he calls.

5

Nurit Iscar and Lorenzo Rinaldi first met in 2005 as guests on the same television programme. She had just published *Death by Degrees*, her third novel which, like the first two, had shot up the bestseller list as soon as it arrived in the bookshops. He'd been awarded a prize in Spain for his journalistic output and had a new non-fiction book doing the rounds, *Who's In Charge? Real Power in Argentina's 21st-Century Media*. Their first meeting wasn't on the set but in make-up. When Nurit arrived he was already sitting in one of those high chairs – like the ones barbers use – with a plastic cape over his shoulders to protect his suit from the powder. They put her in the seat next to his. As soon as she sat down Nurit told the make-up artist that she liked to look simple, natural. Cover the wrinkles, definitely, but not so it shows, she asked. Beside her, Rinaldi smiled. What wrinkles? he asked and she, sensing that she was beginning to blush, pointed apologetically to her cheeks a few seconds before her face went completely red: I get rosacea. Ah, he said, and smiled again. They sat in silence as the make-up artists did their work, but two or three times their eyes met in the mirror. Before he left Rinaldi came over, this time openly looking at her but addressing himself to the make-up artist rather than to her: Hasn't she got pretty curls? Beautiful, said the man, shaking out Nurit's black hair so that the curls lay better. She felt uncomfortable and wondered if that was to do with finding herself under scrutiny, receiving a compliment, pre-interview nerves, the make-up or the rosacea. With every interview, as with every plane flight she took, she seemed not to feel more relaxed but instead more aware of the possibility of crashing. And before and during the interview, without fail – the same as when she buckled her belt at the moment of take-off – she'd always ask herself: What am I doing here? And yet there she was again. As a way of distracting herself she began counting the different-sized brushes the make-up artist had spread across the counter: fourteen; and then she counted the colours in the shadow palette: sixty-four. Lean your head back for me, darling, and look up, said the make-up artist, because Nurit hadn't managed not to blink while he was trying to apply her eyeliner. See how well your friend behaved? Now he's all ready, he said with a nod to Lorenzo Rinaldi, who was taking off his cape. See you in the studio, Rinaldi said to Nurit, and went out. She felt somehow relieved not to be under observation any more, and the make-up artist was able to finish his job well enough. Who's he? she asked as the man finished off her look by dusting a little loose powder over her cheekbones. Lorenzo Rinaldi, the editor of *El Tribuno* – don't you know him? Yes, by name, of course, and from the paper, but I've never seen him before, said Nurit. He's one of the most intelligent men in the country, the make-up artist went on, adding, And also one of the most fucked-up. After that day Nurit often asked herself why she had paid so much attention to Lorenzo Rinaldi's reputed intelligence while ignoring the second part of the description, which might have spared her more than a few sleepless nights and crying jags.

This show on which they were appearing followed the model of most cultural programming: it was well-intentioned, low-budget, with two armchairs and a desk as a set and each segment devoted to one guest. The first was filled by a dramatist who had recently taken a version of Copi's *Eva Perón* to a theatre festival in Berlin and won great acclaim for it. Nurit arrived on the set as this segment was ending, and as she opened the door the technicians and assistants fixed her with a look that said, Make any noise and you're dead. Rinaldi, glued to his mobile on Silent mode, didn't even look up, and she took a chair directly behind his, as if they were travelling in a bus. He smelled of perfume or shaving lotion; a good one, expensive, definitely French, Nurit thought. After the first ad break it was his turn. His presence filled the space, his confidence so innate that you might have wondered who was the presenter and who the guest. Nurit watched him from her seat in the studio's darker reaches, surrounded by cables and miscellaneous stuff – tables, stools, a set of cutlery, a plastic fried egg and steak – that had come from the disassembled sets of programmes probably long since gone off-air. Rinaldi spoke about the prize, journalism, his new book and politics; though at that time he was a less bitter opponent of the president than he later became, so the interview was friendly and not as heated as Rinaldi gets nowadays when he starts talking about "el Señor Presidente", spitting out the words with that rasping contempt she knows so well. Nurit was drawn to his strong, wide hands, which sprang into the air whenever some part of his story particularly enthused him. And to the grey hairs that were beginning to show at his temples. And to his voice: thick, firm, but deliberate. She thought of her husband – she can't remember now exactly what she thought, but Rinaldi's voice, his hands and the memory of his cologne brought him to mind for a moment. An assistant asked permission to run a microphone line under her clothes, distracting her, and when Nurit looked up again the interview had ended and Lorenzo Rinaldi was taking his leave with a kiss, holding both the presenter's hands and looking deep into her eyes. If the woman hadn't been ten years older than him, Nurit would have sworn he was making a pass at her. Later, when she got to know him better, she discovered that he often looks like that; that Lorenzo Rinaldi is the kind of person who seeks to seduce whomever is front of him: man, woman, young, old, tall, short, fat or thin. As Rinaldi walked past her on his way out of the studio, Nurit faltered, caught her foot in a cable lying across the gangway and had to grab his arm to avoid falling. Careful, Betty Boop, Lorenzo Rinaldi said with a smile. What? she asked. Hasn't anybody ever told you that you look like Betty Boop? And without answering, Nurit Iscar wondered if this might also be meant flirtatiously. Look, I don't know if you wear suspenders, I'm saying it because of your black curls and your figure – especially the curls, he clarified, looking her in the eye, and instinctively she reached up to touch them, as though checking they were still there. Next time get them to do your lips redder and then you'll be the authentic Betty Boop, he said, tracing the outline of her lips in the air, and then he took a business card out of the inside pocket of his jacket and handed it to her. At your service, he said. Nurit asked him to wait while she looked in her bag for one of her own cards, but this was a much less graceful manoeuvre than the one with which Rinaldi had extracted the card from his pocket. If there was one area of Nurit's life where disorder reigned it was in her handbag: supermarket tickets; three packets of paper handkerchiefs, all open, plus more lying loose; tampons – because even though her period had started to be irregular since she turned forty-eight, it hadn't yet abandoned her altogether; two lip pencils; three pens, two of which worked; her house keys; a toothbrush; tweezers; pliers; an electricity bill that needed to be paid within the week; a book; a diary; her phone; and a pair of silk tights in case she got a ladder in the ones she was wearing. She blushed again, fearing for a moment that Rinaldi may have seen the tampons or the tights, but this time she knew there was no need to make excuses: in that murky part of the studio and with the foundation they'd put on her, nobody would notice. Over the speaker came the irritated voice of the director: Guys, why is nobody bringing Nurit Iscar on set? Nurit looked up when she heard her name and realized that while she had been rummaging in her bag Lorenzo Rinaldi hadn't been the only one waiting for her; there were also two assistants, a producer and even the presenter, who had come over to see what was going on. Don't worry about it now, Lorenzo said, we've got your contact details at the paper. He said goodbye, then the assistant walked her over to the relevant armchair and she sat down. The presenter greeted her with the same smile she had used to dismiss Rinaldi. You look lovely, she said. You've lost weight, haven't you? I don't know, Nurit said. Maybe. Yes, yes, you're looking great, said the woman, and arranged the books on her desk for the camera to take a close-up. It seemed as though they were about to start, but the presenter made a sign to the cameraman then looked intently at Nurit as though something were wrong. It's your lips, she explained. They've put on way too much lipstick. They're very shiny, and a lot of shine doesn't look good on-screen. Tissues, please, she yelled, apparently to someone miles away, and then, turning to Nurit: Do you mind if I take a bit off? No, of course, if you think that's best, Nurit said, and obediently pressed down on a paper tissue the woman placed between her lips. That's better, the presenter said. Then the woman pulled her suit jacket straight, fluffed out her hair a little with her fingers, checked her reflection in a monitor and finally called: Bring my lipstick and a mirror over here for a second, please. An assistant sprang up to get these things for her, then the presenter touched up her own lips until they were as glossy as Nurit's had been before she had made her clamp down on the tissue. Ready? she asked, when she had finished perfecting her make-up. And without waiting for Nurit to reply, she got on with the show: In this final part of the programme we're joined by the writer Nurit Iscar, who has just published her new novel *Death by Degrees*, a book I devoured and which I guarantee you viewers will also relish. Nurit was struck by that word, "devour". What would it mean for someone to devour a book? That they chewed it up? Swallowed it? Digested and expelled it? It reminded her of that Fontanarrosa story, "A Literary Soirée", where the protagonists, two scholars of literature, roast classic books in the oven then eat them with potatoes. As Nurit imagined the shiny-lipped presenter sinking her teeth into *Death by Degrees*, tearing off the cover and first few pages in one bite, she completely missed her own short biography being shown on the screen. She was still trying to banish the image as the presenter asked her first question: Do you mind being known as an author of bestsellers? No need to think about the answer; yet again, almost automatically, she rolled out the stock responses she habitually used to answer that question – a stock phrase in itself – which she had been asked too many times: that some of her books have been bestsellers, not all of them; that no, it doesn't bother her, that Saramago, Cortázar, Piglia, Murakami and Bolaño also have published bestselling fiction and that they represent very different kinds of writing and readers; that it is always an honour to be chosen by a reader. That writers themselves never think in these terms – at least she doesn't; that these are marketing concepts that have no bearing on the writing itself, etc. etc. But as she reached the end of her answer she seemed to find herself once again apologizing in some way, for being a bestselling author and for the fact that her books were quick reads, popular with people who generally don't read much. And at the presenter's prompting, she had to take some time to consider if a book that can be read quickly is better or not than one that requires many hours of reading, as if any one single quick-read is comparable to any single slow-read. To which she ended up replying: The truth is that I don't know. She lied just once, when asked, Do you mind what some literary critics say about you? No, I don't mind at all. It was only at the end of the interview, when she gesticulated with her right hand, rounding out some elusive observation, that she realized she was still holding Lorenzo Rinaldi's card. And once again Nurit Iscar thought of her husband.

Later that night, as she ate dinner with him and their children, she felt strange, at fault, as if aware that the afternoon's clumsy manoeuvres had concealed some feeling within her that wasn't appropriate given the circumstances. Circumstances aren't set in stone, Lorenzo Rinaldi said, some time after that day, just before kissing her. And they weren't. Soon after that kiss Nurit Iscar told her husband that she wanted to separate. It took a while; he wasn't ready for it. But neither was he in love with her, any more, by that stage in their marriage. And these days she tends to think that he should be grateful to her. Rinaldi's sudden arrival in Nurit's life served only to prove that their marriage had been over for longer than she'd realized. Juan, her elder son, had been living with a friend since he went to university and Rodrigo, the younger one, who was also starting university that year, soon went to join them, sparing him the decision of which parent to live with. Nurit was close to both her sons, but their meetings were much less frequent than she would have liked and usually prompted by calls from her and invitations to weekend meals which, as the boys grew increasingly independent, became less and less regular, with last-minute absences backed up by different excuses.

The relationship with Lorenzo Rinaldi lasted two years, the first of these sustained by Nurit's desire – and his promise – that he would separate from his wife as soon as possible. Even once she'd realized that would never happen, it took all of the second year for her to leave him. The end of their affair coincided with the death of Gloria Echagüe. And with the publication of *Only If You Love Me*. After Echagüe's death, Rinaldi asked her to write a series of articles for the paper. But what kind of article? I'm not a journalist. Nonfiction, he replied, like Truman Capote. Capote interviewed two men convicted of murder, she said, and here not only is there no conviction, there's also nothing known, only confusion. That's why it's a job for a writer, Betty Boo. It's always the same in the first stages of a crime case: there are no concrete facts, or they don't come to light and the only option is to invent, imagine, fictionalize. That sounds rather cavalier, she said. It would be cavalier for a journalist to take that approach, but you aren't one. All the same, it doesn't seem right for a newspaper to publish something invented about a real case. People may get confused. People always get confused. Well, I don't want to be responsible for their confusion. Betty Boo, don't go looking for moral arguments where there aren't any. It's not about morals, it's about ethics. Aren't they the same? No, I'm agnostic. Don't overcomplicate this. All I want is for you to sit down in the clubhouse at La Maravillosa and listen to what people are saying, to shop in the store where they shop, to jog down the streets they jog on, to play tennis. I can't play tennis! So take lessons. No,

Lorenzo, that's enough. I've got my new novel coming out, and that's my priority now. I'm committed to readings, festivals, interviews – I haven't got time. Ask some other writer who's interested in doing this, there's bound to be someone. But I want the "Dark Lady of Argentine literature" to do it. No. I want my Betty Boo to do it, he said, coming nearer and kissing her. And she felt that it was the kiss of Judas. A few days later Nurit Iscar left Lorenzo Rinaldi for good. The same day *El Tribuno* ran a long article by Jaime Brena on the Gloria Echagüe crime in La Maravillosa, accompanied by an opinion piece from a young novelist considering what story might lie behind this as-yet-unsolved death. A death that never was solved.

A month later the first review of Iscar's novel, *Only If You Love Me*, appeared in the cultural supplement of *El Tribuno*. The first, and the worst, paving the way for those that followed. They weren't together any more, but Lorenzo Rinaldi called to warn her anyway: Looks like the reviewer didn't like your book, Betty Boo, but if I stick my oar in it'll make things worse. No, don't do anything, she told him, and waited anxiously for Sunday to arrive and with it *El Tribuno*'s cultural supplement. The review's heading was: "*Only If You Love Me*, Nurit Iscar's new novel, fails to deliver". The byline was Karina Vives, a name she had never heard before. A name Nurit may never forget. These days Karina Vives is the editor of *El Tribuno*'s Culture section and sits to the left of Jaime Brena. And every so often goes out to smoke on the pavement with him.

6

During the two years of her relationship with Lorenzo Rinaldi, Nurit Iscar put a lot of thought and a fair bit of research into the character of Betty Boop and the significance of her image. And although she didn't share all her thoughts with her friends, some of their sessions ended in spirited arguments about the character. Nurit's doubts weren't so much about whether the nickname chosen by her married boyfriend (she never liked the word lover) was affectionate or not, but whether she appreciated being called it in the first place. She was familiar with the drawing, of course, both as a cartoon strip and in its animated form, and she could see that the woman with the round face, black curls and big eyes was similar to her in a way. But she was also interested in knowing what Betty Boop represented, now and in previous eras. And if that represented her, because every symbol stands for something and no representation is innocent of associations. Don't complicate everything, Rinaldi told her. You look a bit like the cartoon, that's all. But Nurit Iscar was, and is, complicated, and has no problem acknowledging this. If I weren't complicated I wouldn't still be going out with you, was her riposte. Complicated and prickly. That too, she agreed. In her immediate circle, the nickname Betty Boo had both defenders and detractors. Her children liked it, though of course they had no idea where it came from. Her friends were either for or against, depending not only on their own criteria but on their opinion of Lorenzo Rinaldi and the confusion in his love life, which meant that all aspects of their own friend's life, and not just the love bit, were kept perpetually in limbo. Nurit could never wholly commit to any arrangement in case Rinaldi contrived a last-minute escape from his wife and was free to do something with her: planning holidays or a weekend break, or a trip to the cinema. Carmen said the man was a waster, and that giving this nickname to Nurit was not only akin to branding cattle but also a way to avoid leaving traces of his lover's real name that might be discovered by his wife. You are my wife, Rinaldi would reply to Nurit's misgivings, and she wanted to believe him. Paula Sibona agreed with Carmen, though with her own, choicer vocabulary: That bastard son of a thousand whores. She wasn't so bothered about the cattle or the traces, but she did mind watching her friend wait miserably for Rinaldi to make decisions it was increasingly obvious he had no intention of making. She liked the nickname Betty Boo, though: Because it's true that you look a bit like her. I like her as an archetype of the sexy, submissive woman, and it's definitely better that he should call you Betty Boo than Daisy, Minnie, Barbie or Olive Oyl. And even the bastard son of a thousand whores can occasionally have a good idea, so why not run with it? That was Paula's take. Viviana Mansini, on the other hand, had no opinion on the nickname, limiting herself to saying every now and then: Poor Nurit, and what about the poor woman he's married to, right? Let's not forget her. To which Carmen Terrada replied: The person who shouldn't have forgotten her is Rinaldi.

So intrigued were they by Betty Boop that, on one of their third-Sunday-of-the-month newspaper-reading sessions, the friends agreed to put aside their cuttings and dedicate themselves exclusively to exchanging whatever information each had managed to glean about the cartoon. The best prepared, as always, was Carmen, who had not only brought a sheaf of ordered and highlighted texts, but whose readings came with citations and sources, usually Wikipedia. But don't they tell schoolchildren to do research instead of getting everything off Wikipedia? I don't, retorted Carmen. Wikipedia gets a bad press because it's the most democratic website there is: made by everyone, for everyone, with no editorial line. That's the real issue, that's what annoys people: who owns knowledge, information. And then she started reading what she had found on Betty Boop: She was born – or whatever the word is for the birth of a cartoon character – in 1930. She appeared for the first time in August that year in the cartoon strip *Dizzy Dishes*, in the series *Talkartoon*, produced by Max Fleischer. She was created by Grim Natwick, an established animator at that time, and modelled on the singer Helen Kane – the one who had a hit with "I Wanna Be Loved By You" – who died at the age of 62 from breast cancer after a ten-year struggle through which she was accompanied until the very end by her husband of twenty-seven years. Poor Helen, said Paula Sibona. Kane was working at Paramount Pictures, the distributor of *Talkartoon*, when Betty Boop was created, Carmen went on. Natwick's drawing began as a French poodle and gradually took on human form. It wasn't until 1932 that the character – as yet unchristened – became unmistakably female, when the long ears morphed into her characteristic hoop earrings and the black snout was replaced by her little button nose. That same year, the producers realized that she was much more popular than her boyfriend Bimbo, and she grew from being a supporting character in *Talkartoon* to a central figure bearing the name our friend here would later inherit in its phonetic form: Betty Boop. Betty Boo.

Natwick's creation was the first female flapper to appear in a cartoon. In the 1920s the word "flapper" was coined for young women who cast off the traditional corset or adapted it to the new shape, reduced the length of their skirts and sported unconventional hairstyles. These were women who liked going to private clubs to listen and dance to jazz, a rhythm that most people had never heard, let alone danced to. Flappers rebelled against the stereotype that had been imposed on women up until that era and transgressed the norms dictating how a woman was supposed to behave: they smoked, they drove cars or motorcycles at top speed, they drank hard liquor and wore little make-up. Or – at the other extreme – they made themselves up in a style more commonly associated with actresses and prostitutes. Do they always have to put us in the same category? Paula Sibona complained. A white powdered face with really black eyebrows and eyelashes to emphasize the red lips in "kiss-proof" lipstick. And lots of bracelets and strings of beads. High-heeled shoes for going out and comfortable ones for working. Opinions vary on the origin of the word, but in 1920 *The Flapper* was the title of an American film starring Olive Thomas and depicting the lifestyle of this new breed of woman. Thomas was considered the original flapper, and was remembered not so much for her career in silent films as for her tragic death: at twenty-five in a Parisian hotel, after a night drinking in the bars of Montparnasse with her husband Jack Pickford, Olive Thomas drank a bottle of mercury bichloride (a substance Pickford was using as a topical solution for sores caused by his syphilis), and this was the cause of her death several days later in the American Hospital in Neuilly, on the outskirts of Paris. Pickford and his brother-in-law were with her when she died. In the absence of other evidence, her death was ruled accidental, although suspicions remained about a suicide or murder.

It was only some time after that Sunday devoted to Wikipedia, cartoons, flappers and the women who inspired them that Nurit Iscar was struck by how many coincidences there were between the deaths of Olive Thomas and Gloria Echagüe. And the deaths of so many other women. Do men more often kill their wives, or women their husbands? When the circumstances of a woman's death are in question, does suspicion always fall on the husband? Are the suspicions always well founded? And what about when a woman kills her husband? Is she more likely to go to prison? Which of the two deaths – or murders – was, or is, more socially acceptable? Has any woman ever murdered her husband in a country club or a gated community? Why, after so many years, have we not forgotten the names of certain women whose deaths or disappearances were never explained: Norma Mirta Penjerek, Oriel Briant, Doctor Cecilia Giubileo, María Soledad Morales, or María Marta García Belsunce? How many unresolved or half-resolved cases of murder are lodged in the collective memory?

The appearance of this new style of woman, Carmen continued after dessert, coincided historically with the First World War and some of its consequences: the scarcity of men (Tell me about it, quipped Paula Sibona), the need for women to join the workforce, fashion styles dictated by what actresses, dancers and singers of the era were wearing. But while writers like F. Scott Fitzgerald or Anita Loos popularized the image of flappers as attractive, seductive and independent women, Dorothy Parker dedicated a poem to them with the title "The Flapper: A Hate Song". And as Carmen read the poem, Nurit wondered whether she could really be likened to Betty Boop, since she was also a fan of Dorothy

Parker. Perhaps she was less of a fan than she thought? Dorothy Parker died at seventy-three, a few years older than Helen Kane and much older than Olive Thomas at the time of their respective deaths, but, in contrast to the singer who inspired the creation of Betty Boop and the iconic flapper actress, Parker died in a New York hotel, accompanied only by her dog and a glass of whisky. And Nurit wondered again who had died in better company. Who would provide a more loyal and loving presence: a much older husband, a syphilitic and potentially murderous one, or a dog and a glass of whisky? How will she, Nurit Iscar, die, when her time comes? How old will she be? And where? Who will be there with her? Will she be able to choose the answer to any of these questions? Why does she, a fifty-something woman, wonder so much about her own death? For that very reason: because I am over fifty, Nurit thinks, answering the only question for which she has an answer. More than halfway through life, on the other side of the hill, where the land falls away towards the next valley.

Petting or sexual play without coitus or leading to coitus was an accepted part of life for flappers, Carmen went on. Oh that must be like *peteras* today, said Rodrigo, who was also at home that Sunday when his mother's friends came round. What's that? Nurit asked him. *Peteras*, Mum, girls who'll blow you. Who'll suck you off. Don't be disgusting in front of my friends! You asked, Mum. Listen, young man, Paula Sibona interjected, you can grow up and leave this house a right-winger or a lefty, heterosexual or gay, a graduate or an illiterate; you can choose to belong to whichever urban tribe you like. The only thing neither your mother nor we are going to allow you to be is sexist. What did I say?! Nothing, nothing, I'm just telling you, in case; it seemed to me that when you referred to oral sex just then you were a bit contemptuous of the woman's role. Not at all; I love getting blow-jobs. That's enough! Nurit intervened. You brought up the subject of petting, not me, Rodrigo complained. Because we're investigating something that has to do with flappers. With what? Flappers, a group of women that first appeared in the 1920s … OK, OK, forget about it, the boy interrupted, and went off to watch the television.

Flappers were popular but they were defeated – as is so often the case – by an economic crisis: the 1929 Wall Street Crash and the Great Depression which followed. That decade saw a resurgence in conservative ideas and religious sanctions, and growing disapproval of these women's liberal approach to life, and not only in sexual matters. Even the character of Betty Boop was toned down: they made the poor girl's skirt longer, covered up her cleavage and finally took away her suspenders. But the real Betty Boop survived censorship, and various flapper symbols remained as a nod to future generations. To future generations in the western world, that is, which isn't the whole world.

Betty Boop is and will always be a definitively sensual and sexual woman. That's what matters. She wears short skirts and stockings, she flaunts her breasts in low-cut tops (big breasts, but not enormous like Viviana Mansini's since she went through the menopause, Carmen clarified), other characters in the series try to spy on her when she's bathing, she likes to dance hula-hula, swinging her hips and repeating the phrase "Boop Boop a Doop" as she dances – a phrase Helen Kane tried to prevent her from using, filing a suit against the production company that she ended up losing. Betty Boop was one of the first cartoon characters to make a cameo, appearing in *Popeye the Sailor*. In the 1960s she went into full colour and in the 1980s there was a boom in merchandising; today you can see Betty Boop's image on everything from underwear to Visa cards. In 1988 she made another cameo appearance in the Oscar-winning *Who Framed Roger Rabbit?* In 1994, her 1933 film *Snow-White* was selected by the United States Library of Congress for preservation in the National Film Registry. Is that good? asked Paula Sibona. I don't know if I'd want my image preserved for all eternity in an archive; the thought of my image surviving my living body by such a long margin scares me a bit. But a cartoon's body doesn't age like ours, said Carmen. Well, thanks for clearing that up, said Paula.

Do the secondary school girls who today have her image stamped on their folders, their pencil cases, their backpacks or T-shirts know what Betty Boop represents? Do they know that she had to be toned down in the 1930s? Why is a cartoon woman re-emerging so strongly in the twenty-first century? Is Betty Boop simply another marketing product for our unthinking consumption? Nurit Iscar doesn't think so. She doesn't believe that Betty Boop's ubiquity is merely commercial. She still believes in the strength transmitted by the icon, even if it is working subconsciously on those who look to her eighty years later.

7

At half past six Lorenzo Rinaldi calls Nurit Iscar again, and this time when she hears his voice she picks up. She's nervous, but prepared. After his first call an hour or so earlier, she's spoken twice with Paula Sibona, once with Carmen Terrada and exchanged a volley of emails with both of them. Don't act as if I were about to screw up my life, we're not twenty any more, she wrote, after the fifth email from Carmen insisting how dangerous it would be to get involved with Rinaldi again. At least ask him if he's separated from his wife first, suggested Paula. So much time has passed – for all we know he might be free now. She was always the most optimistic of the three of them. It's a work call, nothing more, Nurit replied, then shut down the computer so as not to read one more word of advice, warning or reprimand from her friends until after she had spoken to Lorenzo Rinaldi.

This time you have to do it, Betty Boo; it's been years since anyone heard from you or read you. When was the last time you had a new book in the shops? More than three years, the same length of time since we last saw each other, she thinks, though she doesn't answer the question. A feature piece like this in a paper like *El Tribuno* will get you back in the ring. The thing is, I'm not sure I want to be in a ring again. Though, if I had to choose, I'd probably rather tackle a bull than throw myself to this city's literary sharks again. OK, it'll get you back in touch with your readers, does that sound better? Nurit

Iscar doesn't answer because for a moment she's absorbed by the sound of Lorenzo Rinaldi's voice rather than by what he's saying. His voice is the same; it hasn't changed in these three years. The voice takes longer to age, she thinks. And what about his hands? And will he still have those grey hairs at the temple that she used to stroke, or will his hair be whiter now? She makes an effort to concentrate again on what the voice is saying: How much do you want? A column? Half a page? She says nothing. Can you name me one writer today who can command half a page in a newspaper read by millions of Argentines? She sighs and tries a direct question: Why do you want me to do it? You've got Jaime Brena in the newsroom – who could be better? He must be the journalist who did the most investigating and knows most about the murder of Chazarreta's wife. Jaime Brena is out. What does that mean, "out"? He's moved to another section of the paper. Oh, I didn't know that, she says. Why? An editorial decision, Rinaldi says. "Editorial decision", that's a nice way of saying nothing; look, tell me really: why me? For the same reason – an editorial decision. No, you don't get round me with pat phrases. True, I'd almost forgotten how stubborn you are. Let's see, Betty Boo, it has to be you because in a case like this, especially at the beginning, nobody knows zip because of the gagging order; at this stage, there's no point in investigating and then repeating the few things everybody can say. We need thoughtful, imaginative and – above all – great writing. The way to pull people in at the start is with writing, not with information. You're the Dark Lady of Argentine literature, and only the Dark Lady can provide what *El Tribuno* needs at the moment: I know all there is to know about the world of news and I'm the editor of this newspaper, that's how I know that you're the best option, just as you were three years ago, even though you didn't accept the commission then. That's what "editorial decision" means – do you like it better now? A bit more. So will you do it? If I did, what I could offer wouldn't be journalism. I know that. I want you because you're a novelist. Young journalists are getting worse and worse; you'd think they write with their feet. I want somebody who writes well, it's as simple as that. Brena writes well, she says. But he has other issues. Who doesn't? Look, Betty Boo, I've got a place for you in La Maravillosa; one of the paper's directors bought a house there a while ago with the idea of using it at weekends, but he never goes. Move in there tomorrow with whoever you want – try not to make me jealous – and start writing. Listen, watch, think, invent and write. It's not the truth I'm after, it's writing that captivates, it's your interpretation of that world, your description of the people you see around, all those things you do so well. Think it over and I'll ring you back in two hours for an answer. She's silent for a moment, then says: OK, call me in two hours.

"Try not to make me jealous"? The shameless reprobate said that? says Paula Sibona incredulously. Yes, says Nurit, who has summoned her friends to an emergency meeting at her house. You know what? I can see that you want to do this, and that's really alarming, says Carmen Terrada. But I swear it's not because of Rinaldi. No, no, of course not, says Paula sarcastically. It's for me, Nurit insists, because it's a job, because in two weeks I'll have finished untying the knots of Mr Transport's ex-wife and there'll be no visible means of support, because it could be an opportunity to change what happened three years ago. Is Rinaldi still married? Carmen asks. I don't know, she replies. If he's still married you're not going to change anything, Paula asserts. I don't mean to change my relationship with him, I mean to change a decision regarding my career that was probably wrong; I think that if I had accepted that job at the time I'd probably still be writing my own novels now. It looks better viewed from that perspective, says Carmen. But only from that perspective. Would one of you mind coming over to water my plants? Holy shit, you're actually going to do it, Paula says. I don't know; I just think that this would move me towards more fulfilling work than writing other people's books. You're right about that, says Paula. But be careful where Rinaldi is concerned, begs Carmen. I will be. Not just for your sake but for ours – how are we going to get you out this time if you fall back into that man's clutches?

As agreed, two hours after making Nurit his original offer, Lorenzo Rinaldi calls for the third time. Her friends are still there with her. Be careful, Carmen repeats, before Nurit picks up the receiver. And ask if the house they're going to give you has a pool, says Paula.

An hour later Rinaldi is making arrangements with his colleague, *El Tribuno*'s administrative director, for Nurit Iscar to move into his weekend house in La Maravillosa the next day. Meanwhile, she packs a small case the size of a cabin bag; it seems insufficient for a month's stay, but Nurit doesn't really believe she'll last in the house that long. They have agreed that, before taking up residence in Chazarreta's country club, Nurit Iscar will drop by the newsroom to pick up the keys and a few instructions about the house, and to have a chat with Rinaldi and the journalist who heads up the Crime section about the details of the case. From there, once they have finished, a car will take her straight to La Maravillosa so that she can get to work right away.

At the very moment Nurit Iscar closes her case and places it beside her bed, the Crime boy is back on Google again, this time in his own house, trying out different combinations of keywords in the hope of finding some vital piece of information to take to Rinaldi the next day: "Chazarreta + slit throat + La Maravillosa". Shit, nothing useful comes up. He looks down the long list of tweets on his timeline, but none of the Chazarreta posts go beyond the fact of his death. Then he makes two or three calls, again without any luck. He'd call his old boss, Zippo, who always has good info; the best. But Zippo is the competition now, and the Crime boy doubts he would be as forthcoming with him – someone he regards not only as a traitor but as an idiot for moving to another paper – as he was in the newsroom. He'd also call Jaime Brena, except that he's tried that three times already and the guy's not picking up. Besides, his girlfriend's waiting in bed for him to come and watch the first episode of *Grey's Anatomy*, so better leave that job for today, the boy thinks, as he closes various programs and shuts down the computer.

In the taxi on the way back to their respective homes, Paula Sibona and Carmen Terrada are discussing their fears of Nurit falling prey again to the devastating Rinaldi effect. Although they can't be sure that they too, in her shoes, wouldn't do the same. That is, they are pretty sure they would do the same. And more humiliating things besides. There are plenty of examples best forgotten, says Paula. And Carmen Terrada adds: I've blanked it all out, believe me. But this isn't about them, it's about Nurit Iscar, and their duty as friends is not simply to understand but to help her not get crushed by Lorenzo Rinaldi again. Meanwhile Gladys Varela, ever since returning from La Maravillosa, can't stop giving exhaustive accounts of what she saw there to all and sundry. It's gone midnight and the neighbours are still round her house chatting about her employer's death. She's become a celebrity. If Chazarreta's death hadn't taken place inside a gated community I'd have been on TV more, she complains. But camera crews can't enter a country club without authorization, as Gladys knows very well; it's not even easy for the police, not without a search warrant, though the governor has promised to get that policy changed – so if anybody wants to interview her it's either going to have to be in her house or in the queue at the entrance to La Maravillosa. Although, now she comes to think of it, Gladys Varela isn't going to be queueing up at the barrier any more, at least not for a while. She no longer has a job or an employer in La Maravillosa. She ought to start looking for a new job; she will soon, but not yet. She's heard that some people from a news programme have been asking for her at the gate to the country club, that they want to take her to the studio, though they haven't come to her house yet. Apparently you can get good money for these appearances. Someone told her that anyway, and someone else said it just now. Perhaps she should swing by La Maravillosa tomorrow, see if the cameras are still at the entrance and introduce herself to the reporter. Yes, that's what she'll do, Gladys Varela thinks, at the very moment that Karina Vives is selecting a classical music track on her computer and preparing to take a shower. Karina remembers what Brena told her about Chazarreta's death and wonders if the news has reached the television stations yet, but she's not interested enough to break the calm of her home by switching on the news. Chazarreta and the circumstances of his death really don't matter to her very much at the moment, and she's bound to hear plenty about it tomorrow in the newsroom. She does wonder if the Crime boy will have known what to do with the pink note in the wastepaper bin to which she drew his attention at Brena's behest. And her fear is that he won't. Actually it's not a fear: she's certain he won't. Anyway, what does she care about what the Crime boy does? In the shower, with Carl Orff's *Carmina Burana* at full blast and hot water cascading over her back,

Karina Vives doesn't think of Chazarreta any more, nor of the Crime boy, nor of Jaime Brena, but of whether the time has come to announce her pregnancy in the newsroom. She hopes nobody will ask whose it is. Because if there's one thing she hates, it's giving explanations. And they'd better not make stupid jokes or ask idiotic questions about what surname she's going to give the child.

As Karina Vives leans into the spray and lets herself be soothed by the hot water, more than thirty blocks away Jaime Brena is arriving home. It's nearly eleven o'clock at night and he carries a packet containing three beef empanadas bought in the delicatessen on the corner. He walked a long way this evening, before going into a cinema to watch a film where he fell asleep; he called Irina to see when would be a good time to come and collect the books that are still in the house they used to share – books he's been asking her for since they separated nearly two years ago – but Irina didn't answer the call. Does she believe that books bought as a reflection of one's own taste, interests, travels and mistakes, that personal library put together over the span of a life, also constitute a joint asset? Do they, in fact? No, no, they don't, whatever she wants to think. No matter what the Civil Code says, he's sure that he could argue in front of any judge that a personal library does not constitute a joint asset. It just isn't. How could it be? Jaime Brena feels that if his ex-wife, or any of the other women there have been in his life, laid claim to his books, it would be equivalent to refusing to return his clothes, his shoes, the notebooks he's kept all these years or the photographs of his mother. They aren't really notebooks, in fact, but jotters, bound at the top. He makes daily notes in them, recording what he's talked about and to whom, as a precaution, in case somebody makes a complaint or asks him to show where he got a piece of information. To cover himself, basically. And at the end of each day he draws a double line across the page. The day he left the marital home he took his shoes and underpants in a bag. He never got the photographs of his mother. He has the jotters: Irina sent them to him in a box the same day that he moved into this apartment, leaving the two-star hotel where he had spent his first days as a separated man. But not the books. Sometimes, as he knows all too well, women choose peculiar ways to exact what they feel is owed to them. He walked past their building once, the one where he had lived with Irina for nearly twenty years, but he didn't dare ring the bell. The concierge recognized him and proffered a stiff greeting, pursing his lips as though to say "tsk" and shaking his head several times, a gesture Brena took as one of solidarity and as a complaint about women generally. His thoughts return to the dog. He pictures himself, Jaime Brena, walking a dog. It's a happy image. He's definitely going to try it – one of these days he'll go and buy a dog. If he had already made that decision, if he already had a dog, it would be here to greet him now as he entered the apartment with the beef empanadas – wagging its tail as it bounded around him, sniffing the packet – and he'd feel the dog's infectious delight in seeing its master back home. And know that it was sincere. A dog never lies. It can't wag its tail untruthfully. Moreover, a dog doesn't keep the complete library it took your whole life to assemble, then, when you ask for it back, keep ignoring your calls. A dog would never do anything like that, nor its canine equivalent. Jaime Brena drops the empanadas onto the table and turns on the light. When he goes to put the keys on the entrance table, he sees a brown envelope to one side of the door; he must have walked over it without noticing a few seconds before. For: Jaime Brena, From: Comisario Venturini. He opens it; inside there's an

A4 sheet of paper with scribbled writing and over it, attached with a paperclip, a brief note which says: Brena dear, you're going to have to bathe me in Dom Pérignon. I've got you the forensic officers' *in situ* observations. I jotted them down and I'm sending them to you via a colleague from the Buenos Aires division who's going your way. Obviously they don't carry the weight of an autopsy report, we still have to wait for that, but this gives you the data a few days earlier and, going on what I'm told by people who know, the autopsy is going to reach roughly the same conclusion. There are already a lot of idiots barking up the wrong tree. Warmly, Comisario Venturini. Now Jaime Brena doesn't know whether to get started on the contents of the envelope or on his dinner, but since the microwave hasn't been working very well the last few days, he elects to eat the empanadas before they go cold. He can't remember any more how you heat something in a bain-marie. And he can't use an ordinary oven, nor does he plan to learn how in his remaining years on this earth. He pours out the last of a bottle of Cabernet Sauvignon that he opened two nights ago and switches on the television, looking for news. As expected, Chazarreta's death is still making the headlines, but evidently there still isn't that much to say because they're filling the space with old pieces about the murder of Gloria Echagüe and on one of the channels he even stumbles on himself talking about that case, with a little more hair than today and a lot less gut. There's nothing new, though, nothing important. After watching his own report, he takes the few implements he's used to the sink and washes them, then picks up the envelope Venturini sent round and goes to the bedroom. He's tired, and hopes to get off to sleep quickly. He takes off his shoes and clothes. The boxers he's wearing are in a disgraceful state – once they were black but he'd hesitate even to call

74

them grey now. He'll have to buy himself a new pair. Irina used to buy them for him. But it can't be that difficult to buy a pair of pants. He places a large cushion at the end of the bed to elevate his legs and aid circulation. He picks up Comisario Venturini's brief and reads: The body is positioned in a green velvet armchair; in the right hand is a carving knife and there is a glass of whisky at its feet. The whisky bottle, almost empty, is on the chair, between Chazarreta's body and the right armrest. The neck wound is approximately six inches long, with an entry in the left sternocleido-mastoid and an exit in the right lateral cervical region. The exit site is longer than the entry site, and more superficial. The wound is straight and horizontal, except at its exit point, where it runs upwards. The cut has severed the cricothyroid membrane, revealing the laryngeal vestibule. Its lips are well separated, forming an acute angle. Its margins and its walls are clean without any bridging. There are no tentative cuts nor any wounds that might suggest an attempt at self-defence. The bloodstain at the foot of the chair is not, at the time of observation, bright red, indicating that some time has passed since the attack occurred. Not many hours, though, because coagulation has only recently begun. It is likely that death was caused by air embolism and not by haemorrhage alone, given that the depth of the incision would very likely have allowed blood to enter the airway. Once he's finished reading the notes, Brena leaves them at the foot of his bed. He's too tired to start mulling over theories. He may not even remember what he read tomorrow morning. But what does it matter, since it's not his job to report on this anyway? His job is to enlighten the world tomorrow with the revelation that while 65 per cent of white women sleep facing upwards, 60 per cent of men sleep facing down; he's already written it up as a filler piece and filed it today. That's his mission as a journalist now, after more than forty years' work. He feels a surge of contempt and doesn't know whether it's for himself, for Rinaldi or for that strange thing his profession has become. His profession. Tomorrow he'll have another look at the voluntary redundancy form. He sits on the edge of his bed and opens the drawer in the bedside table. Before he goes to sleep he ought to return the Crime boy's call, he thinks, to see what he wants and pass on the information he's just read and which he can no longer remember. He's not sure that the boy really deserves this, but you can never be sure who deserves what. And Comisario Venturini's gone to so much trouble that it wouldn't be right to slight him. Yes, he must call the Crime boy. Jaime Brena gropes inside the drawer of the bedside table until he reaches the tin where he keeps his compressed marijuana, a small tin that once contained lemon drops. He'll leave the call for later. He opens the tin; there's not much weed in it, enough for two or three joints, four if he's lucky. He checks in the drawer to see if there's anything left from the last lump he bought, his hand sweeping back and forth over the wood, but finds nothing. He'll have to track down his dealer before Friday if he doesn't want to go the whole weekend without a smoke. And this time, when he calls, he's going to complain about the quality: too many sticks and seeds. He grabs the packet of Virginia Super Slims, takes one out and empties the tobacco into the ashtray. He'd like to know how to roll a joint, but he's always been clumsy and it's too late to learn now. Refilled Virginia Super Slims do the trick. He lays the empty cigarette case on the bottom of the tin and moves it forward like a shovel, trying to make the marijuana go in. Then he lifts the cigarette and shakes the grass down to leave space for a little more, repeating this action a few times until the joint is ready. He twists the end. He lights it, takes a drag, retaining the smoke then letting it out slowly. Then he calls the Crime boy, who doesn't answer because he's busy screwing his girlfriend. Brena puts the phone down beside him on the bed and draws again on the joint. He gets under the covers, tries to relax. He notices his body softening, especially his lower back. He smiles. After one last drag he puts the cigarette out, carefully, conserving the rest of his bogus Virginia Super Slim for another time. The pages Comisario Venturini sent fall off the bed and glide along the wooden floor. The Crime boy holds his girlfriend for a moment before giving her a kiss and going to the bathroom. Only when he gets back does he see the phone's screen lit up with a missed call from Brena. Didn't you hear the phone ringing? he asks his girlfriend irritably, as if it were her fault the call went unnoticed. The Crime boy calls Jaime Brena, whose phone rings somewhere amid the crumpled bedsheets; he's already asleep. The answering machine cuts in. The boy hangs up without leaving a message and rings again, but gets the answering machine once more and swears. Turning his back to his girlfriend, he pulls the sheet over himself. He closes his eyes but keeps the telephone in his hand in case it rings again. The girl also turns away. Jaime Brena sleeps soundly, deeply, insensible to Chazarreta, redundancy packages and the bedtime rituals of white men and women. If he is dreaming, it isn't about them. If he were dreaming about any of them his face wouldn't look so peaceful. Next to him his phone screen lights up: *Two (2) missed calls, number unknown.*

8

Black trousers and a diaphanous top, suggestive, but not transparent. That was Paula Sibona's pronouncement on what outfit Nurit Iscar should wear for her meeting with Rinaldi the following day. Never mind that there isn't anything between them any more. Never mind that Nurit has taken the job for reasons that relate purely to work. And to subsistence. And to historic reparation. Nobody would go to meet an ex-lover – years later, at fifty-something, such an unkind age for a woman – without some minimal grooming, her friend said. And Nurit Iscar knows that Paula Sibona is right. She expects Lorenzo Rinaldi to look the same as always, though, having the absurd feeling that these last three years have passed only for her. He looks the same in the photo byline on his editorials, but she doesn't know if she can trust that. After a certain age journalists stop updating those thumbnail portraits that accompany their newspaper articles. Writers are the same with the author photos on their jacket covers. When one comes out well, they keep it for ever. And yet, even knowing that photographs can be deceptive, Nurit can't escape this ridiculous idea that he will be the same old Lorenzo Rinaldi. Men don't have their crisis at fifty: at that age life has either already ruined them or will get to them later. But if she's changed she must try to conceal the fact. Or make up for it. Or find the right clothes to enhance what needs enhancing and hide what needs to be hidden. For example, she's lost her waist. She doesn't have a tummy, and she's grateful for that, but she has lost her waist. Her arse has fallen, not a lot, but enough to produce two or three folds in the jeans below her buttocks. Her thighs are worse: they've spilled outwards and acquired wrinkles. The skin on her legs has started to go transparent, and not baby-transparent but old person-transparent. Apart from a varicose vein that she hates and that she's had for some time (she once considered getting it operated on, but when they explained that it would need pulling up with something like a crochet hook, because it's a vein that runs over the whole leg, and that this would be inserted into her body through her vagina, she almost fainted and ruled out any surgery there and then), she also has spider veins on her calves. But by way of compensation, she's much less hairy than she used to be, which is one of the few advantages of ageing. She has one or two marks on her face and means to have these removed one day with diamond-tip micro-dermabrasion or pulsed light therapy, like Viviana Mansini did. She'll do it some year when there are various books to write like *Untying the Knots* – bad for the brain but good for the savings account. She hasn't, however, got any liver-spots on her hands, nor does she have many wrinkles on her face. Nor on her neck which, while mercifully free of jowls, has lost elasticity. Wrinkles don't run in her family; neither her mother nor her grandmother had many, so she expects to follow in a line of taut women. Taut in every sense. Her tits haven't fallen, but they have expanded equidistantly: up, down and sideways. She feels them protruding ever closer to her clavicles and knows, too, that there's a marked line between her breasts, which never used to be the case. On balance, Nurit feels she's pretty good for fifty-four. She's not like Betty Boop, after all; not a cartoon. An animated drawing can keep her curls, her mouth, her legs the same but Nurit Iscar's body is bound to change, year after year. What would a fifty-four-year-old Betty Boop look like? she wonders. Would they draw her fretting – as Nurit is today, minutes away from seeing the last man she ever loved – about how her body looks? Recently she hasn't given much thought to age-spots, to her long-lost waistline, or her thighs. In fact, she has never particularly worried about these things. But today, when Lorenzo Rinaldi sees her, she'd like to look – no point denying it – respectable, at the very least. With a respectable body. When does it end, this obligation women always feel to look "pretty"? She'd like to be a little younger – not twenty or thirty, but forty-four or forty-five, a decade less. She should have ended her marriage then; the children were quite young, but she'd still have brought them up well, she's sure of it. That was her best age. But she didn't know it at the time, and now it doesn't matter. You can't go back. You can only enhance what needs to be enhanced and hide what needs to be hidden.

For that reason she accepts her friend's suggestion of black trousers, although, bearing in mind that she'll be going on to a country club, it would make more sense to wear jeans. A country club calls for jeans, shorts or Bermudas and she hasn't worn shorts or Bermudas for a long time, thanks to that cursed varicose vein. Black trousers will have to do. But she swaps the sheer blouse suggested by Paula Sibona for a white T-shirt with three-quarter-length sleeves and a generous, round neckline that enhances her bust, the part of her body Nurit considers most promising, despite its expansion.

She gets out of the taxi with her suitcase and goes to the newspaper's reception. There's a brief argument with the receptionist about whether or not she can take the suitcase into the newsroom, but finally Rinaldi's secretary comes to fetch her, pouring oil on troubled waters. How are you, Señora Iscar? It's a long time since I last saw you here, this woman says as they walk towards the lift, and Nurit can't decide whether the observation contains a hint of irony or not. Perhaps it is just that she feels paranoid about the past. Yes, it's a long time since I was last here, she replies. The secretary who accompanies her is the same one who worked for Rinaldi when they were together, and on various occasions she'd call in her boss's stead to pass on messages that were invariably humiliating for Nurit, such as: Señor Rinaldi says not to wait for him, he won't be able to go. Or she sent things on his behalf: tickets for some show they were going to see together and then Rinaldi cancelled at the last minute, or plane tickets, flowers, chocolates. Nurit Iscar realizes that the fact that her relationship with Lorenzo Rinaldi was clandestine, on his side, still makes her feel uncomfortable today. As if this woman were somehow judging her. Or as if she were once more judging herself, through the woman's eyes. Even though Nurit did separate, didn't deceive anyone and therefore didn't need clandestinity, she feels annoyed all the same. Or is what really annoys, worries and embarrasses her the thought that this woman knows Rinaldi didn't choose her; that he, unlike Nurit, preferred to remain in his marriage and let their secret relationship run its course? He didn't choose her. And it's not easy accepting that you haven't been chosen, she thinks; you always dream that you will be. The secretary has her sit down in the reception area outside Rinaldi's office and offers her a hot drink. No thanks, Nurit says. If her stomach is already in turmoil, a reheated coffee from an office machine that's plugged in twenty-four hours a day won't make her feel any better. Minutes later a young man comes dashing down the corridor, blurting "Rinaldi's waiting for me", and heads for the office door without waiting for the secretary's say-so, apparently not thinking that he needs anybody's permission. But the woman stops him in his tracks: Señor Rinaldi also has an appointment with this lady; take a seat and he'll call you both in soon. Together? he asks, perplexed. Nurit doesn't question the remark. Together, the secretary confirms, then busies herself with some photocopying. The man turns towards where Nurit is sitting, looks at her and, making a movement with his head that falls just short of a greeting, says: I guess we'll just have to wait, then. She smiles and repeats: We'll just have to wait. The Crime boy doesn't sit down next to her, however, but takes a seat opposite the window and stares blankly outside.

A few minutes later they are both in Lorenzo Rinaldi's office. I expect you've already introduced yourselves, he says, and although they haven't he keeps talking, assuming each knows who the other is. Nurit Iscar's going to come at this case from a bit of a non-fiction angle, Rinaldi says, give it some high-quality writing. Non-fiction, the Crime boy repeats. And you're going to handle the investigative, criminal aspect of it, the pure journalism. Do you understand? I think so. She's going to move into La Maravillosa, I've rented her a house there. She'll mix with the residents, listen, observe and write. I'd be up for that kind of fieldwork too, says the Crime boy in a level tone, trying not to let this sound like a complaint, although it is one. You can make up for that with good contacts, and of course if Nurit finds out anything relevant she'll let you know. The same goes for you: any important, concrete piece of information you get, you call her right away or send an email. There's a computer there with wi-fi and everything you need to be in constant contact. Send your articles straight to me, he says to the boy. Not to the chief sub; I'll edit them myself. Nurit's pieces will start coming out tomorrow, or the day after if she hasn't got something by today's deadline, says Rinaldi, adding: Keep half a page for her. Half a page? repeats the boy. Yes, does that seem like too little or too much to you? Rinaldi counters, though he knows the answer. No, the boy complains, I'm not saying it's too much or too little in relation to what she's got to say, but if we fill half a page with her articles there won't be any room for other pieces, that's the thing. Well, if you've got so much great stuff to publish and not enough space for it, we'll give her a special page outside your section, don't worry, says Rinaldi and looks straight at the boy, who holds his gaze as best he can. Nurit feels uncomfortable witnessing the stand-off, but decides that it isn't her place to intervene. She doesn't want to get off on the wrong foot with the Crime boy, especially since she doesn't yet know whether it will be him or Rinaldi editing her copy, making cuts, choosing images, writing the standfirst, or even changing the head-line. Nothing will be more important for our readers than a piece written by Nurit Iscar, says Rinaldi, putting an end to the discussion. Nurit, send everything to me with a copy to him but – and he addresses the boy directly – her stuff doesn't get edited or cut. OK, says the Crime boy, who now wants nothing more than to leave. And Lorenzo Rinaldi's next question gives him that opportunity: Have you already got something for today? I'm working on it, the boy lies, and then says: If that's everything, I need to go and make a few quick calls.

You're just the same, Betty Boo, Rinaldi says to her when they're alone in the office. And, even though she knows it's a lie, Nurit smiles. You too, she returns. No, I don't think so; this president we've got now has made me age two or three years for every year he's been in office. So the president's to blame for that too? For what? For your grey hair and wrinkles? Yes, of course, nobody has enraged and disappointed me as much in the last few years as this country's so-called leader. Ah, I can just picture the headline: "Editor of *El Tribuno* newspaper suffers premature ageing thanks to president, who refuses to pay damages". Very funny – don't tell me you still believe in him? Not in him nor anyone else, your lot included. Seriously? Very seriously. So how do you form ideas about what's happening in this country of ours, or don't you care? Of course I do – I care very much; I read all the papers, including yours, and then I base my opinion somewhere around the middle, taking my own beliefs into account, too. What an effort. But that's the way things are now; you journalists have left us with no alternative. You always were a mistrustful girl, Betty Boo. Clearly not mistrustful enough, she says, standing up. I'd better get going – it's a long way to that blessed country club. Do you think you'll have something for today? Don't put so much pressure on me, Rinaldi. There was a time when you liked me pressuring you. Once upon a time, she says, but we're grown up now. It's only been three years. Ah, but I measure them the same way you measure presidential years, she says, and smiles. He smiles too. Lorenzo Rinaldi walks with her to the door of his office, and before she leaves he says: I've missed you, Betty Boo. And even though she feels the words pierce her like a knife between the shoulder blades, she tries to walk on as though she hadn't heard him. As soon as I have something worthwhile I'll send it to you, she promises, and goes out.

Nurit Iscar walks along one side of the newsroom making more noise than she would like with the little wheels of her suitcase. Can you get an alignment and balancing service for suitcases? she wonders. The Crime boy sees her coming and deliberately turns his back to avoid having to say goodbye. Karina Vives, standing at the photocopier, recognizes her, but Nurit barely glances at her; she doesn't know that this woman is known to her, she doesn't recognize her face, and yet if someone said: that's Karina Vives, she would instantly identify her as the person who wrote that damning review in *El Tribuno* of her last novel *Only If You Love Me*, destroying her career in the process. Jaime Brena, coming out of the lift, crosses her path too. Good morning, he says. Good morning, Nurit Iscar replies. They don't know each other; or, rather, they've never been introduced, but each knows who the other is. They both have memorable faces, and both have been interested, to a greater or lesser degree, in the other's work at different times. Jaime Brena steps aside so that she can pass with her suitcase. She thanks him. But the wheels don't behave as they should and the suitcase ends up rolling over Brena's foot. Oh, I'm sorry – how clumsy of me! Don't worry, he says, I've been needing to see a chiropodist for a while anyway. She returns his smile, still feeling embarrassed about her gaffe. Bon voyage, he says as they walk away from each other and, as she gets into the lift, Nurit Iscar says: Thanks. Brena sits down at his desk. Immediately, the Crime boy comes over. You called me last night, he says. Yes, there was no answer and then I went to sleep. What was Betty Boo doing here? Betty who? Nurit Iscar. Oh, Rinaldi's commissioned her to write reportage on the murder of Chazarreta, says the Crime boy, dressing the word "reportage" with light sarcasm. It's not a bad idea; she'd be very good at that, says Brena. Why? Who is she? Where have you been hiding, kid? I don't know her. Well, you should, she's one of the few female crime writers in Argentina. You mean you haven't read *Death by Degrees*? No. You have to read it – that and anything else you can get your hands on – to open up that head a bit. I haven't got time. Sometimes I read a bit of fiction in the holidays. Make time, then, make time. If you want to be a good journalist you have to read fiction, kid; there's never been a great journalist who wasn't also a good reader, I can assure you. Jaime Brena takes out of his satchel the envelope he received the previous night from Comisario Venturini. Here, have a look at this. It's from a reliable source and it may be useful to you, he says. The boy takes the envelope and casts an eye over its contents. He knows, for all his inexperience, that what Brena has just given him is priceless. Thank you, he tells him. Enjoy, Brena replies and gets to work on his next piece: Male babies cry more, earlier and louder than female babies. Bunch of poofs, he mutters, and starts writing. The Crime boy comes back and asks: What did you say her name was? Who? The chick who writes crime novels. Nurit Iscar. Yes, but you said another name first. Ah yes: Betty Boo. Because of the curls? I suppose I can see the similarity, agrees the Crime boy. A few years ago she was identical to Betty Boop, and that's when we gave her the nickname. You and who else? That's a professional secret, kid, Brena says, sternly. Then he turns towards Karina Vives' desk and asks her: Did you know that baby boys cry more than baby girls? And she says: No, I didn't know, and her own eyes fill with tears. Are you all right? he asks. It's an allergy, she says. This time of year my eyes always stream. Jaime Brena doesn't believe her but respects the fact that, for the moment, his newsroom colleague would rather not tell him why she's crying. There will be time enough to find out why later, when they go outside to smoke.

The taxi that picked up Nurit Iscar soon after her bungled exit from *El Tribuno* is now turning onto the Pan-American Highway. It's a cool day, but with lovely autumn sunshine. She hasn't come down this road for ages, not for years. Nurit Iscar hails from the south of Greater Buenos Aires, a very different part of the metropolis to the one she's entering now. She goes back down there every so often to see her high-school friends. But what she sees travelling south on the ring road is very different to the views on either side of the Pan-American. The ring road is lined with tyre shops, garages, swimming pools run by trades unions for the benefit of their members and a university. In the last few years a hypermarket and even a golf driving range have sprung up. From what she remembers the Pan-American used to have a lot of "love motels" offering rooms by the hour. There aren't so many now – or maybe they are just less obvious amid the proliferation of buildings on both sides. The cars around her are also of a different order to the ones she sees on the ring road. When she travels south it's in the company of aged fleet vehicles, rickety cars with broken lights and registration plates with letters from the beginning of the alphabet. The cars she sees around her now, on the other hand, seem to get newer and more luxurious the further they get from the capital, with registration plates that start with H or I. There are shopping centres, cinemas, restaurants, factories, banks and businesses, health centres. And when they turn onto the Pilar road, she's surprised by how green and kempt the embankments are, the grass on both sides of the road recently cut. The service road that runs alongside the highway is still an unpaved dirt track in places, but it is lined with home interior stores, antique shops, private cemeteries, car dealerships, small office complexes, "strip malls" – that American innovation, offering basic services such as pharmacies, mini-markets, newsagents, etc.: a support system for suburbs and exurbs – as well as a sushi restaurant from the same chain that has a branch in Puerto Madero near the office where her ex-husband works. Thinking of sushi leads to her ex, and thinking of him leads to the children, and only then does it occur to Nurit Iscar that neither Rodrigo nor Juan has answered the message she left to let them know that she was going away for a few days and where they could reach her. They're big boys now, she thinks, but somehow that's not a comfort.

A little before reaching the tollbooth she starts seeing the first country clubs. The club you're going to can't be seen from the road, says the driver. We have to go in. We have to go in, she repeats, more to herself than to him. At some point on the Pilar branch, the car takes a right turn and leaves the highway to travel along a side road perpendicular to the Pan-American. They continue for at least ten blocks then turn left, crossing a road that seems to be disused, and continuing a few more yards before arriving at the entrance to La Maravillosa. There are still two outside broadcasting vans from news channels standing sentry at the gate. And then comes Nurit Iscar's first challenge. "First trial of strength" was how she described it later, on the phone to Carmen Terrada. There's nobody in the house to authorize your entry, the guard on duty says. No, of course there's nobody in the house, because I'm the person who's going to be living there, she replies. But nobody has given me authorization to let you in. Look, I've got the keys. How would I have the keys without authorization? You wouldn't be the first, Señora. Please call the owner, Nurit asks. We are trying to call him, but there's nobody at home. Of course there isn't anybody. Call somewhere else; call a mobile. We don't have his personal details, only the home phone. OK, I'll try to get hold of him, she says. By all means, says the guard, but please free up the entrance until we have authorization. We're freeing it, we're freeing it, says Nurit Iscar, and while the taxi driver parks to one side of the entrance she calls *El Tribuno* and explains the problem to Rinaldi's secretary, who assures her that she'll sort it out straight away and tells her it's not a problem. Nurit Iscar lowers the window and lets the sun bathe her face. She sighs. Don't worry, Señora, the taxi driver says, any minute they'll let us through. It's always the same in these places, you just have to have patience. But patience is not a quality she's blessed with, and she can feel herself losing the little she has. Minutes later a guard approaches the car. The taxi driver starts the engine: They're coming over to give us the go-ahead, he says. But he's wrong. Señor, you can't park here. I'll move, says the driver. Why? asks Nurit, patting the driver's shoulder to indicate that he shouldn't move. Because it's forbidden to park in front of the entrance to the club, the guard replies. I can't see any sign from the National or Regional Highways saying that it's forbidden to park here. It's a regulation of the country club, Señora. The taxi driver sighs. The club can't make rules about property that doesn't belong to it, and the roads are public, Señor. These orders come from above, the guard insists. From above what? she asks. From above, the guard repeats. She looks up at the sky. Above there are only clouds, she tells him. From the club's authorities, the man clarifies. Please explain to the authorities that the club has no jurisdiction over the roads, or over my life and my decision to park in an area that's not prohibited by order of the National or Regional Highways, she persists. But it is prohibited, Señora, you're not listening to what I'm saying. It seems to me that you're the one who isn't listening. Don't get annoyed, says the taxi driver, I'll just move the car. No. She stops him. I'm not moving from here. Señora, can't you see that a car parked outside the entrance to a place like this compromises the security of its members? No, I can't see that. And, anyway, I'm the one who's in danger, from these men who are carrying arms that they may not have permission to carry. Do you have permission to carry them? The man doesn't answer. Another guard approaches. The taxi driver says again that it's no problem to move the car: Let's not make a mountain out of a molehill. The street belongs to everyone, she repeats. I'm just following orders, says the guard who came over first. The lady's been authorized to enter, says the one who has just arrived. The taxi driver breathes a sigh of relief and rolls forward in first gear. Just as well these guys aren't cooking your Sunday lunch, he says. Nurit doesn't grasp his meaning. They'd spit in the food, he explains. It's important to know how to stand up for yourself, she tells him. But there are some lost causes, the driver says. That's also true, Nurit concedes. When they arrive at the barrier, another guard asks for both their identity cards. The driver must also provide his driving licence, registration document and insurance policy. They take Nurit's photograph with a mini camera. It's so that from now on you'll be registered and we won't have to trouble you again, says the man who controls the barrier. Boot, please? the same guard asks the driver, who pushes a button to open it without getting out of his seat. Nurit Iscar wonders what happened to the rest of the sentence; where are the missing words, the unbroken syntax? Why does someone say "Boot, please?" and leave out the verb? What would the verb be: "May I see, or open, or look inside?" Why does the other one immediately understand and accept? There are no tacit verbs. "Boot, please" could mean: can I borrow your boot, take your boot, burn your boot, piss in your boot? Who stole those verbs from the guard, from the driver, who's been de-verbed and doesn't even know it? Why does the theft not matter to anyone? Is word theft not a crime? Is it only the word that's stolen or the action it describes? OK, the guard says finally, and swipes a magnetic card over a reader which raises the barrier in front of them. Have a nice day.

Now they're driving down the main street. Two lines of tall trees occupy the spaces that might have been used for pavements. Some of the uppermost branches meet overhead. See, I really like that, Nurit says to herself. But her pleasure is short-lived, because as they drive on the interwoven branches form a closed tunnel which she feels herself entering with no certainty of being able to leave. Like those children in nursery rhymes who open a door and plunge into another world, or fall into a well that leads into another kingdom or climb into a wardrobe that opens into an enchanted (bewitched?) forest.

The taxi arrives at its destination. The house is by no means one of the grandest in La Maravillosa and yet it is much bigger, more imposing and striking than any other Nurit Iscar has stayed in. The driver opens the boot, takes out her suitcase and puts it down next to Nurit, then gives her a receipt to sign. If you need anything, give me a call, here's my number, he says, and hands her the taxi company's card. They told me that any journey you need to make is to be charged to the newspaper. We always work with *El Tribuno* – they have an account with us, so no worries, just call me. Oh, that's great, I'll call you, then. Absolutely, but call in good time because I live in Lanús and it takes me two hours to get here, two and a half in the rush hour. Lanús? she repeats. West Lanús, he clarifies. And what if I've got a headache and I need to go to the pharmacy to buy aspirin? I'd recommend that for that kind of emergency you get the number of a local taxi company from the guards; then, when you go to buy something, stock up. That's going to be cheaper than ordering a taxi every time you need something. Yes, of course, she says, I'll stock up. The taxi drives away and Nurit is left for an instant on the grey gravel with her suitcase in one hand, the keys of a house that doesn't

91

belong to her in the other, thinking of all the things she is going to need to stock up on so as not to feel that she may at any moment stumble into some kind of insurmountable emergency.

9

It's the end of the afternoon when the Crime boy receives Nurit Iscar's first dispatch from La Maravillosa, sent to Rinaldi and copied to him. He reads it. And feels a rush of hatred. A strong desire to kick something. He looks over to Jaime Brena's desk, but Brena's not there; he's standing chatting at Karina Vives' desk. The Crime boy walks towards them. Seriously, I'm absolutely fine, she's saying. But you always come for a smoke, Brena says. It's because of my allergy – nicotine would only make it worse, she's saying as the boy reaches them. Jaime Brena, his back turned to the boy, says: Well, don't smoke, then, but come and keep me company. She shakes her head. She knows that if she goes outside to smoke with Brena she'll end up telling him about her pregnancy and she didn't wake up today with the heart to announce her news, even to him, her best friend in *El Tribuno*'s newsroom. Why is she so full of doubts again today, when she was so sure in the shower yesterday of what she wanted to do? Unwittingly the boy comes to her rescue. Have you got a minute? he asks Brena. It seems so, Brena says, putting the box of Marlboros back into his shirt pocket with resignation and gesturing the boy over to his desk. The chick's already sent in her piece, the boy tells him. What chick? Brena asks. That writer Rinaldi's put in La Maravillosa. Nurit Iscar. Yes, Nurit Iscar, the boy confirms. Learn her name, Brena says. I know it, but I'm pissed off. What's up?

She's come up with some theory that goes directly against mine, and we can't run my piece alongside hers without looking schizophrenic. Well we are, a little bit. I mean it; I can't publish what she's sent. What points don't you agree on? Jaime Brena asks. She's saying, on the basis of some rubbish she's heard in the supermarket, that Chazarreta's death was a murder, and I'm absolutely clear that the man killed himself. Why so sure? He was holding the weapon in his hand. That's not sufficient proof: it could have been planted. There are no signs of violence in the house. You don't always get signs of violence in homicide, especially not if it's been well planned. There are no defence wounds on Chazarreta's hands. They could have cut his throat while he was sleeping in the armchair, all boozed up; you're still not giving me anything solid. Does the forensic report say if the right hand was covered in blood? Brena asks. The boy's surprised by the question. No, it doesn't say anything about that – why? If it doesn't mention it that must be because there wasn't any blood: it's a murder, kid. Internet news sites are leaning towards a probable suicide, and there have been loads of tweets and retweets, the Crime boy insists. In Spanish we call them *tuits* and *retuits*, admonishes Brena, adding: You know what your problem is, kid? Too much Internet and not enough legwork. A crime reporter is made in the street. How many times have you hidden behind a tree to watch something? How many times have you called a witness to a crime or a victim's relation posing as Chief Inspector Bloggins? How many times have you disguised yourself in order to gain access to a place you've been barred from entering? The boy doesn't answer, but it's obvious that he's done none of these things. Remember, kid, get out in the street, think on your feet, learn to assimilate: you have to be the thief, the murderer, the victim, the accomplice, whatever it takes to be inside their heads. And get away from the computer a bit; all that Google isn't good for you. You know why the Chinese have banned it? The Internet's going to be the new opium of the masses, the new religion. Come here, take a seat, Brena says, and offers the boy his own chair. He opens his desk drawer, pulls out an old twelve-inch wooden ruler and, standing behind the boy, holds it against his neck as though he were about to cut it but without making any movement. The boy shudders at the touch of the ruler on his skin. Brena asks him: What sort of cut was it? Parallel to the floor? Upwards? Downwards? Parallel to the floor, then slightly upwards at the end. Then he was murdered. Why? Brena hands him the ruler. Cut your own throat, he says. The boy stares at him without doing anything. Cut your throat, kid, Brena says again. Without much conviction, the boy moves the ruler from left to right. Where did your hand end up? Slightly downwards. If you're slashing your own throat the action is inevitably downwards. It's actually impossible to cut your own throat in an upward motion; it's unnatural, kid. Find out if the right hand was bloody; when the blood starts spurting, it's going to land there, on the hand that's cutting the arteries. But there are no defence wounds on the hands, the boy insists. It doesn't matter. The upwards slash and the absence of blood on the hand are stronger pieces of evidence. If there are no defence wounds it must be because Chazarreta didn't have enough time to wake up and react. You'll see when the definitive autopsy comes out – it's going to say that there was a lot of alcohol in his blood, doubtless that he was asleep, drunk, and they may even have put something in his whisky, a tranquillizer, for example, or a cocktail of tranquillizers. So the chick could be right. Nurit Iscar, not the chick. Nurit Iscar, or Betty Boo. Or Betty Boo, yes, she must be right; does she have those notes from the preliminary autopsy that I sent to you? No, I didn't give them to her; I was planning to use that info in my own piece. Fair enough, you have to be selfish with your material, Brena agrees. She's basing her ideas on such stupid observations, like I said before, says the boy, things she over-heard when she was buying yogurt in the supermarket, for example. Street, you see, kid? The Maravillosa supermarket may not seem very street to you, but in this case it counts. Can I read what she's written? I'll email it to you, says the boy. No, kid, print it out. I'm from the paper generation.

A few minutes later the boy comes over with a printout of Nurit Iscar's piece and hands it to Jaime Brena, who reads it immediately:

> All is calm in La Maravillosa. Walking around here, in the shade of its trees, smelling the scent of flowers and freshly cut grass, you might believe that nothing bad could ever happen to you behind these walls. Children walk around on their own, ride bikes, electric cars, even tricycles. People still leave their keys in the ignition and their houses unlocked. There's no noise of screeching brakes or buses, no exhaust fumes to pollute the atmosphere. You won't hear a car horn sound unless it's one resident greeting another. And yet I am reminded how in Brian de Palma's film *Carrie* (based on the novel by Stephen King), at the moment where serenity prevails and the unsuspecting viewer finally begins to relax, Carrie's hand shoots through the earth, out of the grave, grabbing the wrist of the friend who was bringing flowers. Here too, even in such a bucolic setting, death bursts in, abruptly ending a life, this time the life of Pedro Chazarreta at his home in La Maravillosa. The setting says one thing, and the

reality something else. Reality had already spoken, three years ago, when Gloria Echagüe was found dead. For a while we were led to believe that her death had been the result of an unfortunate accident, but it was murder, pure and simple. A murder like any other, with a murderer, a motive and a body. As simple, and as terrible, as that. The difference being that it happened in a place where these things don't happen. Not here. Here in the same place where, three years later, with no culprit having been brought to justice, another crime has been committed. Another person's throat has been cut. So far, so coincidental, but there's more: let's say that these two murder victims were husband and wife. And that the man had been accused of killing his wife. And that the case was dismissed for lack of evidence. For that reason perhaps, and because of their shock and surprise, the first response of La Maravillosa's residents when they learned of Pedro Chazarreta's death yesterday morning was that the widower of Gloria Echagüe must have committed suicide. This rumour sprang from a fundamentally weak piece of evidence: the deceased was holding the knife that had been used to inflict the wound in his right hand, as though he had wielded it himself. *As though.* But the rumour ran wild, until it reached some of the people who had known Chazarreta best. And these friends and relations are adamant that if the knife was in his hand it is because somebody put it there. In La Maravillosa's grocery store, I heard two residents observing with total conviction, as they picked out yogurts from the chiller cabinet, that the death of Pedro Chazarreta was no suicide. And the reasons they gave were the ones that I heard repeated later at the newsagent and in the clubhouse bar. That there is absolutely no way it could have been a suicide. That only someone who didn't know Chazarreta would credit that theory. Those close to him don't need to wait for the results of the autopsy or for the secrecy order to be lifted. Why are they so sure? Simply, they say, because Pedro Chazarreta would never have left the Maravillosa Cup, a four-ball golf tournament played over two consecutive weekends, halfway through. Especially not if (as was the case) he and his partner had achieved on the first weekend the highest score ever registered in the ten years since La Maravillosa had opened its golf course. Nobody in this place of trees and flowers and freshly-mown grass cares if there was a knife in Chazarreta's hand. All that matters to them is the certainty that he would never have abandoned a four-ball, let alone the club's most important tournament, and especially not considering how well he was playing. Nobody would do such a thing, least of all Pedro Chazarreta. Consider that, three years ago, the Maravillosa Cup coincided with Gloria Echagüe's funeral. The decision was made to hold it back a week, and the following weekend Chazarreta was there as usual.

I, like the residents, don't believe the suicide hypothesis. I don't know anything about golf, but I do know about character profiles. If Pedro Chazarreta were a character in one of my novels he wouldn't have considered suicide, because pride and the urge to compete and win wouldn't allow him to abandon a club tournament in which he was the clear front runner. Besides, from a psychological perspective, he was exhibiting none of the feelings that typically lead someone to that decision: guilt, depression or regret. Not even pain. He always presented himself as someone who was strong, calm and absolutely sure that he was right, either because he really did not kill his wife or for reasons of self-preservation: to protect his reputation and hers, the family's honour, or simply his property. Pedro Chazarreta always gave the impression of knowing more than any of us, including the prosecutor and the judge. And by his attitude he also made it crystal clear that he didn't believe that anyone had the right to demand explanations from him. Why would a man like that commit suicide? Especially now, when his case had just been dismissed once and for all due to lack of evidence? And when he's on the point of winning the Cup again? No, if Pedro Chazarreta were a character in one of my novels, he certainly wouldn't have killed himself. So why did someone try to make us believe he did by placing the murder weapon in his hand? Was it some kind of joke? A mistake? An underestimation of us all?

The two theories circulating La Maravillosa are that the motive was either revenge or the same motive – still unknown – that dispatched Echagüe. Thus:

1. Whoever killed him wanted Chazarreta to experience what his wife had gone through; in other words, the murderer considered him guilty, responsible or complicit in the murder of Gloria Echagüe and, for that reason, took justice into his own hands.

2. Both murders were committed by the same assassin, hence the same modus operandi. The knife was placed in Chazarreta's hand to throw would-be sleuths off the scent.

It's still too soon to incline towards one or the other of these two alternatives. Moreover, I suspect that once we have the autopsy report, and as the investigation progresses, other hypotheses will appear. As we walk beneath La Maravillosa's trees, breathe her pure air and revel in her silence, more theories, inevitably, are going to come to light, like Carrie's hand coming out of the grave.

It's a question of patience, and waiting.

You're in trouble, kid. Why? Because Iscar knows more than you. Change your article, tweak it a bit to say something like some people are still entertaining the suicide hypothesis but that "official sources" and different versions circulating inside La Maravillosa reject that idea. And then you pop in a cross reference to Iscar's piece and everyone's happy. OK? OK. You're going to have to be her friend. Be intrepid, remember, and learn to pull together or Rinaldi will send you on to a better place. The boy is silent for a moment. He'd like to speak, but doesn't dare. Go on, off you go and work, or you'll never make the deadline, Brena says. Thank you, the boy says with an effort. Jaime Brena merely repeats: Off you go. I see you've adopted him, Karina Vives remarks, passing his desk at the end of the day on her way out. Orphan and halfwit, what else could I do? It's in your nature, Brena; you're generous and you like people to do good work. And I'm also a halfwit. That too, says Karina, and they laugh. Don't forget, he tells her, that I want you to ask all your friends with children if it's true that the boys cry more than the girls, since neither of us has the relevant experience. You can say that again, she says, straining to hide the emotion this remark provokes. Could that be the reason why adult women cry so much more than men – they're redressing the balance? Oh, so you never cry? she asks. What do men do when they feel bad, then? Vegetate in front of the TV, he says. We lie in bed and channel-hop. Karina goes to hug him, more tightly than usual. Brena, though taken aback, lets himself be hugged. See you tomorrow, Brena. See you tomorrow, gorgeous.

Jaime Brena tidies his desk, gathers up his papers, switches off the computer then notices just as he's about to go that the ruler with which he instructed the Crime boy to simulate his own throat-slashing is lying on the floor under his chair. Jaime Brena has had this ruler ever since he first came to work at *El Tribuno*. He has a tendency to form slightly fetish-istic attachments to certain objects. He picks it up and puts it back in the drawer. Looking up, he sees that the Crime boy is still working at his desk, and he goes over to him. How's it going? Fine, says the boy. I'm just finishing up. OK, I'll see you tomorrow, then. See you tomorrow. Jaime Brena starts to walk away but after a few steps he turns back and says: Can I ask you something? Yes, of course, says the boy. Who would you like to be like? What? says the boy. Who would you like to be like, who's your role model, your favourite journalist? Ah, from here, or anywhere? From here, kid, here, and in Crime, because if you're going to write about crime that's where you need to look for your role model. I don't know, I've never really thought about it. I got into Crime a bit by chance; my role models are in other areas. It shows, kid. Not to bring you down, but it shows. Have you heard of GGG, the *Crítica* journalist? No, the boy says. Check him out: Gustavo Germán González. Find out who he was, how he worked. There's probably something on the Internet about how he got into a morgue when he was investigating the assassina-tion of the Radical party councillor, Carlos Rey, Brena goes on. The piece he wrote the next day was called "There is no cyanide". You should read it. What a great title, kid. And read Osvaldo Aguirre's *The Undesirables*, which is a novel that has GGG as its protagonist. Mark my words, you're never going to get anywhere on the Internet alone – it's not enough. So, lesson number one: read everything you can get your hands on about Gustavo Germán González. That's an order, OK? OK, the Crime boy says. Jaime Brena takes his leave with his favourite gesture, raising his hand to his head as though tipping an imaginary hat. Then he goes.

The Crime boy watches him leave. He finishes his piece and gets it in just before the deadline. Before turning off his computer he types "GGG + Crítica newspaper" into Google and waits for the results. He suspects that Jaime Brena's words constitute good advice. Never mind suspects; he knows it. What he doesn't know is how to find out who Gustavo Germán González is, if not via the Internet.

10

In the following days it became clear that Chazarreta's death had not been a suicide, just as the neighbours on whom Nurit had eavesdropped in front of the chiller cabinet suspected. The results of the autopsy confirmed (in more technical language) the details Comisario Venturini had advanced to Jaime Brena in his handwritten note: severing of the sternocleidomastoid muscle, severing of the common carotid artery about an inch below its bifurcation, severing of the jugular vein and complete severing of the larynx at the level of the cricothyroid membrane, with opening of the laryngeal vestibule, and severing also of the inferior horn of the thyroid cartilage. Although there were no defence wounds on the victim's hands, there was a small, shallow cut on his chin surely caused by an instinctive reaction on Chazarreta's part to lower his head as he felt the knife at his neck. And there was indeed a high level of alcohol in his blood. It was also shown, crucially, that the slant of the cut was slightly upwards and that there was no blood on the hand that had been holding the knife when the body was discovered. Told you so, Jaime Brena says when the Crime boy confirms these details. So what theories are going around? Score-settling or avenging his wife's death, the boy replies. Score-settling was also mooted as a motive for Gloria Echagüe's death. When he sold the bank, Chazarreta got into loan collection, Brena explains. That must have made him a lot of enemies, says the boy. Yes, above all because of the way he operated, says Brena. He'd take on any debt and used some pretty ugly methods to recoup it. He had a posse of heavies, muscle-men, pack dogs who'd descend on some debtor, for example on his daughter's fifteenth birthday, grab the microphone and announce to all the guests that the man paying for the party – assuming hc was paying for it – owed them money. The guests would get antsy, the waiters would whisk away the wine, the disc jockey would demand payment in cash before he continued the set, and the poor girl whose birthday it was would end up in tears. I've heard that they could really put the screws on if necessary, but nobody ever reported them. What do you mean by "put the screws on"? Kneecapping, face-slashing, breaking the odd bone – fingers, for instance. Chazarreta couldn't take his debtors to court because the people he was lending money to were involved in some pretty dubious or even illegal business: buying properties with dodgy paperwork, pornography, sex tourism, money laundering. I asked him about it when I interviewed him and he told me that his business was lending and collecting money; that what the other guy did with the cash didn't concern him. But that wasn't true, because while it might not interest him from an ethical point of view, it certainly inter-ested him from an economic one; otherwise how could he evaluate the business's ability to pay back the loan? I should have looked deeper into that side of things. If that question had been cleared up, we might have started disentangling the threads and found a clue to lead us to Gloria Echagüe's killer. Because one version of events said that she had to be shut up, that she didn't agree with some of these activities and that she was being very difficult about it, threatening to leave him or even report him. But I don't know; sometimes I think that was a red herring. At any rate, Brena concludes, the score-settling motive keeps coming back, and if we have to go in that direction we'll get bogged down again in a few days. And the other theory, someone taking the law into his own hands to avenge Chazarreta's wife's death, strikes me as too heroic for the cast of this movie we're watching – no? So? asks the boy. We have to keep thinking. Sometimes we cling onto a hypothesis then can't break free of it, says Brena, almost at the same moment as Rinaldi irrupts furiously into the newsroom and hurls a copy of *La Primera de la Mañana* onto the Crime boy's desk. Jaime Brena moves aside; he's not the object of this outburst, but for a long time now seeing Rinaldi furious with anyone has made him tense up. Would you like to explain to me why Zippo has got information on this story that we haven't? The boy looks at the newspaper Rinaldi flung on his desk, picks it up and quickly scans Zippo's article. I don't know. I put in everything they gave me at the police station and in the district attorney's office. Well they obviously gave him more; just as well we have Nurit Iscar's pieces, says Rinaldo, and departs as furiously as he arrived. Only when Lorenzo Rinaldi is safely back in his office does Jaime Brena return to pick up the copy of *La Primera* from the boy's desk and look for the article. Lesson number two, kid: where did Zippo get hold of this classified information? I don't know, I swear I'm doing the best I can. Look at the piece and tell me where he got the information from. I read it just now and I don't know. I didn't say "read the piece and tell me", I said "look at the piece and tell me". Look at it, kid. Doesn't anything jump out at you? No. Don't just trust your eyes, assimilate, get inside his skin, inside Zippo's skin. I swear I don't know. The photo of the attorney is the same size as the text, see? With a big caption. Then Brena brings the paper close to his face and from under his glasses reads: District Attorney Atilio Pueyrredón making progress, thanks to his meticulous work and that of his team. I'll ask you again, kid: Who gave Zippo his information? Attorney Pueyrredón. Exactly. Zippo's doing his publicity, see? Yes, how weird. Zippo's better than that. Times are hard for everyone, even the best people, says Brena. He must have some favour to repay; I always preferred to pay with an *asado*. Doing publicity for the police, judges and attorneys sticks in the craw, kid. It's different with prisoners because they don't have a voice. But, as for the others, if they're after fame let them earn it on their own.

Jaime Brena returns to his desk. Today he has to write about the opening of a state-of-the-art nursery school in Mataderos. Rinaldi's asked him to do it, and doubtless the mayor asked Rinaldi. Not that Rinaldi and the mayor are close friends, but these days they are united in hatred of the president. Having to write about a nursery school isn't all bad, Jaime Brena decides, since it means taking a trip out to Mataderos in order to get the piece done by mid-afternoon. Just knowing that he's going to spend part of his working day outside, idling around some neighbourhood of Buenos Aires, makes him feel happy. How little it takes to please you these days, Jaime Brena, he says to himself, and starts typing. Let me take you out to tea in Mataderos, he suggests to Karina Vives, who has just arrived. Tea in Mataderos! Since when are you so cool, Brena? Would that be Mataderos Soho or Mataderos Hollywood? She sits down at her desk. Mock me all you like, girl, one of these nights I'm going to take you dancing with the gauchos at the rural fair on Avenida de los Corrales and then you'll really see what a good time is. She smiles again.

As Jaime Brena is writing the title of his puff-piece for the mayor, yards away the Crime boy is looking online for information about all the people who work with Attorney

Pueyrredón to see if by chance he knows any of them while, over in La Maravillosa, Nurit Iscar is trying to write a new piece for *El Tribuno*. None of the names the boy finds sound familiar; nothing she writes satisfies her. She looks out of the window: everything is green. She closes the curtains and switches on a light to recreate the feeling of being at home, in the boys' room – which she turned into a study when they went to live on their own – sitting in her own chair and leaning on the big cushion with the knitted rice-stitch cover that once belonged to her mother. She should have brought it with her, the cushion at least, to feel more at home here. And one of the plant pots from her balcony; her plants may be less spectacular than the ones that surround her here, but at least they are hers. She could stare at the moon now, like ET, whispering "go home" in a shaky voice, but Nurit Iscar finds a crisper articulation for her predicament. What if I fuck up? This fertile line of thought is interrupted by a call from Carmen Terrada. You don't sound yourself today, her friend says. I'm going through my second trial by fire at La Maravillosa. The first was getting in the entrance gate. Yes, I remember, Carmen says. Who are you picking fights with now? Nobody yet. So? What's the problem? City withdrawal syndrome: the trees are stressing me out, the greenery is stressing me out, the 6 a.m. morning chorus is seriously doing my head in, not to mention the noise of crickets and the frogs merrily croaking all night. Do you know what I need, Carmen? A man, my love. No: concrete. Lots of concrete and a café on the corner of my street, Nurit says, and she goes on: Imagine what it's like to go out for a stroll and know that you're not going to meet anyone intriguing, that everything around you is nature, sport, so-called healthy living, and empty houses. Because even though there are people, you never see them unless they're engaged in some sporting activity. Even if only jogging. Imagine what it's like feeling that nothing is going to surprise you, that nothing unusual can happen to you, Nurit says. Well, I don't know – I suppose you could get your throat slashed from ear to ear; or had you forgotten the original reason for going there? Of course not, but I tell you, give it a couple more days of solitude and birdsong and I'm going to be running out into the street begging someone to slash my throat, Nurit says. Don't worry, Paula and I will come over early Saturday morning and stay with you all weekend, her friend promises. Thank you, Nurit says, that would be really great. Another thing, Carmen Terrada asks, did the house turn out to have a pool?

The Crime boy's typing his piece, still shell-shocked after Rinaldi's outburst in the newsroom a few minutes ago. Jaime Brena is writing about the facilities at the Mataderos nursery, which so far he has only read about in the press release sent from the mayor's office. And I've got the nerve to tell that boy that I don't do publicity for anyone, he thinks, banging the keys with disgust. Rinaldi is composing the next morning's editorial, starting with the title: Another of the President's Lies. Karina Vives is transcribing an interview she's just done with the Egyptian/Italian/Mexican poet, Fabio Morabito. Nurit Iscar is typing her second piece.

> Day after day, in this place, silence is the winner. The residents are frightened and perplexed: two murders, so strange and so similar, in the same house, inside the same "country club" (the self-styled name of this and other similar places, which have come together in loose association). But they don't say anything, they don't talk about it any more as they did during the first days. They try to think of something else and

carry on with their lives as usual. Many people, most people, are content to think: this is something to do with them, the Chazarretas, and not with us. As though the person who entered the house to kill for a second time had come to finish off some business that only implicated Pedro Chazarreta and Gloria Echagüe. Or at least them and their family. Or them, their family and their closest friends. Or them, their family, their closest friends and their business partners. So the circle widens. But not too much. It doesn't reach "us". "We" are safe. And who are "we"? We are all the other residents, still alive, still living in La Maravillosa. There are questions, however, that make those residents uncomfortable and which they therefore neither want to be asked or to ask themselves. Because everybody living in this place, whether or not they acknowledge it, knows that there aren't that many possible answers: either the murderer lives in La Maravillosa; or he entered and left through the security gate, with the authorization of a resident; or (and this is what makes the residents especially anxious) the club's security measures failed. Today, anyone who wants to come into a private community like this has to provide: authorization from an adult resident (a seventeen-year-old cannot bring in a friend, nor can a maid authorize anyone to enter unless she has written permission from the owners of the house); an ID card (before, it was enough to give the number without necessarily showing the document itself, because people regularly entering the club have their photographs stored on the computer and can be checked against records on the spot, but since a recent burglary in a neighbouring private community, documents must now be shown, even if the face at the gate is identical to the one on the screen); a third-party insurance policy in the name of the person driving the car (a man driving his wife's car would be in trouble); a photo (if it's the first time the person is coming in, and even though this is redundant now that ID also has to be shown; "better too much than too little" is one of the head of security's many sayings; others are "prevention is better than cure", "better to be safe than sorry" and "everyone's a suspect until he can prove otherwise"); inspection of the car boot on entrance and exit and now also under the bonnet – in case a visitor conceals some stolen object between the radiator and the engine? Who knows. For a few weeks now it has also been obligatory for a vehicle entering at night to turn off the external lights and turn on the internal ones until the guard has approached and checked who is travelling inside, which is exactly the same procedure for inspection of vehicles as prevailed during the military dictatorship. But even with all these safeguards – authorization, insurance, photo, document, boot in order and lights off, Chazarreta's murderer got in. So either he was already in, or a resident authorized his entry, or he bypassed security without the guard noticing anything strange. And that is what's really making "us" feel bad.

Nurit Iscar saves the text and sends it to Rinaldi, but this time without copying in the Crime boy. He gets the same piece in a separate email addressed only to him. She tries to make her covering note friendly, dispensing with all formalities in favour of a breezy Hello! Then: Here's the piece for tomorrow. I really liked your article yesterday. Warmly, Nurit

Iscar. And then she adds a PS at the end of the text: If you'd like to see the scene of this crime we're both writing about, you could come some time over the weekend, or whenever suits you. And so that there can be no suspicion that the invitation conceals some secret intention to throw herself at a boy who must be nearly thirty years younger than her, she adds another line to the PS: Feel free to bring someone else.

The Crime boy opens Nurit Iscar's email as soon as it pops up in his inbox. The invitation to La Maravillosa surprises him. Without even reading her latest dispatch, he stands up and walks over to Jaime Brena's desk. What do you think the chick's game is? The chick? Betty Boo. She's just sent me her piece without sending it to Rinaldi and she's inviting me over to La Maravillosa. She's just being friendly; now and then you meet someone whose first thought isn't to screw you over to get to the top faster or to get your job. Like me, you mean? No, kid, it's not your fault that I am where I am, or rather that I'm not where I ought to be. Anyway, are you going to go? It's a great opportunity and I shouldn't waste it but – I don't know. Remember the first lesson, kid, get out into the street. You have to go and be there, even if the streets inside that place are very different to the streets of Mataderos. What's Mataderos got to do with it? Nothing, just that I have to go there in a minute to cover the opening of a new nursery. Want to come with me? If you'll come with me to La Maravillosa at the weekend. I can't just turn up at the chick's house. Not the chick, Brena: Nurit Iscar – practise what you preach. Quite right. Nurit Iscar. Betty Boo. And yes you can, the boy insists, because she said in the email that I can bring someone if I like. She means your girlfriend, numskull. But she didn't spell that out, so I can go with whoever I like. I already know La Maravillosa, says Jaime Brena. I went there to interview Chazarreta. He

111

hated me after that interview. Why? Because I didn't say what he wanted me to say; because he couldn't control me. The bastard was an arch-manipulator, and those are the types that scare me most. I can defend myself in a fist fight; manipulation is much harder to tackle. So will you come with me? the Crime boy insists. If you've been there before, that's even better. It will be a privilege to go with someone who knows the lay of the land. Jaime Brena's gaze stays on the boy. This kid is nothing like how I was when I started working at *El Tribuno*, he thinks, but there's something in him that makes me want to help him, even if it's the same instinct that prompts someone to help a blind man across the road. Then he smiles and agrees: OK, you're manipulating me, too, kid, but I like you. Thank you, that's quite a leap forward in our relationship, the Crime boy jokes. And if it turns out that Nurit Iscar was expecting you to come with a girl, I can always squeeze your hand and give you a little kiss. You're a bit old for me, Brena. José de Zer would have done it if the situation called for it, Brena says. You see, this can be your third lesson, kid: find out which city very close to the capital, birthplace of one of our greatest football players, got its name thanks to José de Zer and why he became famous for the catchphrase "Follow me, Chango, follow me!" I'll find out, the boy says with enthusiasm. I'm just going to finish this piece and then I can go with you to Mataderos. Great stuff. The boy goes off and Brena looks over to Karina: See? I've found a colleague who's prepared to accompany me to Mataderos even though it isn't cool. How quickly you replace me, Brena. You're irreplaceable, gorgeous, even though you've abandoned me. She smiles but says nothing, knowing he's half-right; she's not avoiding him because she doesn't care about him but because spending time with him would force her to make a decision and tell him her secret. Why does Jaime Brena's gaze affect her so powerfully? She has a father and older brothers. Why, if she could choose a father, would she opt for Brena over her own? She looks at him and smiles again. He smiles back but doesn't say anything; he has no doubt that she's going through something that she doesn't yet want to tell him about. The Crime boy stands up and walks back to Brena's desk. What's up, kid? Brena asks. I owe you something, the boy says. I don't understand. What do you owe me? An answer to the question you asked me in the first lesson of this crash course for lamebrain journalists. Ah, come on! It's not such a big deal. The boy continues: Gustavo Germán González, of the *Crítica* newspaper, disguised himself as a plumber in order to gain access to the morgue and find out what the forensic specialists were saying about the body of the Radical councillor, and afterwards wrote: "There is no cyanide". No traces of cyanide were present in the corpse, and he was the first to publish that. Jaime Brena smiles with a certain satisfaction. Have I passed? the boy asks. Yes, kid, you've passed and you're learning, says Brena. You're going to learn a whole lot more, too.

11

Nurit Iscar decides that it might be as well to get some help in for the weekend. Her friends are like family and good at mucking in, but the house is big and gets full of dust and tree pollen. Besides, if the Crime boy does come, she'd like everything to be looking nice and not to worry about food, drink, washing up, replacing toilet rolls and all those other household chores, so that she can concentrate on him, take him around the neighbourhood and over to see Chazarreta's house (which is still sectioned off with *Do Not Cross* tape and guarded by a police inspector from the Buenos Aires division and a guard from the club's private security team) as well as any other places he may want to see. She guesses that the best way to find help would be to ask a neighbour's maid if she has a friend, relation or acquaintance she can recommend. So Nurit goes outside and waits for a maid to walk past. But none does. A car goes past, though, and another one ten minutes later and fifteen minutes after that a four-by-four. There must be a quicker method than this; perhaps it would be better to knock on some doors. Nurit tries the house on the right, with no luck. Nobody comes to the door of the house opposite, either. She can't bring herself to ring the bell of the house on the left: if no living being comes out of that one either (dogs and other domestic animals don't count) the sensation of absolute solitude could plunge her into a state of anguish from which she might never recover. If she, Nurit Iscar, is the only human being in the immediate vicinity, she'd rather not know about it. She lets a few minutes pass, trying to project a sense of calm she doesn't feel. But waiting only makes her more anxious. In order to see people, she fears, it's going to be necessary to go to the store, the tennis courts, the gym or the bar in the golf clubhouse. And Nurit Iscar really wants to see people. She's on the point of succumbing to another bout of city withdrawal syndrome when she sees a maid come round the corner walking a chihuahua. Nurit takes a deep breath, as though having narrowly escaped a peril only she can recognize. The woman seems rather annoyed by the task she's been given and not surprisingly, given the hysterical behaviour of the dog. Devil's spawn, she says under her breath as she walks past. Nurit nods sympathetically then takes advantage of the exchange to ask if the woman knows anyone who could help her at the weekend. The maid tries to stand still to answer her, but the dog starts barking furiously, so she's obliged to keep walking, with Nurit beside her. I've got a daughter, she says, but she can't do weekends; her husband wouldn't let her. Weekdays she can do, if you like, but he won't let her do weekends. And the woman is about to launch into a diatribe about her son-in-law, but Nurit Iscar interrupts her to say that unfortunately she only needs someone to help for a few hours on Saturday and then again on Sunday and that the rest of the week she can manage alone. There won't be many of them: just her, two friends and a work colleague, but even so she'd like someone to give her a hand. That's a shame; her husband won't let her do weekends, the woman repeats. That is a shame, agrees Nurit. The maid, still struggling with the chihuahua, waves to a gardener who's cycling past carrying a load of cut grass on the handlebars and, without Nurit saying anything, asks the man if he knows of anyone. He stops and they try to stop too, but the dog's hysterical barking makes any kind of conversation impossible. So the man turns his bike around and walks with them for a few yards in the direction the chihuahua wants to go. I did have someone, the man says; my wife, in fact, but she's just found something, she got a job yesterday after three months with no work. It's been really tough but yesterday she found something. Then, as though just remembering this, the man tells Nurit that at weekends women seeking casual work tend to gather at the other side of the club's entrance barrier, and that she'll probably find someone there. Sometimes the guards chase them away, but it's a public street, so they can stand there if they want, can't they? Yes, they can, Nurit Iscar says, remembering her contretemps with the guards over the ownership of streets on her first day at La Maravillosa. It's true, says the maid. I've seen them too. They come early on Saturdays. And if you need them, there are also men who can prepare an *asado* or wash your car, whatever you need, says the gardener. Nurit thanks them for this information and returns to the house. The man goes on his way. The woman has no option but to follow the dog, still griping about her daughter's husband as she goes.

Early the next morning, Nurit puts on the only trainers she owns, a present from her ex-husband – not yet "ex-" back then – on her forty-ninth birthday, the last one they spent together before separating. You spend too much time sitting in front of the computer, he'd said; you're going to end up with an arse like a pancake pan. She would have preferred a more romantic present and a less graphic metaphor, but her husband always was a pragmatist and by then she no longer had very high expectations either of him or their marriage. Or of metaphors. But five years on, the trainers are coming in handy. Although she still can't bring herself to go jogging. So she puts on jeans (an Argentine staple that when combined with something smart works just as well for a party as for a picnic) together with a T-shirt and sunglasses, and just before leaving applies some sun cream and sprays herself with insect repellent. Evidently the club's authorities haven't found a way to kill or keep out mosquitoes. Or are the ones here trained to recognize outsiders and, having identified Nurit as an intruder, biting only her? She looks at the map they gave her on the day she arrived and tries to work out the shortest route to the entrance gate. There are too many curves in La Maravillosa, culs-de-sac, roundabouts and circular streets that require careful navigation if one isn't to end up like the Minotaur, trapped in Daedalus's labyrinth. She works out the best route to the entrance and memorizes it, but folds up the map and tucks it into a pocket, anyway. Just in case she gets lost despite her good memory. She picks one of the books she brought with her – Muriel Spark's *Memento Mori* – to read as she walks and puts her mobile in one pocket and some money in the other, in case she feels like buying something in the store. What else? she thinks. And finally she leaves the house. I should have worn a hat, she realizes, a few yards from the house, but she isn't going to turn back now.

Today being a Saturday, Nurit sees more people than she has in all the time since she moved into La Maravillosa. She knows nobody; some people say hello, others don't. She has the feeling that something about her appearance is drawing their attention. As though there were some dress code with which she's failed to comply. But she can't think what. The jeans can't be wrong, nor the trainers. Perhaps the book? But it bores her to walk without reading. Maybe people think it's a dangerous habit because it takes her attention off the road. If that's the case, they don't know that Nurit Iscar is accustomed to reading in any situation: walking, travelling on the bus or underground, in a queue at the bank; even in a cinema when the lights are still on before the film begins. And with her eyes fixed on the book – and behind sunglasses to boot – she feels protected. She wouldn't like anyone to recognize her, to know that she is here masquerading as one of the residents while secretly spying on them. Even though anyone who reads *El Tribuno* must suspect that Nurit Iscar is here, it's not the same as knowing for sure that she is, or as recognizing her face. A spy. The non-fiction angle, as Lorenzo Rinaldi would say. Two days ago a woman came up to her in the supermarket and said: I know you, don't I? And stared at her. Possibly, Nurit replied. The woman smiled. From the Pilates class, right? Yes, Pilates, that's it, Nurit lied. She wants to remain anonymous for as long as possible. Not that people have told her very much yet, but as soon as they learn that she's not one of them, they'll tell her even less. And they'll look askance at her. She hates getting funny looks. If that's what people mean by "the evil eye", she believes in it, in the idea that people can hurt you by looking at you with hatred, anger or contempt. For all those reasons, Nurit Iscar walks along in sunglasses with her eyes fixed on her book, because she likes reading while she's walking and to avoid anyone recognizing or staring at her. Not that anybody is looking. Most people she passes are jogging. A few walk. Two young women rollerblade by. Quite a few are on bikes. A boy no older than twelve passes, driving a quad bike at an alarming speed. Electric golf buggies, mopeds, skates, motorbikes. The non-car traffic component in La Maravillosa is the most diverse she's ever seen, to the extent that she doesn't even know the names of some of the vehicles that pass her.

As Nurit Iscar is reaching the halfway point of her walk to the entrance of the country club, Carmen Terrada is getting into Paula Sibona's car, in preparation for a weekend at La Maravillosa providing company for their friend, as they promised. Are you taking a bathing suit? Paula asks. Yes, I've brought one, Carmen says. It's one of those end-of-March days that often count among the best in the year: sun, clear sky, unoppressive heat.

Meanwhile, Jaime Brena is sleeping. The Crime boy calls him: he wants to arrange a time to come by and pick him up. Give me an hour or so, kid, I've got some business to finish here. The boy's wise enough to know that the business involves Jaime Brena still having a pillow stuck to his face, but he says that it's fine, that there's no hurry, he can wait. His girlfriend complains that she's going to be on her own all weekend. I'm going for work, says the boy and switches on his computer to fill the time until he goes to Brena's. He types "José de Zer" into Google, discovering that the neighbourhood named for him is Fort Apache, birthplace of Carlos Tévez. It had previously been named Army of the Andes by Cacciatore, its mayor under the dictatorship, who had either forgotten or scorned the fact that its first inhabitants had named it Carlos Mugica, after the activist priest who was murdered in 1974. While covering a gunfight in the neighbourhood de Zer unwittingly excised the dictatorship's choice of name and rechristened it with the one we know today. This is like Fort Apache! he shouted at the camera, as bullets whistled around him. He deserves a place in history for that alone, the boy thinks. Today people all around the world know Tévez as "El Apache", never imagining that they have José de Zer to thank for that. If de Zer hadn't renamed the barrio, what nickname would the Argentine player have today? Little Soldier from Army of the Andes? The Crime boy learns, also thanks to Google, that one of de Zer's first jobs was in the ticket office of a theatre and that he was sacked for stealing. The anecdote appears in almost all the biographies returned by his search, as though knowing it were a necessary part of understanding his personality. And the words, "Follow me, Chango, follow me" were spoken by de Zer to his cameraman Carlos "Chango" Torres, when they were following the lights of supposed UFOs that had come to Mount Uritorco and were later revealed as a hoax: the lights in fact came from portable lamps placed there by de Zer himself and his team. "Follow me, Chango, follow me", and the two men had followed the light of those lamps. It was a practical joke, like that inflatable toy that fed the legend of the Loch Ness monster for so long. The boy laughs. He wonders how come he never heard that story of the lamps before. De Zer was ahead of his time, Jaime Brena will say to him later as they drive towards La Maravillosa, a forerunner of every lamp that one of our colleagues lights today with less grace and greater impunity, presuming to think of themselves as defenders of journalism and getting offended if anyone dares compare them to de Zer. And he'll confess that he respects José de Zer, despite his flaws; even if he was playing a game, the rules were clearer then and others could decide whether or not to play. That clarity is harder to achieve these days, kid, Brena will lament; our profession is one in which the clarity is getting darker all the time. An observation worthy of de Zer himself.

The Crime boy's girlfriend is asking again why she can't go with them. Without answering, he dials Jaime Brena's number. He knows that ten minutes haven't gone by yet, but he doesn't feel like waiting any longer. Brena's phone rings; it isn't the Crime boy on the other end, though: Comisario Venturini got in there first. Hello, my dear, how are you?

Well but poor, Brena replies. When are you taking me out for that *asado* you owe me? the police chief asks. Not today, Comisario – I'm going to La Maravillosa. *El Tribuno* has rented a house there for Nurit Iscar and I'm going over with a friend to see her. What perfect timing – I'm going to be in the area too. If I have time I'll drop by for a chat. Absolutely. Give me a call and I'll come and meet you, Brena says and hangs up. The phone rings again: All right if I come by to pick you up in ten minutes? the Crime boy asks. Make it fifteen, Brena says. I want to go too, says his girlfriend and, just to shut her up, the Crime boy says: OK, come then. Shall I take a swimming costume? the girl asks.

Nurit Iscar is nearing the entrance to La Maravillosa. Even before reaching the barrier she can see the women waiting outside. As she leaves the compound, one of them, faster than the others, runs up to her. "Need has the face of a heretic" was the title given by Lorenzo Rinaldi a few days ago to an editorial in which he reproached certain opposition governors mired in funding conflicts with the president. Are you looking for an hourly cleaner? asks the woman who's come up to her. Nurit Iscar doesn't know it, but the blonde woman speaking to her is the very one who was shouting in the line that day that Gladys Varela was waiting to go into La Maravillosa, that last day she came to work, moments before she found Pedro Chazarreta with his throat slit. Yes, I do need a cleaner, Nurit says. Could you work today until mid-afternoon and the same tomorrow? Whatever you need, I can do, says the woman. Great, let's go, Nurit says, and turns back towards the entrance. As they approach the barrier, the guard stops them. Does this lady have a work permit or an entry card? he asks, referring to the maid while addressing himself directly to Nurit. She looks at the woman inquiringly. No, says the maid, who seems uncomfortable. Then she needs to go to the office and fill in an entry form, which you can sign as authorization. Of course, says Nurit, and goes with the woman to do the paperwork. The woman presents her name and ID number, showing her document and handing over her bag to be examined. A guard asks her if she needs to declare anything she's bringing in and she says no, then quickly changes her mind and says: Yes, the mobile phone, which she hands to him so that he can make a note of the make and model. The guard enters her details into the computer and sees something on the screen that catches his eye. He prints off the permit, but before giving it to Nurit Iscar to sign he asks the woman who was shouting in the entry queue the same day they found Pedro Chazarreta's body to wait outside. The woman does as she is told and stands grudgingly outside the door, looking in through the window. Waiting. The guard looks at Nurit Iscar and says: I asked to speak to you alone because a warning came up on the screen just now. And what does that mean? asks Nurit. The system is asking me to advise you that Anabella López – the guard nods towards the woman waiting outside the door – used to work for a neighbour and resident of La Maravillosa, Señora Campolongo: do you know her? No, I don't know anybody here. Right. Well, Señora Campolongo has asked for this woman to be barred from the club, do you see? No. Señora Campolongo has requested that Anabella López not be permitted to enter La Maravillosa. Why, though? Because Señora Campolongo had an issue with López. But is that legal? Legal in what way? I'm asking if Señora Campolongo has made a formal complaint, or if there's a court order preventing the maid's entry. No, this is just a courtesy to members of the club. A courtesy. Yes, that's how we manage things here: we put an alert on the system. Señora Campolongo couldn't make a "legal" complaint, as you put it; because she has no proof, then these girls go straight to a lawyer who'll start some interminable, cripplingly expensive suit. There was a federal lawsuit brought against a resident a few years ago for denying the constitutional right to free circulation and work. We remember it very well here because it almost cost us our jobs. They asked us if the woman had worked for that member and we had to say yes, because it was in the register. It was a nightmare. That's why Señora Campolongo didn't report this to the police. But she did report it here at the gatehouse so that we could prevent anyone else falling victim to this situation. Ah, says Nurit, and what is "this situation"? That Señora Campolongo doesn't wish this woman to enter. But what's she accused of, even if it hasn't been proven? Apparently Anabella López stole from her. She stole something? Yes, a cheese. A what? A wheel of cheese. A wheel of cheese. The man looks at her blankly and she looks back. If you like we can call Señora Campolongo in and she can explain things better to you. She can tell me about her cheese being stolen? She can tell you whatever you need to know. And tell me, if I decide to run the risk of this woman stealing my cheese and employ her anyway, will you and the other guards let me bring her in or will you bar the way with rifles? They're shotguns. OK, with shotguns, then. No, we can't prevent you from bringing in whoever you'd like to work in your house, because of free circulation and the right to work; this is merely a piece of friendly advice from Señora Campolongo to her neighbours. A courtesy. Yes, a courtesy. How kind. Yes. Where shall I sign? Sign what? The authorization to work. So you are authorizing this woman's entry? Yes; I don't really like cheese, you see. I understand, says the security officer, and then says nothing more. Nurit goes out with the signed permit and hands it to the woman. Here you are, she says, and they start walking. After a few yards she stops, looks at her and says: I'm going to ask you something, and whether I let you work in my house or not depends on your answer, so think about it carefully. Did you steal a wheel of cheese from Señora Campolongo's house? The woman looks at her. Be careful how you answer, Nurit warns her again, looking at her hard. The woman holds her gaze without saying anything. She waits. Well? says Nurit, moving her head in an invitation to speak. Finally the woman says: Yes, I took the cheese. Nurit waits for a moment in silence then says, OK. OK? Yes, OK, you're hired, she says, and starts walking. If you feel the need to take anything from my house, let me know and I'll decide whether or not you can take it, agreed? Agreed, says the woman, but she seems to fall behind, as though this exchange had distracted her from the natural action of walking. Come on, hurry up, because people are about to arrive at my house and I haven't sorted out the kitchen yet. The woman catches her up and they walk in silence for a while until Anabella López says: And it wasn't a whole cheese, just a half. A half cheese, that's all. That fat cow ate the other half. Which fat cow? asks Nurit. That fat cow Campolongo, says the woman.

They walk the rest of the way in silence.

12

First to arrive at La Maravillosa's entry gate are Carmen Terrada and Paula Sibona. Somebody calls from the gate-house for Nurit to authorize their entry. Ten minutes later the women step out of Paula's Ford Ka in front of the house where Nurit Iscar has taken up residence at Lorenzo Rinaldi's request. That entry procedure's more rigorous than a medical check-up, says Paula. All that's missing is a cervical smear test. Don't give them ideas, says Nurit. By the way, that journalist who works on the Crime desk at El Tribuno is coming too – you don't mind, do you? Not at all; I'd love to meet Jaime Brena, says Carmen. No, it's not Jaime Brena, it's a young guy, someone I've only met recently. Brena's moved to another section, Nurit explains. Which section? Carmen asks. Jaime Brena was the best Crime correspondent left. I prefer Zippo, Paula interjects. You prefer Zippo because he's dark and hairy, but Brena's the better writer, says Carmen. Yes, Nurit agrees. You read his articles and it's like reading a story. How strange that they moved him – which section is he in now? Carmen asks. No idea, but I'll find out, says Nurit and, changing the subject: I didn't have the energy for an *asado,* so I've bought some empanadas and I asked Anabella to make some salads. Who's Anabella? The lady who's helping me in the house. Swimming pool and domestic help on the weekends – what luxury, says Paula. Where can I get changed into my costume?

Half an hour later there's another call from the gate-house. Carmen answers and passes the phone to Nurit: They're calling from the gate for you to authorize someone to be let in. It's the Crime boy, she tells her friends, then says into the receiver: Hello, yes? But the name they give her at the other end confuses her: Who? No, I was waiting for someone else. What did you say his name is? Matías Gallo, the guard replies. He says he's a friend of your son Rodrigo. Ah yes, but what's he doing here? Fine, yes, tell him to come in. Nurit's worried now. Why has one of Rodrigo's friends come to La Maravillosa? Something must have happened. Could he be the bearer of bad news? Her friends try to reassure her, but Nurit's face is testament to their failure. Oh, please, why do you always have to get so dramatic about your children? Paula chides. I'm sure it's nothing important. He was probably at somebody else's house and he's coming by to drop something in or to say hello, says Carmen. No, we're not that close – he's a friend of Rodrigo's from university. I know him, I know who he is, but we don't have the kind of relationship where he'd feel any obligation to come and see me. In that case he's probably dropping something off for Rodrigo, Carmen insists. He'd have let me know. You really think so? Kids can be very flaky. Nurit calls her son's mobile, but it's switched off. Carmen tries evoking the principle of Ockham's razor. Whose razor? Paula asks. It's a philosophical principle devised by one William of Ockham, Carmen explains, stating that when there are two possible reasons for the same occurrence, the simplest theory is most likely to be right; for example, if the person you're waiting for doesn't arrive, it's much more logical to think that he's missed the bus or got held up at a friend's house than that he's been killed in a traffic accident. Paula and Nurit both stare at her. OK, admittedly that wasn't the best example, but Ockham's razor, when properly applied, is a useful tool for keeping calm. Carmen decides it's safer not to say anything else. At Paula's suggestion, they go to wait for Matías at the door. They don't know from which direction he'll come; the road Nurit's staying on is a perfect semicircle and the house can be approached from the left or right. They keep looking both ways, as though watching a tennis match in slow motion. Time seems to stand still. How can it be taking the boy so long to travel from the entrance to here? asks Paula. What's he coming in – a horse-drawn carriage? Would you like us to take the car and go look for him? Maybe that would be best, Nurit agrees. Her friend's about to go and fetch her keys when the boy appears around a left-hand bend about twenty yards away, walking unhurriedly. Is that him? Carmen asks. And without waiting for an answer, all three of them run out to meet him. The boy, backpack on his shoulder and iPhone plugged into his ears, looks disconcerted by their approach. Nurit reaches him first and plants herself in front of him, grabbing his shoulders and saying: What's happened? The boy stares blankly at her. Tell me what's happened! she insists. What's happened when? her son's friend manages to ask. When whatever's happened happened, she says. But what's happened? Matías repeats. That's what I'm trying to find out! Nurit shouts back. Matías looks at the other women as though to say: "Throw me a line, I don't know what to do with this madwoman". Nurit starts crying. Paula, although inclined to believe that this is an overreaction, hugs her and lets her cry on her shoulder. The boy, sweating, wipes his brow with his arm. Carmen, in an effort to keep calm, states firmly: If you have something to say, whatever it is, say it now. The boy thinks for a moment; it's clear from his face that he'd like nothing better than to give these women something they could identify as the right answer, but he hasn't the slightest idea what they expect of him. Come on, speak, Carmen insists, spit it out, whatever it is. Thank you? hazards Matías. Thank you for what? says Carmen, not understanding. Thank you, Señora Iscar, for inviting me to spend the day at your country house, the boy recites. Nurit leaves the shoulder on which she's been sobbing and says: What? I invited you to do what? Well, not you personally, but Rodrigo invited me to spend the weekend at your country house. My country house. Yes, me and a few friends. Haven't they arrived yet? No, says Nurit with a deep breath, feeling calmer now but also murderous. Oh right, they set off in a van from Plaza Italia, but I made my own way here since I was coming from my grandfather's house in San Isidro. The women and Matías have been standing in the street and the driver of an Audi sounds his horn, a discreet beep to usher them out of the way. Everyone moves to the side to let the car past, and then they follow it towards the house. So tell me, Nurit asks Matías, exactly how many are coming in the van. Well… not many: four or five. Four or five, Nurit repeats. Without counting Rodrigo, the boy clarifies. No, we'd better not count Rodrigo, because I have a suspicion he may be about to have a nasty accident, Paula says. Seeing that the boy doesn't get the joke, she looks heavenwards and murmurs: Thank you, Lord, for giving me only nephews and nieces.

Back inside the house, Anabella tells Nurit that Viviana Mansini has called to say that she'll arrive after lunch (Who invited Viviana Mansini? asks Paula) and that the security guard has called again: There's someone at the entrance who needs authorization to enter, the maid says, then carries on cutting up lettuce. I'll call through now, says Nurit, sizing up the quantity of salad and realizing it won't be nearly enough. We've got more guests coming than I expected, she says, so throw in another lettuce and two or three more tomatoes. I'll

128

go and get some more empanadas in a minute. Nurit calls the security guard: Yes, apparently I have to authorize someone to come in. She listens to the name of the new visitor. Juan? she says. Yes, yes, let him in. He's my son. It looks like Juan is coming too, she tells the others. They never answer my calls, then they descend on me unannounced. Do you mind if I put on my trunks and swim for a bit while I wait for Rodrigo and the boys? Matías interrupts. No, go ahead, please make yourself at home, says Nurit, with a light irony that goes unnoticed by her son's friend. She looks pointedly at him without adding another word, leaving the boy to deduce that the best thing he can do is go and throw himself into the pool. Looks like I won't be gracing the swimming pool today, says Paula, once Matías has disappeared to get changed. Why? Nurit asks. Did you see that body? That skin? That youth? All that's going to be multiplied by five when Rodrigo arrives, and by God knows how many more when Juan turns up, and I'm just not braced for the contrast. Oh, cut the crap; we're past fifty, nobody's expecting youth from us, Carmen says. Maybe not youth, but self-awareness, respect for others and dignity. Dignity above all. I agree with you there, says Nurit, and she remembers herself standing in front of the mirror a few days ago, ashamed that Lorenzo Rinaldi should see how her body has aged in these last three years. I should have followed the example of Greta Garbo, says Paula. Or Mina. Women who chose their moment to retire from public view. Mina who sang "Parole, Parole"? asks Carmen. Yes, Mina. I didn't know she'd retired. She shut herself away. Old age is frightening for us artists: we're aesthetic beings, young souls in bodies that age. And somewhat narcissistic, Carmen adds. Call it whatever you like, but I was once a renowned artist, even if that boy didn't seem to recognize me, Paula complains. Do you realize he's got absolutely no idea who I am? He walked right past without even noticing me. All the more reason to get in the pool – you can safely assume the boy won't spare you a glance, Carmen says. Yes, I'm aware the risk is low, but it's there all the same. What if one of Rodrigo's friends happens to have seen me in an old film on cable, recognizes me, takes a photo and it goes viral? I'll get in the pool tomorrow; after all, the boys aren't staying the night, are they? I got the impression this Matías guy was talking in terms of "the weekend", says Carmen. The three women exchange glances. Paula walks over to the window to touch wood.

Juan, who arrives in a car borrowed from his father, isn't alone. I almost persuaded Dad to come, he says, greeting his dazed mother with a kiss. Instead he's brought his girlfriend – whom Nurit has never met before today – as well as his girlfriend's sister and his girlfriend's toy poodle. Bingo! cries Paula Sibona when she sees the dog jumping about in the garden. You never told me you were coming, Nurit says to her older son. I lost my mobile and I couldn't remember your phone number. Are you pissed off that I came without letting you know? No, of course not, darling, she says and, despite the inevitable complications that arise from unexpected visitors, Nurit Iscar isn't lying. If she is always silently bemoaning how little she sees them, then this sojourn at La Maravillosa has delivered an extra bonus. It's a lovely place, Mum, Juan says, pulling up some loungers so that his girlfriend and her sister can lie down. The toy poodle runs off to bark at someone who's just emerged from behind the privet. A dark man with a moustache, who isn't Zippo, Paula tells Nurit. Excuse me, says the man, coming forward and trying to ignore the hysterical yapping of the dog jumping around him. Well, things are looking up, murmurs Paula, as Nurit goes to see who the man is and what he wants. Comisario Venturini, delighted to meet you, he says. I'm an admirer of you and your novels, Señora Iscar, and I'm anxiously awaiting the next one. Thank you, but I don't write novels any more. What do you mean, you don't write them? Not at the moment; perhaps some time in the future. I'll keep waiting, then, in the hope of having another of your books in my hands one day. I like Moustache Man, he seems like a bit of a gent, Paula says to Carmen, who's standing with her a few yards away. I could already tell you liked him, she replies. I was in the area, Comisario Venturini is telling Nurit, and I arranged to meet up with Jaime Brena for a quick chat in your house. If that's not inconvenient, of course, he adds. Jaime Brena? Yes, he told me he was coming here. I didn't know that. How can that be? Well, anyway, take it from me; I rang him an hour ago and he was just setting off. If you say so; I seem to have lost track of who's supposed to be coming today, Nurit says with a sigh. Please do come in, anyway. No, not to worry, I'll come back a bit later. There's something I need to look at with a colleague in Chazarreta's house. The remark piques Nurit's curiosity; since arriving at La Maravillosa she's been to Chazarreta's house several times but has never managed to get past the red- and white-striped tape placed around it by police on the first day and now supervised constantly by a police officer from the Bonaerense and one of the club's own security guards. I don't want to compromise you, Comisario, but is there any chance you could take me into the house, too? Well, it isn't standard procedure. I understand. But since it's you – the police chief pauses, then grins – I think we can find a way. I'll let you know for sure when I come back later to see Brena. Thank you; you can't imagine how much that would mean to me. Before leaving Comisario Venturini says: Forgive me, I don't want to be impolite to the ladies, and goes over to greet Nurit's friends, clasping each of their hands firmly between both of his own, a gesture that irritates Carmen and thrills Paula. Comisario Venturini, he says, twice, holding Carmen's hand first, then Paula's. And that "Comisario" is like a knife twisting in Paula Sibona's stomach, leaving her speechless. Aren't you Paula Sibona? he asks. She takes a few seconds to react, then says: Yes, I'm Paula Sibona. Well, what an unexpected pleasure to meet you; you're one of my favourite actresses. I remember seeing you in that film – what was it called? – the one in which you played the wife of a very powerful man … *The Way to the Lake*, something like that. *The Way to the Lagoon*, she corrects him. That's it, *to the Lagoon*. I loved it, he says again, with Paula's hand still pressed between his. Anyway, I'm off now, but I'll be back later so we can talk more then, Paula, says the police chief; may I call you that? That's my name, she says. The Comisario says goodbye to the three women and leaves. You really liked him, says Nurit. The bitch is burning up! Carmen says. I confess that I've a weakness for men with a good strong handshake, especially when they're dark and hairy, too. I think you'd like him to squeeze more than your hand, darling, says Carmen. What's that supposed to mean? She means you'd like to screw him, Nurit translates. I fancy him, for sure, but I can't. Why not? What do you mean, why not? I studied at the Conservatorio. I've been Medea and Lady Macbeth at the Teatro San Martín. I did experimental theatre during the dictatorship! Do you understand? I can't fuck a Chief of Police… it's a question of ideology. And since when have you ever let ideology get in the way of sex? Carmen laughs. Since forever. Would you like me to run through a list of all the ideologically incorrect men you've laid? Nurit asks. No, I'd much rather forget them. And anyway, in each of those cases I found out afterwards: sex first, ideology later. He seems like a nice guy, though, plus he reads, says Carmen. Didn't he say he'd read all of Nurit's books? Don't push me, girls, I wouldn't be able to do it with a policemen; I'd freeze up, honestly.

Twenty minutes later Rodrigo arrives with his friends – five of them in total – and ten minutes after them come the empanadas. Nurit is seasoning the salads and asks Carmen to settle up with the delivery man: Get some money from my wallet, on top of the microwave. The toy poodle comes into the kitchen and makes a beeline for Nurit, rubbing against her legs. Can somebody sort out this animal? she asks, trying to shake the dog off, but Juan, his girlfriend and her sister are basking in the sun like lizards and nobody answers. Returning with the empanadas, Carmen says: Will two dozen be enough for so many hearty appetites? I forgot to call and order more! Is that Alzheimer's or mental strain? Strain, darling, relax, says Carmen. Nurit picks up the phone and orders four dozen more empanadas. How long? An hour and a half! she wails into the phone. Well, do what you can, she says, and hangs up irritably. Thank God the Crime boy still hasn't arrived, she says, just as the telephone rings again. Leaving the salad, she answers the phone, listens to the voice at the other end and then says: Yes, let him in.

13

Jaime Brena and the Crime boy are waiting in a long queue behind the barrier marked *Visitors.* Nurit Iscar has authorized their entry, and a guard has already checked the boot to speed up the process and indicated on a map which road to take to the house they're visiting. But they still need to show their documents and have their photographs taken at the gate. And there are six cars or so in front of them, which means a wait of at least fifteen minutes. The Crime boy's girlfriend got left behind at the first red light they hit en route to Jaime Brena's flat. She had wanted to swing by her own home to pick up a bikini, and her boyfriend had told her (and reiterated several times) that it was too late, that people were waiting for them and that they were going to Nurit Iscar's house for work, not for a pool party. But what am I going to do out there all day while you're working if I can't sunbathe? the girl had said as they waited at a junction for the light to turn green. You're right, the Crime boy said. Then he had got out of the car, walked around to her side, opened the passenger door and helped her out, saying: You'd better not come after all. The girl was astounded. I've never been so insulted, she said, as he gave her a hand out. There's always a first time, he said, then got back into the car and drove off. Jaime Brena wasn't surprised to see the Crime boy arrive on his own, because he'd never known that the girl was meant to be coming, but he did notice the boy's tense expression, his furrowed brow and awkward attempt to behave as though nothing were wrong. Is something up? he asked. Bit of a domestic, said the Crime boy, and they didn't mention the subject again.

As they travelled along the Pan-American Highway, they talked about football, the newspaper, the voluntary redundancy package that Jaime Brena might take, José de Zer, Karina Vives (Is it just me, or is she hot? Brena asked; the boy appeared bemused, saying only: She's a pretty girl, but very disagreeable, to which Brena responded, You have to know how to handle her), and also Pedro Chazarreta, Lorenzo Rinaldi and Nurit Iscar. The traffic was heavy that Saturday afternoon, and Brena had to ask the boy to stop slamming on his brakes so close to the car in front unless he wanted him to vomit on the upholstery. They left the Pan-American two bridges before the exit to La Maravillosa and it took them more than one attempt to rejoin the highway and leave by the right one, but finally they managed it. To think that there are people who do this journey every day; they must be out of their minds, said the boy. Don't underestimate them, Brena replied. Membership has its privileges, as American Express would say.

Finally it's their turn: documents, photos, registration number, car insurance, boot again – "But you've already checked it", "Ah, my apologies" – and they're inside La Maravillosa. Jaime Brena immediately recognizes that tree-lined road, the highest branches meeting above it to form a green tunnel through which the midday sun filters. He's always remembered that green tunnel. Brena lowers the window and unfastens his safety belt, filling his lungs with air. Have you been here before? he asks the boy. No, not to this one, the Crime boy says. I haven't been here for over a year, but it's exactly the same as when I came to interview Pedro

Chazarreta. Or it looks the same; it's not really, of course. At that time he was still a suspect in his wife's death. From the very first question he was trying to manipulate me, trying to turn the interview into a publicity campaign. He was a difficult man: cold, calculating, calm and very intelligent. What do you think happened? the boy asks him. You mean the murder? Yes. I think that he killed her or had her killed; or at least that the guy knew who killed her and why, and that he was the one ultimately responsible for her death. The Crime boy brakes to let some unsteady roller skaters – a woman and her daughter – cross the road in front of them. Do you know what Chazarreta said to the operator when he rang for an ambulance after finding his wife dead? No, says the boy. The call was recorded – I've heard the tape. He said: Please come straight away to Lot 23 in La Maravillosa. My wife's cut her throat and is bleeding everywhere. She got distracted then slipped on a wet floor and smashed into a glass door. Can you believe it? It seems like a very long and complicated sentence for someone supposedly in a state of shock, says the boy. And it's a sentence calculated to lead the listener to a particular conclusion: that it was all a terrible accident, Brena explains. Besides, unless he actually touched the body – and in his first statements he said that he didn't until the doctors came – he couldn't have known that the cut was across her neck because his wife was lying face down. So why was the case against him dismissed? I'll never be able to understand that. The ruling stated that the evidence was "inconclusive", but I'd convict him on what I've just told you alone. Then again, I'm not a judge.

An electric buggy driving ahead of them forces the Crime boy to drop his speed. The buggy is carrying a couple with their golf equipment in bags behind them, the man's clubs longer than his wife's. One of the wife's irons has a kind of cover on it designed to look like the long-eared head of a toy dog. Observing the couple, Brena says: It's another world, isn't it? Yes, agrees the boy, but there are a lot of different worlds. The trick is making sure you live in the one you like best. Quite right, says Brena, still studying the couple, then he adds: Turns out you're not such a dick in the end. The boy shoots him a look of hurt surprise and Brena laughs. It's a joke, kid; of course you're not a dick, you're just short on experience. Speaking of which, do you want to continue with the training? Yes, I'm ready for my next lesson. I already know all about José de Zer, Fort Apache and the UFOs. Who's next? Enrique Sdrech. You must know Enrique Sdrech. Yes, I think I've seen some old report they show on TV every so often. One report isn't going to tell you all you need to know about Sdrech. You need to find out more. For instance, did you know that someone shot at his house with an Ithaca 37 in 1992? No. Right, get hold of his book *Giubileo: An Open Case*. Do you remember the Giubileo case? Vaguely, says the boy, rather than admitting that he knows nothing about it at all. Vaguely, repeats Brena, good God; she was a doctor who disappeared off the face of the earth in 1985, leaving no trace. How old were you in 1985? I hadn't been born yet, replies the boy. Jesus wept, murmurs Brena, looking out of the window for a few seconds. You hadn't been born yet, he repeats, gazing across the golf course that's appeared on the right. Then he goes on: Doctor Giubileo was a young woman who disappeared while working at the Montes de Oca community neuropsychiatric hospital, also known as Open Door, where it was later discovered that organs were being trafficked and patients used as guinea pigs for new drugs. It was a tragic case, never solved. Sdrech was obsessed with it – and with all unsolved cases: Oriel Briant, Jimena

Hernández, Norma Mirta Penjerek. A lot of women whose murderers weren't brought to justice. He was a passionate man, and a great reader. You know what I learned from him? That crime news isn't written the same way as other kinds of article: you never put some juicy detail, some revelation in the intro. You leave that for the end, as if it were a story.

Three boys on bicycles are ranged across the road and don't seem willing to move to the side. The Crime boy waits; he doesn't dare hoot at them: that might be a contravention of the code here. You'd think they owned the road, says the boy. Well, they are the owning class; at least they're going to be, Brena says. One of the boys moves to the side, swerves and falls off his bike. The others rush to help him and the Crime boy takes advantage of the gap to slip past. Do you think he hurt himself? he asks. That's his mother's problem, says Brena. They drive one or two more blocks in silence before the Crime boy dares to ask: What's your obsession, Brena? Jaime Brena looks at him, not certain that he's understood the question correctly. Like Sdrech, like de Zer: there must be something that's come to be an obsession with you too, in such a long career. What obsesses me? I don't know any more. Years ago I wanted to be like Rodolfo Walsh, you know? He was my inspiration; not exactly an obsession, but certainly a model. Later I realized that I didn't have what it takes to be like him. Nobody, not me nor anyone else in this country today, can come close to Rodolfo Walsh. Why not? Because Walsh – before he was a journalist, before he was a writer, before anything else – was a revolutionary, and journalism has nothing to do with the revolution any more. We turned bourgeois, kid. We got paunchy. We do what they ask of us, within certain limitations, and collect our paycheck at the end of the month. We get by on a minimum of effort. And there are some charlatans who've got the nerve to think they're brave because they criticize the president, or the media. Or the president *and* the media. Do you think Walsh was scared? I would have been, in his shoes. Today the high priests of journalism, or "intellectuals", in inverted commas, are happy to sound off from the safety of their studies or their holiday homes. And they think they're important because they're "opinion-formers". But the question is: how do you form that opinion? What values do you respect? What scruples do you have? Many of them will offer up as an irrefutable truth something that's nothing more than their own opinion. Or the opinion of the people they work for. When a journalist departs from the facts in order to give his own opinion, he has to be clear about what he's doing or there's no integrity. It's fine to have opinions, but don't pass them off as facts. The bourgeois ideology tries to present the interests of its own class as natural or normal. Am I disappearing up my own arse, kid? No, not at all, says the Crime boy. Jaime Brena continues: But Christ, nothing compares with writing a letter to the military junta in the full awareness that the next day they're going to come for you. That was Rodolfo Walsh. Who would be today's equivalent of the junta? The president or the powerful corporations that pay your salary? Neither of them. If you don't agree with the editorial line of the newspaper you work for, what should you do? Follow their line, or resign? Is there room for a third option? I don't know. Anyone who can answer these questions with conviction is lying. We're all too cowardly to come close to Walsh, kid. But don't listen to me; take this as the windbaggery of an old cynic. Your generation doesn't agonize over these questions. I mean, you weren't even born when Doctor Giubileo disappeared. That's incredible, kid. Try to be a good crime reporter; get out into the street and produce great writing – writing that informs, that has teeth, that draws people in. And without any spelling mistakes, which is already a lot to ask for these days.

They've arrived at Nurit Iscar's house, but the sound of reggaeton coming from the garden is disconcerting. The boy looks doubtful as he turns into the gravel drive. Are you sure it's here? Brena asks. The boy consults their map again and checks the address written down by the guard: 675 Calandria. It's here, then, Brena confirms. Our Betty Boo must have very contemporary taste in music. They park, get out of the car and the boy rings the bell. You know how Enrique Sdrech would start this piece, kid? Like this: "Here we are ensconced in the heart of the La Maravillosa country club, more specifically at the house of the writer Nurit Iscar". He loved words like "ensconced".

A toy poodle rushes out to greet them. Brena contemplates it with disdain: This dog is nothing like the one I imagine myself having.

14

The introductions, the empanadas (once the second batch has arrived) and the puddings are duly dispatched. Thanks to Comisario Venturini's early warning, nobody is surprised to see Jaime Brena arrive at the house with the Crime boy. Carmen Terrada, somewhat overwhelmed to meet him face-to-face, manages to say no more than: Hello, pleased to meet you. To Nurit Iscar it doesn't feel altogether comfortable having so many (and so many different sorts of) people in her house, or rather in the house where she's staying, but she tries to manage the situation with calmness and aplomb. Even though aplomb has never been one of her strong suits. The youthful contingent takes over the pool and the area around it. The old are consigned to the shade of the veranda. I don't know how these kids can stand the sun beating down on their heads, says Brena, using his hand to comb the little hair he has left across his own head. Nurit watches him; she remembered him as having more hair. How much time has gone by? she wonders. She doesn't mean since she last saw Jaime Brena, mere days before, nor since she stopped visiting the newspaper offices regularly after her relationship with Rinaldi ended more than three years ago. How much time has gone by since they – Nurit, Brena, Paula, Carmen – were the age their children are now and could cavort in the sun without worrying about having to put their costumes on in front of the others, or about the heat, or about skin cancer. The time that's passed and the time still to come: both concepts cause her disquiet. That's why Nurit prefers not to let her thoughts go in either direction. But you can't always stop yourself thinking, and soon she's wondering again what Jaime Brena must have been like when he was the same age as her sons, more than thirty years ago. The memory makes her uncomfortable now, but Nurit Iscar remembers celebrating at the Obelisk the day Argentina won the 1978 World Cup, jumping up and down with her friends from that time. What would Brena have been doing that day? She seems to remember reading somewhere that he belonged to a militant group during the dictatorship. Carmen Terrada had been a militant too; that was why she had to go abroad for a time. How different their twenties had been to that of their children's. If she had to choose, Nurit doesn't know what kind of ending she'd choose to follow those years of adolescence and high-minded ideals. Any answer runs the risk of being either naive or politically correct, and she isn't sure what her answer would be anyway. Nor does she want to be sure. The Crime boy is certainly young enough to ally himself with the pool contingent, but work allegiances keep him on the veranda. The toy poodle prefers the shade too, but Nurit tells her son firmly: Get that creature away from me, and the dog ends up shut in the laundry room, despite the protests of Juan's girlfriend.

At three o'clock in the afternoon there's a call from the guards to say that Viviana Mansini is at the gate but can't get in because she hasn't brought her most recent car insurance policy document. As Vivi will tell them later, it did her no good to explain several times (and in great detail) that she had no paper receipt because her policy is charged monthly to her credit card, or to show the insurance company's laminated card or to suggest – implore, even – that they ring her insurance broker. The regulations changed this week, the guard explained; if you had come last week I would have let you in, but today I can't, because, like I said, the procedure has changed. Now we need the receipt as well as the card: what a shame you didn't come last week. And for that reason, because she's come this week rather than last, and doesn't have her insurance receipt, Viviana has the guard call the house where Nurit's staying so that Paula or Carmen can come to collect her from the entrance, a request that prompts a great displacement of cars because the Crime boy's car is behind Juan's and his car is behind Paula Sibona's. And while it doesn't occur to Juan to offer to go and fetch his mother's friend from the entrance to the club – in fact, he hands his keys to Paula so that she can move his car herself and then her own – it does occur to the Crime boy, but Paula turns down his offer, asking Carmen to go with her instead: Can you imagine how many indiscretions Viviana could fill that boy's ear with between the entry gate and here? Carmen agrees, and once they are in the car she asks her friend: Why do we still love Viviana when she drives us up the wall so often? Because she grounds us and that, in itself, is also guilt-inducing. Everyone needs someone to take things out on, but someone who stoically puts up with everything – and she never gets fazed – deserves a bit of recognition. Having someone to offload on is the only way we other mortals can protect ourselves, Paula contends. Absolutely; it's almost as if Viviana were our sacrificial lamb. Almost. We should almost feel sorry for her, then. Almost. But I don't. No, me neither. She still irritates the hell out of me. Me too. Guess we're not going to heaven, then. No.

And almost as confirmation of her ability to irritate her friends, some time later, when Comisario Venturini reappears in search of Jaime Brena, Viviana makes it clear that his dark, moustachioed looks are as appealing to her as they are to Paula – and she's prepared to let him know as much. How difficult your job is, Comisario; you must be very brave, she says, barely five minutes after meeting him (this observation being completely irrelevant to the rather aimless conversation the others are having). Carmen shoots Paula a knowing look and says under her breath: What a bitch. Paula adds: She'll end up screwing him. She won't let ideological qualms get in the way. Viviana Mansini? I doubt she even knows the meaning of the word ideology. She's not the only one. Look at the boys' friends in the pool. Paula follows her gaze and sighs: Young skin, young bodies, young laughter; any ideology? Wouldn't you swap a bit of ideology for some sex? For sure. Me too. We're definitely never going to make it to heaven. No. Nor are we going to make it into the history of great women. No, not that either.

Soon afterwards, the police chief proposes a visit to Chazarreta's house, and of course Viviana Mansini tries to join the group. But Carmen stops her firmly. They're going for work; don't stick your nose in. So Viviana stays back, albeit grudgingly: All I did was ask. Is it against the law to ask? The group that goes to the house where Chazarreta died – and his wife before him – comprises Nurit Iscar, Jaime Brena, the Crime boy and Comisario Venturini. Nurit suggests they walk there, to get a better feeling for the neighbourhood. As they walk, the Comisario fills his lungs, extravagantly swinging his arms as though the walk, the surroundings, the country air, the evening light or whatever were a tonic he's rarely able to enjoy. What's the smell here? he asks. Eucalyptus? Wood? Flowers? It's the smell of wealth, Venturini, Brena says, and nobody contradicts him. The Crime boy takes some pictures on his BlackBerry. Nurit Iscar stops to remove something bothersome from her trainer. She can't tell what it is – a stone, a seed or a clod of earth. Jaime Brena also stops and waits for her. The pebble she finally tips out of her shoe is tiny. How could something so small be so annoying? she wonders, showing the stone to Brena. It's like the story of the princess and the pea; remember it? he says. No, I don't know that one. Oh, well it's a nice Andersen fairy story: some young damsels had to undergo a test to establish whether or not they were really princesses. They had to lie down on twenty mattresses, under which the Queen Mother had placed a single pea – there's always a mother-in-law fretting about which woman's going to carry off the jewel of her son, even in fairy tales. Only the true princess felt the pea through all the mattresses and couldn't sleep all night, Brena concludes. So you're saying I'm a princess? Something like that. How gallant; thank you. Not at all, Betty Boo. She finds it awkward that he should use her old nickname, and Brena notices. You don't like being called that? Betty Boo isn't exactly the name of a true princess, she says. She's much more interesting than a true princess; she's almost a real woman, says Brena, looking at her. She says nothing, so he asks again: Does it annoy you when people call you that? No, it's not the nickname I mind, it's the story of how I got it that sometimes bothers me. Where did the name come from? Brena asks. Then Nurit, without knowing why and as though confiding in a life-long friend, says: Lorenzo Rinaldi picked that name for me, years ago. Lorenzo Rinaldi; is that what he said? That you look like Betty Boop? Yes, the day we first met in a TV studio. Well I never – so Lorenzo Rinaldi says he gave you that name! No, I say that he did. He was the first person to call me that. Intellectual property is always a contested area, says Brena. Why do you say that? Nurit asks. Oh, no reason, he replies, and changes the subject – What does it feel like living in La Maravillosa? – just as the Crime boy, walking a few yards ahead, turns around and takes a photograph of them. I don't really feel that I am living here, she says, only working. But you're on a full-time regime. Yes, and that's not easy, she admits. I can imagine, says Brena. Although it's not such an ordeal to spend a few days in a place like this. No, I suppose not; once you've got over the symptoms of city withdrawal syndrome, you start to see it all with a kinder eye. Relax and enjoy it, then. I'll certainly try, she says. Their eyes meet and they smile, then they look away from each other and walk in silence for a time.

There's something about their group that seems to draw the eye of the people they pass. Nurit's experienced this on other occasions too – that look that distinguishes "them" from "us". She'd thought that it was down to her habit of reading as she walked. But she hasn't got a book now, so what is it that marks them out to passers-by as outsiders, intruders, aliens? Perhaps it's Comisario Venturini's sports jacket, which isn't quite appropriate for a country club on a Saturday afternoon, much less so the silk handkerchief with Bulgarian motifs tucked into his breast pocket; or it could be Jaime Brena's leather moccasins that scrape against the asphalt, threatening sparks, or the white dress shirt he wears unbuttoned at the neck but with stays in the collar. The two who blend in best with their surroundings are the Crime boy and Nurit Iscar – who selected her clothes this morning with that specific aim. She's been studying the dress code these last few days at La Maravillosa and although she isn't quite ready for sweatpants, she's noticed that jeans and trainers don't attract attention, so this is what she wears, day and night. The Crime boy blends in because he's wearing khaki trousers – like fatigues, with lots of pockets – plus trainers and a white round-necked T-shirt. Designer sportswear would have been the best apparel in which to pass unnoticed.

The group walks on. Back at the house, Carmen Terrada is making maté, Paula Sibona – fully dressed – is trying to harness the last of the afternoon rays to get at least her face tanned. Nurit's sons and their friends are kicking a ball about in the garden beside the pool. Juan's girlfriend and her sister are attending to the toy poodle, who's suffering from stress after his long confinement in the laundry room, and Anabella is picking up the wet towels, dirty glasses, leftovers, dog poo, half-smoked cigarettes and butt-ends that have been scattered the length of the garden.

Meanwhile, after about ten minutes, the party walking through La Maravillosa sees Chazarreta's house appear around a bend, at the bottom of a cul-de-sac. The property's boundary is still marked off with that red-and-white barrier tape which, though it has no writing on it, clearly indicates that you'd be an idiot to go further. They aren't idiots, though; they are empowered by the presence and authority of Comisario Venturini. Before they can go in, however, Venturini has to give even more explanations to the private security guard employed by La Maravillosa than he's already given to the Buenos Aires police officer on duty, with whom, he says, this visit was arranged two hours earlier. It's not that the security guard has too much respect for the laws of this great nation to honour the arrangement, but that he's unswervingly committed to following the orders of his superiors – in this case, the manager and owner of the security firm contracted by La Maravillosa – and his superiors have ordered that nobody must enter the house. And nobody means nobody. So it takes two or three bad-tempered phone calls on the Comisario's part for the guard to get the necessary authorization from his superiors by walkie-talkie and finally allow them to duck under the police tape. Sorry, but I'm only following orders, says the security guard once more.

It's fine, it's fine, my dear, says Venturini, and he's about to cross the tape too, but then turns back to say: Do you know the anecdote about San Martín, the hobnail boots and the powder keg? No, I don't know it, says the guard. Remind me when I come out, and I'll tell you it if I have time, my dear, Comisario Venturini promises, and squats down again to pass under the barrier.

Now they're walking along the veranda, as Gloria Echagüe supposedly did the evening she died. And they enter the living room by the glass door through which she fell. Comisario Venturini takes out a handkerchief and uses it to turn the handle without leaving new prints. Just in case, he says, with a wink to Brena. In fact, please make sure you don't touch anything, he says to the others. Even though the forensic work has been completed, everything must stay exactly as we find it, OK? OK, say Brena, Nurit and the Crime boy, in unison. They begin the tour in the living room on the ground floor, the scene of the crime. Around them are expensive wooden fittings, polished to a shine, silver ornaments, glassware, paintings that may not be worth much but are displayed in ornate frames in distressed gold to make them seem old. The decor isn't what one would expect of a country club, but instead reflects a more traditional, conservative aesthetic, like something you'd find in an apartment in Belgrano or Recoleta. There's a polished wood and bronze bar with different kinds of drink: gin, mango vodka, whisky – the same label that Chazarreta drank the night of his death – and Baileys; a kilim under the cherrywood dining-room table and another, smaller one under a coffee table made out of the same wood; and two three-seater corner sofas, upholstered in beige velveteen with oversized cushions striped in different shades of green, brown and burgundy. At the side of each sofa stands a little Carrara marble table bearing a bronze-based lamp with a white lampshade. But the group's inevitable focus is the green velvet armchair (there's only one) facing the window and stained with blood. The place where Chazarreta met his end in the hours before dawn. Without planning it, Nurit, the Crime boy and Jaime Brena converge in front of the chair at the same time. Nurit is more affected than the men; not because of the blood, or the death it inevitably brings to mind, but because of the literary coincidence. Could Chazarreta have realized, before he died, how closely his final scene resembled the one in that Julio Cortázar story, "The Continuity of Parks"? she asks and, without waiting for an answer, continues: Chazarreta wasn't reading when he was murdered, but perhaps while he was sitting there drinking his whisky he was thinking of a crime, like the character in that story. He was imagining an intruder breaking into a house and cutting somebody's throat and finally, seconds before he died, he realized that it was going to happen to him, that somebody would come up behind him and cut his throat. But would Chazarreta have read Cortázar? Brena asks her, while the Crime boy takes pictures of the armchair and then types "Continuity of Parks + Cortázar" into his BlackBerry and runs an Internet search. I believe in fate, and that the scene could still have happened even if he'd never read Cortázar. Anyway, he probably did read him, at secondary school, Nurit goes on; we all read Cortázar at secondary school. Then she thinks for a few seconds and a chain of thoughts prompted by free association makes her ask: Which secondary school would Chazarreta have gone to? Jaime Brena says: It never crossed my mind to find that out. Would knowing make a difference? I don't think so, she says. Yet for some reason you thought of it, he says. Curiosity, no doubt, Nurit says. Or fate, says Brena: You just said you believe in fate, and thought works along the same lines. Nurit Iscar looks at the boy and says: Did you read Cortázar in secondary school? And the boy says: Yes, deliberately avoiding Brena's gaze because he knows that his colleague from *El Tribuno* will identify this as a lie. Or a half-truth, at any rate, because he has in fact read Cortázar, but only "House Taken Over", which is less than two hundred words long. And if he's ever read anything to do with a green velvet armchair and the continuity of parks, he can't remember it. The text of the story appears in the list of results his Google search returns, but it doesn't seem quite right to start reading it now in front of everyone and on such a small screen. Comisario Venturini walks over to them and suggests they continue the tour around the rest of the house. First they go to the kitchen, impeccably appointed, with white tiles, a brick-coloured floor and a black marble-topped island in the middle over which hangs a variety of pots and pans in different shapes and sizes, none of which appear to have been used more than once or twice. The boy goes over to them and swings some of the stainless-steel utensils: a ladle first, then a slotted spoon. No touching, I said, chides Venturini, and the boy quickly pulls his hand away. The appliances are the same as you might find in any house in La Maravillosa: a double-door fridge freezer, microwave, Nespresso coffee maker, waffle maker, electric hob and oven. How strange to have a washing machine in the kitchen, Brena says. It's a dishwasher, Nurit corrects him. Oh, I could definitely do with one of those, Brena says. What you could do with is a wife, not a dishwasher, my dear, says Venturini with a laugh. That's what I think, too, ventures the boy. Nurit, of course, doesn't appreciate the comparison: Well, how flattering to know that you put women and dishwashers on a par with each other. The three men exchange glances, and nothing more is said about the respective merits of wives and dishwashers. Not even as a joke. Second stop is the utility room, which is almost as immaculate as the kitchen. An industrial washing machine that must have far exceeded the household's needs, even when Chazarreta's wife was still alive. A dryer. Two sinks. Above one of the sinks there's a metal sign, like a small street sign, that says *No bleach to be used in this area.* Shelves. And through the window, clothes lines hidden behind a fence as per the regulations of La Maravillosa. Barbecue area, swimming pool, storeroom. They continue to the first floor. At the top of the stairs is a chill-out area with an LCD television, DVD, sound system and squashier, friendlier armchairs than the ones downstairs. A small bathroom. And then a corridor with two rooms leading off it: a study and a guest room (presumably the Chazarretas had found new uses for rooms they had once hoped would be filled by children, Nurit thinks). Finally the master bedroom suite: a severely ordered room and obviously one that is – or was, until recently – occupied by a man. You can tell from the dark scheme of the bedspread, the articles of perfumery in the bathroom, the lifted lavatory seat. Nurit wonders if the room would have been like this when Gloria Echagüe was still alive, but she doesn't raise the question with her male companions. Would Echagüe have allowed such masculine domination of this shared room? Did she give in to it? Or is this decor the product of the change wrought in Chazarreta by widowhood? They leave the room and walk back down the corridor. In the guest room there are two single beds, two bedside tables, a wardrobe, a TV set (much smaller than the one on the landing, but also LCD), a rocking chair and a chest of drawers. And in the room that Chazarreta used as a study there is a big table, and on top of it: a computer, a printer, a tray (presumably for papers still to be dealt with), a few outstanding bills, and a diary.

Two chairs, one on either side of the table, an old globe, and a small bookcase in which the few shelves are divided equally between books and ornaments. The ornaments look like souvenirs from foreign trips: Peruvian earthenware; three gold metal pillboxes in different sizes with black drawings typical of Toledo on them; glass miniatures from Murano; some stones and shells. The books are novels by bestselling foreign authors (Sidney Sheldon, Irving Wallace, Wilbur Smith); investigative works on current affairs, written by journalists, ex-civil servants, politicians and economists; and a few blue-leatherette-bound classics of national and world literature from a series that was produced in association with the newspaper *La Nación*: *One Hundred Years of Solitude, The Leopard, The Inverted Cross, The Tunnel*. On his BlackBerry, the Crime boy takes photographs of the books, first all together, then close up, or in groupings that allow the titles to be read. He takes a few more random shots and, by the time he's finished, realizes that Jaime Brena and Nurit Iscar are no longer standing behind him waiting but have moved to the window, where there's a side table crammed with framed photographs. Chazarreta and Gloria Echagüe; Gloria Echagüe alone; the two of them with other couples; Chazarreta receiving a golf trophy with a partner; Gloria Echagüe in a tennis tournament; Gloria Echagüe and two children; those same two children but older this time, standing with a couple who may have been her parents; Gloria Echagüe with a group of friends in a picture taken years ago, perhaps at the time of their school graduation trip because the Andean background scenery looks like Bariloche. The boy watches them; they have their backs to him and are standing still, without talking. He isn't sure whether it's a pleasing or unsettling scene, but he takes a photograph of it: their backs in front of a table full of photographs next to the window. Brena hears the camera click behind him and turns around. Come here, kid: get a photo of this. The boy comes closer and Nurit moves aside to make room for him. Of all the pictures or one in particular? All of them, says Nurit. Everything, agrees Brena. But when the boy steps forward ready to take it, his position suggests that he's about to leave one photograph out of the composition. The frame on the end, too, says Nurit. Yes, kid, don't leave that one out, Brena agrees. Even though there's no photo in it? he asks. Even though there's no photo, Brena confirms. The boy steps back to alter the focus, then takes a shot incorporating the frame which has glass edges and backing, but contains nothing.

Then without saying a word the three of them leave the study, and the tour is over. Comisario Venturini is waiting for them in the garden, having left earlier to smoke a cigarette. The guard is talking to a Maravillosa neighbour. This man, dressed from cap to trainers in Nike sports apparel, intently observes the party emerging from the house, making no effort to disguise his interest. But he leaves before they have all ducked back under the police tape, slapping the guard on the shoulder as he goes. A few yards further on he pauses to do some stretches. See you later, dear, says Comisario Venturini to the guard. Aren't you going to tell me that story about San Martín and the soldier? the guard asks. Ah yes, I'll tell you, but it'll have to be a short version because I'm a bit pressed for time: the soldier had to guard the powder-keg, and it was San Martín's order that nobody go in wearing hobnail boots, because they could cause sparks, see? Spark plus gunpowder equals explosion, right? But that night San Martín himself came along in his boots, wanting to go into the store, and the soldier wouldn't let him no matter how much he insisted and pulled rank. What do you make of that? The guard says nothing. Would you have done the same? The guard hesitates. Do you know what San Martín did the next day? He decorated the soldier, that's what he did. See? He gave him a medal. So – was that a good anecdote? Yes, yes, says the guard, thank you. As he turns to leave Comisario Venturini says: It was another age, dear, another age. That's the lesson: that times have changed. Then he raises his hand to say goodbye and hurries to catch up with the rest of the group. But now it's Nurit's turn to stop and walk back to the guard. Who's that man? she asks, gesturing in the direction of the Nike-clad neighbour, who is still doing his stretches. That's Luis Collazo, a friend of Chazarreta, says the guard. He comes by the house every day. You can tell he isn't coping well with what happened. Nurit stares after the man, who seems to sense her gaze and turns around to see her looking at him. Rather than avert her eyes, she keeps looking, trying to match the face with one she knows she's seen on several other occasions since arriving at La Maravillosa. The man turns away again and clumsily speeds off. He seems like an anxious type, Nurit observes to the guard. Maybe; since Chazarreta was killed things have changed here. Not for everyone; some people carry on as though nothing had happened. For other people life has changed. I understand. Do you mean it's changed more than when Gloria Echagüe died? Nurit asks. In all honesty yes, says the guard. Nurit hesitates for a moment, studying the house until Jaime Brena comes back looking for her. Another stone in your shoe? he asks. Either that or a real pea; we'll soon find out, says Nurit Iscar. And they start walking again.

15

On the way back to Nurit Iscar's house, Jaime Brena tells
Comisario Venturini about the suspiciously empty photo
frame. But Venturini is unmoved: Sounds like hooey, dear.
Don't you have the odd empty photo frame in your house?
Neither empty ones nor filled ones: there are no framed
photos in my house, Brena replies. Well, I certainly do.
There's been one on my bedside table for three months that
I can't find the right photo for; do you think I'm about to
be murdered, too? Nurit thought it was significant as well.
Oh, you writers and your fantasies! I'm not a writer, I'm a
journalist. Same thing, Brena. No, don't waste your time
chasing red herrings. Stick to writing, since that's what you
do well, and let us do what we know how to do. Unto Caesar
what is Caesar's; right, my dear?

Comisario Venturini takes his leave and the others go
back into the house. Why do you care so much about the
empty photo frame? the Crime boy asks when the three of
them are sitting in the living room. Because it's a break in
the sequence, says Brena. Because what's there speaks to us
and what isn't there raises questions for us, says Nurit. We
need to know who originally occupied that space, why they
ceased to occupy it, and when. Where is that photograph
now? Who took it? She isn't expecting answers to these
questions, but the boy tries to find an explanation anyway:
There could be a mundane reason; for example, somebody

could have given Chazarreta the frame very recently, just a few days before his death, and he hadn't yet chosen a photo to go in it. It wasn't new, says Nurit. The glass was scratched on the bottom left-hand corner and the bronze frame had the kind of marks that old metal gets. Besides, it's identical to the frame which had the picture of Gloria Echagüe and her secondary school friends in it, says Brena. I'd be willing to bet that the relationship between the two frames was also shared by the two images and that the empty one once contained a photograph of Chazarreta and his school friends. The Crime boy takes out his BlackBerry to confirm the descriptions that Nurit Iscar and Jaime Brena are able to make with such confidence, as if they had the collection of frames in front of them now. Also, says Nurit, Chazarreta's house is the home of an obsessive: the T-shirts are organized by colour, bottles in the bar are ordered from tallest to shortest, the towels are all white, the dishtowels are all tartan. And an obsessive doesn't put an empty frame on a table intended to display photographs. He keeps it wrapped up in its box until he's decided what to put in it, Nurit concludes. That frame contained a photograph that, for whatever reason, has been removed, says Brena, and Chazarreta left it there because it speaks, because it's saying something; otherwise he wouldn't have kept a frame with scratched glass. The boy says nothing, dazed by so much logical argumentation. I wouldn't want to leave this area unexplored, no matter what Venturini says, says Nurit. I'd never forgive myself. I agree with you, Betty Boo, says Brena. Without knocking, Viviana Mansini opens the door and asks: And Comisario Venturini? He's gone to work, says Jaime Brena. We're working too, Nurit says meaningfully. What a shame, says Viviana; I've made some banana fritters I wanted him to try. Would you all like some? Go on then, says Nurit. Tell Anabella to bring them through with some drinks. Maté? she asks the others. Yes, maté, the Crime boy and Jaime Brena agree.

Nurit suggests asking Luis Collazo about the missing photograph. She gets his phone number from the gatehouse and calls it, but as soon as she introduces herself – It's Nurit Iscar, from *El Tribuno*: we saw each other this afternoon in front of Chazarreta's house – whoever said "hello" at the other end immediately hangs up and Nurit is left listening to the dialling tone. She tries again: no response. She tries once more: nobody answers. It seems that Collazo isn't keen to speak to us. Who else might know what photos used to be in the frames of a man who lived on his own? Nurit wonders aloud. Some relative? Some other friend, more sociable than Collazo? From what I know, his relations were few and far-flung, and I doubt Chazarreta would have brought many friends up to his study, says Brena, but we could try asking – if we knew who his friends were, of course. Nobody speaks for a moment, as if they need to let their brains work in silence. The Crime boy stares at the empty frame on the screen of his BlackBerry, looking for clues. Then he gets up and goes over to the window, drawn by the game of football Nurit Iscar's sons and their friends are just finishing. It's tempting. His feet itch to get involved. But he's here to work and learn, even if he does feel like a hindrance some of the time. And in the last few hours this intensive course in crime journalism he's on has gone from fast to high-speed. The door opens and Anabella brings in the fritters and maté. Do you need anything else? she asks. No, thank you, says Nurit. Don't forget to let me know if I got them right, the woman says. Oh, did you make these yourself? Nurit asks, unsurprised. Yes, of course, replies Anabella. Who else would have made them? As she's about to leave the room, the Crime boy stops her. There is one other thing, he says. Do you know the woman

157

who was Chazarreta's housekeeper when he was murdered? Gladys Varela, says Anabella. That's her name. It was on the news. Yes, I saw it on the news too, but do you actually know her? Could you find her? I don't know her very well, but I've got her number in my phone. Could you call her, says the boy; call her and tell her that we're journalists, that we work for *El Tribuno* and that we'd like to have a quick chat? Nurit and Brena look on, startled by the boy's shrewd intervention; not because they wouldn't have thought him capable of it, but because he finally seems to have woken up. I'll ring her, sure, says Anabella. I'll go and get my phone from the kitchen and call her. She leaves the room and the boy smiles with satisfaction at his beginner's luck. Don't get too big-headed, Brena tells him, but you're learning. That's all there is to it: if a person wants to learn, he'll learn. And the boy, without letting it go to his head, feels good.

Minutes later, Anabella appears at the door with the phone in her hand. Gladys Varela is asking how much they're going to pay her. Tell Gladys that we're serious journalists and that serious journalists don't pay for their pieces, Jaime Brena says quickly. But she got paid for going on television, the woman insists. Precisely, says Brena, because that was television, not us. Tell her that *El Tribuno* doesn't pay its sources, but if she can help us we'll take a lovely photo of her and she'll come out in one of the most widely read newspapers in the country. A nice big photo, quarter of a page, tell her. Did you hear that, Gladys? Anabella says into the phone, then waits for the other woman's response. There's a short silence, and then: Fine, I'll tell him, Anabella says into the phone. Addressing herself to Brena, since he seems to be leading the negotiation, she says: Gladys says she'll come, for the photo in the paper, even though you're not paying her, because she doesn't like how they treated her on television – she'll tell you all about that. Anyway, she's coming for the photo, and on one condition: that you let her enter through the visitors' gate. Brena stares at her, uncomprehending. That you let her in through the same gate you use, Anabella tries to explain: Gladys will go up to the road, catch a taxi and come into the club through the visitors' entrance; otherwise she's not coming. Because she's not coming to work, like she used to. She's coming because you've asked her to; you're inviting her. And you have to pay for the taxi. Yes, of course, Nurit answers hurriedly; after living here for a week she's quicker than the others to grasp the niceties of the woman's request. But let somebody at the gatehouse know, Anabella cautions, otherwise they'll make her go through the staff entrance, and if she thinks you haven't kept your word she'll go away and never come back. I'll tell them, and I will keep my word, don't worry, Nurit says. Are we good to go, then? Anabella says into the receiver, and then confirms: She'll be here in half an hour or thereabouts. Then she closes her mobile and leaves the room. Why is coming through the visitors' entrance one of her conditions? asks the boy. So that she can feel that she gets to use the same door as everyone else, even if it's just the once, Nurit replies. I have to say, they didn't make us feel all that great when we came in through the visitors' gate, Brena says. It's not about how they treat you, but what they call you, says Nurit.

An hour later Gladys Varela rings the bell. Nurit Iscar ushers her in and introduces her to the others. There weren't any taxis; I had to wait twenty minutes, the woman explains apologetically, so I've told him to wait outside, otherwise I'll be stuck here for ages. You'll pay for him to wait for me and take me back, won't you? Yes, of course, says Brena. It's obvious that the woman has put on her best clothes: black skirt, shiny white shirt, high heels, faux leather bag. Gladys Varela sits down and prepares to be interviewed again. Shall I tell you what happened that day? she asks. No, we already know about that, says Brena and although he simply meant to speed up the proceedings, Gladys is momentarily disconcerted by the bluntness of his manner. Why have you asked me to come here, then? It's the boy who steps in to smooth her ruffled feathers. We saw you explain what happened that day on television. Oh, so you saw me, she says, noticeably proud. And on YouTube, says the boy, I saw you on YouTube, too. Yes, my kids told me I'm on it. They saw it in the cybercafé. Lots of people have seen it on YouTube, it's had loads of hits, the boy enthuses. But the TV people weren't true to their word. They gave me less money and they didn't pay my travel expenses, the woman complains. And they only put me on one day when we had agreed that I'd be on three times. Three: do you see what I mean? Including once on the evening bulletin. More people watch television in the evening. I mean, even my husband never got to see me. The kids are going to take him to the cybercafé so he can see me, but there hasn't been a good time. There never is with my husband, says Gladys Varela, sadly shaking her head as if letting the movement speak for some grievance she's decided it would be better not to articulate. So? she asks. What have you brought me here for? We asked you here because we want to ask you about one detail, something we noticed in the house, says Jaime Brena. You've been into the house? Gloria asks. Yes, with the police. When? Just now. It must be very dirty. Not particularly, Brena says. But it must be. Nobody's been in there to clean since I stopped going, and all the dust gets in and gathers. Men don't notice these things, Nurit interrupts, but yes, there was a lot of dust. Like you wouldn't believe, says Gladys Varela. The dust here is

160

terrible. We wanted to ask you specifically about a photo frame in Señor Chazarreta's study, one with no photo in it, says Brena, getting to the point. The woman visibly stiffens, and looks like she's considering leaving. Do you know the photo frame I mean? Gladys doesn't answer, but clutches her bag, ready to rush out at any moment. Is something wrong? the boy asks. What does the frame matter to you? she says. It's the photograph that matters, Brena says. The woman gets more upset. Are you Chazarreta's lawyers? she asks. No, Brena says vehemently, and he can't understand why she would think this – for him, for Jaime Brena, to be taken for a lawyer is far from flattering. We're journalists; what makes you think we could be representing Chazarreta? He said that if the photograph wasn't found he was going to call his lawyer and the police. When did he say that? When the photo went missing. But when was that? A few months ago, or a year, I don't remember any more. I thought the whole thing was cleared up, or at least that Señor Chazarreta knew that I had nothing to do with it. With what? With the missing photograph. He blamed me to start with, until one day he said that he'd realized I didn't have anything to do with it. He acknowledged that, but he never actually said he was sorry, and afterwards he never mentioned it again. I was very upset: I never touch anything that isn't mine. Not anything. What would I want with someone else's photograph? She looks at each of them anxiously and says again: How can I be sure that you aren't lawyers? She's a writer and we're both journalists from *El Tribuno*, says the Crime boy. If you don't believe us we can call the newspaper now. Gladys Varela interrupts him: No, it's fine, I do believe you, she says to the boy. She asks for a glass of water, and Nurit brings her one. The woman drinks. I thought the whole business was over. I forgot about it. I didn't like what Señor Chazarreta had said to me, but I let it go. You can't work in a place and have bad blood with your employer, she says, leaving Jaime Brena to think over just how much bad blood he has with his. What would I want that photo for? And what was that photo? What was it of? the boy presses. It was a photo from years ago, of him and some friends: there must have been four or five of them, friends from secondary school. Jaime Brena and Nurit exchange glances. There were two matching frames; one of them had a picture of his wife and her friends and the other one had a picture of Señor Chazarreta and his friends. Do you happen to know which secondary school he went to? Nurit asks. Well, the name was in the photograph, but I can't say I paid much attention to it. There was a flag they all held among them, and it was a saint's name, but it wasn't San Pablo, San Pedro or San Agostino; I don't know, it was an odd saint. A lesser-known saint, do you know what I mean? That's why I can't remember it. And why do you think that it was so important to Chazarreta? I don't know. But to make things worse, soon after it was lost one of the friends who was in that photo died. Such a shame. And that it should be someone from that photograph, too. Do you know the name of that friend? Brena asks. Yes, Gandolfini. He was a member of this club too, of La Maravillosa. He had a weekend house here. He was killed on the Pan-American. He liked driving fast, apparently, and one day he drove straight into a pillar. Chazarreta was in pieces, as you can imagine. He was never one to talk, he wasn't chatty, but he let the odd thing slip sometimes, after a whisky. And with good reason. I mean, first his wife and then his friend. I think somebody used that photo to fix him. Because it's a big coincidence. You'd have to hate someone a lot to do a fix like that, says Gladys Varela and then she falls silent, pressing something she's wearing under her shirt and which they can't see. A fix, she repeats.

I told him that somebody must have fixed them up. What exactly do you mean by a "fix"? the Crime boy asks. Those things people who know about black magic do – voodoo. A curse, a hex. You pray to someone, you ask for something bad to happen to a person. I'm sure it was a fix – what else would it be? At the beginning I didn't realize, because the wife was already dead when I first went to work there. But then there was Gandolfini, Chazarreta himself and a little time before that the one who died in the snow. Somewhere snowy in the United States, I think, because it was summer here. What? Nurit asks, but in her enthusiasm the woman doesn't hear her. That's not down to coincidence, that's down to someone praying and willing bad things to happen to you; it's a curse, Gladys Varela concludes. Who died in the snow? Nurit insists. Another of Chazarreta's friends, says the woman, in a skiing accident. I don't understand, says Brena. Was the one who died in the snow also in the photo? Yes, Chazarreta, Gandolfini and the snow one, all three of them dead, says the woman. Can you remember the name of the one who died skiing? the Crime boy asks. No, I don't remember, but he had a house here too. It was a few months after Gandolfini. Anabella probably remembers, and if not we can ask around; someone is bound to remember. Everybody was talking about it. Imagine – he went on holiday with all his friends and wound up dead. And the guy really knew how to ski; he had prizes and everything, apparently, such a shame. Gladys pauses and drinks more water. Nurit, Jaime Brena and the Crime boy, while trying to appear calm and composed, can barely contain their astonishment. The Crime boy does his best: So, to sum up, you said that the photo showed five of Chazarreta's friends from secondary school. Four or five at the most; it would have been five including Chazarreta, I think. Or was it six? the woman

163

wonders. And of those four, five or six, three are dead, states Jaime Brena, though this is really a question, and then he speaks the names aloud: Chazarreta, Gandolfini and the skier. Yes, three dead, Gladys Varela repeats. Three dead, Brena says again. Three dead, whispers Nurit. That's why it must be a fix, a curse, Gladys insists; they wouldn't just all die for no reason. Added to the fact that the wife was already dead. And who knows if the thing will end there, says the woman, and Nurit shivers. Somebody prayed for misfortune to befall them. And so it did.

They're shaken by the revelation, but Nurit Iscar, Jaime Brena and the Crime boy are also prey to an odd mixture of excitement and puzzlement. The Crime boy is awed, too, by his colleagues' powers of intuition. Setting aside any logical explanation they might bring to bear, he's beginning to suspect that in all this (and if he thinks "this" it's because he can't yet be sure of those other words: death, crime, murder) there's a connection, a special perception that made Nurit and Brena sense – sense, not think – when they stood at that table full of photographs that the empty frame contained the key to the mystery. It's a gift, he thinks to himself; those two have a gift.

Gladys Varela has to go, she says, they're expecting her home. Nobody stops her; they don't have much else to ask at the moment and need some time alone to organize their thoughts. There's too much information, too many leads to follow, too many new doubts. And the photograph? Gladys asks before leaving. At first they don't understand what she means, they're still fixated on the missing photograph of the dead friends that they've recently found out about. Then the Crime boy reacts and whips out his BlackBerry. Let's do it now, he says. You're going to take it with that? the woman asks. Yes, it's better than a camera, the boy says defensively, and he shows her how she looks on the screen when he frames it to take a photograph. Ah, she says, better than a camera? Way better, the boy confirms. Also, since it's connected to the Internet I can send it from here straight to the newspaper and you'll be able to see it in the paper edition as well as online. Ah yes, I can see it online, she says, and then, Where shall I stand? Next to the window, says the boy, and he arranges her in the right position, steps back, sets the frame and takes the photograph. He shows it to Gladys Varela: Do you like it? Yes, what do you think? she says. I think it's come out very well, he says, but I'll take a couple more anyway, just in case. And when is the piece going to be published? the woman asks. In a few days, the Crime boy says. We'll have to check a few facts first, but it'll be out in a couple of days or so. We'll give you a call to let you know, Gladys, don't worry. The boy offers to show her out and arrange payment with the taxi driver and Gladys Varela accepts, says goodbye and stands up ready to go. Before they leave the room, Nurit Iscar stops them. Just one more question, she says to Gladys, and I promise it's the last. Could one of the other men in the photograph have been Luis Collazo? Yes, yes, Señor Collazo was in the photograph, Gladys confirms, but that one's still alive, as far I know. Yes, Nurit replies. He's still alive.

16

The improvised and multitudinous social gathering taking place at Nurit's temporary home has been ravaged by events. The sons, friends, girlfriends and dog, realizing that nobody is going to minister to them for the rest of the day, that nobody is planning a dinner for that night and that nobody is making up beds for them to sleep in, decide to accept a last-minute invitation to a barbecue in Banfield, promising to come back on Sunday if the fine weather continues. Viviana Mansini complains that nobody told her the party included an option to stay over: I haven't closed the windows at home, I haven't left food for the kids. Luckily my kids can cook for themselves, says Carmen. I never leave the windows open, because of the bats, you know? says Paula. The word alone makes Viviana Mansini shudder. There are no bats round my place, she says. How strange, says Carmen, considering that the rest of Buenos Aires is full of bats. Nurit accompanies the Crime boy and Jaime Brena to their car. So what next? the Crime boy asks. I think we should keep this new information to ourselves until we've checked it out, says Jaime Brena. I agree, says Nurit. But I'm the loser who's going to get his balls cut off by Lorenzo Rinaldi when someone breaks this exclusive ahead of us, the boy protests. Jaime Brena looks at him thoughtfully. For the first time it dawns on him that, like it or not, he has no control over the way information about Chazarreta's death is managed. That being the case, he says, without anger or empathy but with resigned conviction, the decision is yours to make, because you're the Crime Editor. It's up to you and Nurit; I'm no longer part of it. You're our honorary adviser, Brena, says Nurit. Honorary and *ad honorem*, the boy adds. Do you accept? Brena says nothing for a moment, and then: You mean there's not even a fiver in it? All three laugh. He doesn't say it, but the truth is that Jaime Brena would pay to do this job: for a long time he's felt nothing when working on a report or a feature – or rather he does feel something, but it's apathy, frustration, weariness, anger – and now he's rediscovering that vertigo, that passion that drove him to become a journalist in the first place. My honorary and *ad honorem* opinion is that you need to sit on this exclusive until it's fleshed out, kid, you can't go ahead and publish with so few concrete facts. What about the police? the Crime boy asks. Should we say something to them? All we know is that some time ago a photograph was stolen from Chazarreta's house, and I've already mentioned that to Comisario Venturini himself and he didn't give a damn. I don't think it's necessary, at the moment, to tell him that three people in that photograph have died, either coincidentally or otherwise, and two of them in accidents. I don't believe in coincidence, says Nurit. I don't believe in the curses Gladys Varela referred to, says the Crime boy. I don't believe in either of those things either, says Jaime Brena, but I do believe that there are murderers in the world. I propose we start by establishing which school Chazarreta went to and who his closest friends were. I don't want to push too hard on the Venturini side of things. He'll get annoyed and cut off the flow. I'm going to try to be more sociable with my neighbours in La Maravillosa; one of them, other than Collazo, must know something, says Nurit. Whereas I, of course – and the boy addresses himself to Jaime Brena, as though dedicating what he's about to say to him – plan to submerge myself in the Internet. Somewhere on the Web it's going to say where Chazarreta went to secondary school. The men kiss Nurit goodbye and get into the car. She stands there, waiting for them to pull away. She feels cold. The evening dew, added to a light, intermittent breeze gathering right in front of the house, prompts her to cross her arms over her chest, rubbing them at the very moment that Jaime Brena is lowering his window for a bit of air. Men and women have different thermostats, he says. That's what they always say, she agrees. You must be one of those people who prefer an overhead fan to air conditioning, Jaime Brena says. And you probably keep the air conditioning on even in winter, says Nurit. You mean we're doomed never to live together? Brena asks, and she blushes. You never know, Nurit Iscar would say, if she were the heroine of one of her own novels. But since she isn't she doesn't say this; she merely thinks it, and smiles. Why must she always keep a distance – especially, it seems, with men she really likes? Even at this age, she doesn't understand it. Now Viviana Mansini, who's suddenly remembered that her car is parked at the entrance to the club, comes running out of the house. Could you drop me off at the gate? she asks. Yes, of course, says the boy. She gives Nurit a kiss and gets into the car. Jaime Brena waves goodbye, tipping an imaginary hat, and the car moves away over the grey gravel before disappearing.

Back inside the house, Nurit makes herself a coffee. Paula Sibona and Carmen Terrada are practically sisters to her, but tonight she would prefer to be on her own. Their conversation drifts over her as though it were the English dialogue on some television drama with subtitles she can't quite read. She decides to make her apologies – I have to go and write a piece for *El Tribuno* – and goes to her room.

She switches on the computer. Nothing she writes holds her attention because now the only important thing, really, is that missing photograph and the people in it. And she can't say anything about the photo. Not yet. So she sets to writing about Chazarreta's house: inside and out, all the details, everything she saw, the colour of the walls, the texture of the fabrics covering chairs or hanging at windows, the smell of the house, the sound and weight of its emptiness: the hum of the fridge, which is still connected, and an alarm clock on Chazarreta's bedside table that marks the time with a dry tick-tock. Everything. Except for the empty photo frame. She reads over what she's written, dissatisfied: it isn't as good as the previous pieces. She knows why: it's the silence, what's unsaid or hidden, that part of the iceberg which Hemingway, talking about fiction, said stays submerged beneath the surface of the ocean, enriching the story, but which, in the case of reportage, a piece of journalism for a newspaper, simply highlights the impossibility of saying what she should be saying. It's what there is, she thinks. This is what there is today. She types two or three lines more before rounding off the piece, which is almost exclusively a description of Chazarreta's house, with the following:

If houses could speak, we would know who murdered Pedro Chazarreta. Because this house was the sole witness to that crime committed within its walls. The truth is in there. In its floors, its walls, in the furnishings and ornaments that still grace it. All of them silent witnesses.

If the ghost of Pedro Chazarreta could come before us, as the ghost of Hamlet's dead father appeared to speak his truth, we would know who killed him. Assuming that the ghost wanted to tell us, which, in a case as riven with secrets, lies and obfuscation as the one in which the deceased was involved, seems less clear even than in the case of the King of Denmark, Hamlet's father.

If the murderer were to crack, if the person who killed Pedro Chazarreta couldn't keep his secret any longer, if he came before us and said, with or without remorse: "I did it", once again, we would know the truth.

Which of these three alternatives is the most likely and which the least?

This kind of murderer rarely cracks.

Houses don't have voices.

Ghosts don't exist.

After meeting the ghost in Act I of Hamlet, Marcellus declares that "Something is rotten in the state of Denmark". And after being in Pedro Chazarreta's house, I say the same. Something is rotten; something smells bad.

Houses may not have voices, but can they find another way to speak?

Something smells bad, and not only in that house. Something smells bad in La Maravillosa.

She saves the file. She'd like to send it to Jaime Brena for his opinion. But Nurit Iscar realizes that she doesn't have his email address, or even a telephone number. Nothing. Nor does he have hers. If she wants to get in touch, she's got no option but to call him at the paper on Monday. But why would she; what excuse would she use? Actually, does she need one? Does she need an excuse to call him? No, Nurit tells herself; after all, they're in this imbroglio together. And she tries to think of something else. She attaches the file to a new email and sends it to the Crime boy. This time she entirely forgets to send it to Lorenzo Rinaldi.

At the moment that Nurit is shutting down her computer and going downstairs to have supper with her friends, Jaime Brena is in the kitchenette of his apartment grilling a steak he found lurking in the fridge and which, though it looks grim, is going to save him going out to buy something for supper. The lunchtime empanadas and the afternoon's banana fritters are a distant memory, and his stomach is once again demanding attention. He leaves the steak cooking and wanders over to the dresser which houses the few books he's bought or been given since the separation, along with his DVDs. The DVDs are something he was able to hang onto after the separation, doubtless because Irina never liked the same films as he did. Then again, what sort of films would appeal to his ex-wife? Does she even like cinema at all? He isn't sure any more, and it surprises him how he's gradually losing the memory not only of Irina's face but also of her mannerisms, her taste, the anecdotes they shared. Is that what people mean by "the grieving process"? Or has he finally come through that? At any rate, he can't let go of the fact that she still has his books. No way. Jaime Brena rummages in the disordered pile for the DVD he wants and stands looking at the cover for a moment. He reads: *Betty Boop and Friends: 90 Minutes of Cartoons*. He turns it over and looks down the titles: "No, No! A Thousand Times No!"; "Poor Cinderella"; "Betty Boop and Little Jimmy"; "Betty Boop and the Little King"; "Swat the Fly"; "Musical Mountaineers"; "Mother Goose Land". The steak is spitting on the hob and Jaime Brena walks back to it, still reading the DVD: "So Does An Automobile"; "Cupid Gets His Man"; "Pudgy the Pup in 'Happy You and Merry Me'"; "Grampy in 'House Cleaning Blues'". Smoke and the smell of cooking meat fill the kitchen; Jaime Brena salts the steak, flips it and salts the other side. He pours himself a glass of wine, then leaves a plate beside the griddle, ready for the steak, and puts the Betty Boop DVD to one side. In a while, when he goes to bed, he's going to smoke a joint, put on this DVD and let himself drop off to sleep with Betty Boop singing "Boop, Boop a Doop" to him like a lullaby. Will he ever be bold enough to tell Nurit Iscar that he was the one who thought of that name for her? Will he tell her that he used to have her photo stuck to his desk – the one that came out in the paper's weekend magazine when she brought out *Death by Degrees*, his favourite novel? Will he tell her that Rinaldi was only copying him? Will he ever tell her, Nurit Iscar, Betty Boo, that he has loved her from afar – like someone in love with a movie star – and not only the curls but the head that invented those stories, that chose those words, that created those characters? No: he doesn't believe he ever will tell her. And he certainly won't tell her that on the afternoon he learned that Rinaldi and she were lovers, he tore the photograph off his desk and threw it into the bin.

As Jaime Brena settles down to his steak, pouring more wine and casting sidelong glances at the DVD still lying on the work surface, the Crime boy is starting up his computer. He opens his mailbox and sees that Nurit Iscar has sent a piece. He reads it. For all her qualms, of which he knows nothing, the Crime boy thinks it's good. He forwards it to the newsroom to get it in ahead of the deadline. Then he forwards it to Jaime Brena, adding a postscript: The guy who died skiing was called José Miguel Bengoechea – I found it on the Internet, obv. But Jaime Brena never looks at his emails at home, not unless someone calls specifically to say that it's something needing urgent attention and he has no choice but to oblige. And the boy doesn't call, just sends on Nurit Iscar's email. He, in contrast to Brena, finds it hard to walk away from his computer once he's switched it on. For him it represents unconditional company, like Jaime Brena's fantasy dog. The boy logs on to Twitter to see if there's anything new and important. He scrolls through the tweets quickly; most of them, as on any weekend, are more egocentric than interesting. Then he clicks on Google to look for information about Pedro Chazarreta's school. He types "Chazarreta + Gandolfini + Collazo + secondary school" into the browser. Nothing useful comes up. He decides to remove one of the variables, a surname first. Still nothing. He takes out another surname instead. Still nothing. He removes two surnames together. It doesn't work. He swaps "secondary school" for "college", then "institute", then puts in "school" on its own, then "secondary" on its own. No. Changing tack, he searches for all the schools that have a saint's name. The list of results is endless, even if he limits himself to the ones within Buenos Aires. He refines the search by excluding schools named after "known" saints, as Gladys Varela put it. That leaves San Ildefonso, San Bartolome, San Anselmo, San Viator, San Silvestre and San Hermenegildo. Now he tries these, looking at each school's website in turn, but without finding any lists of leavers. The boy gets up to make a coffee, looks out of his apartment window, stretches and thinks. It occurs to him that his girlfriend hasn't called all day and that he doesn't care. Night has descended on the street, and traffic going in both directions makes a muddle of car lights. He'd like to go out for a walk. The night is generous, he thinks; it always throws you something. That's what Cynthia, his ex-girlfriend said a while ago, a long while ago. What became of Cynthia? he wonders. He ought to go out for a bit. He's spent all Saturday working, after all. Back at the computer he logs onto Facebook to see if anyone has organized anything for this Saturday night. He answers two

173

or three surveys, watches a video, looks through the album photos of a friend he hasn't seen for years. And through the photos of a friend of his friend. Nothing interesting. What if he just goes out to see what's happening, without any particular plan or destination in mind? No, he's not much given to those sorts of spontaneous nights out. They can end in tears. He doesn't think to ring his girlfriend. Or rather he does think of it, but rejects the idea immediately, almost with contempt. Can he really feel contempt for someone he slept with less than twenty-four hours earlier? No, it must just be that he's still annoyed with her about that business with the bikini, or tired. Or generally hacked off. Actually, perhaps he really does feel contempt for her. He types Cynthia's full name into Facebook's search box and locates her among various other possibilities. He knows it's her from the photo, because she hasn't changed at all. Perusing her "wall", he sees that she's in a relationship and decides not to add her as a friend – what would be the point? What about asking Karina Vives out, though? Stupid idea – he hasn't even got her telephone number. And she must be about five or six years older than him. Is that a problem, though? He looks for her on Facebook too, finds her and checks her birth date: seven years older. Well, it's not that much, he thinks, but he doesn't dare ask her to be a friend, or at least a friend on this social network. Sometimes he gets the impression that she thinks he's an idiot. He looks at her wall, looks through her photos; it surprises him that these aren't restricted to her friends. If he were brave enough to admit that he'd been looking her up, he'd advise changing her security settings. But he doesn't send a friend request. He refreshes the page to see if there are any new updates – and there are. A friend of his has joined the group "I'm a Fan of Agent 99 and I hate Agent 86". It makes him smile, but

174

isn't it a bit childish? If so, what does that say about him? Is he childish too? There's a group for anything you want on Facebook, he thinks. And for things you don't want. He types into the search engine: "I studied at San…" and a list of 28 possibilities comes up. Leaving out once again the more popular saints, he selects San Ildefonso, San Ansclmo, San Jerónimo Mártir and a few other schools. All the comments are from users looking for old school friends, trying to organize reunions, get-togethers, tributes. There's nobody from Chazarreta's generation. As he scrolls down through old stories, the Crime boy remembers his own secondary school. It's frightening to think that his contemporaries may be trying to plan a reunion. He can't think of anything worse. Secondary school was not a happy time for him. Two or three old school friends have tracked him down on Facebook, but he didn't reply to their friend requests. If he only ever hung out with them at break times, or on a handful of stultifying evenings out, why look them up now? He looks them up. And there they are. Reading a few of their comments is enough to confirm what he thought at the time: he's got nothing in common with these people and no interest in their news. And yet he keeps reading it all the same, and looking at their photographs and thinking "what a bunch of pricks". He returns to the list of Chazarreta's potential schools, and on San Jerónimo Mártir's page a comment catches his attention. It's not the comment itself that's arresting – "Go for it, San Jerónimo Mártir, for fuck's sake!!" – but the person posting it. It's one of the members of the group: Gonzalo Gandolfini. Gandolfini. Going into his page he sees that the guy is young; according to his profile he was born in 1983. He doesn't understand why people put their birth date in with the year and everything; he always leaves that out, along with the city where he lives and his relationship status. This 1983 Gandolfini could be a relation of the dead man, maybe even his son. He scans the comments for more information or familiar names and finds nothing else. But under "Friends" is another Gandolfini – Marcos. He goes onto Marcos' page. This person also went to San Jerónimo Mártir, and was born in 1987. Brothers? Cousins? He's starting to suspect that this is one of those schools that educate successive generations from the same family, that pride themselves on "traditional values". He sends a message to Gonzalo. Hello, how are you? I used to be friends with a Gandolfini who went to this school (if the Crime boy knew the first name of the dead Gandolfini he'd put it in the message, but he doesn't know it), a man who would be in his sixties now. Then I left the country and lost track of him. Do you know him, or is he a relation of yours? He used to hang around with Pedro Chazarreta and Luis Collazo. I'd like to get back in touch. I've got a lot of memories of those guys. The boy presses Send and waits for a while to see if there's a reply. In the meantime, he looks at some other pages. It occurs to him that it would be better if Gonzalo turns out not to be Gandolfini's son; if he is, it won't be pleasant for him to get a message enquiring about his dead father. But he doesn't regret sending it, despite this risk; in fact, he feels that he's finally putting some of Jaime Brena's teachings into practice. If Brena asks him again, "Have you ever disguised yourself?", or "Have you ever posed as a policeman and called the house of a murder victim?" he'll be able to answer that yes, he has made a start. In his own way. The new technologies have made thousands of disguises available. Time goes on and the Crime boy begins to feel the weight of his long day. Gonzalo Gandolfini still hasn't answered his message. He's a young guy, the boy thinks, he's probably got plans on a Saturday night. For his own part, the Crime boy thinks it's time to go to bed, that the most logical thing to do on this Saturday night, still glittering through his window, is to close his eyes and sleep.

He stretches, turns out the lights, draws the curtains. But he doesn't shut down the computer. He leaves Facebook open on the screen, in case Gonzalo Gandolfini, returning in the early hours from his night out, checks his page and answers the message. There's always a chance the Crime boy will get up to go to the bathroom during the night and, checking his computer on the way back to bed, find what he's looking for, there on the glowing screen.

17

Sunday dawns rainy. It's not torrential rain; in fact the stuff that's falling couldn't strictly speaking be described as rain at all. It's barely drizzle. But it's thick and unrelenting, the sort that soaks you through. Nurit gets up and looks out of the window. She notices that, far from making the land-scape less beautiful, the spray enhances it: the colours look more intense with myriad greens; even without opening the windows, she can smell the wet earth. Or is she intuiting it? Can you conjure a smell, evoke it as if it were there? Water runs along a tin gutter bordering the roof and down a drain. At the point where it finally falls, it has formed a puddle. The sound of water in the gutter is dimly reminiscent of something. As if she had heard that same rain in another place, a long time ago. Or had dreamed of it. It would have been a rainy Sunday much like this that Gloria Echagüe was murdered; even though Nurit didn't accept the commission that Rinaldi offered her at the time, she remembers clearly that on that day, the day Chazarreta's wife died, it was also raining. Now she goes to the room where her friends have spent the night, opens the door and peeps in at them. They are both still asleep. She makes herself a coffee and picks up the copy of *El Tribuno* that the newspaper boy left on the front step this morning and every morning – just as she arranged when she first came to La Maravillosa. On Sundays Nurit Iscar likes to read the other papers too, nearly all of them. On other days she'll settle for the online editions, it's less wasteful, but on Sundays she wants paper, ink, fingers that get grubby from turning pages. A proper newspaper. *All* the newspapers. She knows that if she rings the newsagent they'll take ages to bring them, especially with this weather and the fact that it's a Sunday, so she decides to walk, telling herself that it may be raining but it isn't cold, and that it will do her good to move a bit. Besides, she's promised Jaime Brena and the Crime boy that she'll make an effort to socialize more with the neighbours, in the hopes that one of them may have information about Chazarreta's schooldays and his friends from that time. She didn't pack an umbrella when she came here, not thinking that she would need one, but she does have a light anorak with a hood. No book this time; it would only get wet. No sunglasses, either. She steps out with determination and, less than a hundred yards later, sees Luis Collazo jogging towards her. Nurit looks at him, but he runs past deep in concentration (or so it seems), breathing deeply in and out not because he's out of breath, but as an explicit part of his training routine. He runs at a steady pace, and on his arm is something Nurit initially takes to be a radio before realizing that it's one of those gadgets for monitoring your heart rate. She walks on a few paces then turns back. He, without slackening his pace, has also turned to look at her from a distance that lengthens with every step. As soon as their eyes meet, however, he turns round again and continues as though this awkward exchange had never happened. Nurit feels tempted to follow him. Very tempted. So much so that she does just that, running a few yards behind Luis Collazo, with short fast strides, like someone running to catch a bus in Buenos Aires. The ground is slippery and she's nervous of landing spilled like an oil stain on La Maravillosa's asphalt. She drops the jog in favour of a

lighter, safer trot. He hasn't managed to get that far ahead
of her, but still she loses him at a bend in the road. Then,
even though it makes her feel ridiculous, she starts running
again. By the time the bend and all the vegetation bordering it allow her a view of the street ahead, she realizes that
Luis Collazo isn't on this road any more. And yet he can't
have jogged fast enough to reach the next bend. Impossible.
Nurit Iscar keeps running, but at a slower pace, wondering
what to do next. She pulls her hood tighter so that her hair
won't get soaked, tucking a few errant curls inside. Humidity
makes her curls, her Betty Boop curls, springier, and she
likes that. But the last time she let herself get soaked in the
rain she caught a cold that took ages to shake off. She zips
her coat right up, the zipper almost touching her face, then
keeps walking. She wonders if any of the houses she can
see on both sides of the road belong to Luis Collazo and
inspects them openly, looking for clues and finding none.
Nurit Iscar fears that if she keeps walking in this direction
she'll get lost; she forgot to bring the map of La Maravillosa
with her and none of the few walks she's been on so far have
brought her to this part of the compound. Better to go back,
she decides, and turns on her heel, only to be confronted
by Collazo, who must have been hiding somewhere behind
her. What do you want? he demands. Nurit doesn't answer,
her heart pounding from the shock. I asked you what you
want! Collazo shouts at her again. Nothing, I was just out
for a walk. You were following me, Señora, I'm not a fool.
OK, I admit that I was. I wanted to ask you a question. I
don't answer questions. It's something silly: I just wanted to
know which school Chazarreta went to – you and he were
classmates, right? Something silly, Collazo repeats, with an
implication Nurit can't grasp. What do you know, Señora?
he says, and grabs hold of her arm. She stares at the man's

hand squeezing her above the elbow but makes no move to free herself, and replies: Nothing, but I would like to know. If it's for my sake, don't waste your time, says Collazo, letting her go. I'm not scared of anything, not even of getting killed, but don't you or anyone else expect me to talk, because I will never do that. Nurit is still trying to understand when a guard drives by in his electric buggy. He looks at them as if wondering whether or not he should stop, but waves instead and asks: Everything OK? while continuing at a slow speed. Everything's fine, Collazo replies. But the guard doesn't appear satisfied with this and pulls up a few yards further on. Then Collazo warns Nurit in a low but firm voice: Don't get involved, and immediately sets off again. Nurit Iscar is left standing, watching him go. The guard puts his buggy into reverse and draws up alongside her, sounding a continuous beep to warn that the vehicle is reversing, which Nurit can't help but find ridiculous in the circumstances. As he glides to a stop beside her, the guard asks: Are you all right? Would you like me to take you home? She skips the first question and goes straight for the second: Not to my home, but to the newsagent. Would that be OK? Yes, of course, the man says, and Nurit climbs in beside him.

For a few yards they drive in silence, then, just before reaching the newsagent, the man says: Did he startle you? A little bit, Nurit says. No, don't be alarmed. Señor Collazo has been very shaken by Chazarreta's death, you see; they were very close friends. He runs and runs all day long, no matter what time it is, but he'll get over it. They reach the newsagent. Right, I'll leave you here, says the man. Thank you, says Nurit, and then: Before you go, may I ask you a question? Yes, of course, the guard says, and stops the buggy, which had already been moving off. Tell me, do you know which school Chazarreta went to? The man is taken aback by the question. No, I don't have the slightest idea. But would you know how I could find out something like that? Nurit persists. Did you ask Collazo? Yes, but he didn't want to tell me, she says. How strange, it's a harmless question. That's what I thought. Well, if I see him to chat to I'll bring it up with him. You're the lady from *El Tribuno*, right? Yes, Nurit replies. I'll let you know what I find out, says the man, but my advice would be not to speak to anyone else about this. My superiors don't like this kind of thing, us giving information to journalists, do you see what I'm saying? Yes, of course. That would be my advice, the man repeats, and drives away. Nurit goes into the shop and asks for the Sunday papers. Which one? the newsagent asks. All of them except *El Tribuno*, she says. A resident browsing among the mints looks at her with contempt. Nurit Iscar knows it isn't because she's not buying *El Tribuno*: he has recognized her. She holds his gaze and the man puts on an expression of "the things we have to put up with in here", chooses two packets of lozenges in the same flavour – menthol – but of different brands, pays for them and leaves. The newsagent looks at her but says nothing, so she volunteers: I get the impression people here don't like me much. Don't you worry, the man says, bundling up the papers and putting them in a plastic bag so they won't get wet. I'm not sure they like anybody very much round here. Nurit smiles, pays for her newspapers and walks towards the door. Then the man, from behind his counter, says: Great pieces, by the way. I really liked today's, that one about the bad smell. Thank you, she says and, before shutting the door, she asks: You don't happen to know where Chazarreta went to school, do you? No, not a clue, says the newsagent, why? Nothing really, just something I was thinking about for a piece; well, if you happen to find out, would you let me know? Yes, he says, if I hear anything I'll tell you.

Nurit walks along in the rain again. She isn't worried about getting wet any more, or troubled by the confrontation with Collazo, or alarmed by the way he spoke to her. She's excited by the certainty that the trail they are following is leading somewhere, and that the missing photograph in Chazarreta's study is the key, that understanding it will finally unlock the mystery of that death. If that were not the case, Luis Collazo wouldn't have reacted in the way he did. What now of that initial doubt over whether Chazarreta's death was suicide or murder? It seems ridiculous now. She'd bet that it was intended as a distraction, the planted knife meant to suggest a link between his wife's death and his own. But his death is connected to something else, she's sure of it, something dark and terrible enough to warrant a particularly grisly reprisal: his murder and his friends', too. She can't wait to get home, write to the Crime boy and tell him what happened. And, while she's at it, ask for Jaime Brena's email. Yes, that too, why not?

Opening the door into the kitchen, she finds her friends having breakfast. You're up early, she says. We didn't have a choice: the telephone wouldn't stop ringing, Carmen says in a reproachful tone that conceals something more than her annoyance at having been woken up. You forgot to take your phone, birdbrain, Paula says. Nurit pats her pockets: You're right, I left it behind. Lorenzo Rinaldi called. He said you should call him urgently. Nurit clutches her head. Shit, I forgot to send him yesterday's piece. But it's here – look, Carmen Terrada says, showing her the page in *El Tribuno* with her article on it. No, yes, I sent it to the Crime boy, he's the one who takes copy, but we'd agreed that I'd send everything to him, to Rinaldi, first, and I forgot last night. There's a lot going on in that little head, says Paula. A lot, Nurit agrees, heading for the door. Where are you going? To call him from my room. No, my friend, you call him from here, we'll act as a restraint. And anyway, we want to supervise, says Paula Sibona. We have a responsibility to look after you, Carmen says. And to supervise, Paula repeats. It's a work call, Nurit clarifies, although she knows that her friends will never be convinced of that. Nor is she. It doesn't make any difference; we all know where a work call can lead – or do you think we've never worked? Carmen says. Just pick up the phone and dial the number: here, in front of your friends. Then, seeing that she's been left no room for manoeuvre, Nurit takes the phone and dials. No need to pretend in front of them that she doesn't still know Lorenzo Rinaldi's phone number off by heart. She waits with the receiver against her ear, Carmen and Paula's eyes fixed on her. Hello, yes, Lorenzo... Nurit, yes... Look, I'm so sorry that I completely forgot to send you the piece yesterday. I had a headache and... oh, no... really? You liked it... I'm so pleased, yes... yes, it wasn't easy, I'm really glad you liked it. Now Nurit listens in silence, looks up at her friends, keeps listening. It's quite clear from the way she looks at them without saying anything that Rinaldi is saying something she'd rather not let slip out. They've realized, though, and watch her all the more hawkishly. Eventually Nurit has no choice but to speak a few words, enough for her friends to see where things are going, for example when Nurit, Betty Boo, says: Aha, yes, yes I can. And they, who know her, start worrying. A lot. And they're also a bit annoyed. Then Nurit Iscar confirms their worst fears: OK, yes, that's fine, that time's fine. And no sooner has she said "that time's fine" and, a second later, "will you come and pick me up here?" than Paula Sibona claps an exasperated hand to her head – open-palmed, to the centre of her forehead – and Carmen Terrada turns her back, opens the newspaper to a random page and buries herself in an article.

18

Shortly before Lorenzo Rinaldi arrives at La Maravillosa to take Nurit Iscar out to lunch, Jaime Brena is preparing his first coffee of the day. The Crime boy, who didn't wake up in the night after all and slept most of the morning too, is pissing ferociously in order to get to the computer quicker to see if there has been an answer from Gonzalo Gandolfini. And there is one. Hello, yes, I'm his nephew. Sadly my uncle died a while ago in a car accident. I suppose that you knew him back in the Little Ranch days. I hope your memories are good ones! (Ha ha). According to my dad not everyone remembers that time fondly. Take care. The Crime boy rereads the message several times, wondering how to proceed. He calls Jaime Brena, who's having his second coffee now. What little ranch? Brena asks. No idea, the boy says. One of them must have had a farm. I think it's something else; he wrote it with a capital L and R. It's a place name, then. Yes, I think so. Have you tried searching for it on the Internet? Hey, Brena, are you really asking me to look online? If you can't beat 'em, join 'em, so long as you remember that the web isn't God. Really, it's not God? Can you think of anything more godlike than the web? Give me a break, kid. I accept that it's a kind of religion, just not God. The boy smiles, but Brena can't see this. Anyway, I did have a look, he says, but I didn't find anything helpful. What about asking him? Asking who? Gandolfini's nephew. OK, I'll try. Tell me, have you had anything from Nurit Iscar? Yes, I emailed you her piece last night as soon as I got it. Oh, I don't turn my home computer on unless it's for a very good reason. This is a special event, Brena, turn it on. Anyway, you can read her piece in the paper today. Jaime Brena opens the copy of *El Tribuno* that's lying untouched on the grey marble work surface and turns the pages until he gets to Nurit Iscar's article. Got it, he says, I'll read it now, and he looks around the kitchen for his glasses. Let me know if you find out anything about Little Ranch. The boy, sitting in front of his monitor, says yes, that he'll let him know, adding that his email also contained the name of the man who died skiing, Bengoechea, something else he found on the Internet. Bengoechea, OK, Brena repeats, and he hangs up. The Crime boy checks his messages again. There's another email from Nurit Iscar, relating in detail the morning's encounter with Luis Collazo and all her thoughts arising from the incident, information that will surely never find its way into the pages of *El Tribuno* but is intended only for the three-man team they seem to have formed without ever setting out to do such a thing. In a postscript, Nurit asks the boy to forward her email to Brena together with both their phone numbers: so that we can all communicate more easily, she says. And she gives him hers. Reading over the text of her message again, the boy feels a physical sensation he can't describe or explain. Could it be that for the first time he is excited by his work? It feels like something fizzing inside him. No woman has ever provoked that sensation in him, no football final, not even the Coldplay gig in the River Plate stadium. The boy has always believed that it was not so much a sense of vocation that drove him to finish his journalism degree but rather obstinacy and a determination not to disappoint his mother. At the time of joining the Media Studies faculty he didn't even know if he was going to specialize in journalism or advertising. But since all the people he liked best were studying journalism, he followed their lead. Or that's what he's always told himself. That he ended up in journalism through a combination of fate and lack of initiative. The same applied to the section he occupies now: he ended up working in Crime because it was the first vacancy he found in a newsroom. And yet now, for the first time, he really believes that he could do nothing else. He doesn't know exactly how the change came about, but right now, on this rainy Sunday, there's nothing in the world more fascinating to him than this case he's working on. He forwards Nurit's new email to Jaime Brena and calls him, too, to tell him to read it. And Jaime Brena, annoyed at having to break one of his most cherished principles of life to use a computer at home but every bit as caught up in the case as the boy is, logs on and reads Nurit Iscar's email. He answers her: Great stuff, Betty Boo, we're on our way. Take care, Brena. At the very moment that Nurit Iscar is pondering those words, "take care", Lorenzo Rinaldi pulls up in front of her house and sounds his horn. She didn't know that he was already inside La Maravillosa – one of her friends authorized his entry – but such is the antipathy they feel for this man that neither of them felt inclined to go up to her room and inform her of his arrival. Nurit leans out of the window and shouts: Just coming. He must not have heard her, because he sounds the horn again. Hurriedly she grabs her bag, and before leaving dashes into the bathroom to look in the mirror. Probably not such a good idea, but she does it anyway. She arranges her curls, puts on lipstick in a muted tone, an intense but dusty pink, almost brownish, definitely not one Betty Boop would choose; a daytime colour that gives her lips moisture and a bit of shine, making them look younger without drawing attention. Can lipstick make lips look younger? She looks at them, turning her head one way and the other, opening her mouth, forcing a wide smile. She isn't sure. She strokes her neck, lifts her chin; while she certainly doesn't have a double chin, her skin has lost elasticity. No, turns out it wasn't a good idea to go into the bathroom and look at herself: now she's only going to feel more insecure. The horn sounds for a third time. Paula Sibona appears behind her in the mirror and says: You can hear that man blowing his horn for you, right? Yes, yes, I'm going now. You look lovely, Paula says. She turns round, smiles and says: Thank you, darling.

As she comes out onto the veranda, Lorenzo Rinaldi gets out of the car, walks round to her side, opens the passenger door and waits there with the door open. She'd forgotten how he always used to do that – getting out to open the door for her. Rinaldi knows and honours all the rules of etiquette governing social interaction between men and women (rules which don't include being faithful to your wife or not ruining someone's life by raising false hopes you have no intention of fulfilling, anyway), the kind that not all men preserve these days. Rules such as walking on the outside of the pavement; opening doors (not only to cars, but also lifts, houses, offices, cheap hotels); getting into taxis first so that the woman doesn't have to slide across the whole of the back seat to the most uncomfortable spot, behind the driver, who's sure to have pushed his seat back; going upstairs behind a woman and going down in front of her; carrying her luggage; serving the drinks in a restaurant. And, of course, paying the bills, all of them. What would a flapper make of these norms? Nurit Iscar wonders. Is it still gallantry when a man honours all these conventions nowadays, or something closer to humiliation? The humiliating ones are the men who claim to be modern to get out of paying the bill, was what Carmen

Terrada always said. But there are different kinds of humiliation, Nurit thinks, as Lorenzo Rinaldi leans forward and
says: Hello, Betty Boo. He kisses her discreetly on the cheek
and puts his hand on her neck, almost at the nape, under
her curls. And she feels it. Feels Lorenzo Rinaldi's skin
against hers three years on. Slipping away from his touch,
she sits down, and he closes the door and returns to the
driver's seat. They drive towards the entrance of La
Maravillosa. Have you noticed that I've got a new car? Rinaldi
asks. And she says yes, but it's a lie because she has no idea
what kind of car she's just got into. If someone put a pistol
to her head and forced her to give the make, the model,
even the colour of the car she's riding in, Nurit wouldn't be
able to give an answer. She can never remember who has
what car. She doesn't notice. She can, on the other hand,
remember people's licence plates if they lend themselves to
forming words. For example, the BRM on Paula's licence
plate, which she thinks of as BROOM. Or the GRL on the
car her ex-husband lets the boys use and which Nurit remembers as GIRL. And the HMD on Viviana Mansini's car, which
stands for HUMID. But she hasn't yet had a chance to look
at Rinaldi's new licence plate. Do you like it? he asks, and
before she can answer, he adds: You wouldn't believe what
it cost – more than a flat in Belgrano, but I've wanted it for
a long time... Besides, I already have a flat in Belgrano, he
says, and laughs. Nurit Iscar glances at her watch and wonders
if she'll be able to bear the hours ahead. All the things she
didn't like about Lorenzo Rinaldi but ignored because she
was in love with him come flooding back to her. How did I
forget this part? she reproaches herself. You've not done so
badly yourself, made some good money from those books
you published, right? he asks, confirming Nurit's misgivings.
She can't believe the direction this conversation is taking – is

this the sort of stuff they talked about when she was in love with him? Had she let love bestow intelligence and importance on Lorenzo Rinaldi's conversation and interests? Or had he made more of an effort not to come across as a jerk? Nurit sighs and gazes out of the window. You still get royalties, right? Rinaldi insists. Nurit Iscar would rather not dignify this with an answer but knows she should, or he'll keep on asking. Some, she says. How much is some? he asks. Oh please, she thinks, you can't be that much of an arsehole. I don't know, Lorenzo, she tells him, if you like, when I get home I'll send you a copy of my latest statement. But he's oblivious to the irony, and goes on: And how much might they give you as an advance for your next novel? Nurit Iscar looks at her watch again. In dollars, he adds, because you're in a strong position; you can send it to various publishers, let them fight over it and then sell it to the highest bidder. Like a kind of auction, you mean, Nurit says ironically, but he takes the comment at face value. Exactly, a publishing auction of your new book. There is no new book, she says. Still not? There never will be: I've stopped writing. You're kidding, right? No, I'm deadly serious – did you never think it was strange that I haven't brought out a book these last few years? No, I suppose I thought that you'd been knocked back a bit by what happened with the last one and that was why you were taking longer. Your last novel didn't do too well, right? No, it didn't do too well at all. What was it called again? *Only If You Love Me*. That's right, *Only If You Love Me*, all the same, they must have paid you an advance, says Rinaldi. They can't have known beforehand how it would go. Nurit doesn't answer but wonders again what she's doing here. She looks at her watch. I can't fathom why, as someone who understands so well what needs to go into a novel to make it work, you didn't stick with what you knew, Rinaldi says. Nurit feels a strong desire to slap him. An overwhelming desire. And she doesn't hide it. But he, being strangely insensible to other people's feelings, blunders on: Anyway, just because you got it wrong once doesn't mean you don't have a gift. A gift for what? Nurit asks, with undisguised irritation. A gift for knowing what to put into a book in order that people will want to buy it: a bit of this, a bit of that. Why don't you fuck off, Rinaldi? Hey, where did that come from? he asks, astonished. Look, I'm not going to discuss with you what I write and how I write it because you know nothing about it, she says, with such force that for the first time Rinaldi sees she's upset. OK, we seem to have got off on the wrong foot. It wasn't a great start, she agrees. They exit the club in silence after answering a few questions at the gate. Outside on the road, Rinaldi tries again with some routine observations: the rain, local restaurants, Nurit's latest piece, the president's murky business dealings, the disastrous state of the country (in his judgement, Lorenzo Rinaldi's judgement, though he states it as a revealed and irrefutable truth), the sensation of being persecuted by the government – I am a victim of political persecution, he says – and the fact that this persecution, far from cowing him, gives him more adrenaline. She agrees with almost nothing Rinaldi says, about the president, the country, or the supposed risks run by someone in their profession. None of it. She doesn't even agree with his opinion of the local restaurants. But Nurit Iscar keeps her own counsel, knowing there's no point in offering up her views. She knows that Lorenzo Rinaldi wouldn't even suspect that she might think differently. As someone who's intelligent, professional and has slept with him, how else could she think? How could she not see the reality of things? Today, reality is an entelechy; a theoretical construction. If she were to observe that "her" reality is very different to his, they'd end up in an argument with no logic or ending. Lorenzo Rinaldi would keep trying to convince her, even if she didn't do the same with him. How could she ever have been so in love with someone who seems so distant now, someone with whom she can't even have a light-hearted conversation in a car? What are the mechanisms of love that prevent us from seeing things we don't want to see? Because Lorenzo Rinaldi is the same person he was three years ago. There's no doubting that. And yet she, back then, only saw the aspects of him that attracted her. And what were they, exactly? His hands, his voice, certainly. But are these enough for a woman to prostrate herself at the feet of a man? If Nurit Iscar had to say now what it was that had made her fall in love with Lorenzo Rinaldi, she would say that it was the fact that he was in love with her – or had said that he was, at any rate. Deeply in love, he used to say. He had still been saying it even at the end – and the fact that she'd believed him. It had been intoxicating to feel that she – named by him, desired by him – had the power to awaken passion, love, tenderness and need in this man. It was a sensation that Nurit Iscar hadn't experienced for a long time in her own marriage. And she had gambled everything on it. She fell in love with being in love. Was she wrong? she wonders as she stares out of the car window while Rinaldi drones on about the downturn in sales since the advent of online news. No, she hadn't been wrong to gamble. But she had got the stake wrong. She had needed to know if her body retained the memory of those feelings from her youth, when love, relationships and marriage were still a mystery to her. And it did. Does it still? She doesn't know. How is your wife? Nurit interjects as Rinaldi is explaining the increased cost of inputs in the newspaper business. She's fine, he says, fine. What's she up to these days? Nurit goes on, as though she were talking about an acquaintance, someone distant but in whom she is interested, when the true nub of her question isn't any genuine interest in Rinaldi's wife but in establishing that he had, has and will always have a wife. She pretty much lives in Bariloche now, he says. We'd like to retire there. When the time comes, of course, not yet. I bought some land there dirt cheap, some inheritance muddle that we ended up resolving for a pittance, and we've built a house there at the bottom of a hill with a view of the lake, it's a dream of a place. A dream. And Nurit wonders for whom it's a dream. For Rinaldi? For Rinaldi's wife? For the deceased who left the inheritance muddle? For people like them? When some-one says "dream", do they suppose that all of us share the same dream? It was a huge lot, he goes on. We divided it up, made log cabins and Marisa – the name rattles her, she's ceased to be "Rinaldi's wife", but someone with her own name, Marisa, a name that Nurit and Lorenzo Rinaldi were always careful to avoid during their relationship – is in charge of running them. She's very happy there because she's got animals and plants, too, and she loves all that. I go down there every now and then, or she comes up to me. It's a dream of a place, he says again. A nightmare, Nurit thinks. It's about twelve miles from the town centre, you know? I know Bariloche, yes, but not where you have your lot. We've already nearly made the money back. Some of the cabins we rent out, but we sold the others for three or four times more than they cost to build; it's proven to be a very good investment, a fantastic investment. Nurit looks back out of the window in silence.

Lorenzo Rinaldi picks an Italian restaurant, one that only serves pasta, where the few tables are complemented with old chairs in different styles and coverings. There's a wine cellar in the basement visible through glass panels in the floor so that the clientele can see the wines without having to move from their tables. The best thing about already being here, Nurit tells herself, is that in a few minutes they will be eating and then in one or two hours she'll be liberated from Lorenzo Rinaldi and his repartee. But the atmosphere improves as time goes by; in hopes of forestalling Rinaldi's dreary conversation, she brings up topics that interest her more – cinema, books, her children, the Chazarreta case. But he doesn't really seem drawn into the subjects she chooses. He answers in monosyllables, nods and smiles but doesn't listen, merely waiting for her to finish so that he can go back to talking about himself and his world. Starters, mains, wine (selected by Rinaldi after a bit of back and forth with the waiter to show that he knows about this), dessert, coffee. Done. They get back into the car. But Rinaldi doesn't start the engine. He looks at her. He smiles. He puts a mint in his mouth to freshen his breath; he offers her one. No thanks, Nurit says, and the fact that he's worrying about his breath rings alarm bells. Did you know that I had an operation a month ago? Rinaldi says. No, I didn't know. A major one? No, nothing serious, uncomfortable more than anything. They signed me off a week ago. I'm pleased to hear it, she says. Prostate, he says. Ah, that's not unusual in men your age, is it? That's what they said, too, but it wasn't much of a consolation, he says, and laughs. He sits back in the seat, as though to look at her better, and it's clear that he has no immediate plan to start the car. I'm a virgin again, he says. What? says Nurit. I haven't tried out the new equipment since the operation, he clarifies. Is this guy really talking to me about his prick? Nurit Iscar wonders, silently marvelling. They told me there won't be any problems, but I can't rest easy until I've tried it. Is that right, says Nurit. He smiles at her, looking her straight in the eye. She fears what is about to come, what is portended by the breath mint. Do you want to help me out, Betty Boo? Rinaldi asks, with the expression of a newborn lamb separated from the fold. Are you really serious? she answers with another question. We were good together; as far as I remember, anyway. Am I wrong? Yes, we were good, says Nurit, until we were bad. Come on, he says, don't you want to be the first? You should consider yourself privileged. No, no, what a bastard! Paula Sibona will say a couple of hours later when Nurit tells her that – the "consider yourself privileged" bit. And so brazen, without even trying to romance you a bit? Carmen will ask. I think that honour rightly belongs to Marisa, Lorenzo, Nurit says. She'll be patient; she's known you so long. Go off to Bariloche, relax in that dreamworld and try out the new equipment with her. Rinaldi shakes his head then says: Don't ask me why, but I'm sure that it's not going to work with Marisa. Then try a prostitute: they're definitely experts in reviving dicks, says Nurit, looking straight back into his eyes and holding his gaze without even batting an eyelid at the word "dick". She doesn't recognize herself speaking to Rinaldi with such brass, but she enjoys doing it. You said that to him? Carmen will ask, helpless with laughter. Son of a thousand bitches, Paula will say again. No, it won't work with a prostitute, either, Rinaldi says and sighs before continuing: You know I never liked having sex with prostitutes. Now's the time to give it another go, she quips. You know how tastes evolve – you might prefer salty food when you're young and sweeter food when you're older. Maybe if you try again you'll be surprised. And there I was hoping you were going to be my Florence Nightingale, he says. You really don't want to be my Florence Nightingale? I don't believe you, Carmen will say, appalled. I don't believe you. Tell me it's not true; he didn't say that. But who does this arsehole think he is? Paula will say. No, I don't want to be your Florence Nightingale, Nurit says.

The drive back to La Maravillosa seems interminable; to her, at least. He drops her at the door of the house, but this time doesn't leave the car. Think it over, he says. On Tuesdays and Thursdays I can be your man. Tuesdays and Thursdays, Nurit repeats. And remember what good times we used to have together. She keeps looking at him. Think it over, he says again, and Nurit smiles and goes into the house without answering.

Well, the guy gets zero points for seduction techniques, Paula Sibona says, handing her friend a cup of coffee. How can you be turned on by someone who invites you to be his Florence Nightingale? If he's proposing something like that it must be because he's sure that there are women who would willingly play the part, says Nurit. You know what? Paula says. What? Up until recently the problems the men we went out with had were pulled ligaments, cartilage damage, at worst a raging appendicitis. Prostate is a one-way ticket, Carmen says.

19

Around the time Nurit Iscar is treating her friends to a detailed recap of her date with Lorenzo Rinaldi, the Crime boy gets an email that surprises him. It's from Gandolfini; not Gonzalo, though, but his father, Roberto, the brother of the dead Gandolfini. Hello, I heard from my son Gonzalo that you knew my brother and his friends. He also told me you asked him a number of questions that he couldn't answer, so he passed on your email to me. But there's so much to say about that time that it would probably make more sense for us to meet for a coffee. What do you think? What are your plans for the rest of this Sunday? Do you live in Buenos Aires, like us? Warmly, Roberto Gandolfini. The Crime boy starts to fizz again. Before answering he calls Jaime Brena again. What if I take things further and ask him to bring along some photos from that time? If he has a copy of the lost one, we'll have a photo of the whole group. It's a good idea, but what worries me is something else, kid: if you weren't born at the time of the Dr Giubileo case, how could you have known Chazareta and his childhood friends? When they were finishing secondary school you hadn't yet been born. Or am I wrong? No, you're right. They think it over for a while, the Crime boy and Jaime Brena, then the boy says: What about if you go in my place? Jaime Brena's first journalism lesson: disguise yourself. How would that work? Gandolfini's nephew knows my name; it's on Facebook, and he mentioned it to his father when he passed on my message. To change it now or contradict myself would put them on their guard, make them suspicious. But they don't have any other information about me apart from my name. My profile picture doesn't show my face, just the Estudiantes de La Plata football shirt. You support La Plata, kid? No, only the student team, nothing else, he clarifies, and continues: But you could have been a friend of theirs, Brena. It's true, God help me; I'm just as old as those poor bastards. There's a risk, the boy says, that Gandolfini will recognize you; even though you're a print journalist, you've been on TV a few times, and to make matters worse, you were speaking about the death of one of his brother's friends. If the guy saw you on one of those reports and recognizes you, what will we say? That I do look like Jaime Brena, and that it's caused me no end of trouble, but that luckily I'm not him. The boy laughs. It's like you said, kid: blend in, disguise yourself, hide, say you're something you're not, whatever it takes – it's all part of the job. Crime journalists are obsessive, neurotic detectives and stubborn, too, because we know what failure is; but we keep at it until the end. And as Walsh said, if there is no justice, at least let there be truth. At least I think Walsh said that. The boy says nothing, but makes a mental note to check this later. On the Internet. Arrange to meet Gandolfini in a bar in an hour or two, ask him to bring some photos. Oh, and forward me all the email correspondence between you and him or his son, so I don't put my foot in it. Can you come and pick me up, then wait in the car while I talk to Gandolfini? Depending on what that conversation throws up we might go and work for a bit at Nurit Iscar's place afterwards, what do you reckon? Fine by me. Shall I mail Nurit to bring her up to speed? I'll call her, Brena says, if you give me her number. I emailed it to you, the boy says. You're not going to make me switch the computer on just to find a phone number, are you, kid? The Crime boy relents, and tells him the number.

Incredible, says Nurit Iscar when Brena calls, echoing his reaction when the Crime boy called with the news shortly before. We're getting close, Brena. Closer, yes, he says, and then: Do you think we could come over to your place after the meeting with Gandolfini? It would be easier to compare notes and see if we can begin to draw some conclusions, however vague. Yes, of course, I'll be here, she says. What time would you be coming? I'm afraid you won't get out of buying pizza for supper, Betty Boo. She says: Worse things have happened to me, Brena. She smiles, and although he can't see the smile, he feels it.

Jaime Brena prints out the emails forwarded to him by the Crime boy, reads them, folds them up and puts them in a pocket. Taking his pad, he writes down the name of each of the murder victims so far in a column on the left-hand side with an arrow from each name to the cause of death in a column in the right margin, sometimes with explanations in brackets. Pedro Chazarreta, arrow, throat slit (ditto his wife). Gandolfini, arrow, road accident. Bengoechea, arrow, skiing accident. Luis Collazo, arrow, still alive. Brena remembers that Gladys had mentioned there being four or five of Chazarreta's friends in the photograph: Five including Chazarreta, I think, she had said. Or was it six? she had wondered afterwards. So he adds two more entries to take account of the maximum number of possibilities. Unknown One, arrow, still alive? Unknown Two, arrow, still alive? Jaime Brena stares at his rough diagram. He knows that it's telling him something he can't yet hear. Or see. Or decipher. He looks at the names and the arrows, one above the other, and the causes of death. What links each of these deaths, besides the photograph? What's the pattern? What game is the assassin playing? Why does he think of a game, and an assassin, if the majority of these deaths were accidental? Or were they? The facts say they were. The only death known to have been as the result of a crime is Chazarreta's. He thinks. And asks himself again: What are these names saying; what are these deaths telling me? What is fate (or coincidence, or destiny) saying when three people from a small group pictured together in an old photograph that's disappeared from its frame are now dead? He thinks. The intercom buzzes. He goes to the kitchen, picks up the receiver and says: I'll be down in a minute. Although he can't hear anything, Brena knows that it's the Crime boy; for months now the system hasn't been working properly and he can't get the building's administrator to fix it. He can still open the door to people buzzing up from downstairs, but he can't hear them speaking. He'll have to give the administrator a bigger tip; the intercom doesn't matter too much, but it'll be a pain if something else breaks. He goes to look for a leather jacket and matching cap that he hasn't worn for a long time. He puts them on and studies his reflection in the bathroom mirror. Recognizing this get-up as a kind of camouflage, he laughs gently at himself. In this hat, and bearing in mind the time that has passed since his last TV appearance and the weight he's put on since then, he would defy anyone to say that the man looking back from the mirror is Jaime Brena. The buzzer sounds again as Brena is opening the door of his flat. He doesn't pause to assuage what he takes to be the Crime boy's impatience, but carries on out and summons the lift. When he arrives at the ground floor, however, he's surprised to see that the person waiting outside is Karina Vives, with unmistakably red eyes. He opens the door quickly and says: What's happened, gorgeous? But she doesn't answer, just hangs onto his neck and sobs disconsolately. He lets her cry. A long time ago he learned that when a woman cries the best thing is not to try to solve her problem but to give her time to unburden herself. After a while he leads her over to a sofa in the lobby, sits down and gets her to sit beside him. What's happened? Jaime Brena asks again, as the frequency of hiccups and sighs begins to abate. I'm pregnant, the girl says. He looks at her. He waits without saying anything to give her time to say more, but she doesn't. Questions come into his mind that he won't ask, questions that he could never ask. If Karina Vives doesn't mention who the father is, for example, he's not going to ask her. Jaime Brena strokes her hair. He smiles at her. She still says nothing. He says: What do you think you'll do? That's the problem, Karina Vives says, and starts crying again as she speaks: I don't know what to do; one day I'm sure that I want it and the next I'm just as sure that I don't. Jaime Brena takes her hands. How can I help you, gorgeous? Like this, by holding my hands, says Karina, and she lays her head on his shoulder. Brena puts an arm around her back and she moves more comfortably against his shoulder, drawing closer to him. Jaime Brena looks into the street and sees the Crime boy, standing on the other side of the glass watching them and clearly unsure how to interpret the scene in front of him. Or more likely misinterpreting it. Brena gestures to him to wait a minute. He holds the girl's chin and lifts her gaze to meet his: I have to go on an assignment with the Crime boy, he says, nodding towards the door so that she can see that the boy is waiting there. Would you like to come with us? Karina twists round to look at the boy. Don't tell him, she asks Brena. No, of course not, he says. Without explaining any further, he gets her to stand up and guides her towards the door, opening it with the keys that were in his jacket pocket, then greets the Crime boy and, also with no further explanation, announces:

She's coming with us. The three of them get into the car and drive towards their rendezvous.

Ten minutes later the boy is parking the car at a street corner across the road from the bar where they have agreed to meet Roberto Gandolfini. Jaime Brena gets out and the others wait for him inside the car as agreed. Brena crosses the road and, before going into the bar, stops at a kiosk to buy cigarettes. The Crime boy follows him with his eyes, which then come naturally to rest on the face of Karina Vives. She notices and smiles, and he feels like someone caught spying through a keyhole. To cover his awkwardness, he feels compelled to say something: Your eyes look very irritated. This is an observation he regrets as soon as Karina explains: I haven't stopped crying since last night. Now the boy's even less sure what to say. Being in such a small and as inevitably intimate a space as a car can only make matters worse. She's the first to break the silence: Don't you guys ever cry? Us guys? You men. The boy says nothing, but makes a gesture with his mouth that could be interpreted as a hesitant "no" or "occasionally" or "some of us may cry, but not me". But he doesn't say any of that, limiting himself to the gesture. So what do you do when you feel bad? Karina wants to know. We surf the Web, chat rooms, Facebook, Twitter, all that. I asked someone the same question a while ago and he said: We lie in bed, zapping through the TV channels. You must have been asking someone from another generation, an older guy, right? So the technology that stands in for men's tears depends on the generation, Karina says. Yes, the boy answers. But whether young or old, they never actually cry, she persists. The boy makes an ambivalent gesture and turns on the radio in hopes of putting an end to this uncomfortable exchange.

As the boy is tuning into some song that, while not much to his taste, will allow him to say nothing and pretend to be listening, Jaime Brena is entering the bar. He looks around him, trying to work out if any of the people sitting at tables may be Roberto Gandolfini. He sees two couples, a woman with her children, a young man – almost as young as the Crime boy – and a woman of about fifty crying beside a window. This is no time for gallantry, he thinks; he's had enough of crying women for one Sunday afternoon. Irina wasn't much given to crying: she preferred shouting, and tears would only spring into her eyes sometimes after a lot of shouting – tears of rage, mind you. Why would he think of Irina now? Why does he think of her every so often, especially on a Sunday afternoon? Jaime Brena picks a table close to the door. He glances around him again. Nothing. Then a man comes out of the toilet, talking on the phone, and sits down at another table diagonally opposite Brena's. He says something like "OK, so I don't need to worry? One last push and we're done." Jaime Brena catches only a few syllables, guessing the rest from reading his lips. Brena watches him. He's a short man in his fifties, perhaps a little too young to be Gandolfini's brother. The man snaps his phone shut and plays with it on the tabletop, spinning it one way and then the other. He's wearing glasses and his clothes are expensive: good quality but rather old-fashioned. High-waisted trousers, the shirt buttoned up to the top, classic moccasins and a beige twill jacket. Under Jaime Brena's scrutiny the man appears nervous, anxious even. Now he takes some photographs out of a brown manila envelope and looks through them one by one. Is it him? Brena wonders. It must be. That face looks familiar. But Jaime Brena doesn't know what either Gandolfini looks like – neither the dead brother nor the living one – so if he does recognize him it must be from somewhere else. The man looks at his watch and fans the photographs in front of him as though to cool himself. Jaime Brena is increasingly persuaded that the man sitting diagonally to him is the one he's here to meet, but he bides his time, watching him and studying his movements. This wait, he soon realizes, is agonizing for the man. So much so that finally he stands up, looks around him and says, almost shouting: I'm Roberto Gandolfini; is anyone here to meet me? Everyone – customers, waiters, the cashier – looks at him as if he were mad and now they're on their guard, caught in mid-action, alert to what this nutter may do next. Everyone except Jaime Brena, who also stands up and says: Yes, I am. And he walks towards the man's table. May I sit down? he asks. Yes, of course, take a seat, says Gandolfini, and normality prevails in the bar once more. Hurriedly he shuffles the photographs back into the envelope, perhaps still undecided whether or not to show them to a stranger. What would you like to drink? he asks, and Jaime Brena says: A milky coffee. The man says: I'll have the same, and then smiles, waiting for Brena to say something else. Thanks for coming, Brena adds. No, on the contrary, Gandolfini replies. I'm grateful for an opportunity to talk to someone about my brother; it was all so quick, so unexpected. Well, what accident isn't? Brena says. The man surveys him in silence for a few seconds and only after an uncomfortable pause asks: But you weren't at school with him, were you? I don't remember your surname (it's the Crime boy's surname, not that Gandolfini knows that). No, I wasn't at school with them; I met them on the school-leavers' trip and then I stayed in touch for a while. Not with the whole class, just that particular group – Chazarreta, Collazo, your brother. The famous Chazarreta, Gandolfini says. The famous Chazarreta, that's right, says Jaime Brena, feeling his way. In that case we must also have met back then, Gandolfini says. No kidding? I was that horrible brat who

204

tagged along everywhere with them. Don't you remember? Even on the school-leavers' trip. One of my mother's crazy ideas. She said that everything my brother did I must do too, to be fair; can you believe it? She had a rather peculiar concept of justice. Sometimes mothers try so hard to get things right they get them wrong. Can you imagine how pissed off my brother was with me? Gandolfini says, and laughs. They send him on his end-of-school trip with a little brother and a nanny to look after him. Quite a woman my mother was, quite a woman. The man stops, staring at his hands, as though looking at them helped him to remember. Brena says: I was very sorry to hear about your brother. Gandolfini makes a sad face, a strange, melancholic smile, and nods his head. Yes, it was a terrible accident. It was raining and my brother loved driving fast, you know? Somehow we all knew that one day that would be the death of him. Gandolfini takes out the photographs again and this time he does show them to Brena. The first, top of the pile, Brena suspects is similar to the one missing from Pedro Chazarreta's photo frame: it's of six friends, in a mountain setting, most likely Bariloche, holding the flag of their school: San Jerónimo Mártir. Brena's seen this photograph somewhere else, he's sure of it. Or is it déjà vu? Little Ranch, says Jaime Brena, with the photograph in his hand. I never knew why they called themselves that. The man stares down at the image, inverted from where he's sitting. Then you were lucky, Gandolfini laughs. I don't understand, says Brena. Nothing, just a joke, the man says, and resumes his melancholic smile. Brena waits. They called themselves Little Ranch because it was at the Chazarretas' farm that they held their initiation ceremonies. Initiation ceremonies? says Jaime Brena. You know, those things kids do when someone comes into the gang, a new member. Joining rituals, says Gandolfini, trials that you had to

205

undertake, that kind of thing. I don't remember it very well; it's such a long time ago. You were part of the group? Brena asks. Of which group? Little Ranch. Oh no, no, they didn't let me into that one. They said I was too young. I went everywhere with them like a ball and chain, a tax on my brother's freedom to go out, but they didn't include me in anything; although they did use me as an errand boy whenever they could. My brother was nearly ten years older than me. And we didn't have the same mother. My father had been a widower when he married my mother, then some time later they had me. So we had the same father but a different mother. Half-brothers. I see, Jaime Brena says. They are silent again for a moment, openly observing one another. Brena is wondering where he knows this man from, but Gandolfini is the first to ask the question. You look familiar to me, he says. Could we have met before? Well, Jaime Brena says, tackling the question head-on to avert suspicion, some people say I look like a journalist from *El Tribuno*; people have even stopped me in the street because they think I'm him. Ah, yes, that's it. You look like Jaime Brena. Jaime Brena, that's the one. And is there somewhere I might know you from, Señor Gandolfini? I'm in business development. We start up companies, get them running, and then we sell them on. We also do feasibility studies, analysis of national and international markets, future trend studies, that kind of thing. We do a lot of consulting work for big economic groups, even for a few politicians, so I've often been on television programmes or news reports where they ask me to speak about some aspect of my expertise, says the man, adding with undisguised pride: I'm the go-to man on several areas in this country. Especially relating to economic matters, you know? Yes, yes, now that you say it I think I've seen you on some show on cable. Very likely. The men are silent again for a moment, then Gandolfini gets to the point: Why don't you ask me those questions you sent to my son, now you've got me in front of you? OK, though really it wasn't so much that I wanted to ask questions as that I wanted to get back in touch with that group of friends from my youth, find out what became of them. All the stuff that happened – first with Chazarreta's wife and then with him – have brought my memories of that time flooding back. The man observes him with an expression that's accommodating but also penetrating, and then he says: Yes, the death of Chazarreta's wife brought us all together again; at the time of her death we hadn't seen each other for a while. Or I at least hadn't seen the others for a while. I saw my brother, of course. Not as often as we used to, because of our respective commitments, but we were in touch, we kept up with each other's news, we were a family. But not the others. And then there were the other deaths, one tragedy after another. The man breaks off for a moment and stares down at his hands again. Jaime Brena watches him; time passes and it's as though Gandolfini has no awareness of the length of time he's been in this attitude, silently staring at his hands. Finally he says: Fate is a strange thing, isn't it? Yes, Brena nods; then he points to the photograph and says: Out of six friends, three are dead. The man corrects him: Not three, four are dead. The remark stuns Jaime Brena. What do you mean, four? Gandolfini picks up the photograph and points to each of its subjects: My brother in a car accident, Chazarreta apparently murdered, Bengoechea in a stupid fall while he was skiing and Marcos Miranda (he points to the tallest man in the group of friends), who's just died in the United States in one of those absurd attacks where a guy goes crazy and shoots some random person coming out of a supermarket pushing a shopping trolley. So another of the friends has just died?

Yes, Marcos Miranda, a couple of hours ago. I saw it by chance on CNN. An Argentine who had lived in New Jersey for years and was the CEO of an important bank. You haven't heard anything about it? No, Brena replies. You will for sure; it'll be in all the papers. It's one of those stories everyone gets on to. Luckily only a couple of people were injured, and not seriously. There are a lot of mad people around these days. Yes, a lot of mad people, says Brena, still stunned by the news. So the only two friends still living are Luis Collazo and… What was the other one called? His name's slipped my mind, Brena lies. Gandolfini looks at him, scratches his head as though that might help him to remember, looks at him again and then says: Vicente Gardeu? That's it, Vicente Gardeu, says Brena.

Gandolfini nods his head a few times, as though confirming the fact to himself. And once again the men fall silent, watching one another, appraising each other, but this time Brena senses that Gandolfini's expression has changed; only slightly, but enough to notice. Gandolfini checks the time on his watch. Well, if there's nothing else you wanted to ask, he says, and starts putting the photos away. Brena stops him: Not ask, as such, but tell me, is there any chance you could lend me that photograph so that I can make a copy then give it back to you? No, look, it's one of the very few mementoes of my brother and his friends that I have left, Gandolfini says. It would mean a lot to me, Brena insists. I'd like to have something to remember them by. It's not a very good photograph, says the man; it's just a snap. That doesn't matter. No, I'm sorry, not this photo. If there's another one you'd like I'll think about it, but not this one. Gandolfini closes the envelope containing the photographs as though to put an end to the conversation. Then he reaches into an inside pocket of his jacket, takes out a card holder and gives Brena his personal card. If there's anything I can do for you, this is a more direct way of getting in touch than via Facebook. OK, thanks very much, says Brena. One last favour – could I take another look at the photograph? The man hesitates before reaching into the envelope and taking out the picture. Jaime Brena studies it as though trying to imprint it on his memory. He's sure he's seen this photograph somewhere else. Positive. He curses his memory, which used to let nothing escape but which he feels has been waning for some time. Gandolfini puts out his hand for the photograph and Brena returns it. Thank you, Brena says, and let me pay for the coffees – it's the least I can do. It seems like a fair deal, agrees the man. Thanks, then, and he leaves.

Jaime Brena watches him through the window. Where has he seen that photograph before? He takes out his pad, crosses out Unknown One and puts in "Marcos Miranda". Then he crosses out Unknown Two and puts in "Vicente Gardeu". To the right of Marcos Miranda's arrow he writes: killed in the US by a gunman. He puts the pad back in his jacket pocket. He thinks of Chazarreta and the other dead men. He thinks of Gloria Echagüe. He thinks of all the work he did on the story of that woman's death. He thinks of himself, a few years ago, reconstructing that crime, interviewing Chazarreta, putting together reports – even some for television. Television. That's it, on television – that's where he's seen the photograph, on the report that went out not long after Chazarreta had been killed, when they still knew nothing, that report in which he had done a piece to camera, and which ended with a series of photographs of the Chazarreta couple: photos of Gloria Echagüe, photos of Pedro Chazarreta, photos of them both together, photos of when they were young, recent photos. Photos of Gloria Echagüe with friends. Photos of Chazarreta with friends.

And other photos, although he doesn't care about those any more. He only cares about the one in which Chazarreta appears with his friends. He'd be willing to bet that it's the same photograph. He has to get hold of that tape; if this weren't a Sunday it would be easy, but if he calls someone now they'll boot it into Monday. Or even Tuesday. He's going to mention it to the Crime boy. He must know some magic way to locate it in a corner of the Web. Jaime Brena has no idea where or how, but he has faith in the boy in these matters; a lot of faith.

Finally he leaves money on the table to cover the coffees and goes out. Crossing the road in the direction of the Crime boy's car, he wonders how soon it will be before he's putting down a cause of death in the right-hand column for Vicente Gardeu and Luis Collazo.

20

By the time Jaime Brena arrives with his party at La Maravillosa,
around eight o'clock, the entrance gate is closed. From his
booth, the guard asks the Crime boy to turn off his exterior
lights and put on the ones inside the car. The boy doesn't
understand these signals, though; all he sees is a man making
hand gestures, opening and closing his fingers as though
imitating a duck's beak; a man who isn't opening the barrier
and apparently has no intention of explaining why but is
simply going to wait until the Crime boy does whatever it is
he wants him to do. Jaime Brena, who does understand the
gestures, explains: Turn off your headlamps and put on the
inside lights. The boy does this. But even though he, Jaime
Brena, has understood what the guard was asking (or perhaps
because of that), he feels irritated, despite being a patient
man. The process smacks of abuse of power and reminds
Brena of another era. During the years of his marriage he
often argued with Irina about what she considered to be one
of his many inconsistencies and contradictions: that he was
essentially patient and yet so quick to become irritated. If
you're annoyed, do something about it; if you're going to
sit back and be patient, then don't get so annoyed, his wife
would complain. When a mosquito bites you, you feel it
right away; that's nothing to do with patience or impatience,
he'd reply. Besides, if it's already bitten you, what can you
do other than scratch yourself? Jaime Brena was patient in

those days, when he was married to Irina, and now he sits patiently facing the entry gate to La Maravillosa because he knows that losing patience would help very little, that anything he might do won't help and may even delay their entry further. But that doesn't stop him from feeling as irritated as if a swarm of mosquitoes had bitten him. When the car draws level with his window the guard asks the boy for his name, ID number, registration number and the model and colour of his car. The colour? says the Crime boy. The colour, repeats the guard. Green, says the boy in the tone of someone giving an obvious answer to a stupid question. Green what? insists the guard. What? the boy asks. What green? says the man, inverting the order of the words as though that might make the question easier to understand. Green, the boy says again. Another guard prowling through the area with a rifle against his shoulder comes close, and like someone at the races furtively passing on a tip for the next race, he says: Tahiti green. OK, Tahiti green, thanks, says the guard who's registering the visitors' entry and, with two fingers on the computer keyboard, confidently types the word "Tahiti". The boy looks at his companions and says: The worst thing is that this isn't even a joke. Don't get me started, says Jaime Brena. Now the guard asks the boy for his registration number, his ID card, car insurance document and proof of payment for the car insurance, then asks him to open first his boot and then his bonnet. The boy does this, obeying each of the guard's commands in turn, but pointing out that he'd been here yesterday: I came as a visitor to the same house; you've already taken my photograph and entered all this information into the system, apart from the colour. Yes, that's new, says the guard, you must have given those details to my colleague. So is it necessary to write it all down again? the boy asks. Not normally, but the system's gone down, so we have to input all the data by hand. Jaime Brena can feel his temperature rising. Karina Vives laughs: These guys are incredible; they're not for real. Do you think this man doesn't realize that it makes no earthly difference whether your car is Tahiti or moss green? Brena fumes: It's the people they answer to, not them, that we need to thank for this brainwave. Every time there's an assault on a gated community they add some new security check that will do nothing to prevent another incident, but which nobody dares to question. Karina says: I think they should take apart the seats like the drug squad, pull up the carpets, test the fire extinguisher to make sure that it doesn't contain some substance that can be used in the preparation of home-made bombs, frisk us, check my bag, make us walk through a metal detector. Just give it time, Jaime Brena interrupts, more resigned now than irritated, as the barrier rises before them, finally permitting them entry to La Maravillosa.

In her house (or rather the house where she's staying) Nurit Iscar – who knows that Jaime Brena and the Crime boy are on their way because there's already been a call from the gatehouse asking her to authorize their entry, but who doesn't yet know that Karina Vives is also in the car – brushes her hair, puts on some perfume, applies gloss to her lips and feels like an idiot. She goes back into the kitchen to join her friends. What time did you order the pizzas for? Paula Sibona asks. For nine o'clock. I should have got them for earlier, right? No, nine's a good time to eat, says Carmen. And what if they're hungry? Shall I get some snacks ready? Nurit asks. Betty Boo, is it just me or are you even more nervous than when Lorenzo Rinaldi came to pick you up? Paula asks. It's just you. The sound of car wheels on the gravel outside saves her from further explanations. Nurit Iscar goes to the front door to receive her guests. The darkness outside prevents her from seeing that there's someone else besides the Crime boy and Jaime Brena until Brena opens the back door and Karina Vives steps out of the car which, as its passengers now know, is Tahiti green. I hope you don't mind, but we've brought a friend: Karina, says Jaime, introducing the women. Hello, I'm Nurit, she says, kissing the girl and then the two men. And for some reason it doesn't cross her mind that this woman is Karina Vives as she kisses her, or as they walk along on the veranda before entering the house, assuming from her age that she's a friend of the Crime boy, not Jaime Brena, and it will be a couple of hours before the penny drops, when her friends ask her, Don't you know who that bitch is? Because even then she won't have guessed that this is the woman who tore apart her novel *Only If You Love Me* three years earlier, thus hastening her exile to the realm of ghostwriters. It's true that nobody uses her surname during the introductions, nobody mentions that she's a cultural journalist, nobody even says "she works with us". But isn't there such a thing as female intuition? Gut instinct? A sixth sense? Clearly not, unless Nurit's excitement – fuelled not only by the evolving Chazarreta case but also (as we should acknowledge now) by the fact that Jaime Brena is here – has clouded her perception. At any rate she's entering the house now, chatting with the girl, friendly, amiable, making introductions: Paula, Carmen, this is Karina. And they all kiss each other, smile at one another, sit down in living-room armchairs and say nice things to one another as if (even though some of them know each other very little) each for her part believes wholeheartedly in that popular saying "My friends' friends are my friends too".

The first thing the Crime boy does is carry out Jaime Brena's request: he goes up to Nurit's room and searches on YouTube for the news item on Chazarreta's death which was shown a few days ago on the channel that belongs to the same media group as *El Tribuno*. It's not difficult to find, nor is it hard to print off the photograph that appears at the end of the item in a montage of different images and which Brena believes may match the one that was in the empty frame. Although the definition on the image is frustratingly poor, it does seem likely that this is the missing photograph, and the men's faces can be seen fairly clearly, albeit in fewer pixels than he would have liked. He takes the printed picture down to Brena, who confirms his hunch: This is the one; thanks, kid.

A while later, when they're all comfortably installed in the living room, Jaime Brena takes from his pocket the notepad and the photo the Crime boy has just given him, finds the page with the last set of notes he made and beckons to Nurit Iscar. She comes over, takes the printed photograph from him and studies the men in it one by one. Each man offers up a posed smile apart from Gandolfini, whose expression is different, stiffer, as though he were talking to the person taking the photograph – or not so much talking as giving him instructions or upbraiding him. Nurit and Jaime Brena exchange a few impressions, the Crime boy following their conversation closely. The others listen but keep their distance, not knowing whether it's appropriate or not for them to be a party to this conversation. Jaime Brena sees this and makes an effort to involve them: If you're interested in our strange deliberations, by all means join in. The others lean in. Brena gives a summary of his meeting with Gandolfini's brother, pouring praise on the Crime boy and the computer skills that helped locate the man. And the photograph. Then he puts on his glasses to read aloud the part that matters to him most, his chart detailing each victim and the cause of his death. Nurit puts the photo down on the table and reads Brena's notes over his shoulder. The Crime boy, in search of a signal for his BlackBerry, has moved to the doorway between living room and kitchen. He doesn't exactly know why it unsettles him to be without a signal, but it does. When Brena has finished reading through the chart, Carmen Terrada, hesitant in the way of a person who realizes she's about to give an opinion on something she knows little about, ventures: If you don't mind me saying something that sounds a bit half-baked, this reminds me of a Carnival death. Jaime Brena nods. What do you mean by "Carnival death"? asks the Crime boy, although in fact this question could have come from any of them, since only Brena knows what Carmen is talking about. She explains: Things are more tightly controlled these days, but years ago at the Rio Carnival lots of people used to die in fights that were supposedly caused by alcohol, excessive partying and general mayhem. The deaths were taken as an acceptable cost of the celebrations. They weren't really investigated; there were a lot of deaths and not many clues. It meant that a criminal who wanted to pick somebody off for whatever reason would wait until then so that the murder would get included in King Momo's yearly tally and go almost unnoticed. Well, some of what you've been saying reminds me of the Carnival deaths. I don't know if I'm explaining myself; it's more a feeling than anything else, Carmen says. Jaime Brena, listening intently, nods. He also has the sense that somebody is trying to pull the wool over their eyes, that they are being outwitted, that somebody, somehow, is still pulling the strings of these dead men. And of those yet to die. However complicated the situation, he doesn't believe that the accidents are, in fact, accidental. He asks the Crime boy to look up information about the latest fatality, Marcos Miranda, the one who was killed a few hours ago in a shoot-out in the United States. Are these all "Carnival

deaths"? Are any of them? Are any of them not? What link
could there be between a ski accident, a fatal crash, a throat-
slitting and a gun crime? Jaime says, sharing his thoughts
with the group. What's the pattern, the one constant in every
case? The boy says that it's odd that there's still nothing from
the news agencies about the shooting in New Jersey. Karina
Vives, who's forgotten her pregnancy worries for the time
being, is kneeling at the coffee table looking at the photograph of the Little Ranch men. Nurit Iscar is still focused
on Jaime Brena's notepad, tracing lines with her finger
between each victim and the cause of his death. She seems
to have cut herself off from the rest of the group, so deep
in thought she doesn't hear what the others say. She keeps
poring over the list of victims and crimes, looking from left
to right and right to left, down and up, up and down. Until
finally, as though she had had a revelation, she interrupts
the conversation she hasn't been following and says: Each
one got the death he deserved. Meaning? says the Crime
boy. That they died in the way you'd expect, says Nurit Iscar.
Then she stands up and, just as though she were giving a
class at the university, she paces around the living room
explaining, as she refers by name to each of the men in the
photograph which she has snatched from the hands of Karina
Vives in a gesture that's impulsive and enthusiastic rather
than arrogant: The guy who drove like a madman and who
everyone thought would come a cropper dies in a car accident; the daredevil skier dies skiing; the one who went to
the United States dies the ultimate American death: shot by
a crazy. And Chazarreta, whom so many people considered
to be his wife's murderer, died like her, as he should die, as
it was to be expected that he might die. Each one of them
got the death he deserved, Nurit concludes. But it wasn't
fate, or karma, or coincidence or a curse, not even a "fix",

217

as Gladys Varela would put it, Jaime Brena adds, and Nurit nods in agreement. Who's Gladys Varela? Karina Vives asks, but nobody answers. So what was it then? Paula Sibona asks. Contract killings, says Jaime Brena, without a moment's hesitation. Somebody wanted all these people to die, and set out to find someone who could make that happen. That's the pattern. Does that really exist? Carmen asks. Can you really get someone to kill another person so easily? I thought it was an urban myth. I don't know about easily, but it's no urban myth; hitmen exist, says the Crime boy. You'd better believe it, says Jaime Brena, continuing: a "proper" job, in quotation marks, clean, done by professionals, can cost between 3,000 and 5,000 dollars, but you can also find guys who'll take someone out for 300 pesos. If only I'd known that before, says Paula Sibona with a wink to Carmen Terrada, who ignores the joke. Whoever wanted this job done must have paid a lot of money for it, says Brena. This isn't the work of a lone hitman, there's a firm behind this; a series of murders like these demands logistics, information, international reach, even a script. Quite an operation. I once wrote a piece on something similar to this, says Karina Vives. Oh – are you a journalist as well? asks Paula Sibona, who has seemed the least engaged in the conversation so far. Yes, says Karina. I wrote about a company that specialized in organizing fake courses or conferences for men or women who were unfaithful to their partners. The cheaters would say that they were going off to a conference in some part of the world and they'd get sent fake publicity material, folders with coursework, fake photo ID, diplomas, etc., etc., all impeccably done. There are a lot of bastards out there, says Paula Sibona. For sure, agrees Karina. This seems similar, no? An organization to create a lie which, instead of concealing infidelities, conceals something else. A string of deaths, says Jaime Brena, but providing execution – the murder itself – as well as cover. A truly professional job in the worst sense. And Brena would be happy to keep explaining and talking about the case but he can't help noticing that the three women who have joined their working party are intrigued by the concept of the organization for unfaithful men and women and are still talking about this under their breath without paying much attention to his ruminations. Over on the other side of the living room, that conversation is getting lively. But Jaime Brena, the Crime boy and Nurit Iscar aren't a part of it. They're worried – very worried. They move away from the others so they can speak freely without alarming them. I think we do need to tell the police now, says the Crime boy. Yes, Jaime Brena agrees. Nurit nods, but her mind is still working away. Who could contract a firm of assassins, and why? Someone with a lot of money, for starters, says Brena. And she says: Clearly it's someone with a lot of money, but what can those men have done for someone to expend so much energy and money on planning their deaths and carrying them out in such a sophisticated way? Those are the two things we need to find out next, says Jaime Brena, who and why. But either way we need to inform the police.

They're interrupted by the bell. The pizza? says Nurit. How strange that they didn't ring from the gatehouse. I wonder if any of us will be able to eat now; I've got such a knot in my stomach, she says as she walks towards the door. But when she opens it, it's not the pizza delivery man standing outside but the guard who gave her a lift to the newsagent in his buggy that morning. I'm sorry to bother you, Señora, he says. No, not at all; what is it? she asks. I… I don't know if it's right for me to be here, but… What's happened? Nurit insists. It's Señor Collazo. Do you remember how we were saying that he's been on edge recently? Yes, says Nurit, already sensing what's coming. Jaime Brena and the Crime boy, realizing that the guard is about to reveal something important, have come to the door. Señor Collazo has killed himself. A colleague told me a little while ago, and I've just seen his body. Nurit feels as though she's been thumped in the chest. How did he die? Brena asks. He hanged himself from a tree. He's still hanging there, in his garden; they can't bring him down, they have to wait for a judge to come. Nurit grabs hold of Jaime Brena's arm, and he holds her but also puts his hand on hers and squeezes it. The Crime boy rubs his face as though trying to wake up from a nightmare. Please don't tell my superiors that I let you know, the man asks Nurit. They don't like any gossiping... but I swear it's such a shock, you never expect such a thing... I wanted to tell you, I'm sorry. No, you did the right thing, she says, you were right to come and tell me and don't worry, I won't let anyone know how I heard the news. He was very agitated, the guard goes on. You could see it coming, right? Nurit Iscar tries to say something, but her voice cracks. Noticing her distress, Jaime Brena spares her from having to give the answer the guard is waiting for. Instead, he speaks the words she would have spoken if her throat hadn't tightened around them, words that, though they sound like confirmation, mean something different to what the man standing in front of them will hear. Yes, you could see it coming. Collazo died how you'd expect him to die.

21

Jaime Brena and Nurit Iscar are about to go over to Collazo's house, where his body is still hanging from a tree. The Crime boy, who had intended to go with them, is persuaded by Brena that he should concentrate now on trying to locate the group's only survivor: Vicente Gardeu. At least they hope that he has survived the others. Nurit Iscar suggests he use the computer in her room, which has a bigger screen and a keyboard less likely – she hopes – to bring on osteoarthritis than the tiny one on her BlackBerry. Karina Vives, Paula Sibona and Carmen Terrada will stay at home awaiting pizza and news. So at the moment that Nurit and Jaime Brena are walking in the dark of a moonless night (at the last meeting the residents of La Maravillosa voted against a proposal to increase the number of street lights so as to preserve a feeling of being in nature, "otherwise we may as well go and live in Buenos Aires", one of the residents is supposed to have shouted, and everyone applauded) the Crime boy is in Nurit's bedroom typing "Vicente Gardeu" into the Google search box, and Nurit's friends are chatting to Karina Vives in the kitchen while waiting for the pizza delivery man, whose arrival has already been announced from the gatehouse. We should put the oven on to keep them warm until the others get back, right? says Paula. I doubt they'll still feel much like pizza but yes, cold ones would be worse, Carmen says. Then she turns to Karina Vives: So you're a journalist too? Yes, the girl says. And where do you work? At *El Tribuno*, like the others. Ah, so the three of you are colleagues, you work together. Yes, almost literally: our desks are very close to each other. Did you only start working there recently? Paula Sibona asks. No, Karina says, and she laughs. I've been there way too long, like eight years. But how old are you? Thirty-five. You seem much younger. Thanks. So you've been there for ages. Yes. And which section are you in? Do they always make you write about unfaithful men and women? No, thankfully not, that was right at the start when they had me filling in and covering all kinds of things, then I moved on to Entertainment, and for a few years now I've been in Culture. Carmen is the first to hear alarm bells, and to confirm her suspicions she repeats: You work in *El Tribuno*'s Culture section. And immediately asks: In the main body of the newspaper or in the supplement? In *Tribuno 2*, Karina Vives confirms. And you're called Karina. Yes, she confirms again, a little disconcerted now, not only by the questions but by the tone of voice in which Carmen is putting them. She works in Culture at *El Tribuno* and her name's Karina, Carmen says to Paula with an emphasis that isn't lost on her friend. Out of interest, what's your surname? Paula asks. Vives, says the girl. I don't believe it, says Paula. Karina Vives, says Carmen, with an expression that says "I might have known". Tell me, Karina, Paula says, do you know whose house this is? Yes…, says the girl, not understanding where the question is leading. So whose house is it? Paula insists. What do you mean? It's Nurit Iscar's house. Is this a joke? she replies. And it doesn't make you feel a bit funny to be here? Funny how? Funny in the sense of embarrassed, ashamed, remorseful, or, to put it another way: don't you feel a bit shit? Paula Sibona says, going in for the kill. Karina looks uncomfortable, still not understanding if this strange conversation constitutes a joke, a misunderstanding or something else and struggling to find an explanation for the aggressive way Nurit Iscar's friends have suddenly turned on her. If it's because… I'm not involved with Jaime Brena or with the boy — No, darling, it's not that. This has nothing to do with men. The review she wrote three years ago and which signified something very different to her than it did to Nurit Iscar and her friends doesn't even cross Karina Vives' mind. A review which, for other reasons, she tried to forget – successfully, until today. Paula Sibona is about to remind her of it, though: You write a book review that rips Nurit apart and now you turn up here as if it never happened. Was this recently? A new book? No, not new: three years ago. Is your memory that bad? Let me help: the review of *Only If You Love Me*. Ah yes, that review. But that was three years ago, says Karina, finally understanding what they are talking about. Don't you have anything to say about it? Paula presses. Look, you're both making me feel really bad. I was asked to write about that book and I did. It was a piece about a book, not a person, it was my first job as Culture editor, and I didn't know Nurit Iscar at that time, anyway. What? So if you'd known her you'd have written something different? Carmen says. Is that how you people operate? I'd rather not talk about it. There are things related to my work that I'm not going to discuss outside it; it was a review, that's all. A review doesn't change anyone's life. It changed Nurit's, says Paula, unflinchingly. That will have been down to something else, not the review, says Karina Vives, defensively. Does one person's opinion of a book really matter so much that it can affect the life of whoever wrote it? Well, each one of us is affected by different things; or does nothing affect you? Carmen asks and continues:

Maybe it doesn't affect you if someone talks down your work, or doesn't value the time and effort you put into it, but something in life's got to affect you, something must make you cry – or do you never cry? Karina Vives holds her gaze for a few seconds, teeth clenched, breathing fast, eyes hot with anger, then noisily bursts into tears. Hey, don't cry, it's not that bad. We're not getting at you; we're just respectfully saying something that needs to be said. Isn't that right? Paula says, looking at Carmen. Totally respectfully, Carmen agrees. If what you want to do is make us feel bad — I'm not crying because of that! I'm not crying because of you, or because of Nurit, or because of that bloody review. I'm crying because I'm pregnant! Now Paula Sibona and Carmen Terrada are the startled ones. Isn't that a bit more important than churnalism? Paula and Carmen look at one another and then at her. Karina Vives struggles to control her breathing, choking on her sobs. And I don't even know if I want it or not, she stammers. Paula Sibona fills a glass of water and takes it to her. Here, sweetheart, let's start at the beginning. What is "churnalism"?

At the moment that Paula Sibona is passing Karina Vives a glass of water, the Crime boy is discovering that Vicente Gardeu was the founder of the order that brought the San Jerónimo Mártir school to Argentina, and that if he were still alive he would be 109 years old. Should they be looking for someone else with the same name? He keeps searching, but every entry returns the same Vicente Gardeu. Some of the results mention suits against him for accusations of pae- dophilia and sexual abuse. He clicks on one of them: more than fifteen seminarians who passed through his order claim to have been the victims of abuse perpetrated by Gardeu. Others defend him, however. There are statements from parents who have sent their children to schools belonging to the community saying they aren't affected by what may have happened in the past, because "the achievements of the foundation surpass any private failings of the founder". What's certain is that Jaime Brena must have got the wrong end of the stick: Vicente Gardeu is not the sixth friend. He can't be. The Crime boy returns to the news about the shooting in New Jersey. The websites are on to it now, all of them carrying more or less the same information in English, which he translates as he reads: Today, a few minutes after three o'clock in the afternoon, an unidentified gunman opened fire from a building next to the car park of a Walmart supermarket in New Jersey, leaving one man dead and three with superficial injuries. The police are still trying to determine from where the shots were fired. The victim is thought to be a sixty-year-old Argentine national who had lived in the United States for several decades and was the manager of a large company. The Crime boy prints out three pages from different online newspapers, knowing that Jaime Brena, when he gets a chance, will want to read them on paper. He tries to get at least one of three options in Spanish and feels that he's gradually getting to know Brena.

As the third page on the New Jersey shooting is coming out of the printer, Nurit Iscar and Jaime Brena are arriving at Luis Collazo's house. They know that they won't get much further, that they won't be permitted to approach the inert body still hanging among the shadows from the branch of an oak tree. The two entrances to the property are blocked respectively by a Buenos Aires police patrol car and La Maravillosa's chief of security's van; the club's security personnel are turning away anyone who comes within a few yards of the house. A woman is crying and clinging on to a man in his late twenties. Approaching one of the guards, Jaime Brena gestures towards them and asks: Who are they? Collazo's wife and son, he replies. They're in a terrible state, aren't they? says Brena. And how would you feel if your husband or father had just hung himself from a tree? retorts the guard and goes off to speak to his boss, not caring that he may have left Jaime Brena formulating a response to this question. But Brena doesn't mind being rebuffed; it may have been a stupid question, but it served his purpose. Now he has the information he wanted: the police don't doubt that Collazo's death was a suicide, that he hanged himself. He says as much to Nurit, who's not shaking because she's cold, but from the shock of this latest dark development. And Jaime Brena, though he knows that her trembling has nothing to do with the temperature, takes off his sweater and puts it around her shoulders. Here, take this, Betty Boo. Thank you, says Nurit, and attempts a weak smile. The guard who broke the news of Collazo's death to them minutes before has arrived now in his buggy. He acknowledges Nurit briefly from afar, barely moving his head as if he doesn't want anyone to see this greeting. She responds in kind. Jaime Brena observes the exchange, stroking his chin so hard he's almost squeezing it. We need to see the body close up, he says, finally. There's no way they'll let us, Nurit replies. Not us, no, says Jaime Brena, but they'll let him, and he signals towards the guard. Do you feel able to ask him to take a photograph on your mobile? He's more likely to say yes to you than to me. I don't think a phone photo is going to show us very much in this light. You might be right, it may not show what I want to see, but you could ask him to focus on two things: where the knot is on the rope that Collazo is supposed to have used to hang himself and what colour his face is. To be more precise, we need to know whereabouts on his neck the knot is – at the front, at the nape or at one side – and whether Collazo's face is white or blue. OK, I'll convey all of that to him exactly as you've said it, and later on you can explain to me why I'm asking it; I don't think I can handle a disquisition about the marks on a hanging victim's neck at the moment. Of course, I'll explain it to you later. Charily Nurit Iscar approaches the guard, and only when he sees her and signals that it's fine to talk does she approach him with more confidence. She says hello, then passes on Jaime Brena's instructions. The guard agrees to take a photograph, and walks in the direction of the oak tree. Nurit Iscar walks back over to Brena. He sees her rubbing her arms again, as though she were cold. You can put on my sweater if you want. No, it's OK, it's fine over my shoulders. I never thought that these murders would come so close to us, says Brena; in crime journalism you're always arriving after the event, later, treading on the heels of death. And on the murderer's heels. It's different this time. Yes, this is different, Nurit agrees. We have to do whatever we can to find the last survivor, even if only to feel that we were able to make a difference. Do you think we'll be able to get there in time? When we get back to your house I'm going to call Comisario Venturini, Brena announces. We can't carry the burden of another potential death alone. I hope to God Collazo did commit suicide and we're wrong, Nurit says. I hope so, but I very much doubt it, Brena says. The guard who went to see how Collazo's body was hanging from the tree has come back, and he makes his way over to where they are waiting. The knot is to one side, under the left ear, he says, and his face is white as a sheet. Thank you, Brena says, and asks nothing more: he doesn't need to. When the guard has left them, Jaime Brena says to Nurit: Let's go back to your house, there's not much more we can do here. They definitely killed him.

What makes you so sure? You're ready now to hear about the effects of different hanging methods? Not really, but my curiosity is killing me. So Brena explains: There are white hanging victims and blue hanging victims. The white ones have a symmetrical hanging, that is to say that both carotid arteries and both jugular veins are compressed simultaneously, he says, demonstrating this action on his own neck. The blood supply is cut off, causing cerebral anaemia and a white facial pallor. For this symmetrical compression of veins and arteries to occur, the knot has to be below the nape of the neck or the chin. Nurit's beginning to feel dizzy, but Jaime Brena is so absorbed in his explanation that he doesn't notice. If the knot is under the jawline or beneath the ear, he continues, the compression is asymmetrical. The circulation is interrupted in both jugulars, but only in the carotid artery where the loop of the rope is, not where the knot is. Shall we get going? Nurit suggests, taking him by the arm. Yes, let's go, he says, and they start walking away together. But Brena hasn't finished his lecture: There's less compression at the point of the knot, so the blood can still flow into the head but can't return to the heart, and that's why you get what's called cyanosis, where the face goes blue. Jaime Brena and Nurit Iscar keep walking slowly, putting distance between themselves and the dead man. If Collazo were blue, there'd be room for doubt. But he's white and has the knot below his ear, which makes suicide an impossibility. He notices her shiver and glances over at her; she's shaking, in fact. So Jaime Brena puts his arm around her, takes her shoulder and brings her close to him. That's how Nurit likes to think of it, anyway. Those are the words she would use to describe the gesture if she were working on her own novel, because if she wrote "Jaime Brena embraces me" or "Jaime Brena holds her", the held person – that is her, Betty Boo – would shiver even more. And she certainly wouldn't write: "Finally, for the first time in three years, a man holds her."

Nurit Iscar would never put one of her own characters through something like that.

22

The half-eaten portions of pizza are congealing on their plates. Nurit Iscar has no appetite and no desire to talk, despite her friends' efforts to make her feel better. But the image of a dead man hanging from a tree isn't something that goes away without leaving its mark. Not if you knew that person, had spoken to him, and even had argued with him. Not if you had feared that something like this was going to happen. And especially not if you believe that the decision to hang himself was not his but forced upon him. Or even that he was killed first and hanged later. It's one thing to write about death and something else to observe it at first hand. Paula Sibona hands her the blanket which, after searching through the unfamiliar house, she has finally managed to locate in a wardrobe on the landing at the top of the stairs. Karina Vives is still red-eyed from crying, but in the midst of so much death nobody pays her any attention. The Crime boy passes Jaime Brena the page he printed off a while ago with the news (in Spanish) of the death of Chazarreta's friend in New Jersey; he waits for Brena to put on his glasses to read it, and once he's finished that, he translates the English news stories for him, skipping any redundant details. Next Jaime Brena calls Comisario Venturini, but doesn't get through. He leaves a message: It's Brena here, please call urgently. It's about Collazo's death; I don't know if you've been told about it. It's nearly midnight on Sunday and everyone looks at each other without knowing what to do, what the next move should be. Nobody dares to propose a plan of action: that they get some sleep; that they write down the new facts so as not to forget anything important; that they try Comisario Venturini again; that they decide what information can be published immediately on the Crime pages of *El Tribuno* and what must be kept quiet. Nobody says anything: silence rules. Then Paula Sibona, employing a method of free association that she's explained many times in drama classes when teaching her students to improvise, says: Hey, has anyone got a joint? Carmen Terrada's surprised by her friend's directness. Nurit Iscar looks disapprovingly at Paula, who notices but doesn't let herself feel inhibited. Karina Vives, her mind elsewhere, doesn't hear the question; if she had she would gladly offer up the one that's in her bag and which she hasn't wanted to smoke since learning of her pregnancy. Jaime Brena smiles and says: I only wish I did. On hearing that, Paula relaxes and winks at Nurit, making a gesture, a sideways smile that between them signifies something like "See? I wasn't wrong". The Crime boy gets up and says: I seem to remember I've got one in the glove compartment of my car. And off he goes.

Waiting for the joint slows the scene even more. Nurit Iscar isn't going to put up any resistance: she knows that in a few minutes everyone will be smoking in her house. And it's not that she's in any sense annoyed about that. Envy is closer to what she feels. They'll have a good time, they'll laugh, they'll relax, they'll discuss trivialities as if they were immensely important and find sage conclusions to banal questions, or banal conclusions to sage questions; they'll discover solutions to problems they've never even considered before, looking lovingly at each other while she, Nurit Iscar, Betty Boo, tries yet again to get some sort of hit off the marijuana. And once again, marijuana will do nothing for her except tickle her throat, make her want to cough and disappoint her. It's like not being able to laugh at a joke everyone else finds funny, or not being moved by a poem which those in the know have recognized as exceptional, or – after really working at it – failing to reach orgasm. The Crime boy comes back into the house, twirling the joint between fingers and thumb. Anyone got a light? he asks. And Brena passes him a lighter. The boy lights the joint and draws deeply on it until the tip glows red. Then he passes it to his right. Paula Sibona smokes with pleasure, greedily, as if she's been wanting this for a long time. She has, in fact, been wanting it for a long time. Carmen Terrada takes one short puff and apologizes: not too much for me, otherwise I'll either fall asleep or get silly. Brena takes the joint with almost as much enthusiasm as Paula Sibona, but smokes it differently, more serenely; smoking is a daily act for him, every night he smokes to unwind and send himself off to sleep. He gives time to the act: pressing his lips to the fingers that are holding the joint and breathing in over them, half-closing his eyes. He holds onto the smoke, gradually releasing it, and only after all that ceremony passes it to Karina Vives. Not for me, thanks, she says. You don't smoke? You don't like it? says Nurit, almost cheerfully, as though she's found a kindred spirit in this woman whose identity she has yet to discover. Everyone is quiet, guessing at another reason for Karina's abstinence. They all, apart from Nurit, think they know why she's not smoking, but nobody knows that the others know. So they dissemble, waiting for Karina herself to respond. Jaime Brena still has the joint in his hand. Paula comes closer and takes it from him, ending the impasse and taking another toke. I'll have a smoke to be polite, but I don't like it much either, it has no effect on me, Nurit says, apparently to Karina Vives. And true to her word Nurit accepts the joint Paula Sibona passes her, takes a half-hearted puff and hands it on. No, it's not that I don't like it, Karina clarifies, but I'm pregnant and I don't know if I can. Nurit coughs. The Crime boy looks at Brena and says: She's pregnant. Yes, I know, he says. But she hasn't decided what to do yet, says Carmen to Nurit. Jaime Brena's phone rings. It's Comisario Venturini. Jaime Brena listens closely, then says: It wasn't suicide, Venturini, believe me, I know. His expression suggests that the Comisario doesn't share his theory. Ah, so you're at Collazo's place now? And he moves his head as if to say that if it's his turn with the joint they shouldn't skip him. Yes, I've been there too, says Brena, but I didn't see him, Comisario. Yes, I'm still at Nurit Iscar's house. Something of what's being said down the line seems to irritate him. Nurit coughs. OK, OK, I understand, but a white hanging victim with a lateral knot – that doesn't add up. Paula takes the joint from Nurit with the excuse of knocking off the ash before it falls on the floor, though she uses the opportunity to take another drag first – her third. Brena says goodbye to the Comisario and hangs up: What a dick, he says. I think you'd probably be fine to have a bit, Carmen says to Karina Vives. I smoked when I was pregnant; not very much, but it doesn't harm you any more than a few sips of wine. I never drank wine when I was pregnant, Nurit says. But you're very controlled, darling, that's why marijuana doesn't affect you, says Paula, laughing. Nurit doesn't find the observation amusing. The order of rotation changes and the joint goes to Jaime Brena. Now it's no longer clear whether it should be passing from right to left or left to right. From Jaime Brena it goes to the Crime boy. Then back to Paula Sibona. After her, Nurit has another try, putting it between her lips. Breathe in deeper, says Brena, and he tries to encourage her by imitating the gesture she should make. More, he insists, it needs to light up, the end needs to go red. Paula laughs. Nurit passes the joint to Carmen and exhales the smoke. Hold on to it, Brena tells her. Don't breathe out so quickly; let it go gradually. Carmen smokes. It's got nothing to do with breathing out too soon, Nurit says, weed just doesn't affect me. But are you drawing the smoke into here? asks the Crime boy, touching his chest. Yes, says Nurit, I'm not completely stupid. Paula laughs. Support for the frustrated smoker. Carmen laughs too, then curls up in the armchair as if wanting to sleep. Right, give it here, I'm going to have a quick toke, says Karina Vives, and takes the joint from Carmen before Paula can grab it again. She inhales and passes it to the Crime boy, who takes a drag then neatens the end of the joint in the ashtray. The ash is a bit like a cloud, isn't it? says the boy. I don't know if it's because of the colour or that inconsistency it has so if you touch it, it falls apart, it vanishes. It vanishes, Paula murmurs. Now the boy plays with the ash quietly and seconds later says: Like a cloud, just like when you go through a cloud in an aeroplane. It's a clouuuud, there's no douuuubt, chants Carmen, who's almost asleep. Vox Dei, says Brena. Vox Dei, Carmen agrees, and she sings: Light as a… clouuuud. My uncle Luis was always singing that song and playing it on the guitar, says Karina. The Crime boy has never heard the song, although he thinks he knows who Vox Dei were; he's not altogether sure. But he says: A cloud, yes, like a cloud. Meanwhile the joint is still journeying from hand to hand. Because ash comes from fire, says the boy, and in a way, so do clouds. Paula takes the joint from Karina Vives. Have you worked out yet who this chick is? she asks Nurit, and laughs. Nurit shakes her head. Karina stiffens. Karina Vives is that bitch from *El Tribuno* who wrote the review of *Only If You Love Me*, Paula Sibona informs her. Light as… a clouuuud…, sings Carmen, and settles herself more horizontally on the sofa. Karina Vives starts crying again. Nurit feels something between confusion and annoyance, or is perhaps both confused and annoyed. Don't worry, says Paula, she's not crying because she's a bitch, she's crying because she's pregnant, and she's already done that before: she cries and cries. Nurit takes the joint from her and inhales much more deeply than on the previous occasions, her eyes fixed on Karina Vives, though she can't think of what to say. Then, because nothing else comes to mind, she repeats: This is having no effect on me, and coughs. Jaime Brena stretches out his spine and his neck, one side and then the other, and smiles. We're all good, right? he asks. Through her hiccups, Karina Vives says to Nurit Iscar: I didn't read your novel. Carmen, who had seemed to be asleep, sits up straight: What did you say? And she laughs. The Crime boy breaks up the ash with his index finger, barely touching it: Facebook and the other social networks are sort of ashy, sort of cloudy. Sort of, says Brena. Yeah, says the boy. Didn't you all hear this girl just say that she never read Nurit's book? Carmen asks. I didn't either, says the Crime boy. But you didn't write a review that completely destroyed her career, says Paula, and she's about to let out a guffaw but makes an effort to contain it. I didn't write the review, Karina Vives says. What? says Nurit, and asks for the joint. I said, I didn't write that review, Karina says again, and blows her nose. I didn't read your book and I didn't write the review. I did put my name to it, though. I'd just started on Culture and it was my dream, what I'd wanted ever since joining the paper, and Culture didn't have an editor, so Rinaldi gave me the job; I couldn't believe it, she says, crying. And soon after that he came over to me and gave me that review and said that I should run it under my byline, and so that's what I did. Rinaldi wrote that review? asks Nurit, astonished. No, not Rinaldi, his wife, Marisa, he said. Rinaldi's wife is called Marisa, right? Well, Marisa was trying her hand at journalism, but she didn't want to publish anything under her own name until she felt more confident because she knew there would be a lot of attention on her as "the wife of". The wife of the biggest bastard of all time who, by the way, has prostate problems, says Paula, and laughs. Rinaldi's got prostate problems? asks the Crime boy, still playing with the ash. Sometimes we're told to run a review with a particular slant. It happens every now and then and you just have to accept it; usually the aim is to lift a book, not bury it. If you want to bury it you just don't mention it, don't write about it, you act as though it doesn't exist. And why might they want to bury a book? Carmen asks, and yawns. For political reasons, or because the book bad-mouths the newspaper or attacks someone related to it, or because the person who authored it wrote a review in the past which damaged a friend of someone at the paper. How depressing, says Carmen. Or because the author is a lover of the newspaper's editor, says Paula, laughing. Paula... Nurit remonstrates, in a vain attempt to get her friend to show some self-control. I didn't know that that review had hit you so hard, Karina says, regretfully. Weed doesn't affect her but reviews do, says Paula, quickly covering her mouth by way of apology. Who told you it hit me hard? Nurit asks. They did, says Karina, pointing to Nurit's friends. In a metaaal caaaage, Carmen sings, then adds: Sorry. That's why I never read your novel, Karina says, because I didn't want to know if the piece I'd put my name to was justified or not. In other words, my friend Nurit Iscar has spent three years not writing because of a review written by the bitch who's married to the bastard who used to call himself her lover? summarizes Paula Sibona. Paula! says Nurit. I'm sorry, says Paula, and laughs. Jaime Brena, drifting off in his armchair, seems to be talking to Comisario Venturini in his dreams. The Crime boy tries to offer him the last drag on the joint, which is all but finished. Is there anything left? Brena says, stretching to take it. The wife sent in two or three more reviews after your one, Karina continues, then she never sent anything else. I asked Rinaldi about it and he said that she was working for the Travel supplement, that it was more her "cup of tea"; I remember that he used those words. What would be the right cup of tea for a woman like that? Paula wonders aloud. Because not everyone likes the same tea: for me the perfect cup of tea might be peppermint and for the next person chamomile. What cup of tea would suit a scheming, deluded bitch like her? Some people put bark in tea, don't they, says Carmen. And some people put in marijuana leaves, but that really does hit you hard, adds Paula, smiling. I once ate grass fritters, she begins, but she can't finish the anecdote because laughter overcomes her and she forgets what she was about to say. So, just to get this straight once and for all, everything that's happened to me is the result of a review attributed to someone who hadn't actually read my book, Nurit concludes. It happened to you because you let it happen, says Carmen; you should have listened to us in the first place. But you aren't critics, you're friends. I promise you I'll read it, Nurit. I want to be your friend, says the Crime boy, and stubs out the joint, drawing clouds with it in the ashes. I'm really sorry, says Karina, and blows her nose again. Nurit doesn't answer. Amazing the turns that life takes, says Carmen. Has anyone got anything sweet? Paula asks. A chocolate, a biscuit? On the pretext of looking for snacks, Nurit goes to the kitchen for some breathing space, returning with two bars of chocolate and a half-eaten pot of ice cream. She passes one of the chocolate bars to Paula and takes a bite out of the other one. The boy grabs the ice cream and spoon. Thank you, my friend, says Paula. The Crime boy, while eating ice cream from the styrofoam pot, says to Karina: Facebook is going to end up being the ash of the Internet, you heard it here first. Jaime Brena snores. Carmen makes herself comfortable again and seems about to go to sleep. Paula, eating chocolate, asks Nurit: While we're here, can I confess something to you, Betty Boo? Why not, says Nurit, nothing can shock me now. Are you absolutely sure? I'm sure, yes. Well, now that we know that the review that led to your banishment was written by Rinaldi's wife, and that this poor maligned girl's biggest mistake was letting herself get screwed by the system… she says, then stops. Yes, go on, Nurit urges. You sure? I'm sure. In my opinion, dear friend, I have to tell you, I feel obliged to tell you, that *Only If You Love Me* always, always seemed to me, from the first line to last, a steaming pile of horseshit. Nurit looks at her with surprise. Carmen tries to shake off her somnolence and sit up. Paula, you're stoned, she scolds, this isn't the moment for confessions. I may be stoned, but *Only If You Love Me* is still by far Nurit's worst novel. You said so yourself – remember? Paula! Carmen remonstrates. I never said that, she says to Nurit. I said that I liked the others more, which isn't the same thing. The Crime boy asks: Is it just me or is Jaime Brena snoring? Paula Sibona goes on: But everyone has the right to do something that comes out shit, once in a while. Or have you forgotten my Nora in *A Doll's House* at the San Martín theatre and how, when I stormed out, slamming the door, someone in the audience shouted "Good riddance, lunatic!" And he was right. I had turned her into a lunatic.

You think *Only If You Love Me*'s shit, right, Karina? Paula asks. I don't know, I never read it, the girl repeats. I'm going to read it, I promise, says the boy. Nurit, take it from me as a friend, it's a terrible novel – you know why? Because you were in love, your head was somewhere else and love and art don't get on well. Sex and art do, but not love and art. Tortured love works. But not that stupid, cuchi-woochi, love-of-my-life stuff. I never went cuchi-woochi love-of-my-life, Nurit bristles. You need to get writing now, Paula goes on, ignoring the complaint. I know you've got another good novel in you, you'll see. Carmen, still prostrate on the sofa with her eyes closed, clutches her head and asks: Has anyone here got a Vox Dei CD? Nobody answers. And there's another confession I need to make, Paula says to Nurit. No, begs Carmen, don't confess anything else. What is it? says Nurit. No, no, that's enough, leave it, Carmen says. Somebody put some music on, it doesn't matter what, any kind of music. You don't know what it is I'm going to say, says Paula, defensively. It doesn't matter, says Carmen, it's bound to be something you'll regret. It's now or never, Paula warns. Never, says Carmen. Tell me, says Nurit. Come on, let her say it, the Crime boy chimes in. Well, remember that bald guy with the goatee who wrote the article saying that the last time he moved house he left your book *Death by Degrees* behind because he was short of space and he knew he'd never read it? *Death by Degrees*, or *Only If You Love Me*? *Death by Degrees*, like I said. No, I don't remember that. Of course you remember, you remember everything everyone says. I don't remember the bald guy. That bald guy who thinks he knows about cinema, says Paula. Someone who's supposed to know about cinema but writes about literature? says Karina, I can think of two or three, but they aren't bald. Anyway, I don't remember, says Nurit, but what happened?

Well, just that; he said that every time he moved house he took the opportunity to cull his book collection, that he only took the worthwhile ones with him and that the last time he moved he left your book *Death by Degrees* still wrapped in plastic and everything, just how it came from the publisher, because he knew in his whole fucking life he was never going to read it. Actually that "fucking" bit is my own addition, Paula says. I don't remember it, Nurit repeats. Well we do; we remembered then and we still remember, and you know what we did to him? Do you really have to tell her? begs Carmen. We sent him a new copy, signed by you, or rather by us but with your name, of course, and with this dedication: This is to replace the copy you lost in your last move, Baldy. Paula laughs. I'm really sorry, says Carmen. Sorry, sorry, says Paula. I don't believe this, says Nurit, taking the ice cream away from her. I don't believe this, she says again. How many other things am I going to find out about tonight? The boy throws himself onto the rug. The boss really knows how to snore, he complains, and closes his eyes. Sorry, Carmen says again. It doesn't surprise me, coming from this madwoman, but from you… Nurit says. Paula laughs and says: I'll take "mad" as a compliment. Madness sets things alight. But be careful with the ash, says the boy, and laughs. Can you shut up for a bit? says Nurit. Not you, she says to the boy, I mean Paula. Paula obeys. Carmen and Karina, perhaps taking the order to be directed at them too, also keep quiet, waiting to see what Nurit will do next. Betty Boo is scraping the bottom of the styrofoam pot with a spoon to extract the last remnants of ice cream. She licks the spoon, deposits the empty container on the table and hurls the spoon into it. Then she stands up and looks around to see who's still awake. I'm off to sleep in a bed. She takes two steps and turns back: And you know what? Whoever wrote whatever and whoever did whatever they did to me or whatever I did to myself... She pauses for effect, then declares: Yes, *Only If You Love Me* is a piece of shit, the worst book I've written by a long chalk. It just goes to show that you should never write with your cunt.

And she leaves.

23

When Nurit Iscar goes downstairs to make the coffee that's
going to help her face a new day, none of her visitors remain.
She doesn't know at what point they left, nor in what condition, but she imagines that everyone who ended up spending
Sunday night in her house will by now be back home and
struggling to get a grip on Monday morning, just like her.
Beating sweetener into a paste of instant coffee and water to
make *café batido* (you should use real sugar for this, the kind
that comes from canes, not labs, but she got into the habit
of mixing coffee and sugar granules together this way back
in the days when she wasn't worried about her weight and
was happy to consume the high-calorie version), she thinks
how the quotidian – banal, even – elements of daily life
can get mixed up with crime in a fusion that both robs the
horror of any drama and makes simple things more horrify-
ing. Is it right to be making coffee when last night a corpse
was hanging from a tree? Is it defensible to go calmly about
breakfast in the belief that that death may be part of some
greater criminal plan or project? To blow on your too-hot
coffee while suspecting that if you don't act quickly enough
there may be yet another death? It must be, because that is
what she's doing at the moment. Our days are full of coffee-
making and other small actions that can be passed over in
a story, but not in real life. Penélope Cruz also goes to the
bathroom for a crap, Paula Sibona likes to say when they're

talking about the differences between imaginary worlds and real ones. Fiction and art dispense with coffee-mixing and toilet bowls. Untrue, as her friend Carmen Terrada would say. Duchamp didn't, nor did Jacques Prévert: "*Il a mis le café. Dans la tasse*". Why does she still remember that poem she learned at school at sixteen, in a language of which she can now barely stammer a few words? Nurit Iscar sits down to drink her black coffee. She looks out of the window towards the area where this property's garden dissolves into grassland. She wonders how many different shades of green the pasture contains, but she doesn't try counting them. That would take away the magic, it would mean treating something individually that can only be appreciated en masse. She'd like to go again and see the oak from which Collazo was found hanging, but isn't sure she'd be brave enough. What links the deaths of all these men as the pasture links different greens in a series of undifferentiated tones? Is there something behind the deaths, or are they – Jaime Brena, the Crime boy and she – a bunch of paranoiacs looking for a crime where there's only a string of coincidences? Why do we always need an explanation for death? It's true, though, that we don't demand the same answers of a natural death as of a violent one. In the case of natural death one immediately comes up against the impossibility of finding an ultimate meaning, a why. Why is life finite? What happens after death? Is there another chance, another life after this one, eternal life or whatever you want to call it, something to elevate the concept of death beyond rotting flesh for worms to eat? And she rues her own rational, untrusting nature, the scepticism that means she can only believe in what she sees: worms are what she believes in. Sometimes she regrets being agnostic, too, and envies people who have faith in something. In whatever. Only for a moment, though. Then she quickly reverts to trusting in her own beliefs. Or rather in what she doesn't believe. Now Nurit stands gazing out at the pasture, not drinking her coffee but with her hands around the cup; she likes warming her palms this way even when it's not cold. But the coffee doesn't stop her thinking about death, violent deaths in particular, and all the questions they raise. The search for a meaning shifts, locating itself in something that ought to be easier to decipher than "the hereafter", something earthly, a death ordained not by nature or some god, but by a person, someone like us. And the fact of that death being decreed by someone like us seems to put us on an equal footing with the assassin, making the moral imperative to find an answer all the more urgent. Even if there are no answers. We may even prefer to accept a conclusion we know could be false than to have to bear the uncertainty of not knowing who, and why.

Nurit finishes her coffee, rinses out the cup, dries it and puts it away. Some families are marked for tragedy, she thinks. Some groups and businesses too. Tragic fate is the acceptance of death in people connected to each other as part of an unchangeable destiny. Could Chazarreta and his friends have been one such group marked out for tragedy? Putting that aside, is it a coincidence that the friends died one by one, or is there a man or woman, not so different from herself, who decided their fates, someone Nurit Iscar feels compelled to find? She doesn't know yet, but this will be the subject of her next piece, and she goes up to her room to write it.

At the moment that Nurit is switching on her computer, the Crime boy, still a little sleepy, is entering the reception of San Jerónimo Mártir College. In the hall there is a portrait of Vicente Gardeu, complete with habit. Beneath it, a plaque bears his name and the dedication: To Father Gardeu, this school's founder and guiding light, on the anniversary of his death. Incredible. He imagines the same portrait over the caption "Wanted for paedophilia". He's absolutely sure, since going online at Nurit Iscar's house yesterday, that this can't be the name of that unidentified friend in Chazarreta's photo. But only now does he wonder how Gandolfini made such a mistake, given that Gardeu was someone so present in the lives of San Jerónimo students. Brena was certain that that was the name he gave. Could Gandolfini have been pulling his leg? In his pocket the boy has the photograph of the group of friends that he printed for Brena and which Brena handed him early that morning – they had dragged themselves away from Nurit's and he was getting out of the car at his house – with the instruction that he make copies for all three of them: Nurit, Brena and himself. It wasn't strictly necessary, since the boy could always get it off YouTube again and make all the copies he wanted. But at that time of day and after that Sunday, neither he nor Brena was in a state to distinguish between what was strictly necessary and what wasn't. The boy, sitting in an antique, impeccably restored Gobelin chair, takes the photograph out of his pocket and studies it while waiting to be seen. Several minutes go by without anyone coming. He notices that there's a bell beside the door of what seems to be an office or study and, putting the photograph back into his pocket, goes towards it. He rings the bell, not knowing for whom he'll ask when the door opens. If possible, he'd like to speak to the school's longest-standing priest, someone who was here at the time that Chazarreta and his friends were students at San Jerónimo Mártir. The Crime boy doubts his chances, but it's worth a try. Just as he's about to ring the bell for the second time, the door is opened by a secretary, not much over twenty, who asks him what he wants. The boy spins him the line he invented

245

on his way there: that he's the nephew of Luis Collazo, who has just taken his life, and that among his rambling last words was a request for this photo to be given to one of his friends – and the boy points to the man they haven't yet located, the one Gandolfini said was called Vicente Gardeu. We didn't manage to catch his name, and my uncle died soon afterwards, the boy explains, and the secretary nods sadly as though to convey his condolences. Of course you wouldn't know, you're too young, the boy says, and the teachers from that time must all be retired, but I thought there might still be a priest in the order who remembers his name. The secretary lets him talk without making any gesture to confirm or contradict what the Crime boy is saying. Then, with the same impassive face, he offers: There are no longer any priests or teachers from that era, but if you come this way, there is something that might be helpful. The secretary leads him down an apparently endless corridor paved with grey flagstones which have lost their lustre but are still beautiful. They come to a door that says *Order of San Jerónimo: Meeting and Reading Room* and the secretary opens it. In the centre of a large room there is a cherrywood table and around it a great number of chairs. More importantly, the walls are covered in photographs, one next to the other, of each of the school's graduating classes year by year and under each photograph is a wooden plaque bearing the name of every boy in the respective image above, in order and engraved in gold. Today is my lucky day, says the boy, and he isn't joking. The secretary leaves him alone in the room with the instruction to take his time looking. The Crime boy feels a little overwhelmed to be surrounded by men who were born several decades before him yet are frozen here at the age of eighteen, each cohort posing behind a blackboard upon which the year of their graduation is chalked in white. He remembers that Chazarreta was close to sixty when he was killed, and calculates that he must have left school about forty-two years ago. While he's not bad at maths, he's never been good at doing calculations in his head, so the boy settles on a round figure of forty and starts with the leavers from 1970 with a margin of five years on either side. He locates the group of friends in 1966. The first he recognizes is Chazarreta, probably because that's the face he knows best. Then he looks for each of the others in turn, consulting the photograph he brought with him before searching on the wall. The wooden plaque confirms the names of the other members of the group. There's Collazo, in the back row. Gandolfini, on one side, almost out of shot. Bengoechea, two along from him, towards the middle. And below him, holding the blackboard, Marcos Miranda, the one who was shot dead in New Jersey. Miranda's flanked by Chazarreta on one side and on the other by that man whose name the boy doesn't yet know. He scans the plaque, following the roster with his index finger for fear of making a mistake: Emilio Casabets. The boy makes a note of it on his BlackBerry. He checks again: there's no doubt about it. He counts all the pupils in the front row until arriving at the one holding the blackboard; he counts along the names on the plaque again: Emilio Casabets. He goes out of the room, the door closing behind him with the kind of click that denotes heavy wood and a good-quality latch. He could go straight onto Google to search for Casabets – "google" him, a verb Brena would surely deplore – but he would rather leave this place as soon as possible and conduct his search over a coffee in some nearby bar. Back in the hall he thanks the secretary, who's handing some admission forms to a couple. Any luck? the secretary asks. Yes, he says. Now all I need is to track the man down. His name is Emilio Casabets. That doesn't ring a

247

bell. He must not have had sons or grandsons at the school, but we'll certainly have his details here. We keep a register of all leavers with their personal information and a note of their current workplace. It gets consulted a lot – it's useful for contacts. I'd be interested to see that, says the boy. I'm busy at the moment, but if you call me later I'll look it up for you, the secretary says, and hands him a school brochure similar to the one he's just given the couple. You'll find my number in here. Thanks, says the Crime boy, and goes off in search of coffee. His first instinct on finding Casabets' name was to google him. If Jaime Brena had been in his shoes he'd have gone back to the secretary to get more information on that one, he thinks. He can almost hear Brena's voice saying "Legwork, kid, legwork". But, for better or worse, he isn't Jaime Brena.

Two seconds after the Crime boy enters a bar three blocks away from San Jerónimo Mártir College, Jaime Brena is arriving at the newspaper. It's earlier than usual – his working day generally starts an hour later – but he slept badly, woke up at dawn and didn't know what to do, alone, in that apartment. God knows enough time has passed since he stopped living with Irina, but his flat still doesn't feel like home. So he decided to get dressed and start the day. He began wondering about getting a dog again. Waiting on his desk is a cable with today's possible feature piece: a French institute of sexual health, having analysed 250 cases, claims that women who are multi-orgasmic tend to have more pubic hair than women who aren't. Jaime Brena reads it and roars with laughter. He reads it a couple of times more and can't stop laughing, tears coming to his eyes. Then, when he's managed to contain himself, he pictures hundreds of French women screwing behind a one-way mirror while scientists observe and log every orgasm they have. Or fake. And then examining each of them and counting, one strand at a time, how much pubic hair is on each woman's sex. Double-entry table, orgasms in the x column, number of pubes in the y, he says to himself. They're laughing at us, he thinks. And if that's the case, I'm going to laugh at them, too. He types out the cable's basic information and adds: *El Tribuno* had hoped to test the conclusions of this study against the experience of local women, but all the ones we consulted claimed to have abundant pubic hair, so it hasn't been possible to investigate what happens when the reverse applies. He considers titling the piece "In Praise of Big Bushes", then decides that would be too much. Then he also types: The great wave of Italian and Spanish immigration to this country has led to Argentine women becoming sexually active and hirsute down below. He's quite sure that someone will kill his piece before it runs, or at least cut it, edit it. That is, if anyone bothers to read it. In the bustle of the newsroom sometimes pieces written by the very experienced journalists – such as Brena – go through unchecked, so long as they are exactly the right number of characters for the allocated space. He's going to make sure that this one is precisely the right length. He types another title he knows will never run: "An Ode to Pubes", and emails it to Karina Vives for her to read and give him her opinion. He looks at his watch: his shift has only just begun and he's already finished the day's work. He wonders if Nurit or the Crime boy have managed to turn up anything new and looks in his Inbox, but there's nothing from either of them. He calls Comisario Venturini. Impossible to avoid the greeting ceremony – How are you, dear? Well, but poor, Sir – but with that out of the way, he gets straight to the point: Have you found out anything more about Collazo's death? Suicide, Brena, there's not much more to know, says Venturini. But there are indications… Listen to me this time: don't get involved, let it go. I don't understand, Brena says. Then don't understand, says Venturini, just let it go. Forget it, dear. Don't waste energy on this; I assure you that it's not worth it. Look, I've got a lot on here at the moment, but I'll talk to you later. And he hangs up, leaving Brena staring at the handset. He's never known Comisario Venturini to be so evasive, so ungracious. Perhaps Venturini should be thinking about taking voluntary redundancy too, he thinks, and goes outside to smoke his first cigarette. Or rather, his first cigarette of the working day; he's already had one at home and another on the way to the office. He wonders again what Nurit Iscar and the Crime boy are up to. He doesn't know it, but when he finishes the cigarette and goes back to his desk there's going to be an email from the Crime boy in his Inbox containing the name they've been looking for, Emilio Casabets, along with Nurit Iscar's latest dispatch, sent with her express request that he read it and give her his opinion.

Is there really such a thing as "tragic destiny", that unchangeable force which, according to the Greeks, it was hubris to try to oppose, something akin to arrogance or insolent pride? To oppose it, they believed, could only ever be in vain because the journey towards one's fate is as incomprehensible as it is unavoidable.

"What's this woman talking about?" you'll be asking yourselves, not unreasonably.

Well, I am talking about the Chazarreta case. And perhaps also the Gloria Echagüe case. But I am also talking about the deaths of four of Chazarreta's friends, which all took place in the months before and after his death and all as a result of different kinds of accident. At least they seem to be accidents.

Successive deaths in a group of people who are all connected to each other, as these men were, unless clearly planned by one assassin or several, could be ascribed to tragic fate. But the fact that tragic events have taken place in their lives does not preclude those events also serving to conceal a crime by disguising it as another tragedy.

Take the Kennedys. A family whose members were powerful in the fields of economy, politics and government, in the United States, no less. Joseph Kennedy and Rose Fitzgerald had nine children. Their son Joseph Jr died at the age of 29, piloting a plane in the Second World War. John Fitzgerald, President of the United States, was assassinated at the age of 46. Kathleen Agnes died at 28, when the plane in which she was travelling crashed in the French Alps. Robert was assassinated at the Hotel Ambassador, in Los Angeles, at 42, minutes after winning a primary election. One of the grandsons of the clan, John-John, the son of JFK, also died tragically in a plane accident at the age of 38.

Three brothers, a sister and a grandson were either assassinated or died in plane accidents. Could that be read as a coincidence? As fate? As tragic destiny? We try to find explanations for death, and they elude us. Sometimes there is no choice but to live with the discomfort of not understanding why a life has reached its end. Today we still don't know who killed Gloria Echagüe. I realize that many people reading these lines are convinced that they do know, that the murderer was Pedro Chazarreta. I certainly envy them that, because it spares them from the unease I feel. But even if we do not agree on this point, I know that you readers will share my anxiety for some explanation to make sense of Chazarreta's own death. And I, having seen a photograph of his best friends, of whom only one is still alive, feel increasingly uneasy. I ask myself whether the deaths of Luis Collazo, José Miguel Bengoechea, Arturo Gandolfini and Marcos Miranda are the products of fate, of a tragic destiny brought on by their own hubris, or if there is another explanation behind these deaths; a more human, more earthly explanation, to do with people rather than gods, like all crime. An explanation that would terrify me but would also save me from the uneasy feeling that these deaths have no meaning.

Jaime Brena stops reading and thinks: This woman's good, very good. Is that all he's thinking? Then he writes his reply to her email: Excellent work, Betty Boo, very well put. One of these days I'll ask you to lunch at my house. Warmly, Jaime Brena.

24

At three o'clock in the afternoon, back at the *El Tribuno* newsroom and having discarded the scant information he found on Google, the Crime boy calls San Jerónimo Mártir College and asks for the secretary. As it turns out, there isn't much information about Casabets in the register. The most recent entry states that Casabets has for several years been managing a rural establishment in Capilla del Señor, where he also lives. Is there an address, a telephone number or anything? the boy asks. All it says is that the establishment is called "La Colmena", but I'm sure if you google it — Yes, yes, the boy interrupts, thank you.

Its website describes La Colmena as one of the first ranches in the province of Buenos Aires to be adapted for tourism: it can cater for traditional *asado*s, cavalcades, weekend packages, foreign groups and special events. There's a map showing directions. First you take Route 6, then the road to Arroyo de la Cruz, and a few miles beyond the historic centre of Capilla de Señor – so the page promises – signs for La Colmena will start to appear. It doesn't take much for the Crime boy to persuade Jaime Brena to go with him. You bet I can, I've already filed my copy and I doubt anyone will miss me. Are you two abandoning me? Karina Vives asks when she sees them getting ready to leave. Jaime Brena answers with a joke: Don't go off smoking with someone else; you know ours is a monogamous relationship. But the Crime boy doesn't hear Brena's joke because he's thinking about how Karina Vives included him when she referred to "you two". She wasn't only speaking to Jaime Brena but to him as well. He likes that.

Shall we ask Nurit Iscar along? Brena asks the boy as they're getting into the car, and the boy decides to call her and ask. He doesn't get her, though, because as they're setting off towards Capilla del Señor, Nurit is walking through La Maravillosa and, yet again, she's forgotten her mobile. She was distracted as she left the house by the thought that once her latest piece appears in *El Tribuno* she won't be able to walk around these streets so easily. The public naming of residents of this club – in one of the country's highest circulation newspapers – and her suggestion that their deaths conceal a mystery that ought at least to be investigated won't come without a cost. She wonders if the Crime boy or Jaime Brena have found out any more information that will help them reach Chazarreta's missing friend. The only one still alive. Or at least that she believes to be alive. She's surprised that they haven't called her yet, and it's only when she pats her pockets to check for the mobile that she realizes she didn't bring it with her. Just as well, she thinks; it won't do any harm to walk for a while without being connected to anything, to walk aimlessly, even, choosing a path because of the colour of its trees, or the scent of a particular flower, or its silence. She's aware that these ruminations sound a bit sentimental. She always did have a sentimental side, but she used to be better at hiding it. As the years pass one's worst flaws don't deepen exactly; it's more that they finally reveal themselves. You can't keep up the pretence in the way you once could. It's annoying to admit it, but she likes this place, La Maravillosa. If you could forget about the wall encircling it, or all the bureaucracy at the entry gate, or the expression on some neighbours' faces, or that to buy antibiotics you've got to travel at least six miles, that there's no public transport, no corner bars or seven-day-a-week cinemas, you could say that La Maravillosa is a lovely place. She's thinking about all the things it's hard to forget and the reasons why someone chooses one path over another when she realizes that she's in front of Collazo's house. It's strange that there's nothing to mark off the area, nothing like the red tape around Chazarreta's house to bar access. If she wanted, she could easily get to the cobblestone path that passes the tree where Collazo was still hanging yesterday; she could get as far as the tree itself, the exact branch. Cautiously, she starts off along the path, walks as far as the oak and looks upwards, scanning for traces of the rope which had held that lifeless body, for marks, for signs of damage to the tree. There they are: the flayed bark, the white trunk glistening, as though sweating. She imagines Collazo hanging right above the spot where she's standing at that moment. The feet dangling above her head. If there's no longer anyone at the house, if they haven't posted a guard in front of it or surrounded it with plastic tape, it's because they consider this an open and shut case: suicide. She imagines how much it must hurt to hang like that, suspended in the moment between life and death. It must hurt. And she wouldn't know how to tie the knot. Thinking that reminds Nurit that she hasn't been in touch with the transport tycoon's ex-wife about *Untying the Knots*. She ought to call and put her mind at rest, tell her that the manuscript will be ready in a couple of weeks. When she's finished her work here. Soon. She looks up to the tree's crown. No, she wouldn't choose to hang herself from a tree. She wouldn't jump in front of a train or shoot herself, either. It would seem wrong to shatter the body that has been her shelter. She would take pills, for sure, a lot of them, thus easing the transition from sleep to that other state about which we know nothing. Is there a specific method of suicide reserved for each person? If Collazo had committed suicide, is this the one he would have chosen? At the moment that Nurit Iscar is arriving back at her house, the Crime boy and Jaime Brena spot a sign by the road indicating the entrance to the La Colmena ranch and turn off towards it. There's something contrived about the scenery, which is of a neat prettiness that doesn't happen naturally but has to be worked at. They drive on past an area signed *Coaches and Visitor Parking*, and stop in front of the entrance to what must have been the original homestead. Before they have even got out of the car, a woman has come forward to introduce herself as the person in charge. We don't receive visitors on Mondays, she says. We're not visitors, strictly speaking, says Jaime Brena. We're looking for Señor Emilio Casabets. On what business? asks the woman. It's personal, Brena says quickly. We have some mutual acquaintances and we'd like to chat, to talk over a few things. Emilio isn't one for talking, the woman replies automatically, and it sounds as if this is something she often says. Emilio is my husband. He went out riding but he should be back any minute. The woman shows them in and offers them a drink, which they decline. Please don't go to any trouble, Jaime Brena says. He can sense the woman's wariness when she looks at them, as if she doesn't trust them, or as if he and the Crime boy represent some kind of danger to her. He tries to draw her into conversation but she's reticent, giving succinct answers then clamming up, making no effort to continue the exchange. Emilio isn't one for talking and neither is she, Brena thinks. The wait becomes tense. The Crime boy asks if he may take some photographs. The woman says: Yes, you may. And doesn't add a single word more.

Hanging on a brick wall within view is a collection of stirrups. And in a glass cabinet different types of receptacles and gourds for drinking maté. The rugs scattered around the room are all animal hides: cow, sheep, lamb. On a high stool there's a photograph of a horse saddled up and beside it two silver embellished belts typically worn by gauchos and a long knife in its sheath. It doesn't get more Argentine than this, the Crime boy tells himself. All they need now is some *zamba* music, he thinks, and guesses that if it were the weekend there would indeed be *zamba* playing. Behind what appears to be a bar, hanging on a wall which still shows the outline of a door that has been filled in, there's a large shield with the words *Exaltación de la Cruz* embroidered near the top. That does strike the boy as different; it's not something he's seen before. It's not an object he would choose to include if someone told him to draw the elements of a typical farm or ranch. The boy snaps it from several angles. Casabets' wife watches and suddenly seems alert, not to the boy and his photographing but to some noise coming from afar; she cocks her head, like one of those dogs that can hear a sound before their owners. He's coming now, she says, and soon they hear the galloping of a horse. A few minutes later the door opens and a man walks in, dressed from the waist down for the country (gaucho trousers and espadrilles) and from the waist up for the city (a sun-bleached Chemise Lacoste T-shirt). In his hand he carries a shapeless wide-brimmed hat. The man looks at his wife as though nobody else were present and says: Yes? He waits for her to explain who these people are that he neither greets nor even looks at. These gentlemen know some people who know you, and they want to talk to you. And who are these people that know me? Casabets asks, still not looking at them. Luis Collazo, for example, says the Crime boy. Luis Collazo, the man repeats, then walks over to the bar and pours himself a whisky without offering one to them. So Luis Collazo speaks about me and counts me among his acquaintances. The man sits down in an armchair beside the window and crosses his legs, his eyes fixed on the whisky as he swirls it in the glass. The woman looks at him. The Crime boy looks at Jaime Brena, waiting for him to make the decision about what to tell and what not. Brena, seeing that they can't continue in this elusive vein, says: Look, Casabets, I'm going to be honest with you. We know Luis Collazo, but we're not here because he sent us. We're journalists investigating a series of deaths, all of people that you knew. Does anyone still care about the deaths of Gloria Echagüe and Pedro Chazarreta? the man asks. Lots of people care, yes, but I'm not just talking about them. So who else? Gandolfini, who died in a car accident, Bengoechea, who died skiing, and Marcos Miranda, who died in a shooting in New Jersey. Marcos Miranda is dead too? the man asks. Yes, says Brena, and also Luis Collazo, who's just been found hanged. Casabets looks at him impassively, expressionless, as though he hadn't heard him. But he has heard, because he then looks at his wife and makes a face, a barely perceptible smile, and says to her: There's nobody left. She doesn't answer, but it's clear that she knows what her husband is talking about. Nobody left, Casabets says again and grins openly. But Brena corrects him. Yes, there is someone left: you. And he gestures to the Crime boy to hand over the photograph of Chazarreta's friends. What is that? asks the woman, and tries to take it before it reaches her husband. Leave it, he says, let me see. And don't worry, I've already explained to you that there's nothing to worry about. Casabets looks around the room for his glasses then sits back down. He studies the photo and nods several times. We're concerned that the deaths of the men in this photograph were not accidental and that you may be in danger, the Crime boy says. The woman looks anxious. Casabets laughs. He points at himself in the photograph. Nothing can happen to this guy here; he died a long, long time ago, if I'm not mistaken, a few days after this photograph was taken. Emilio, says the woman, perhaps — but he cuts her short: Perhaps nothing. Have you also failed to understand that the man in this photo is dead? No, I understand, but — she begins and he interrupts her again: If everyone in this photograph is dead, it's because they deserved it. Apart from this boy, he says, pointing to himself again. He didn't deserve to die, but they killed him anyway. One day someone was going to get him justice. Justice for what? Brena asks. The man scowls at him: Don't you listen? he says, and knocks back the rest of the whisky. Who got justice? the boy asks. It must have been God, the man replies. It seems to me that these deaths are the result of a man's actions, not God's, Brena ventures. If it was a man, who could it have been? Casabets considers the question, not wanting to enter into Jaime Brena's game but unable to avoid it, either. He takes the photograph back and examines it more closely. He looks thoughtful, but not worried. If it was necessary to get justice then there must have been a crime; what was the crime, and who got justice? Brena presses. If it wasn't God…, says Casabets, who seems to have accepted the challenge and, still looking at the photograph, starts to smile as if he finally knows the answer. If not God… Who? Brena tries again. The man knows; they can tell he knows. Brena is sure, now they've got God out of the way, that he knows. This photograph was taken on a date very close to that day, Casabets says. Which day? That's enough, says the woman, please don't take this any further. Leave them alone, Casabets tells her, let them. Then he looks at the Crime boy and says:

How many men are in this photo? Six, the boy replies. Wrong, says Casabets. And what about you? He turns to Brena. You have a more experienced eye – how many do you think there are? I'm sorry, even to my more experienced eye there are only six. What a shame, says Casabets. You're missing the most important thing: seeing what isn't there. On that day, the day that I'm not going to bring back to mind, we were all there, he says, the ones you see and the ones you can't see. The same as in this photo. Casabets throws it onto the table and continues: Sometimes the witnesses get the worst of it; the pain can be more intense even for them than the victim. They feel so guilty for not having been able to avert the tragedy, for not having done anything. The man stands up. How could I have forgotten about him? About who? Brena asks. Either he or I was going to kill them... and I'm a coward. Casabets doesn't go on. He knocks back his whisky in one go, leaves the glass on the bar and acts as though he hadn't heard Jaime Brena's question. He looks up at the shield of the Exaltación de la Cruz and stays in this attitude for a moment, with his back to them, contemplating it. Or perhaps he's contemplating the boarded-up door. Who do you think embroidered this? he asks. Then he turns to face them, smiles and says: Isn't it incredible? What is that shield exactly? Jaime Brena asks. It's the shield of Exaltación de la Cruz, the region to which this town, Capilla del Señor, belongs. In 1940 the mayor, a man called Botta, commissioned a shield to depict local historical events. A shield is like a heart, don't you think? Two atria, two ventricles. I was going to study medicine, I was going to be a doctor, but that was before... Casabets seems waylaid for a moment by this thought that he doesn't share, then takes up his story again: It was the municipal secretary José Peluso who came up with this design. What's in the left atrium? asks Casabets, pointing to the shield's first quarter. It's a cross, says Jaime Brena. Yes, very good, a cross, representing the founding of the town by Francisco Casco. And in the right atrium? he asks the Crime boy, in the tone of a secondary school teacher. Is it a wagon – or a cart? A wagon, yes, the wagon that carried the image of the Virgin Mary and that came to a stop at the other end of Route 6, so giving rise to the legend of the Virgin of Luján. Because, in truth, all stories are legends – yours, mine, the Virgin Mary's, right? he says, looking at Brena. I agree with you there, Brena says. Left ventricle, two ears of corn representing the fertility of the land, and right ventricle, a pen, because this is where Rivadavia founded the first state primary school in 1821. What else can you see? he asks. Give us a clue, says Jaime Brena. A silver thread, says Casabets and points. See this grey line separating the left and right sides? That's a stream, the Arroyo de la Cruz. Emilio Casabets sighs and seems tired. I'm going to have a nap, he says, walking over to his wife. He kisses her on the lips. Don't worry, he says, don't worry. It's all over now. And he goes off towards the bedrooms, calling back to her: Go with them as far as the cattle gate. The woman stands up. I'll take you now, she says. Jaime Brena looks at her for a moment. Can you explain any of this to us? There's nothing to explain, she replies, my husband has already said everything he had to say. Come, I'll take you up to the cattle gate. Jaime Brena tries again: Look, I respect your and your husband's silence on this, but the truth is that he may be in danger. Why wouldn't the person who killed your husband's friends not come looking for him next? They weren't his friends, she says, bitterly, and nobody will come for him because Emilio didn't do anything. So what did the others do? The woman says nothing. Now it's the Crime boy who says: Somebody who kills five people or who arranges for them to be killed doesn't think like us, doesn't use the same logic. We're talking about a murderer. Do you really believe, Señora Casabets, that you can know what's going through the mind of a murderer? Do you think there's always an explanation for murder that's comprehensible to the rest of us? The woman begins to look doubtful. Seeing this, Jaime Brena gestures to the Crime boy to keep up the pressure. If the murderer thinks that your husband could give him away, the boy says, don't you think he might come for him even if he hasn't done anything? The woman looks at him for a moment, then says: Wait for me at the cattle gate, I'll follow behind.

Five minutes after Jaime Brena and the Crime boy get to the cattle gate, Casabets' wife arrives in an old Ford Ranger with mud-caked wheels. When she sees Jaime Brena smoking, she asks him for a cigarette: Emilio doesn't like me smoking, she says, taking her first drag. Do you also believe that my husband could be in danger? she asks Brena. On my honour, Señora, I truly believe that he could be, Brena says intently. She thinks for a moment, takes two or three more puffs on the cigarette and then begins to tell them what she knows.

Little Ranch was a group of friends in their late teens, the ones you saw in that photograph. They had fun just like any other boys that age, but they also used to enjoy being provocative. That was their greatest pleasure: bothering people. The woman draws deeply on the cigarette. Jaime Brena and the Crime boy wait for her. She exhales the smoke and continues: Whenever the Little Ranch boys arrived at a party or a get-together everything would stop and soon the party would begin to revolve around them. Maybe because the people there admired them, maybe because they were scared of them. They were a gang of "bad boys", and if you couldn't be part of the gang, you certainly wanted it on your side. And Emilio, even though he was scared of them, wanted to belong. The woman takes two more drags then throws the cigarette butt on the ground and crushes it with the tip of her shoe. Before any new member could be accepted into the gang, she says, the candidate had to submit to an initiation ceremony: break into the carriage of an abandoned train, drink urine, walk down the most godforsaken street in the dark, go into a graveyard at midnight. But when it came to Emilio, Chazarreta asked for more. The woman falls silent now, and it's clear that she isn't pausing but saying that the story ends there, or that she wants to end it there with those fateful words: Chazarreta asked for more. Her eyes are red with anger. She asks for another cigarette. Jaime Brena passes her the packet, waits for her to take one and put it in her mouth, then lights it for her. The woman still says nothing. What did they ask of him? Brena prompts. She continues with difficulty: It wasn't a request as such; it's not what they asked of him but what they did to him, she says, and her voice breaks. Forgive me, but I need to ask: what did they do to him? Brena says. Don't make me say it, the woman begs, her lips pressed together in rage. Brena stares into her eyes, trying to gauge if he should say this or not, trying to ascertain whether the woman really wants silence or for someone to say the words aloud once and for all, for someone to find words to describe what happened so that it will hurt less, if such a thing is possible. Then Jaime Brena makes his decision and says: Chazarreta raped him. The woman tightens her jaw and tears start to roll down her cheeks, big, hot tears, shed for someone else's pain. Then she corrects him: Not just Chazarreta – all of them. And once she's said this, she really does weep with abandon. The words and the weeping get mixed up. All five of them, she seems to say between sobs, all five of them raped him. Though inevitable, the woman's distress make them uncomfortable. The Crime boy moves as though to comfort her, but Brena stops him with a gesture and mouths the words: let her cry. When she's managed to calm down, she continues: We've been married thirty years, but I knew nothing about it; he never told me, never. He told me only recently, one night not long after Gloria Echagüe was killed. He couldn't tell me before, you see. Then these people started appearing on the news, in the papers, in magazines, and the memory of that horror which had been dead and buried came back to him. The woman dries her tears, breathes deeply and makes an effort to speak calmly, in spite of what she has to say. He told me everything, how they took it in turns to penetrate him, he told me all the details, the smell of the place, the beating, the shouting, his face scraping against the brick wall, the pain, the laughter and then the shame, the silence. He made me promise that we'd never speak about it again. Emilio had never told anyone, do you understand, not even his parents. He never could. She starts to cry again. How can somebody keep something like that quiet for so long? He had buried everything, he'd killed the boy he was and been reborn as someone different, as far as he could; as another person. That's how I knew him, as another person. I'm never going to know how he was before, at the time of that photograph. When these people reappeared, it brought back all the dead memories and didn't resuscitate the Emilio who had died, but instead reminded him that he was dead. He looked for them, all of them – he needed to look for them, he spoke to them, he even met Miranda when he was on a visit to this country. They denied everything. As if it had never happened. As if he were mad. Emilio wanted only for them to recognize the damage they had done, for them to say sorry, but no: the bastards wouldn't even give him that, they wouldn't make even the smallest atonement. That was a very hard blow for my husband. It was then that he thought of buying this house and land. It wasn't for sale but he set his sights on it, made the owners a very good offer and got it. I didn't want it, I fought him all the way, but eventually I realized that I wasn't going to be able to stop him. It had to be this farm. This and no other. Why this place in particular? the Crime boy asks, almost dreading the reply that he can already feel coming. Years ago this was the Chazarreta family's farm, the woman says. Her chin trembles, but she doesn't want to give in to the tears; she contains herself and speaks through the tremors: The place where they raped my husband, the place where they killed the man he had been until that day, for ever. After the others had denied everything, he came here, he went back to the basement where they had violated him. He needed to confront those mute witnesses, the walls, the bricks. He needed confirmation that he was not mad. And there it was. The same place, same smell, same damp. We bought the farm and soon afterwards we came to live here. He spent a whole week holed up in there, not speaking to anyone, barely eating. And when he came out, he bricked up the door himself, the one that's hidden behind the Exaltación de la Cruz shield. He covered it over for ever. Since that day he's never spoken another word about what happened and he's never left the farm except to go into town with me, to the bank or the doctor, then back. Now the woman does cry again. The Crime boy gets a bottle of water from the car and offers it to her. She drinks, then awkwardly dries her eyes. I knew nothing. I lived alongside him and yet I knew nothing until the cursed day Gloria Echagüe was killed and they all came crawling out of the woodwork. Do you know who your husband believes to be the murderer? No, and I don't think he'd tell me; he won't talk about it again. Try to get him to talk anyway, Brena urges. I swore to him that I would never raise the subject again, she says. But this is a case of *force majeure*, he insists. I don't know if I'll be able to. If you can, if he happens to give you any information that you think could be useful to us, please call me, says Jaime Brena, and he gives her his card. And if you discover anything that may endanger my husband's life, tell me, too, the woman asks. Don't worry, you can be sure that we will.

For a few miles they drive in silence, not because they have nothing to say but because they can't say it. It's getting dark and in the rear-view mirror the Crime boy sees the sun, still blazing, about to set. Why would he have wanted to live there? he asks, only once they have left the Pan-American Highway and are on the road that leads to La Maravillosa. I don't know, says Brena, I really don't. I have a theory, the boy admits. Can I say something awful, even though it's not politically correct? Go ahead, I'm sick of political correctness. Sometimes I think women are more equipped to cope with something like that than we are, says the boy, that they fear rape but also have more awareness of it. Somebody, at some point in their lives, has warned them that a man can hurt them, that they need to be careful, that they should avoid places that are dangerous or dark or close to the tracks – I don't know, all those things that my mother used to say to my sister and never to me. Men don't talk about stuff like that, it doesn't belong to us, nobody warns us that we could also be sexually assaulted or raped so, when it happens, we're completely lost, we go to pieces or we feel dead, like Casabets did, because what's happened could never happen, not to us, and so we even doubt our own perception: what happened didn't happen, it's impossible, it isn't real. For Casabets, the fact that they lied to him so many years later, that they made him doubt what he had gone through, that the men who had raped him continued to deny that what had happened, happened, must have affected him like a second rape. First they raped his body, and then his mind and his memory. And his pain. He couldn't heal the first rape, but he could heal the second by going to the place where the outrage took place, recognizing the walls, finding those complicit witnesses, silent and faithful, recovering those memories that he had tried to kill for years. In order then to kill them himself, this time as a deliberate act, his own decision, to wall them in behind a door and hang a shield over it, a shield that looks like a wounded heart crossed by a silver thread. The boy stops talking then and Brena looks over at him. Am I talking crap? the Crime boy asks. No, you're speaking the truth and you put it beautifully, with feeling, almost poetically. You're going to be a good writer one day, kid, if you read a little more, one day you'll really write something.

When they get to the entrance gate, they don't care about the guards wasting their time or about the different controls through which they have to pass. Not today. Today there's no room for arguments or even irritation. The Crime boy complies with everything they ask of him. And Jaime Brena waits without getting annoyed. When they arrive at Nurit Iscar's house, she's waiting for them on the gravel drive. One look at the men tells her all she needs: You look as if you've been hit by a truck. She makes coffee while they tell her everything. Is there no possibility that the murderer is Casabets himself? Nurit asks. No, I've totally ruled that out, Brena says. All my years of seeing murderers and victims have taught me something, and that man isn't capable of murdering anyone. Besides, if we believe his wife, Casabets hasn't left the farm in three years, the Crime boy adds. His reaction to the deaths of Miranda and Collazo seemed genuine, as did the fact that he made no attempt to seem the slightest bit sad about that, or about the deaths of the other members of the group. Now I see why Collazo was more worried about the truth getting out than he was about the possibility that he might also be killed, says Nurit. Yes, it makes sense now, Jaime Brena agrees, and asks the boy to take out the photograph again and show it to her. The key is in this picture; I saw that in his face. Casabets says that there is a seventh person out of shot, and he implied that that person, besides being a witness to what happened, is also the murderer. Have you got a magnifying glass? Brena asks. Perhaps there's some detail too small to see, like a foot or a hand hidden behind one of them. Nurit doesn't answer; she doesn't know whether or not there is a magnifying glass in the house, nor does she care – she's intent on the image in front of her. Have you seen something? Brena asks. Yes, you've seen something, he answers himself. It's not what I'm seeing, she corrects him. Hasn't it occurred to you that what we're looking for may not be hidden behind them but in front? Where in front? says Jaime Brena. How do you mean, in front? asks the Crime boy. A photograph is testimony to something real, and the witness is the photographer. There's always a photographer. He's the seventh man, says Nurit. The photographer, Brena repeats. We have to find out who took this picture, says the Crime boy, we can put pressure on Casabets' wife to tell us. We don't need to ask anyone, says Jaime Brena. I know who took this photograph. Who? asks Nurit. Roberto Gandolfini: he went everywhere with them, they let him tag along but he didn't belong to the group. He took this photo. Are you sure? Nurit asks. Almost, says Brena. The mother used to make his half-brother take him everywhere, even on the school-leavers' trip. She made him into a kind of hobble. Can you imagine how fondly those guys would have looked upon the boy? I can well imagine, says the Crime boy, and he'd have had to endure them, too. I'm convinced that he was also at the Chazarretas' farm that night, says Brena. He is the witness. The avenger. But would the pain of witnessing the barbarities they carried out really have been so great that it warranted killing all of them? the Crime boy asks. What constitutes a sufficient motive for murder, and what doesn't, is a question that has no logical answer for us, kid, Brena says. If it was him, that would also explain why all the news stories about Miranda's death in New Jersey only broke a few hours after he told you about it, says the Crime boy. He knew about it before anyone else. What I don't understand is why he said that the sixth friend was called Vicente Gardeu. Gandolfini knew very well who the sixth friend was and who Vicente Gardeu was. He was sending a warning to Brena, says Nurit; if he got close to the truth, he wanted him to know. Know what? the boy asks. Who he was getting involved with. Gandolfini went to that meeting to size you up, to see who it was who's going around asking questions about him and his victims, Nurit Iscar concludes. Then, looking at Jaime Brena, she says: He wanted you to know that he knows, that he was already on to you that time you met in the bar. He knew who you were and why you wanted to see him. He was putting out a warning. Or perhaps it was bravado, says Jaime Brena, a way of bragging about what he had done. It was more than that, says Nurit. I think he meant to threaten you. The three of them sit in silence, nobody refuting Nurit's theory. What next? the Crime boy asks after a while. So far we have conjectures, says Jaime Brena, but we may not be far from the truth. Gandolfini is a powerful businessman, with enough money to pay a hitman, or several of them. He could have taken out a contract for his brother and friends to be tidily dispatched, he could have contracted someone to kill each of them in the most suitable manner. And if that was the case, we'll have our confirmation tomorrow, Brena concludes. What's happening tomorrow? the Crime boy asks. I'm going to drop in at his office and run our theory by him. You're mad, says Nurit. Didn't I just say that the guy was threatening you and you plan to turn up there, just like that? Don't think about it, Brena, the boy agrees, he's a dangerous guy. Not to me; why would he do anything to me? Because you know. I don't think he cares about that; after all, we've got no proof. He warned you off that evening in the bar, he threatened you, Nurit insists. But he didn't kill me. He's known that I know for a while and he hasn't done anything to me, Brena says. I don't think it's sensible for you to confront him. To say what, to confirm what? says the Crime boy. Jaime Brena interrupts him: It's my job, kid, he says firmly. The boy looks worried, Nurit too. It's crazy for you to go, she says, he's waiting for you. It's my job, Brena repeats. The boy looks at him, hesitates, then says: No, it's not your job, it's mine now. You're not on Crime any more. Jaime Brena is not only surprised by the boy's retort, but disarmed, almost offended. It's not as if he'd forgotten that he no longer works on Crime, but these last few days with the boy and Nurit Iscar he's enjoyed the illusion that, despite everything, despite the transfer, despite Rinaldi, despite the stupid reports he has to read and rework, he's been back where he most wants to be. But no. It really was only an illusion. Jaime Brena looks at Nurit Iscar but she says nothing, and it's clear by her silence that she endorses what the boy has just said, even if only as a means to protect him. He shakes his head a couple of time, sighs, seems about to say something then thinks better of it. Then he opens his wallet, takes out the card that Gandolfini gave him a few days ago and tosses it onto the table. If it's your job now then there's the address, he says to the boy. If you've got the balls for it. Then he puts away his wallet, puts on his jacket and says: I wish you both luck. Where are you going? Nurit asks. Home, he says. How, though? I'll walk to the gate and call a taxi or a minicab. Don't be an arse, says the boy, I'll take you home. I am an arse, agreed, says Brena, but sometimes being an arse isn't such a bad thing, if it means maintaining your dignity. And dignity is important on those occasions when everything around you is shit. Jaime Brena makes the gesture of tipping an imaginary hat, this time only for Nurit Iscar's benefit, then leaves the room. The boy is fretful. I just wanted to protect him, he says. I know that, says Betty Boo, and Brena knows it too. He knows very well. But he's pig-headed and he thinks he's immortal, which isn't a good combination. So what next? the boy asks again. I don't know, Nurit says, I still don't know. Perhaps we need a few hours to think things over. Let's get some sleep and then decide what to do tomorrow afternoon. As Brena said, we only have conjectures, however plausible. What do you reckon? I think that's a good plan, says the Crime boy. Come to the kitchen, says Nurit, and have another coffee before you hit the road. She shows him the way. You go and plug in the coffee maker while I draw the curtains; I'll be down in a minute, she says. The boy nods and goes out. But she doesn't do what she said. Instead she walks back into the room, picks up the card Jaime Brena threw onto the table with Gandolfini's address, reads it, tucks it into a trouser pocket. Only then does she go to the kitchen to make coffee.

25

At eleven o'clock the next morning, the minicab used by the newspaper comes to pick Nurit Iscar up from La Maravillosa. The night before she had asked if it could be earlier, but the taxi driver reminded her that he lived in Lanús and that from there it was a "nightmare journey". Nurit found herself considering this use of a noun as an adjective. She wondered if it should, strictly speaking, be a "nightmarish journey", or if it would be better to invert the phrase and add an article: "it's the journey of nightmares". She can't decide. While she's lost in pointless disquisitions about the use of language (ever since childhood, she's concentrated on words as a way to ward off anxiety and not think about what's really bothering her) the minicab driver is warming to his own theme: Do you know what Avenida Pavón is like at this time of day? She doesn't know what it's like, but she can imagine. In fact there is no reason for Nurit to feel hurried, other than nerves and a fear that the Crime boy may ring to ask for Gandolfini's business card, which Jaime Brena left and that he forgot to take. She's asked Anabella to come to the house again for a few hours and leave it looking spotless; although their arrangement was that she would work only on the weekends, she imagines that she won't be in La Maravillosa much longer and before leaving she wants to be sure that everything is as she found it. Or better than she found it. She's got her mobile in her bag in

272

case of emergencies, but it's switched off: she doesn't want Jaime Brena or the boy to find her or they'll try to stop her, as she did them.

At the barrier, the driver hands back the card he was given upon entering the compound, then the guard checks the boot – "Boot please?" – and they are out. It's always easier to get out than in, says the driver. And again Nurit finds herself latching onto something as abstract as a sentence, an eight-word observation and wondering if this would make a good title for her next piece (perhaps her last piece?) from La Maravillosa. "It's always easier to get out than in."

Just as the car is exiting La Maravillosa on its way to a meeting with Gandolfini, the Crime boy is leaving his house to set off for the newspaper. It upsets him to think he's dam-aged his relationship with Jaime Brena, but he had to stop him, whatever it took. Perhaps he should have found another way to do it, explaining his reasons better rather than resort-ing to cheap shots, and especially without mentioning his banishment from the Crime section from which, as the boy now knows, Jaime Brena should never have been forced out. But yesterday the only thing that came to mind was: "No, it's not your job, it's mine now. You're not on Crime any more." Of course, now that it's too late he can think of a hundred better ways to put it. He could even have suggested that they go to see Gandolfini together. He was scared, though; he sensed that Jaime Brena was hurtling towards disaster. He had to be firm. But – and he can't forgive himself for this – he knows that as well as being firm, he was cruel.

As the minicab carrying Nurit Iscar passes through the tollbooth, the boy is getting into a taxi and Jaime Brena is leaving his house, having decided to walk to work. It's twenty blocks and he isn't in the best shape, but he feels like walking. He needs to walk. To think. Waiting on a corner at a red light, he finds himself sharing the kerb with a dog-walker. And with his pack of canines: a confusion of leads and barks. That's something he'd never do – have a dog then get someone else to take it out, in the middle of an inevitably resentful pack. Jaime Brena would like a dog so that he could take it out for walks on its lead. And take it to some park, and have it wag its tail when he got home. It's the only kind of company that he could stand to have living with him. He has gradually been turning into a solitary man, Jaime Brena thinks as he observes a Dalmatian looking at him with its head to one side and its tail wagging amiably. It occurs to him that he was solitary even before separating from Irina. Solitude comes from within and can be experienced even in the company of others, he believes. Of course those other people, if they aren't solitary like you, end up losing patience, as Irina did. And he believes it is that, his solitary nature, paradoxically, that links him to other people. The solitude that bonds. Or that joins. A fellowship of loners. With Karina Vives, for example. With the Crime boy, though he doesn't even want to see him today. With Nurit Iscar. Nurit, he'd be willing to bet, is a solitary woman, even if she is surrounded by friends. A loner to the core; you can tell. Just as you can tell with him. Being solitary is constitutional, a matter of nature, and not something that changes with the passage of time or whenever the house fills up with people. If he and Nurit Iscar had something, some day, if they got together as some kind of couple, they would still continue to be loners at heart. Happy, perhaps, enjoying each other's company, tenderly demonstrative towards one another, with great sex, but still two loners. And that doesn't sound so bad to him, he almost thinks that may be the kind of relationship he needs: to share what is left of his life with a woman who's as solitary as he is. Only a solitary person is able to be at the side of another without feeling the need, the obligation to possess him or to change him. And what's suddenly brought on these thoughts of Nurit? I'd better stick to the dog, he tells himself.

Gandolfini's office is in a tower block in the Catalinas business district, on Avenida Leandro N. Alem, one of several clustered around one side of the Sheraton Hotel. To avoid going the long way round, the minicab driver leaves her on the other side of the road and tells her that he'll wait for her there, but that if she doesn't see him when she comes out it will be because someone asked him to move, in which case he'll drive around the block and come back. Or maybe around several blocks, because a lot of the streets are pedestrianized, you know? Any problems, just call the mobile, the man says. I'll call if I need to, she promises. As Nurit Iscar crosses the street, the wind almost knocks her sideways. She hadn't realized that it was such a blustery day. Perhaps it wasn't. She's always found it curious how strongly the wind blows in this part of Buenos Aires, and she's no longer persuaded that the proximity of the sea is the only cause of this climatic phenomenon. She remembers a friend of Paula Sibona – an actress who's been living in Spain for some time now – who, whenever she felt depressed, would put on a full-skirted dress, stand on the corner of Leandro Alem and Córdoba and wait for the wind to produce a Marilyn Monroe-like effect on her skirt that lifted her spirits and seemed also to lift those of passers-by. Since Betty Boo is wearing black trousers and a white shirt, the worst the wind can do is ruffle her curls, which she keeps trying to pat down: a reflex action, and hopeless in these conditions.

Gandolfini's building is all polarized glass. Black when looked at from outside. There's as much security here as in La Maravillosa. No sooner have you got through the revolving door than you're stopped by one of the guards sitting behind a long desk and asked for your name, ID and the floor and office that you want to visit. When it's her turn, Nurit says that she wants to see Señor Gandolfini, but can't remember which floor his office is on. Floor 17, the guard says and asks: Have you got an appointment? Yes, of course, she lies. The man writes down her details on a form and passes her a visitor tag; it seems strange to Nurit that this stage of security should be so easy to breach, requiring only a brazen lie. Although having the right face, skin colour and clothes (and the fact that she's a woman) also surely play a part. The security guard tells her that she must leave her ID at the front desk until she hands back the tag on leaving the building. And although Nurit doesn't like leaving the document with anyone, she hands it over. Before passing through a turnstile she also has to show her bag (like the maids at La Maravillosa, although in this case a different fear is at work), walk through a metal detector and then press her visitor tag against a reader. Everyone's identities have been reduced to a given number of cards for different uses, she thinks. She feels as though she's in an American film, entering the CIA, or in the series *24*, going into the building where Jack Bauer works. It seems excessive, especially bearing in mind that all these measures are to protect, among others – if she, the Crime boy and Jaime Brena suspect rightly – a murderer. Someone who pays for other people to be assassinated to order. Like commissioning a suit from a tailor. A made-to-measure murder, she thinks, and wonders if this would be a good title for her next novel. Or perhaps *The Tailor of Death* or *Death XXL*. But is she really thinking about writing another novel? She stops in front of the lifts and, when the door opens, gets in among a group composed of men in impeccable suits, women in office clothes and high heels of the kind she stopped wearing years ago, a motorbike courier holding his helmet on one arm and assorted packages under the other, and a woman holding the hand of a little boy who asks: Is this where Daddy works? Nurit gets off on the seventeenth floor and looks around for a secretary. She finds one behind a frosted glass door on which in white letters, difficult to make out, are carved the words *RG Business Developers*. She introduces herself to the secretary: My name is Nurit Iscar, I'm a writer and I've come to interview Señor Roberto Gandolfini for a book of journalism I'm putting together. The secretary looks down at her diary: I can't find a note of any appointment with you, could you repeat your name, please? Nurit Iscar, just as it sounds – but how strange, they told me at the publisher's that everything was arranged. Which publisher? Nobody has spoken to me about this. They probably spoke to Señor Gandolfini directly and he forgot to let you know. I don't think so; he always tells me. Well, would you be kind enough to ask if he can see me anyway, even though it isn't in the diary? I doubt that will be possible, Señor Gandolfini has a very full day. Could you try? The woman looks doubtful. Please could you try? Nurit presses. You said Nurit Iscar, is that right? the secretary asks. Yes, she says, and tell him that Señor Collazo suggested I speak to him, don't forget that – to mention Luis Collazo. The woman dials through to her boss and there's an exchange at the end of which she repeats: Yes, yes, Luis Collazo. She hangs up and says, He'll see you in fifteen minutes. Please take a seat in reception, and as soon as his meeting is over he'll call you in. OK, says Nurit Iscar, and feels as though her legs may buckle. There is nothing she wants more than to be here at this moment. But there is nothing she wants less, either. She thinks of Jaime Brena and the Crime boy, of what they will say when they find out that she came here. She imagines the dressing-down. On the coffee table in front of the chairs there's a copy of *Newsweek*, a Sunday newspaper magazine that's two months old and the directory of an Argentine business association. She closes her eyes and waits.

At the very moment that Nurit Iscar is closing her eyes, Jaime Brena is arriving, sweating and out of breath, in the *El Tribuno* newsroom. The Crime boy, who sees him come in, watches his movements closely, trying to read into them whether or not Brena is still annoyed with him. Brena issues a general greeting and sits down at his desk. He's still annoyed, the boy thinks. Jaime Brena settles into his chair, rubs his face and stretches his neck a little while the computer starts up. There on the screen, waiting for him, is the wire story for his next piece: a clinical study in Lyons, France, has found that people who are allergic to penicillin are 64 per cent more likely to divorce before they turn forty than people who are not. Can someone really have gone to the trouble of studying the link between penicillin and divorce among the under-forties? He reads it once, twice, three times. Then he shuts down the computer, takes out the voluntary redundancy papers from his drawer and starts to fill them in. The Crime boy comes over to his desk. Jaime Brena quickly turns the forms over so that he won't see what he's doing. Have you got a minute? the boy asks. Jaime Brena looks at him without saying anything; the boy, on the other hand, says: Sorry. Jaime Brena still says nothing. Sorry, the boy says again. I was scared that you would go and see Gandolfini without considering the risks and it seemed like the only way to stop you. OK, Jaime Brena says. Anything else? The boy, wrong-footed, makes an effort and continues: Yes, there is something else. Do you remember that question you asked me back when you first started teaching me about crime reporting? No, says Jaime Brena, I asked you a lot of questions; I've got no idea what the first one was. It was the most important one of all: you asked me who I wanted to be like, who my role model was, but I didn't know at that point. I'd forgotten that, Brena says. Well, I know now, the boy says, and waits to be asked who it is that he would most like to be like. But Brena doesn't ask him, so he gives the answer anyway: I want to be like you – like Jaime Brena. Brena keeps looking at him, with no other reaction than a barely perceptible tremor of the lower lip, like an involuntary pulse; if the boy knew him better he would understand that if Brena's lower lip quivers this way it's because these words have struck some part in his body, we don't know which, but somewhere he still has feeling. Shall we go to see Gandolfini together? says the boy. What? Let's go together, it'll be less risky. We definitely can't wimp out of it, but this way we can look out for each other. Shall we go? And Jaime Brena, as though this were just another workday and yesterday's altercation, the half-completed redundancy forms, even the boy's declaration of admiration, had never existed, asks: Where is it? Did you look at the card I gave you? The boy curses: I left it at Nurit's house, like an idiot. Call and ask her for directions, Brena suggests. The boy does as he's told: It's switched off, he says. Why does that woman even have a mobile? Brena grumbles, as though he weren't every bit as difficult to reach by mobile as she is, then says: Call her house. I don't have the number; I'll go and ask Rinaldi's secretary for it. The boy goes off and comes back along the corridor moments later, talking on the phone to Anabella. The Señora has gone out, she's telling him. A minicab came to pick her up; why don't you call her on the mobile? It's switched off. I don't suppose you know where she was going? She said she had to see someone in town, I think. The boy strokes his jawbone

279

several times, then claps his hand over his mouth, shaking his head, as though not wanting to believe the direction of his own thoughts. Could you do me a favour, Anabella? Go and see if there's a card that I left behind yesterday on the table in the living room, a card with the name Roberto Gandolfini on it. The woman goes to have a look, confirming his suspicion when she returns to the phone: There's nothing on the table in the living room. Thanks, says the boy, hanging up and returning to Jaime Brena's desk. Nurit Iscar is on her way to Gandolfini's office, he says, assuming she isn't there already. What a nightmare that woman is, Brena groans. Did you speak to her? No, but going on what the cleaner told me, I'm sure that's where she's gone. She must be mad, the boy says. Only as mad as us, Brena points out, but a lot quicker off the blocks. And for all that he admires his colleague, he fears for her, too: We have to get to her. I don't like to think what she may be getting into. Look on the Internet and see if you can find an address for Gandolfini's company. I've already looked, the boy replies, and there's nothing. It's as if it didn't exist. Brena thinks for a moment, then says: Ask Rinaldi's secretary which minicab service Nurit uses; if it's the one the newspaper always uses then we're safe, if not…

A few minutes later the boy speaks to the minicab driver who took Nurit Iscar to Gandolfini's office, but the man doesn't know the exact address, only where he's waiting for her, illegally parked, and that she crossed Leandro N. Alem a little before the Córdoba turn-off and that she went into one of the identikit buildings in that area: Could have been any one of them, how should I know if it was two storeys higher or two storeys lower, they all look the same, he says. And that he has to wait for her there. No, he already said that he doesn't know which building she went into. No, she's going to call him when she's finished. Please stay right where you are, the boy says, we're on our way over. And so they are.

By the time the Crime boy and Jaime Brena are leaving the newspaper office, Nurit Iscar is already sitting opposite Roberto Gandolfini. The view through the immense window behind him is so beautiful that it inspires ambivalence: on one hand, the limpid scene attracts her and she can't stop her eyes drifting towards it – the river, the boats that seem not to be moving, the reflected sun. On the other, the picture doesn't fit with the conversation that she will have to have here with Gandolfini. If this were a Nurit Iscar novel, she'd lose the window and that view. The man is also very different to how she had imagined him: shorter, less portly. His clothes are good quality, but a little dated. If she didn't suspect what she suspects of him, she would not be frightened of the man sitting opposite her. He would strike her as inoffensive. So you'd like to interview me for a book that you're writing? he asks while playing with a ballpoint pen, pressing it at one end to make the nib intermittently appear or disappear. Yes, she says, I'm grateful to you for seeing me despite the confusion about our appointment. Gandolfini nods, with a tightening of his lips, then says: What's your book about? Well, I'm investigating companies that offer special or unusual services. Ah, in that case, I'm afraid I'm going to disappoint you. There's nothing extraordinary about my companies, he says, but she detects a note of false humility. Perhaps not for you, because you work with them every day, but for the readers there is. The man looks at her and she knows that he's studying her. My secretary said that Luis Collazo recommended you come and see me. Yes, shortly before his death, says Nurit, coming straight to the point and watching Gandolfini's face for a reaction. But he says, almost without expression: A tragedy; I heard that he hanged himself. He was found hanged, she corrects him; and yes, it was a tragedy. And which of the companies I manage did you want to ask me about? About the one that can have people eliminated on request, she says, making an effort to look impassive. Eliminated from where? he asks. Eliminated from the world. Gandolfini smiles: And what makes you think I have a company that organizes that? It may not be yours, you may only have contracted it. Once again, Señora, I don't know what has led you to think that. Certain circumstances and coincidences. Circumstances and coincidences can lead to the wrong conclusions. It's striking that all the members of the group known as "Little Ranch", including your brother, have died in very particular circumstances; I take it you remember Little Ranch? When she mentions the name, she looks to see if it makes Gandolfini uneasy in any way, if there is any flicker of recognition. But there's still no sign of any such unease, not that she can detect. Yes, of course I remember; in fact, somewhere round here I think I still have a photograph of them that I came across a while ago, he says, and Nurit knows which photograph he's talking about and guesses that he came across it in Chazarreta's photo frame and took it as the spoils of war. Why should something as mundane as a car accident particularly concern you? Gandolfini asks. Because everyone feared exactly that: that your brother might die in a car accident. Well then, he should have paid more attention to those fears and learned to drive more slowly; my brother never listened to anyone, and the greatest challenge in his life seemed to be breaking his own record for speed. People say he drove very well, says Nurit. Very well, but much too fast, Gandolfini shoots back. And with absolutely no respect for the law, endangering not only himself but also other people. So you believe that I did something to cause or bring about his death on the road?

You or someone that you hired, yes, that's what I believe, Nurit asserts. I cut his brakes, for example. For example. You've got a prodigious imagination, says Gandolfini, smiling. And I got Collazo to hang himself and Bengoechea to kill himself skiing, he says. She adds: You had Miranda killed by someone disguised as an alienated gunman, and you had Chazarreta killed in the same way his wife had died, with his throat slit. Each death took place in the way it should, in the way people would have expected. Gandolfini nods: Now that you say it, yes, I'll give you that: each man got the death he deserved. He gets up, walks over to the window and looks out at the river. Without turning round, he says: Which doesn't mean to say that I had anything to do with their deaths. Nor that anybody else did. It could be nothing more than coincidence, the fate assigned by each one's statistical probability of risk, Señora Iscar. It could even be divine justice, if one wants to take a religious view, for want of a better word. Or it could be that somebody considered that possibility and recognized it as the perfect way to conceal a crime, she says, that each one got the death you would expect for him. He turns round and looks at her: And you think that person was me. Yes. Gandolfini smiles again, returns to his chair and looks at Nurit without saying anything. No, on second thoughts, if this were a Nurit Iscar novel, she'd keep the window in – it's one of the few elements that allow the characters to move. Gandolfini tries derailing Nurit Iscar's theories by retreating into the absurd: So, as far as you're concerned, I'm almost God; or God Himself. I don't believe in God. You're an atheist, he says. Agnostic, she corrects. Gandolfini watches her, but now there's a shine in his eyes that owes more to excitement, it seems to Nurit, than to alarm. Like when someone who is highly competitive in a particular sport discovers that his rival is good, almost as good as him, but that even so he has every chance of beating him. And that being the case, if he can win, beating him will bring great satisfaction. Greater than with any other rival. It's a very good idea you've come up with, Señora, very good. May I steal it? Do you have copyright on it? Let's think about this. I, from the luxury of this office overlooking the river, equipped with the best technology, decorated with excellent taste for which I can take no credit because it came courtesy of my architects, as I was saying, let's imagine that I, from here, manage two or three people in this country plus hitmen overseas, a small team so as to keep my secret well protected, and for a sum commensurate with the difficulty of each case arrange the death of whoever it happens to be to occur exactly in the way that people might expect that person to die. Something like that, says Nurit. It's not a half-bad idea, I have to hand it to you. And as well as hitmen, I'd need to have people who are experts in obtaining information from the victims, right? Gandolfini continues enthusiastically. Old-school spies as well as experts in cyber espionage. People who can even find out a potential victim's make of underwear. Gandolfini smiles, goes to one side of the office and pours himself a coffee. Would you like one? he asks. No thanks, she says. But let's suppose that you are right, that these deaths weren't accidental, let's suppose that there is a mastermind behind them. I ask again: why me? What motive would I have, beyond how nice or nasty my brother and his friends seemed to me, for killing them? Nurit Iscar wants to see his reaction, so she answers directly, avoiding euphemisms: Because you witnessed the rape of Emilio Casabets. Now, for the first time, Gandolfini's face betrays a tiny alteration, and it's as though tension has set into his cheeks, his brow, his mouth. He neither frowns nor smiles, but his features harden. Perhaps that wasn't even the only rape they made you watch. And there came a point when you couldn't cope any more with the guilt of having been a witness, of having done nothing to stop it happening, Nurit goes on. Gandolfini keeps watching her for a while with the same stony expression then says through clenched teeth, almost to himself: I was only eight years old. And I don't judge you for anything that happened at that time, says Nurit Iscar, only for the recent deaths. Those feelings that had been buried for years came to the surface much later, when your brother and his friends started appearing regularly in the papers in connection with Gloria Echagüe's death. Gandolfini walks back over to the window and stands staring out of it for a long time until, finally, like an actor finding focus and reprising his role he says: You have a lot of imagination. I don't deny that, she agrees. Even if years ago something might have happened, and I might have been there, I say again: what proof do you have to show that I had anything to do with those deaths? None, says Nurit, nothing yet. Look, Señora Iscar, all that you say may or may not be true. But nothing in this world exists if it can't be proven. Besides, let's suppose for a moment that you're right, that I do control hitmen in different parts of the world, or even that I have a firm to do that. In fact, let's suppose that I used that firm not only to get rid of the people you've mentioned, but also a few others, like a business, to turn a profit. Let's suppose that something that began in response to a personal need grew to serve other uses. Don't you think that I'd then become somebody supremely powerful and untouchable? Me and my firm. My "people-killing" business. It would be a hugely successful business; every powerful group would come to me, I would lend my services and they would owe me favours. Politicians, other businessmen, even men of the cloth, why not? And I'd become untouchable. Imagine that I, or rather my firm, could have brought down the helicopter of a president's son. Or could have thrown an indiscreet secretary out of a window at her home, making it look as though she were trying to cut a television cable. Or even that we could have induced a powerful businessman to blow his head off with a rifle. What a lot of power I would have, Señora Iscar, don't you think? I would be what they call "an untouchable". Nobody is untouchable, she says. Ah, don't you believe it. Having a lot of favours to call in at the right moment is like a guarantee of safe conduct. But I don't want to tell you any more. I mustn't tell you any more, Señora. I got into enough trouble after my meeting with Jaime Brena the other day. Who gave you trouble? Nurit asks. We all answer to someone, don't we? Have you asked yourself if there's someone above me or if I really am my own boss? Because that can happen these days, no? An investigator – you, for example – thinks she's identified the murderer, but who actually is the murderer? The person who wants someone dead, the person who pays for it, the person who carries out the execution with a blade, a bullet, whatever method you like, the person who organizes the execution, plans it, the person who covers it up, the person who takes payment? Which of these people is most responsible? What does the pyramid of murder look like today? Who in this twenty-first century is the true assassin, Señora Iscar? All of them, she replies. No, that's too easy an answer, too politically correct. And politically correct answers, apart from being contemptible, never speak the truth. Do you know what my answer would be? The assassin is the one who's still alive at the end, the one nobody could kill. The others are merely cogs in the wheel. Replaceable cogs in most cases. But the one who's still alive at the end, he's something different, he's the one with the real power. Gandolfini gets up and paces around the office again without looking at Nurit, his gaze lost in the river. Then he stops and says: Oh dear, oh dear… you were so close, but you'll never know if you hit the bullseye. The only person who can confirm that for you is me, and I'm not going to tell you, Señora Iscar, I'm sorry. Will you be able to bear the uncertainty? Will you be able to bear your question going unanswered, your theory unconfirmed? Will you be able to bear nobody telling you whether this plot you've imagined in so much detail is the truth? I know that it is, I'm sure that it's true, says Nurit, trying to sound resolute, even though her legs are shaking inside her black trousers. No, I don't believe you can be. There's still something inside you that's doubting, that's making you doubt; I can see it. And Gandolfini stares at her as though he really can see that doubt in her. Only after a moment of tense silence does he ask: Is there anything else I can help with? No, says Nurit, there's nothing else. You've been very clear, more than I imagined you would be, I'm going away with a lot of material. I don't think you'll be able to use it, Señora: there are no reliable sources for you to quote. I'm not a journalist, I'm a writer; I can tell a story without quoting sources, I can take as given something that is only in my imagination. All I have to do is call what I'm writing a "novel" instead of a "report" – almost a minor detail, Nurit says. Gandolfini looks at her, studies her, weighing up which piece to move next in deference to his rival rather than the game. There is something else I'd like to say to you, Señora Iscar. Or would you prefer I call you Betty Boo? Gandolfini asks to Nurit's astonishment while removing from his desk drawer a yellow file with two thick black bands across the top right corner, like funereal ribbons. Only my friends call me Betty Boo. Ah, forgive me, I had no wish to appear forward. Not yet opening the file that he has just taken out of the drawer but leaving his hand on top of it, as

287

though ready to swear an oath on the Bible, he begins to recite what Nurit Iscar takes to be its contents. This is what she will tell Jaime Brena and the Crime boy a few minutes later, speaking from memory: Jaime Brena, sixty-two years old, disorganized lifestyle, various excesses – alcohol, ciga- rettes, drugs, though nowadays only marijuana. Takes no physical excrcise. Suggested death: heart attack. Nurit's amazement is replaced by horror. He continues: Paula Sibona: fifty-six years old, actress, no medical problems to date, etc., etc. She likes going out and meeting people she doesn't know. Suggested death: murdered in her apartment after a one-night stand. Juan and Rodrigo Pérez Iscar, says Gandolfini. Your children, right? Stop! she says. You don't want me to go on? No. I can tell you about the other friends. I don't want to know. Seriously? I mean, I'm taking a risk here; I'll have to pay very dearly if it gets out that I've passed this information on to you. She's still terrified. She can't make a sound. He knows it. Don't worry, it's only a game, a theoretical exercise. Nobody's going to die. Not for the moment. It's not right for people to die for no reason; that's never good. My brother and his friends had to die; it doesn't matter whether they died in accidents or were killed. They deserved it. Now they're dead, and for me that's a relief. As if the world were in equilibrium again. Nobody can blame me for feeling relieved at the death of such despicable people, do you understand? Nurit stands up: Yes, I under- stand, she says, and her legs are shaking. Shall I show you out? No, I know the way. Aren't you intrigued to know what the manner of your own "theoretical" death would be? Nurit says nothing, but she wants to know. You're not a straight- forward case, you know? You take few risks. You don't go to meet people you don't know, you don't drink too much, you don't smoke or take drugs. Tell me, are you happy? Once again, Nurit is bewildered by Gandolfini's question, although this is different to the others. Oh, Señora, it's hard to be happy, isn't it? And I say that as someone who has almost everything. If you, if Betty Boo, were to die in the country club where you're staying at present, the most advisable method would have to be carbon monoxide poisoning. Houses that have the boiler indoors, even when it's in a separate room such as a utility room or a laundry, for example, are dangerous. That would work; you wouldn't be the first to die that way in a country club. There have been various cases – and we're talking about expensive houses here, but, you know, people prioritize other things. If you were back in your flat, on the other hand, I'd say it would be better for you to fall into the lift shaft. You leave the flat unexpectedly and with your mind on other things; somebody has called you out for some urgent reason. You quickly grab your things, you forget your phone but you don't stop to go back for it, you can't, the light in the passage isn't working, you call the lift, think it's there, the mechanism fails, and you open the door and step into the void. You could also fall from the balcony while watering the plants, but that would be a bit too similar to the secretary who was cutting the television cable and I think you deserve more of a role, something exclusive.

Nurit wants not to be there any more; she makes her way as best she can to the door and opens it. In a way you've flattered me with your suspicions, believing me capable of setting up a firm like that; that's not something anyone could do. Do you remember the Furies? (The who? the Crime boy will ask a little while later when Nurit Iscar tells him this.) It's almost like striking a blow for them. I always thought Aeschylus was wrong to turn them into Eumenides; they went from being avenging Furies to benevolent creatures, and that was a shame. The Eumenides respect the law and justice, they don't take justice into their own hands, Nurit manages to say. Exactly, that's why it's a shame, says Gandolfini. Don't you think it's right that someone brought those bastards to justice who raped their friend? Put political correctness to one side and tell me exactly what you think. That you scare me, that's what I think, says Nurit Iscar, and she's about to leave but Gandolfini stops her once more: Two last things. She turns to look at him without taking her hand off the door handle. First: not a word of this to anyone. I enjoy talking to you and your friends, but I don't want to have the same problem I had after meeting Jaime Brena. And the second: Maidenform, says Gandolfini, and smiles. What? Maidenform. Then Nurit does leave, flees, almost. On her way to the lift she asks the secretary where the toilets are, and goes straight there.

Inside, she pulls down her pants and sees on the label the name she already knows will be there: Maidenform.

26

Nurit Iscar can't remember what happened from the moment when she got into the lift on the seventeenth floor of the building where Roberto Gandolfini's offices were and the present time, which finds her sitting at a table on the corner of Córdoba and San Martín together with the Crime boy and Jaime Brena. They tell her that she ran across Alem, narrowly avoiding a car, that she was carrying her ID card in her hand and that when she reached the other side she collapsed into Jaime Brena's arms and passed out. But Nurit Iscar remembers nothing: not running, not the car that nearly knocked her down, not even the arms of Jaime Brena. The last clear image she has in her mind is of herself leaning over, knees bent, pants pulled halfway down her legs and the label: Maidenform. And then the lift, but only hazily, something that must have been the lift, and the knot in her stomach from the sensation produced as it plunged downwards. They tell her how they bundled her, still unconscious, into the minicab, how she came to when air entering through the open window hit her but that she was still gone, lost. That they took her to the first bar they found to give her something to revive her. She – stirring the double espresso into which Jaime Brena has poured a shot of brandy and added three spoons of sugar – tells them everything she can remember from before that strange amnesia, what happened from the moment she stood before Gandolfini's secretary until she got into the lift after their encounter: what his office was like, the window, the river, the meeting, what Gandolfini had said and what he'd denied, what she had said. The pyramid of murder. And finally the threat. The yellow file with the two black stripes; a file that Gandolfini never opened but the contents of which, it was obvious, he knew and boasted about: Yellow with two black stripes diagonally across the top right-hand corner, she repeated. The make of her underwear. And the Furies, although, even though the Crime boy asks her about them, she doesn't stop to explain their significance. You can look for it on Google later, kid, Brena advises him. The two men are still shocked. I can't believe you did this all yourself, Betty Boo, Brena says. Don't tell me off, she pleads, I'm more scared now than when I was there. Nurit's eyes fill with tears and Jaime Brena moves as though to take her hand, but she – without noticing this or realizing his intention – moves hers, only a little but enough to give him pause. What do we do next? the Crime boy asks. We don't do anything, says Nurit, almost angrily. I'm not putting anyone's life in danger, especially not my children's. All three are silent for a moment. A party of Brazilians who have come into the bar with bags and packages needs them to move so that they can get to the only free table next to a window, a table that's too small for them and to which they have to pull up two more chairs. Talking and laughing loudly, those Brazilian tourists are the perfect counterpoint to what's happening at the table shared by Nurit, Jaime Brena and the Crime boy. Once the new arrivals have all settled in, Jaime Brena says with resignation: Sometimes one has to settle for having discovered the truth. What does that mean? asks the boy. It's not our job to administer justice, we're journalists. If, in the course of an investigation, we uncover some important, true information that we aren't in a position to prove, that's still a lot more than we manage most of the time. Don't we have an obligation to fill the police in about this? I've already spoken to Comisario Venturini and he wouldn't give me the time of day. But it's not just a question of responsibility: if this Gandolfini carries on killing people, the blame for that is going to be on our heads, the boy says. We always carry some guilt; the question is deciding which kinds of guilt we're prepared to live with, says Brena. I couldn't live with the guilt of that madman killing one of my sons, says Betty Boo, looking at the boy. I understand, the Crime boy says, but it's a shame that we can't find some way to write about this. We have to think it over a bit, says Brena. There may be a way to relay some of it, between the lines, turn things around and tell without telling, like we used to during the dictatorship: coded writing. Who would we be writing in code for today? asks Betty Boo. I don't know, for anyone who wants to know. And where is that person who wants to know? Who reads the articles we publish, the novels we write? Is anyone reading them? Who? The Brazilians erupt in guffaws, and the laughter overwhelms them. A waiter arrives at their table with beer and a selection of aperitifs comprising many more little dishes and pots than these tourists will ever be able to eat. Their laughter gives way to exclamations and wonderment at what the waiter is laying before them. And then more laughter. I'd like to speak to Comisario Venturini in person, says Brena. I get the impression he knows more than he's saying. I don't want anyone put at risk, Nurit warns. Don't worry, I'll be discreet, but we're already at risk, Brena says, then he asks: Do you think you're in a fit state to go back to La Maravillosa, Betty Boo? I don't know, but that's what I'm going to do; I'm going to go there, write my last piece and get my things together. Then I'm going straight home. It doesn't make sense to stay there any longer. Would you like one of us to go with you? Brena asks. No, we all have things to do, she says. OK, let's speak later, then, Brena says. The boy nods without saying anything. What's up, kid? Brena asks him. Is this what being a journalist is? Searching for the truth, believing you've found it although you can't prove all of it, then having to keep quiet to avoid risking your life or somebody else's? Yes, sometimes it is, kid; sometimes not even that, you don't get close to the truth. And sometimes, very rarely, you feel that you're getting things right. But then one day you look at the calendar and you realize that life has passed you by, that there isn't much left ahead of you. I don't want that to happen to me, says the boy. I didn't want it either, says Jaime Brena.

At the moment that the Crime boy is going up in the lift to the *El Tribuno* newsroom and Nurit Iscar is in the minicab passing through the toll on the road that leads to La Maravillosa, Jaime Brena enters the reception area of Comisario Venturini's building and, at the behest of a secretary, takes a seat opposite his office door. He hasn't got an appointment, but he knows that Venturini will see him anyway; he always has before. Soon afterwards the secretary, without having asked first, brings him coffee in a little Tsuji porcelain cup, white with gold edging, a luxury accorded only to the institution's highest ranks. On the tray there is a sugar bowl, also porcelain, but from a different set, with old sugar stuck to the spoon and a paper napkin folded into a triangle under the cup. He'll see you in a minute, says the secretary. Jaime Brena still hasn't decided how much he's going to tell Venturini and how much he'll keep back. He promised Nurit Iscar, Betty Boo, not to endanger anyone. Will he ever dare tell Nurit that he was the one who thought up the nickname Betty Boo for her, and not Rinaldi? When she published her novel *Death by Degrees* he became one of her most loyal readers: a fan, even. After finishing that, he read all her previous novels, eagerly awaiting those still to come. He even liked *Only If You Love Me*, although he thought it a minor work. Around the time *Death by Degrees* came out, one newspaper's cultural supplement published a full-page photograph of her. He'd cut it out and stuck it onto his desk. He had it in front of him as he worked. One day when he couldn't think of the right word to end a piece, he had looked up and asked the photo: What's the word for when someone who's the natural heir to a throne rejects it, Betty Boo? He said it just like that, "Betty Boo", as though that had always been her name, as if no other name did credit to Nurit Iscar and her curls. Betty Boo. Abdicate, came the answer, after a moment, and he snapped his fingers: abdicate. So it was that Nurit Iscar, Betty Boo, became his consultant on difficult questions and everything else important. When around that time Lorenzo Rinaldi – with whom Jaime Brena was still on good terms at that point – asked him what the source was of some of his (in Rinaldi's words) "far-fetched conspiracy theories for certain crimes", Brena would say: Betty Boo told me, and point to the photograph without any further explanation. Until one afternoon Rinaldi passed his desk and told him that he'd just met her, the woman in the photo, in person, on a television programme. And not long afterwards Nurit Iscar started appearing in the newsroom every so often. Sometimes she'd wait for Rinaldi, sitting in one of the armchairs in reception, then they would go off together. She and Lorenzo Rinaldi. Other times they would spend a long time in his office, then she'd leave alone. One day a rumour started circulating in the newsroom. Then Jaime Brena decided to take the photograph down and not consult it any more. Will he ever dare tell her all this? he wonders again. It's doubtful; it would mean revealing too much of himself, and if there's one thing Jaime Brena has been very careful to avoid all his life it's telling any woman anything about himself that (according to his own neurosis) they have no business knowing.

Meanwhile, as Jaime Brena is remembering how he christened Nurit Iscar Betty Boo, the Crime boy, with his computer switched off, is wondering what to do. And what to do doesn't mean what to write about the crimes at La Maravillosa, or even what to write about other crimes of less immediate interest but that he should also be covering. He's wondering what to do with his life. If what he wants is to make a career at *El Tribuno* (assuming they continue to want him) until one day he gets made editor of some section that doesn't interest him or where he has to run everything that departs from the paper's editorial line past Rinaldi or whoever replaces him. Is that where he'll be in ten years? Will Rinaldi still be there? And Jaime Brena? Where will they all be, ten years from now? He looks around him. The Crime boy doesn't want to be like the editors he sees around the newsroom. He particularly doesn't want to be like Rinaldi, who was also a reporter once. He wants to be like Jaime Brena. But Brena was moved from the section that was his natural home to one that has made his life a misery. That's not something the Crime boy wants either. So, is there a place today in *El Tribuno* for him to be the journalist he most wants to be? Is he going to feel freer every day he works there or increasingly hamstrung by interests he knows nothing about but which will be presented to him as immovable objects? Is he prepared to spend his life here, as Brena has, only to find out what he really wants when there are no longer any options left to him but to stay where he is or take voluntary redundancy? He doesn't know; he has no idea. All he knows for sure now is that he wants to be a journalist. A Crime correspondent. And he wants to be like Jaime Brena. But he doesn't want to end up in the place where he is now. Not that.

Nurit Iscar puts her things to one side, switches on the computer and starts typing her last piece. The Crime boy goes looking for Karina Vives, but they tell him that she hasn't come into work today, that she called in sick, and that makes him worried. Jaime Brena enters the office of Comisario Venturini, who greets him with the habitual: How are you, my dear? But this time Jaime Brena doesn't complete the joke with the usual "Well, but poor, Sir". Instead he sits down opposite him, on the other side of the desk, and says: Have you got any further with the Collazo case? Venturini looks irritated. The case is closed; Collazo committed suicide. Why are you trying to make unnecessary work for me, Brena? I'm just wondering why, when Collazo was found dead, you were there, too? What do you mean, "too"? Chazarreta's death took place outside your jurisdiction, Comisario, as did Collazo's. Was it just coincidence? Helping out a colleague? Or were there vested interests? Hang on a minute, since when do I have to explain to you which cases I choose to get involved with and which not? You don't have to, Comisario, I'm just trying to understand why you've been avoiding me recently. Venturini fixes him with a look, as though he'd like to say something and can't decide if he should say it. Finally he says this: Look, Brena, sometimes we have to accept our limitations, sometimes we can't get where we would like to, but that doesn't invalidate everything else that we do. Does the fact that we have to compromise once in a while make us crooks? No, it makes us human. Sometimes we can do things, sometimes we can't. Sometimes we can take the right road, sometimes we have to take other roads without knowing whether or not they are going to lead where we want to go. Do you understand me? No, not really. Don't worry, you can't understand everything. That's human too, but trust me, I assure you that I am someone you can trust. Brena says nothing; he doesn't know if he believes him. He would like to, but he doesn't. There's nothing more to be done here.

Jaime Brena gets to his feet, makes his gesture of tipping an imaginary hat, says: Comisario. And he leaves.

27

It's easier to get out than in.

I bid you farewell. This is my last dispatch from La Maravillosa. I won't be writing any more columns about the Chazarreta case. But I want you to remember what I tell you here: I want the fact that I have freely decided that this is my last piece put on record. I have decided not to write any more about the death of Pedro Chazarreta or any related deaths. And this is my decision, my choice.

I don't want this story gradually to lose prominence and currency until nobody talks about it any more, as often happens with a subject, a news story, a piece of information that one day commanded space and interest. Sometimes that's the intention: for the story to disappear, for us to forget all about it. That isn't the case here. I've decided to stop writing because I'm scared. I'm stopping because I don't have enough proof to say what I think. All I have are fear and conjecture. This case has not been solved. And I can't be the person to solve it. Perhaps nobody will ever solve it. Perhaps soon nobody will talk about the Chazarreta case any more. Please don't let that happen.

What's happening with this crime story has implications for other news items and for the general state of the media today. A news agenda that leaves out certain stories is tantamount to censorship. Don't allow other people to create your agenda, no matter what side they're on. Read a lot of newspapers, watch a lot of bulletins – all of them, even the ones you disagree with – and only then decide on your own viewpoint. Communication today is no longer a matter of passively receiving what we are told: we all help to create it. Choosing a hierarchy for news stories that chimes with our own criteria and not with the imposed agenda is a way to create counter-information. And that shouldn't be a dirty word here: quite the opposite. It means being informed from a different point of reference, outside the centres of power: an alternative media. We have to understand the motives of groups and people; we shouldn't settle for obvious causes but instead look deeper to understand behaviour.

What does this have to with the reporting of crimes? With a murder?

A great deal.

It may be reassuring to think that Chazarreta was murdered for this or that reason, but don't count on me for such a simple analysis. I'm not able to give a deeper analysis, but you should know that it exists and it is being denied to you. I'm denying it to you today, out of fear. Keep looking for it in the crime pages, in politics, international news, entertainment and sports. To name the person who took a knife and slit Chazarreta's throat from one side to the other is to say who killed him, which doesn't say anything. Because behind that action lies a truth that is much older, more complex, more brutal. Abuse, revenge, pacts of silence: these are more complicated and turbid matters than who wielded the knife. Does it matter where Chazarreta went to school? Does it matter that the founder of that school has been accused of repeated acts of abuse? Does it matter what ideologies Chazarreta and his friends followed in adolescence, and what in more recent times? Yes, I believe that all those things matter. Do unresolved past grievances, abuses and crimes influence the grievances, abuses and crimes of today, or of the future? When old grievances are not given their due the wounds stay open, and – what's more dangerous – somebody may feel it's his right to seek vengeance for something that had no justice at the time. But taking justice into your own hands can only lead to another wrong, fuelling an endless cycle of hatred and revenge. When a person kills someone who deserves to die, does that make him any less of a murderer? The only way to save ourselves as a society is to administer fair punishment for wrongdoing, for crimes that have been committed. Don't forget the unpunished crimes, because they always conceal something more terrible than the crime itself.

As of today, I shall no longer be writing in this newspaper. Not because the story doesn't matter to me, but for exactly the opposite reason. Rodolfo Walsh recognized that after 1968 he started valuing literature less "because it was no longer possible to keep writing high-minded works that could only be consumed by the 'bourgeois intelligentsia' when the whole country was going into convulsions." He felt that everything he wrote "should be submerged in the new process, and be useful to it, contribute to its advance. Once again, journalism was the right weapon here". Is journalism, this journalism, still the right weapon today? I don't know; nor do I have a right to answer the question, because I am not a journalist. I'm a writer. I invent stories. And it is to that world of fiction that I shall retreat when I've finished this dispatch. Because it is a place where I'm not frightened, a place where I can invent another reality, an even truer one. That is where I can start a new novel, my next novel, with a woman who comes to do the domestic work at the house of a man like Pedro Chazarreta, for example, and has to pass, as she does every day, through the security checks at the entrance to La Maravillosa not knowing, not suspecting, that when she arrives at her employer's house she will find him the victim of a brutal murder. I can invent an investigation, uncover links to other deaths that nobody saw, say why the murder victim was killed. Invent all kinds of things. I can even say, for example, that the ultimate responsibility lies with a powerful businessman, in a skyscraper, an imposing tower somewhere in Retiro, or Puerto Madero or Manhattan. It can be wherever I like because I don't have to answer to anyone. An office with a vast window. Or with no window at all. After all, this reality is all my own invention. A novel is fiction. And my only responsibility is to tell it well.

So it's back to fiction for me. I won't be writing any more of these dispatches because I'm too scared to write what needs to be said, and too ashamed to write anything else.

I respect my readers highly. And I am confident that you will know what to do in this brave new age of information. You are, after all, an inescapable and active part of it.

*

The Crime boy finishes reading Nurit Iscar's last piece at the very moment that she's passing under the barrier at the entrance – or rather exit – to La Maravillosa, in the minicab sent by the newspaper, with her little case stowed in the boot that the security men opened but didn't inspect, on her way back home. Her real home, that is: the apartment in Buenos Aires. The boy sends the piece on to be run in the next day's newspaper. He knows that Rinaldi isn't going to like it. Especially if Nurit Iscar hasn't yet told him that she plans not to write for *El Tribuno* any more. Mind you, he won't like it anyway, even if she has told him. Lorenzo Rinaldi doesn't like being left. The boy answers a few overdue emails then collects his things together, shuts down the computer and is about to go home when he hears Rinaldi yelling: What the hell are you doing sending this piece through for tomorrow without asking me first? Thank God somebody read it along the way and let me know! The Crime boy feigns innocence: I thought Nurit Iscar's pieces weren't supposed to be cut or edited? Don't push your luck, kid, you know very well this is different. There's no way this is going out. The woman's got some nerve. Did you know about this? Here I am ringing her and she's disappeared off the face of the earth. That's a bad, bad way to end things. How did you ever think this could go out? There are editorial standards in this newspaper; we don't just run any old thing. Rinaldi is furious but making an effort at composure, despite his tone and initial vehemence: Put your computer back on and get writing something to fill this space, he orders, and goes back to his office without another word. The Crime boy is sorry to think that Nurit Iscar's best piece won't be read by the paper's readers. He decides to ask a few friends' permission to put it on their blogs, then put links on Facebook, Twitter and other sites so that a lot of people will see it. He looks at his watch – seven o'clock in the evening – and fires up the computer again; is he really prepared to write something to replace Nurit's piece? No, he isn't. He pulls up Google, types "Furies" into the search box. He reads: "In Greek mythology, female deities of vengeance, primitive forces who will not submit to the authority of Zeus. They return to Earth to punish living criminals. Finally, despite their thirst for vengeance, the Furies accept the justice meted out by Athene because they want the people to stop treating them with contempt. Revenge gives way to justice." The boy looks at his watch again: ten past seven. Why is he still here at the paper? he asks himself, not in reference to the late hour but to his life generally and his career choices. Isn't Rinaldi's decision not to publish Nurit Iscar's piece reason enough to hand in his notice? Back to the Furies and justice. What happens when a murderer and his victims – Chazarreta, his friends, Gandolfini – are all poisonous pieces of shit? Does proving that Chazarreta was a bastard make his death in any way more just? Does it make Gandolfini less of a criminal? Does being murdered make Chazarreta less of a bastard? He looks at his watch: 7.15. He types "counter-information" into Google, bypasses various entries then clicks on one about a book with this title, by Natalia Vinelli and Carlos Rodríguez Esperón. The summary is interesting, and he searches for a copy to download but it isn't online. He'll have to buy it, then, but where? Will it be available? He goes to the MercadoLibre website, finds it and orders a copy to be delivered the next day. Simple. He glances over at the door of Rinaldi's office. He looks at the time again on his BlackBerry: 7.35. He types "alternative media" into Google and gets approximately 2,730,000 results. He clicks on two, three, five of them. He clicks on Indymedia and Radio Sur 102.7, leaving the National Network of Alternative Media,

Antena Negra and Barricada TV for further investigation when he gets home. It's too much: he hasn't got enough time at the moment. He feels giddy and excited, as though he'd taken drugs. A quarter to eight. It's now or never. He turns off the computer, grabs his wallet and BlackBerry and walks out of the office. He gets to the post office five minutes before it closes. I want to send a telegram, he says. And he composes his resignation from *El Tribuno*. They're already lowering the metal shutters as he leaves. He calls Jaime Brena on his BlackBerry: Brena, do you want to leave the newspaper and come and start up a news site with me?

28

A week later Jaime Brena and Nurit Iscar are having dinner in El Preferido. He promised her that you can eat the best *puchero* in all of Buenos Aires there. Unless you prefer those restaurants where they employ pretty teenagers instead of waiters and the food is fusion or some such concoction that you could eat in any city of the world, Brena said when he rang her to arrange the meeting. I love *puchero*, she had said. And here they are, sitting across from each other, choosing a red wine. Does it come with chorizo? Nurit asks the waiter. If it didn't have chorizo, chickpeas and bone marrow it wouldn't be *puchero*, the man replies. With a wink and a thumbs up, she closes her menu and hands it back to him. Jaime Brena selects a Cabernet Sauvignon and also hands back his menu. She tells him that she still hasn't responded to any of Rinaldi's persistent calls, that she knows he's going to haul her over the coals for her last piece – especially after the boy put it up on the Internet – and that she doesn't feel like hearing it right now. He tells her that he plans to keep working at *El Tribuno* for the time being, that he'll help the boy with his news site as a favour, that he'll write a few pieces for him and so on, but that he can't imagine not getting up every morning and going to work at the newspaper. Despite Rinaldi, despite the Society section, despite those stupid statistics about the habits of men and women, girls and boys or women with more or less pubic hair, he would still choose to work in a newspaper office. I don't think I could get used to living without the smell of a newsroom, Brena says. What does it smell like? she asks. Well, it used to smell of cigarette butts, and paper and printing ink; I'm not so sure about these days, but in a way the old smell is still there, in that rank, dusty air that goes in and out of the air-conditioning units God knows how many times a day. And the noise – I'd miss that too, that human engine that sounds like vertigo, like things happening. Today you hear it in the hum of television sets around the newsroom, which are always muted unless something important comes on. The gentle but persistent buzz of computers, like mosquitoes. And telephones which don't ring the way they used to, all with the same melody, but which now all have their own ridiculous and exclusive ringtone. So you get a competition of ever stranger ringtones that's supposed to help people pick out which one is theirs. I don't know if I'd be happy without all that, says Jaime Brena. He asks Nurit if she's started to write anything and she says yes and tells him about her new novel, two pages so far with a lot more in her head. Murders, yes, suspense, and then the real story, running beneath the murder, which is what really matters to me; the everyday life which death never succeeds in holding back. They eat bread while waiting for the *puchero*, both protesting that they shouldn't fill up on carbs, that they already have weight to lose. Both laughing. Should we have done more? she asks. Should we have tried to expose Gandolfini? I don't know; I ask myself that too, says Jaime Brena. For the moment we'll have to live with those doubts: the cost of saying what we know, or what we think we know, is too high. Perhaps later on we'll find a way to say it, sometimes time goes by and an opportunity comes up – I don't know. I don't either, says Betty Boo, but I feel uneasy. The waiter arrives with the wine and serves them; they clink glasses and drink. But they don't toast. Above their heads, on a wall-mounted television switched to mute, the nine o'clock news is starting. They don't watch it – they would have to twist their necks like herons to see it. And they're not interested, anyway; today they don't want to know what's happening to anyone else.

As Jaime Brena and Nurit Iscar are waiting for their *puchero*, Carmen Terrada and Paula Sibona are eating empanadas while checking their phones. Has she sent you a message? Carmen asks. No, you? says Paula. No, me neither. And she promised that she was going to text to let us know how she was getting on, she complains. She promised that to get you off her back, Paula; she can't be expected to relay every single detail of her date as though it were a football match. That's exactly what I was hoping she would do, says Paula. Do you want to watch a film or a series? Carmen asks. Which series have you got? *In Treatment* or *Mad Men. In Treatment*: I love that shrink. Carmen turns on the television and puts in a DVD. They make themselves comfortable on the large cushions scattered on the floor. Do you think they've screwed yet? Paula Sibona asks. No, I don't, says Carmen; knowing our friend, they probably haven't even kissed. I have faith in Jaime Brena, Paula declares. So do I, Carmen agrees, the question is whether you can have faith in her. God, you don't think she'll abandon us if she falls in love with Jaime Brena, do you? Paula asks worriedly. No, not our Betty Boo, says Carmen Terrada staunchly, as she searches for the remote control in order to put on the Spanish subtitles. We ought to have some sort of friendship prenup for when one of us hooks up with a guy, saying they have to leave space for us, Paula says. Well, don't worry on my account; there's nobody on my horizon, says Carmen. And you don't have to worry about me, either, because I have a lot on my horizon, which is the same as not having anything. Do you think Jaime Brena has any presentable friends?

The *puchero* arrives at the table. Shall I serve you? Brena asks. Go on then, she says. At that very moment the Crime boy is opening a beer at Karina Vives' house. So? What do you think of my idea? I love it, she says. It's a shame Brena didn't want to be my partner. Brena's a newsroom guy, she says, you have to understand that. But what I'm putting together is a newsroom. Karina Vives looks doubtful. With no people all working together, with no going outside for a cigarette break with your friends, with no boss to mouth off about: that's too much virtuality for a guy like Brena, she says. And you? Would you come and work with me? the boy asks. Later on, when the moment's right for leaving the newspaper, she says. First I have to decide what to do about this pregnancy. I get the impression it's already decided by now, even if only by omission. She doesn't answer. The Crime boy takes another gulp of beer, watching her over the rim of the bottle. Ink or Link? he asks. What? she says. Which would you go for? Ink or Link? I don't understand. Great content with no link doesn't get seen, the boy explains and goes on: Today people need someone to select the best content for them. But somebody's also got to keep writing that great content, she says. OK, he agrees, both things are necessary, but when there's a superabundance of content, selection becomes all the more important, and I'm going to concentrate on linking people who want to follow me to the best possible content. Do you trust in my ability to do that? the Crime boy asks. Yes I do, Karina Vives says. The boy puts his bottle down on the coffee table. Is it acceptable to kiss a pregnant woman? he asks. I think so, she says. And they kiss.

There's no room for dessert after the *puchero*, so they ask for two coffees and the bill. On the television set above their heads a breaking news item suddenly comes on with the caption: *Business mogul killed. Shot fifteen times. Motive may be revenge.* The picture shown is the entrance to Gandolfini's office, RG Business Developers. But Nurit and Jaime Brena don't see it and will only learn the news tomorrow morning; they don't even look at the television screen, they're caught up in other things. The entrance has been cordoned off by police, who are present in large numbers. The reporter does his piece to camera, an archive photograph of Gandolfini flashes up and now the reporter is interviewing a police chief. The caption says: *Comisario García Prieto, leading the investigation into this crime.* The caption changes: *Frenzied murder: businessman Roberto Gandolfini shot multiple times in high-security office block.* And on the screen, in the background, just visible behind García Prieto, if Jaime Brena or Nurit Iscar turned their heads to look, they would recognize the figure of Comisario Venturini, in an impeccable suit and with the calm demeanour of someone supervising an operation that, yet again, shouldn't really fall to him but which he'll nonetheless manage perfectly, and holding a yellow folder in his hands. A yellow folder with two black lines across the top right-hand corner. A folder he's keeping a tight grip on because it doesn't belong to the crime scene but to him. If they turned to look, Jaime Brena and Nurit Iscar would be dumbfounded; they would believe they finally understood, they would speak that night about the pyramid of murder and that observation made by Gandolfini only days before: that the murderer is the one who's still alive. They would ask themselves whether the folder Venturini is carrying, which now on the screen he's folding in half and slipping into a jacket pocket as though it were a newspaper, belongs to him or has been taken from the crime scene. They would ask one another why he gave Brena so many leads on Chazarreta's murder, even taking them to look around his house. They would tell each other that it was because Venturini wanted it to be very clear that this was a murder: in order for Chazarreta to die as he should, he had to die as the result of a murder, and that's why he was so elusive when the other deaths came to light. They would be talking about all these things now if they had raised their heads and seen what was on the news. But they don't do that, they don't look at the screen, they aren't even tempted to do so by the fact that two or three people sitting at the tables around them are looking over their heads and speaking to one another as though something important were happening. It won't be until tomorrow morning at first light that Nurit Iscar and Jaime Brena ask those questions and begin to answer them. When, having learned of Roberto Gandolfini's death in a hail of bullets, and in search of clues, they rewind that same scene hundreds of times – the one they aren't watching now – because they have found out, or someone has told them, that Comisario Venturini appears in shot. Tomorrow; all that's for tomorrow. Today, Jaime Brena calls the waiter over and pays (Absolutely not, he says to Nurit Iscar when she offers to pay her share), then they get up and leave.

At the moment that they are leaving El Preferido, Lorenzo Rinaldi is entering another restaurant in the same area with his wife and sitting down at a table where some of the ministers closest to the president and his wife are already waiting. Have the political winds changed? regular diners who recognize them ask one another, and Jaime Brena would ask the same thing if he saw them. But Jaime Brena is otherwise engaged, walking through Palermo with Nurit Iscar. The street still feels warm from the residue of that strange heat at the start of autumn. I'll take you home, says Brena, and it isn't a question. Shall we walk or get a taxi? Let's start off walking, says Nurit Iscar, then take a taxi if we get tired. They go on in silence, hoping not to be wrong-footed by the broken paving stones and bulging tree roots. Would you like to know where your nickname came from, Betty Boo? Go on then, she says. So Jaime Brena starts telling her the story that, until recently, he never thought he would, and as he does so he puts his hand around her waist. Tentatively at first, and then more firmly, unmistakably. Nurit Iscar feels a twinge of alarm, but she likes it all the same. It's been a long time since a man held her around the waist. Jaime Brena himself was the last man to put an arm around her shoulder, the day that Collazo was found hanging from the tree. But a shoulder is not a waist. A waist has more G-spot to it. If the G-spot actually exists. Jaime Brena, as if he hadn't noticed the consternation his hand has caused ("as if" because he has noticed it, of course), keeps on talking. He's enjoying telling his story and he makes it funny, he wants her to laugh too, he wants to seduce her. Helping her to avoid a mound of raised slabs which threaten the pedestrian with their broken edges, he deftly pulls her in towards his body. From the waist, like a tango dancer, marking the pace. And she lets herself be led and stays there, in that place, closer to him.

If this were a Nurit Iscar novel, she wouldn't describe what happens soon after that. Especially not after the disaster of *Only If You Love Me*. She'd limit herself to describing how they kiss on a street corner, how he strokes her hair and kisses her again a little before they reach the entrance to her building. That is if she eventually manages to find the right words; if, on reading it over again, she hears the music she's looking for. But she wouldn't describe the rush to the lift, and the liberation of their hands in its confines. And much less what happens when the two of them enter her apartment. No, she definitely wouldn't put any of that in one of her novels.

But she knows for sure that when this story gets made into a film the director won't have any compunction about ending it with a sex scene of his own imagining. He'll tell the story with images rather than words, with naked bodies, deep breathing, panting. He'll even take the liberty of making them more attractive than they really are. She, Nurit Iscar, Betty Boo, and he, Jaime Brena, will become other people in that scene. The director will look for firmer legs than she has and for a male torso with a less prominent gut than he has. And he'll make them do things they don't do. Because even though they do everything they'd like to do, they are a man and woman thinking not about all the spectators watching them from the seats of a given cinema but about one another, and that's the difference.

Nurit Iscar thinks about that: the film that could be made about them, of what would be added and what taken away, and laughs. She looks over at Jaime Brena, who's smiling too.

What are you laughing about? she asks him.

Nothing, just something silly. I was wondering if you sleep facing upwards or downwards. A silly thing. And what are you laughing about, Betty Boo?

About you and me.

About us, then, says Jaime Brena.

Yes, about us, says Nurit Iscar.

Acknowledgements

My thanks:

To Christian Domingo, Laura Galarza, Débora Mundani and Karina Wroblewski, for being meticulous, unsparing and loving readers of this novel's various drafts.

Guillermo Saccomanno, because he lent me Zippo and because he's always there.

To Juan Martini, Maximiliano Hairabedian, Facundo Pastor and Ezequiel Martínez, because they helped me to resolve different elements in this story.

To Nicole Witt, Jordi Roca and their team.

To Julia Saltzmann and Gabriela Franco.

To Marcelo Moncarz.

To Eva Cristaldo and Anabella Kocis.

To Paloma Halac.

To my children.

A CRACK IN THE WALL

Claudia Piñeiro

Reckless ambition and needless violence crack secrets wide open

Pablo Simó's life is a mess. His career as an architect at a dead end; he is reduced to designing soulless office buildings desecrating the heart of Buenos Aires. His marriage seems to be one endless argument with his wife over the theatrics of their rebellious teenage daughter. To complicate matters, Pablo has long been attracted to sexy office secretary Marta Horvat, who is probably having an affair with his boss. Everything changes with the unexpected appearance of Leonor, a beautiful young woman who brings to light a crime that happened years before, a crime that everyone in the office wants forgotten, at all costs.

Piñeiro once again demonstrates her capacity to scratch below the surface, laying bare relationships based on habit and cowardice, and exposing the motives of those driven by reckless ambition.

"Piñeiro's moody, immersive thriller explores personal integrity with an ironic twist, calling to mind Patricia Highsmith's *Ripley* series." *Booklist*

"Piñeiro keeps the reader hooked right up to the wicked, if logical, ending." *Publishers Weekly*

£8.99/$14.95
Crime Paperback Original
ISBN 978 1908524 089
eBook ISBN 978 1908524 096

www.bitterlemonpress.com

ALL YOURS

Claudia Piñeiro

Infidelity and obsession lead to murder...

Inés is convinced that every wife is bound to be betrayed one day, so she is not surprised to find a note in her husband Ernesto's briefcase with a heart smeared in lipstick crossed by the words "All Yours". Following him to a park in Buenos Aires on a rainy winter evening, she witnesses a violent quarrel between her husband and another woman. The woman collapses; Ernesto sinks her body in a nearby lake.

When Ernesto becomes a suspect in the case Inés provides him with an alibi. After all, hatred can bring people together as urgently as love. But Ernesto cannot bring his sexual adventures to an end, so Inés concocts a plan for revenge from which there is no return.

"If you read only one crime book in translation this year, make *All Yours* the one, a book that grabs you from the start and whips along at pace. Piñeiro is a best-selling Argentinean author, and unlike many South American books this one doesn't loiter. It screams out to become a film – *The Postman Only Brings Double Indemnity* perhaps". *CrimeTime*

£8.99/$14.95
Crime Paperback Original
ISBN 978 1904738 800
eBook ISBN 978 1904738 817

www.bitterlemonpress.com

THURSDAY NIGHT WIDOWS

Claudia Piñeiro

**"A nimble novel, a ruthless dissection
of a fast-decaying society"
—José Saramago,
winner of the Nobel prize for literature**

Three bodies lie at the bottom of a swimming pool in a gated
country estate near Buenos Aires. Under the gaze of fifteen
security guards, the pampered residents of Cascade Heights lead
a charmed life of parties and tennis tournaments, ignoring the
poverty outside the perimeter wall. Claudia Piñeiro's novel eerily
foreshadowed a criminal case that generated a scandal in the
Argentine media. But this is more than a tale about crime, it is a
psychological portrait of a middle class living beyond its means
and struggling to conceal deadly secrets. Set during the post-
9/11 economic meltdown in Argentina, this story will resonate
among credit-crunched readers of today.

**Winner of the Clarín Prize for fiction and now a film
by Argentine New Wave director Marcelo Piñeyro**

**"A gripping story. The dystopia portrayed is an
indictment not solely of an assassin but of
Argentina's class structure and the wilful blindness
of its petty bourgeoisie."** *Times Literary Supplement*

**"A fine morality tale which explores the dark places societies
enter when they place material comfort before social
justice, and security before morality."** *Publishers Weekly*

£7.99/$14.95
Crime Paperback Original
ISBN 978 1904738 411
eBook ISBN 978 1904738 589

www.bitterlemonpress.com

DATE DUE

MAR 2 4 2016	
APR 0 9 2016	
APR 2 6 2016	
JUN 1 0 2016	
JUL 0 5 2016	
	PRINTED IN U.S.A.